THE STONE CUTTER
GENIUS

Bedside Books
An imprint of American Book Publishing
5442 So. 900 East, #146
Salt Lake City, UT 84117-7204
www.american-book.com
Printed in the United States of America on acid-free paper.

The Stone Cutter Genius
Graphics by John Colaianni

Designed by Jana Rade, design@american-book.com

ISBN-13: 978-1-58982-644-1
ISBN-10: 1-58982-644-2

Cola, Arthur, The Stone Cutter Genius

Special Sales

These books are available at special discounts for bulk purchases. Special editions, including personalized covers, excerpts of existing books, and corporate imprints, can be created in large quantities for special needs. For more information e-mail info@american-book.com.

THE STONE CUTTER GENIUS

A Legendary Tale
by ARTHUR COLA

Illustrations by John Colaianni

Dedication

Dedicated to my family, who bring legends to life for me.

And especially to my mother who has patiently waited for her son to write a story about Italy. Her consistent love and support is the reality of family closeness which Michelangelo yearned for but never experienced. The grace she brings to any environment is similar to those works of art the Stone Cutter Genius left to inspire and awe generation after generation. Everyone in our family loves her for the beauty and serenity which is mirrored in the Pieta of St. Peter's, the strength of conviction expressed in the Giant David of Florence, the funny expressions as seen in the sculpture of the Bacchus, the glorious appreciation of life as God will's it, as seen in the images of the Sistine Chapel, and most of all, the tender loving care epitomized in the master's Madonna and Child paintings. It is a love she has freely given to her children, grandchildren, and now her great-grandchildren, who are little works of art.

Olivia, Arthur V, Connor, Riley

Madison, Matthew, Samantha, and Ashley

Table of Contents

Chapter 1: Scrawny Will of Stone

The twelve-year-old lad flew across the room, hitting the stone fireplace hearth and bouncing off it onto the brightly polished stone floor. The heavy hands of Lodovico had struck with particular forcefulness. He struck the boy's left shoulder and rapidly followed the blow with another, striking the lad's right cheek and lifting him off the floor, sending his light, willowy frame sailing across the sparsely furnished living room.

"No son of mine shall be a stone cutter," Lodovico had yelled with each swing.

He towered over the boy; who, far from cowering on the floor with his bruised face and aching shoulder, grabbed the stones of the hearth and lifted himself up. Unsteady as he was, the young Michelangelo stood ready to receive further blows from his ill-tempered father, Lodovico Buonarotti. Such was the treatment he received whenever he would speak of being an artist, particularly a sculptor.

Lodovico would try to cajole his son but soon that changed to screaming at him and then ultimately the fury would erupt. Usually all of this took place with the lad's Uncle Francesco at his brother's side to add to his argument and contribute beatings to the lad's backside. When tempers flared the beatings would be severe and damaging to the boy's undeveloped body.

To say that Michelangelo would mature into a tall or large person would be inaccurate. He would be of medium height and build all his life; he would, however, possess the power of a giant in his arms and hands, and the creativity of an artistic genius in his fertile mind.

It was that creativity and artistic genius which on that day had brought grief to Michelangelo. But as usual he would once again confront his father with his will of stone. Indeed his will was unyielding as stone; unless, as with a chisel and hammer, the lad himself deemed to bring forth a new expression of thought. Even then, however, such movement could only be caused by a remark or suggestion from someone he loved.

Despite everything, the lad loved his father. We know this from the correspondence left from those Renaissance days in Italy 500 years ago. Those letters, however, were written in the lad's mature years. Now, in 1487 at the age of twelve, this budding genius was just beginning to set his course. That course would not lay in the same direction as Lodovico had chosen for him.

The lad's father had enrolled him in a fine school to prepare his son for a prosperous life in business. Michelangelo, however, was never to master Greek and knew little of Latin, as he himself would tell anyone who asked. Even at the age of 89, he still had not mastered Greek nor could he read much Latin. So would his biographer, and long time friend, Asconio Condivi, write in his biography about Michelangelo near the end of his days.

That lack of mercantile development however would be in this lad's future. Today, the young would-be sculptor had picked himself up from the floor, trembling in pain and rage, to assert his cause once more and knowing the response he would get from his father and uncle. That knowledge did not prevent him from speaking his mind.

"Does not the milk of the stone cutter, as you call it, flow in my veins?" Michelangelo firmly but respectfully asked. "Did it not come into my very being from my wet nurse whom you yourself gave to me as an infant when my beloved mother, blessed be her memory, could not any longer feed me, her and your second son?"

Lodovico turned to Uncle Francesco, who on this day had not entered into the fray. He stood behind the irate father in the shadows of a tall wooden bookcase containing family artifacts. These were a legacy reaching back into one of the noblest families of Italy, that of the Canossa family, who in the 15th century still held great sway in the Tuscan region of Italy. It was because of that family history, of which Lodovico was so proud, that he insisted that his children should never enter a profession beneath their status of noble birth.

"Stone cutting is next to farming as a profession of shame," he would say to his son. "Own the farm, yes indeed, that would be noble, but plow the field behind oxen, never."

Lodovico looked into his son's eyes; those bark-colored orbs with blue and yellow specks. How can this mere child of twelve be so defiant? Why is he so persistent? And, most of all, how did he come up with this notion that his very development from infancy was changed through the milk of a wet nurse who herself was a daughter of a stone cutter and whose husband was a stone cutter?

For a man of little formal education, and who considered himself to be poor even though he was a land owner, he was hard pressed to answer his son. A son, who, though bruised and hurting, refused to bend to his father's will for him to enter a noble profession.

Even at the tender age of twelve, Michelangelo had had a glimpse of what he could do with stone. That glance, into the Medici Gardens of Florence, Italy, had seared images of stone into his developing brain. Stones yearning to be brought to life, he would say. He would cause such stones to burst from their confinement into almost-living interpretations of humanity, faith and heroism from antiquity. He, Michelangelo Buonarroti of Simoni, would bring the stones to life. Because of that belief in himself and his calling, the boy once again stood up to face the wrath of his father.

That glimpse of his future had just occurred. It was the day before, June 28, 1487. He had run an errand for a very famous Florentine *bottega* run by the Ghirlandaio brothers near the Medici Gardens. In this shop for painters, young men were enrolled to learn the techniques of painting, drawing, frescoing, and sculpting as they studied works of art under the direction of Domenico, Davide, and Benedetto Ghirlandaio. It was just a simple errand of little importance. He was to deliver a message from Domenico to one of his students. That future artist was spending time in the Medici Gardens observing and drawing its collection of statues from ancient Greece and Rome and its original works of early masters, such as the sculptor Donatello.

This student, to whom the message was to be delivered, was Francesco Granacci, an aspiring painter at age 18. He had spotted a boy who came daily to peer into the courtyard of the *bottega*. The boy's eyes would bulge as if to fall from his head and his neck strained so as to disconnect his head from it. Such wonder was demonstrated in these secretive visits that Granacci was moved to speak with the lad. It was during that conversation between the teen-ager and the pre-teen, as one stood inside the gate and the younger one outside, that Domenico happened to pass by. Domenico was about to scold the boy but there was something in those eyes, yearning to soak in all that came into their range of vision, which caused him to inquire as to his name rather than scold and send him off. Michelangelo was so moved to be spoken to by a renowned artist that he was tongue tied. Granacci began to answer for him, but Domenico would have none of it. He opened the gate and invited the young Michelangelo into the *bottega*.

That's when one of the most talented, innovative, and creative artists in stone and paint first stepped into a world foreign to him; yet it was a most comfortable and stimulating world. Granacci became his guide and life-long friend that day despite their difference in ages. From that day on, no amount of beating or haranguing from his father would ever keep him away from the world of art.

On June 28th when Granacci and he planned to meet again, Michelangelo came to the *bottega*. His friend was not there but Domenico saw him at the gate and inquired why he was there. After a short explanation, the painter and teacher sent Michelangelo to the Medici Gardens with a message for Granacci to return to the *bottega*.

The school lay not more than three blocks from Palazzo Medici, home of one of the most influential families in Italy, if not all of Europe. The head of the family was a leader of government in Florence and much of Tuscany. Lorenzo de' Medici was the current head of the family when Michelangelo entered the Medici Garden carrying a message. Lorenzo was called "*Il Magnifico*" by all, due to his well-respected and wide-spread influence in the worlds of religion, art, and government. He was a prince in a republican government.

Florence was a city-state akin to those of ancient Greece. In the fifteenth century, most of Italy was made up of city–states, including the Papal States — a large piece of central Italy ruled by the pope who also led the Catholic Church. The leaders of these various states, and many popes, would have tremendous influence in Michelangelo's life.

Now, however, the almost thirteen-year–old Michelangelo had entered the Medici Gardens with its priceless treasures from antiquity, the Middle Ages, and Michelangelo's time. Walking among recently found statuary from ancient Rome, seeing their human forms as no one had seen for hundreds of years affected Michelangelo so deeply it would be reflected and even improved upon in his own work for years to come. Not that the lad ever became prideful or boastful of his work, but the human form he would create expressed perfection in art. It would writhe, twist, and turn. It would bulge with muscles and bone. It would express agony and joy, strength and weakness, life and death so realistically that whomever he portrayed or carved would seem to live. At least, that's what others who saw his work would say. It was through adding expression and life to the statue or painting which made Michelangelo's future work an improvement over that from ancient Greece or Rome. The art of painting and sculpting would never be the same after Michelangelo made his contributions.

Michelangelo was searching in wonder for his soon-to-be new friend. Through the maze of shrubs and flower beds he wandered; looking for Granacci, to be sure, but soaking in each raised arm of a Roman rendition of a saint, or each turned head of a heroic mythological figure carved in marble. He roamed past countless Roman heads without noses; He touched a torso without arms to feel the life within the stone before he continued his mission. The boy became filled with a spirit which seemed to spill forth from the carved marbles. As any boy just entering the threshold of young manhood, he became excited at one moment, then thrilled the next, and finally confused at what was happening to him.

Walking backwards from the end of a maze still mesmerized by a work of bronze, he stumbled onto Granacci seated before a marble torso with only partial legs and arms and no head. Bumping into Francesco, Michelangelo fell over his lap knocking his drawing chalk out of his hand.

Granacci grabbed the young Buonarroti by his shoulders to steady him. He lifted Michelangelo up and laughed. His drawing fell to the ground. Granacci wrapped his arm around the trembling Michelangelo.

"Why do you shake so, young friend?" he asked.

"Your work, master artist, your work… it lies upon the ground. Aren't you angry?" Michelangelo answered and asked at the same time. As he spoke, he found himself waiting to be beaten.

Instead, Granacci wrapped his arm around Michelangelo. With one arm finally released, he made a sweep of the garden. He was presenting the Medici world, the world of art, to the sponge of a lad ready to absorb everything within.

"Now, my dear…what did you say your name was?"

The boy, still quite nervous, managed to speak. "Michelangelo Buonarotti."

"Well then, Michelangelo Buonarotti, I, Francesco Granacci, insist that you look upon the ground and see what great masterpiece you think you destroyed," he said as he concluded the sweeping motion of his arm.

Michelangelo glanced down upon the chalk drawing. It wasn't that of the torso at all but a banner of sorts flying above a stage.

"Granacci, you were drawing from memory, I mean creating from out of nothing… this scene?"

"Ah Buonarroti, I wish this were indeed a creation," he remarked as he picked up the drawing. "It is but a scene being created for *Il Magnifico*'s jousting match a few weeks hence."

Despite the carelessness of Granacci's explanation, Michelangelo stood in awe that he was creating a scene for Lorenzo de Medici, *Il Magnifico*, himself. Even if it were to be used for the city's festival and jousting match, it was still work done for the sublime leader of Florence.

Granacci stooped down to pick up his sketch and place it into a cloth bag hanging around his neck. Turning, he once again took Michelangelo by his arm and they left through a gate leading them down the street now called Via Cavour. As they walked, they passed the Church of San Marco. The gardens next to it were now used for the sake of art, and had been purchased by the Medici family. The church itself was a favorite of the Medici family who had the walls of the convent adjoining it decorated with a fresco by the preeminent artist of the generation preceding them. That artist was the Dominican, Fra Angelico. He would be the bridge from Gothic art to the new innovations of Renaissance expression. His paintings, which adorn the Convent of San Marco, or St. Mark, were to have significant impact on these two boys, who cut through the Church on their way to the artists' workshop.

During their walk back to the *bottega Ghirlandaio*, the elder would-be artist, and the younger who yearned to sculpt in marble, talked about the upcoming festival and jousting match. These festivals, carnivals, and jousts were grand events filled with music, drama, parades, costumes, and combat so glorified that it staggered the imagination. It was Granacci contributing to their grand style. These events were occasions on which the revelry became lurid and at times vulgar. It was not long after this time that the extremes of the celebrations would come to haunt *Il Magnifico* and indeed the Medici rule in Florence. For now, however, they made pleasant conversation between two young men who saw in them an opportunity to observe wonderful works of art, temporary though they may be.

By the time the young men drew near the shop of artists it was late afternoon and the seeds of a life-long friendship had been planted. That friendship would last until Francesco Granacci died, almost sixty years later.

When they entered the protected area of the *bottega* the boys were noticed by Davide Ghirlandaio. Michelangelo explained that Master Domenico had sent him on an errand to fetch Francesco, and they went on to seek out the Master. Domenico was pleased when he spotted them approaching.

"You found him then, did you?" he asked Michelangelo and then he continued, not waiting for an answer. "Francesco my dear boy, I wish you to go to the Casa Buonarotti. There you are to seek out this lad's father, Lodovico. You will explain to him that the master of the *Bottega Ghirlandaio* wishes to meet with him."

As he spoke these words, Michelangelo's eyes widened so that those specks of yellow and blue floating within his iris seemed to jump out of his head. Granacci grinned ear to ear and obediently agreed to do his master's bidding.

This is why Michelangelo, though stinging from yet another beating, stood firmly before his father, ready to take whatever it took to convince him that he would not be merely a stone cutter, but an artist.

While gazing into his father's furious eyes he watched the window just visible over Lodovico's shoulder. Lodovico raised his hand again to strike, but instead, shook his head and allowed his arm to fall limply to his side.

He turned to Uncle Francesco for support which would not come this time.

The reason for the uncle's inaction was that he saw what his nephew saw through the window: a finely-dressed young man of good posture and well-groomed hair. He wore a cap of green wool matching his hunter-green leggings which fitted snugly underneath his tunic of fine brown silk with threads of silver. The tunic reached mid-thigh and was held at the waist by a brown leather belt with silver studs. In his hand he carried a portfolio which he kept close to his chest, ensuring there was no chance for its contents to spill out prior to being presented to its recipient.

Francesco Granacci had arrived and he was ready to play the part to its fullest degree dressed in what we may term as his Sunday best. No worn woolens of dull brown or cords of rope for a belt today. No leggings with holes on the backside and knees from hours of rubbing against stone benches as he practiced drawing in the *bottega* or Medici Gardens. He had a habit of kneeling in front of his subject so that he might get closer to it. This day, dressed in his best, he was to rescue his new friend, though he knew not how much that friend needed to be rescued, from the Casa Buonarotti.

Uncle Francesco moved quickly to the heavy wooden door as the knock echoed throughout the two-story house. The knock was more of a pounding since Granacci was using his booted foot to create the sound on the door. So strongly did he kick, that the bric-a-brac on the shelves shook.

The door opened and, not waiting for a greeting, Francesco Granacci spoke. "Good afternoon. Master Lodovico Buonarotti, I presume?"

"Regretfully, young gentleman, I am not the one you seek," Uncle Francesco responded. "He is within. May I show you in?"

Granacci bowed and entered. Upon coming into the living room, he made no attempt to greet the lad; rather, he bowed to Lodovico ceremoniously as if he were a Medici prince.

This gesture of respect immediately endeared the young man to Michelangelo's father, who was convinced of his family's noble origins. Thus the messenger was invited most cordially to state the reason for his presence.

"My master, Domenico Ghirlandaio, artist to *Il Magnifico* himself, has bid me to seek you out, kindly gentleman."

Granacci gave the slightest wink to Michelangelo at this point as he gave a slight bow. He continued. Lodovico waited with bated breath as he pondered what possible need a master artist could have with his family. Though Lodovico thought such a profession was beneath his family's noble heritage, he was well aware that one who was in the service to the Medici could not, and should not, be ignored. He smiled; something Michelangelo had almost never seen cross his father's face.

Granacci gently removed a sheet of paper from the portfolio and read from it. It was an invitation to meet with Domenico Ghirlandaio regarding the enrollment of his son, Michelangelo Buonarotti, as an apprentice in the *bottega*. Lodovico could not believe his ears. An invitation to apprentice in the very profession which he felt was beneath his family and certainly one which would bring in little, if any, money to the family coffers.

It would take several more visits and much negotiation until Lodovico finally gave in and recognized "his son's natural bent" and the "uselessness to oppose it any longer" as biographer John Addington Symonds writes of the final agreement to apprentice Michelangelo to the Ghirlandaio brothers' workshop. At the time of his admittance the young stone cutter was thirteen years old.

"So began the journey of an artistic genius who would give us such magnificent works as The Pieta of St. Peter's in Rome, the Giant David in Florence, Italy, and of course the masterful work of the Sistine Chapel ceiling, though painting was not his art as he would often say." And with that, Arthur Colonna turned off the projector which had presented the image of the Sistine Chapel ceiling in the Vatican. The former school administrator and now professor at Loyola University of Chicago, turned off his laptop and disconnected the projector. His students were busily closing their notebooks, but they were not about to leave, not just yet. They knew Mr. C., as they called him, would have some directions to give regarding their next meeting. After the laptop had been gently placed into his backpack, Arthur turned his attention to his students.

In this class, he was introducing them to the wonders of Michelangelo's artistic legacy and a bit of history. It was all part of the celebration of the 500th anniversary of the painting of the Sistine Chapel ceiling. The university had arranged with its alumnus to conduct a series of preparatory sessions which would conclude with a pilgrimage to the land where Michelangelo's creative genius bloomed over five centuries ago. Arthur was only too pleased to conduct such sessions and lead the participants on a tour of Italy, in the footsteps of Michelangelo, as he liked to refer to the trip.

After writing two books, one on the folklore of Ireland and the other on the Legend of King Arthur, he was a recognized figure in the literary world of his hometown, Chicago, Illinois. It was natural for the University to invite him to consider the lecture tour. The board's rationale for deciding whom to invite was lost on Arthur. His delight was to finally introduce his ancestral land to, as he liked to think of them, his former and current students.

They were former, and now current, students because Arthur insisted the "In the Footsteps of Michelangelo Tour" be limited in size and also offered to interested students outside Loyola University. As a result, most of the students in the class had come from the school where Arthur once served as principal.

As the students waited, their eyes looked around the Gothic-styled chapel where the presentation had been made. Arthur had purposely not held the class in Lewis Towers across the street, even though it was in that brick skyscraper where most of the downtown classes of the University were held. The University skyscraper, the Quigley Chapel, where they currently sat, and the university complex were in the shadow of the well-known Chicago Water Tower. The tower was a surviving structure of the famous fire of 1871 which destroyed much of the city at that time.

The chapel location and its proximity to the Water Tower were important to Arthur. Any of his four young grandchildren or five children knew why this site was important to Arthur, as did his wife, Donna and his widowed mother, Wanda. Probably every student in the Quigley Preparatory Seminary Chapel knew as well.

The chapel and the school building of the former high school preparatory seminary is designed in medieval architecture with Gothic stained-glass windows and spires, on one of which St. George is piercing the dragon. The statue is representative of a familiar story told in the Middle Ages. In Arthur's opinion the Renaissance was born from the late Middle Ages. As his students would wander through the ancient, yet quite modern, nation of Italy, they would see many examples of that period called by some, the Dark Ages. Arthur held the presentation in the chapel in order to give his students a sense of that time by being immersed in a Gothic environment.

As for the Water Tower, built in the typical style of the mid-nineteenth century, Arthur was attracted to its stonework. Stonework is an important theme in walking in the footsteps of Michelangelo. The complex, which was a working water-pumping station at the time of the Chicago fire and still is at present, gives one a visual sense of standing outside a castle reminiscent of a Hollywood set for a knights-of-the-round-table scene. Having written a book involving those knights, Arthur was particularly fond of the legend. What all but two of his students didn't know was that their teacher had actually met those famous knights and their king last year. It was that very real adventure with his family which formed the foundation of his pseudo-fictitious work. The two who knew the truth of the battle to save the legendary Holy Grail and the sword, Excalibur, were his sons John and Rich, which he and his wife fondly called "the boys."

During Arthur's presentation of *Il Magnifico's* staged jousting matches, the boys had remembered that they had actually been involved in a joust in the twenty-first century at Warwick Castle in England. In that joust, their adversaries had been followers of Morgan le Fay and the dark forces which sought to keep the light of the message from changing the face of Western Civilization. The Colonna Clan had all been involved in the struggle to save the divinely bestowed message.

This year, all Arthur wanted to accomplish was to introduce his students to the charm, beauty, and wonders of his ancestral land. No jousts, no fights to the death, no clashing of the forces of light and dark, no descendents of legendary figures bent on destroying the goodness of the human spirit or its faith traditions were to be part of the experience of walking in the footsteps of Michelangelo.

He delighted in dramatizing the events of Michelangelo's life in picture and word as he introduced his sons and the class to what they were to see for themselves. The class waited in anticipation to hear of the next venue for the class. They knew that each class would take place in a special locale, one which would represent the art, history and environment with which Michelangelo would be familiar, and yet right in the United States of America. In this way, Arthur hoped to demonstrate the far reaching effects of the Renaissance and Michelangelo over five centuries of time.

As soon as the lap top was closed Arthur began his final direction:

"Our next meeting place will take place at Our Lady of Sorrows Basilica on the near west side of Chicago. On your way out, please pick up the map and background information for the church which educated countless immigrants from Europe in its school, became a shrine for hope during the depression, and a symbol of an age-old faith in the heartland of America to which thousands came to visit in search of solace, comfort, inspiration, and vision. Now, once again, it serves the needs of a new generation of the faithful and a renewing community. There will be a bus available to take you to the shrine. It will be waiting for you at St. Anastasia Parish in Waukegan. See you next week."

Not one of the students left before speaking with Arthur, each expressing his or her excitement for the trip. By 8:00 p.m. all were gone and Arthur, John and Rich carted out the equipment. Luckily, their mother had suggested using a small suitcase on wheels to transport the equipment, saving them the trouble of carrying everything to the hotel.

"Dad, why didn't you tell them about the surprise?" asked Rich.

"Yeah," added John. "I think they'd get a kick out of knowing that they were to be a part of it."

"First things first, boys," responded their father. "They need to get excited about the adventure; the other things involved will kind of… add frosting to the experience."

"Frosting? Dad, how about the dream of your life being realized," the tenacious boys observed.

Arthur didn't give in; he pointed out that the focus was Michelangelo not himself. He was just a sidebar, so to speak. With that, they walked onto Chestnut Street and passed the illuminated Water Tower. Turning north on Michigan Avenue, they made their way to the Drake Hotel where he and Donna had started their honeymoon many years ago; long before the boys were considered, Arthur pointed out. John and Rich had the last word; they surprised their father by arranging to have their mother waiting for him in the lobby.

Chapter 2: The Dream Come True

The Basilica of Our Lady of Sorrows was established in the last quarter of the nineteenth century. Back then it was a parish church. The order of the Servants of Mary, or Servites, as they are familiarly called, staffed the parish then as they do now. When the westside neighborhood exploded with a new immigrant population, a larger church was needed. Not only was a new house of worship built, but one which would be one of the finest examples of Renaissance art in America. It was to be a shrine, as well as a parish church, honoring Mary as the sorrowful mother as she beheld her son, Jesus, dying on the cross.

When the yellow school bus came down Jackson Boulevard and pulled up in front of the basilica, Arthur and the boys were already waiting for the others on the front steps. It was just like the old days, Arthur was thinking, as his mind went back to those days when he would take the eighth graders on his famous Chicago tour. But the students coming off this bus, though bouncing around like a bunch of eighth graders, were young men and women. Most of them were college students and on their way to creating careers for themselves.

Arthur wanted to meet the class in front of the church for several reasons. He wished to walk them around its exterior so that they could get a sense of its size and shape. As with most churches built from the time of early Christianity, through the Middle Ages and the Renaissance, to the nineteenth and early twentieth centuries, Our Lady of Sorrows was built in the shape of a Latin cross. Its nave was long and the transepts crossed it about three quarters of the way down its main aisle. The sanctuary served as the top portion of the cross. Its exterior did not hint at the splendor which lay within. Only its twin towers, soaring into the westside sky and topped by crosses, gave possible witness to the magnificence of its interior. The exterior gray façade with empty niches, where statues may have been intended at one time, was typical of churches of the Renaissance period. Once they circled the structure and noted that it could hold over 2,000 people, they were ready to enter.

Rufus Williams, the caretaker of the shrine, was waiting at the huge oak doors when the group made its left turn and passed the only outside statuary; that of the Sorrowful Mother, Mary. Up the stairs they ascended until suddenly Arthur stopped, causing students to bang into one another.

Arthur had wondered why, when he was talking of the twin towers piercing the westside sky, there had been murmurs. Now it came to him. There was only one tower soaring above Jackson Boulevard. He had not been back to visit his boyhood parish church for years. The stories he often told his children and grandchildren, of his parents being married there, how he was baptized in its font, and received his first Holy Communion and the Sacrament of Confirmation at the white marble altar railing, now filled his ears. "Rufus, there's only one tower...what happened?"

"Well Mr. Colonna..." he began to answer.

"Arthur, if you please," interrupted Mr. C.

"Well, Arthur," Rufus began again with a kindly smile which warmed the heart of its beholder. "We had a bit of a fire here several years ago. No one knew that the tower was made of wood and only appeared to look like the stone."

"Good grief, you mean in over a hundred years no one knew?" a flabbergasted Arthur asked.

"So it would seem," Rufus replied, as he pointed to the flat surface of the tower base upon which once stood the steeple with its bells. The twisted bells distorted by flames would later be seen in the basilica museum on the lower level, where the Novena Shrine, so popular during World War II, is preserved.

Arthur realized that Rufus had just presented a teachable moment and he took full advantage of it. He asked his students to spread across the semicircular stone staircase which fanned out from the façade of the church. He explained how the tragedy of the fire would not be unlike what could have happened to St. Peter's in Rome during its construction had it not been for Michelangelo. To save money, the architect Bramante cut corners and instead of using solid stone, he would use pieces of stone which were then sealed to make it look like a solid surface, not unlike what was done here. The difference being that, in the case of the basilica, it was wood made to look like stone. When Michelangelo noticed Bramante's disregard for the integrity of the building he was constructing, and his lack of respect for the artistic pieces being destroyed as he tore down the old St. Peter's, he could not tolerate the practice any longer. Michelangelo brought it to Pope Julius II's attention. His actions saved St. Peter's from being poorly built but it made Bramante a life-long enemy of the young artist and sculptor. With that, he waved them on to enter the basilica.

Arthur led his class, as they formed lines just from habit and followed him through the doors into a world of spirituality and art which few, if any, had experienced in their young lives. Through the marble-lined vestibule they entered another set of doors into the main body of the church. Rufus had outdone himself in preparing the interior to be shown off at its best. The empty church was lighted. The vaulted ceiling of blossom-like spreading petals, gilded with gold, shone like the sun from the recessed lighting illuminating it. At the end of the long, marble center aisle, the high altar shone brilliantly. Its gleaming, white Carrara marble reflected the light from the fixtures above, to the side, underneath the altar, and in the cupola overhead which held a gold crucifix.

To the right and left of the wooden pews, which still held their polished look for over a hundred and thirty five years, were the recessed shrines. Each of these shrines lay behind a marble arch and was dedicated to a scene from spiritual tradition or to a favored saint. In one was the replication of the apparition of Our Lady of Fatima. Other shrines held statues of St. Francis of Assisi, St. Joseph, and St. Peregrine, the patron saint of cancer sufferers. None of the shrines detracted from one's initial impression. The entire flow of the cruciform structure, each piece of marble, each arch and the angels flanking the high altar, drew one's attention to the sanctuary. Natural light poured in from windows located above the shrine area and just below the edge of the ceiling vault, producing streams of sunlight which, at different times of the day, fell on particular paintings or shrines. On this afternoon there were several such rays. One ray illuminated the station of the cross in which Jesus meets his mother. Another shone into the Fatima shrine others streamed down into the sanctuary itself.

There was not one student who was not impressed by the vision created and the artistic wonders viewed.

Arthur slowly led his students down the main aisle, stopping frequently to point out a shrine and once to talk about the vaulted ceiling itself.

"Sister Constance Mary of the Order of Providence Nuns," he began, "would tell us, when I was a student here at school in second grade, that this ceiling was patterned after that of St. Peter's in Rome. When we visit the mother church of Christendom in a few weeks, I would like you to remember her words and decide if you agree with them."

When they arrived at the intersection of the transepts and nave with the sanctuary before them, Arthur invited the students to climb the few white marble steps to the communion rail, still preserved as it had been carved over a century ago. He invited them to offer a silent prayer and make a wish. The latter was a family tradition handed down to him by his grandmother, Ida Doretti-Stella, who, in turn, had received the tradition from her *nona*, Cleophe Nannini, in Italy, before coming to America.

Rufus had arranged for another surprise. Sr. Mary Catherine was visiting the friars. The aged musician had once taught in the school now long since torn down. She was seating herself in the organ loft to the left of the sanctuary as Arthur and his students made their way forward. As they knelt on the pads lying across the ledge in front of the communion rail, she began to play the pipe organ. Arthur had not heard it since childhood and his students had never heard a pipe organ. She began with Shubert's Ave Maria and then ended with the triumphant Trumpet Voluntary by Purcell.

The young people, accustomed to guitars and a piano during a service, were astounded and moved, but no one spoke. They stood and looked up to the loft barely able to see the elderly nun running her fingers across the keyboard as if she were once again a young novice.

As for Arthur and his sons, they were suddenly brought back to Stratford-upon-Avon in England. It was there, last year, where the boys had been invested as jousting knights by real Knights of the Round Table while the same Trumpet Voluntary played. The whole unbelievable, yet real, experience of that quest to save the sword Excalibur flashed before them once more.

In a resounding flourish the nun ended the impromptu concert and the students applauded her. She peered over the edge of the balcony loft and bowed to them while placing one hand over her mouth in a motion of shyness and humility. Flipping her veil behind her shoulder, she waved and disappeared from view.

Arthur led the group to the left transept shrine which depicted the vision of the seven holy founders of the Servite Order and through large wooden doors leading into the baptistry.

In the baptistry was the shrine of the Pieta, displaying a duplicate of Michelangelo's Pieta located in St. Peter's in Rome. The students were able to walk completely around the statue. The duplicate was carved by an artist from a block of marble located directly in front of the original masterpiece. Arthur would explain, as the students explored the wounds of Christ and the serene look on Mary's youthful face, how the Stone Cutter Genius' early attempt at sculpting a major piece blended the emotional elements of classical antiquity and the reverence of Renaisance Chirstianity. Danny Garcia ran his fingers across the marble belt which crossed Mary from her shoulder to her waist. Onto it were carved the words: this was carved by Michelangelo Buonarroti of Florence. Danny asked Mr. C what the words said and Arthur translated it for the class adding the famous story of how those words got carved onto the original statue in Rome. Arthur explained how the new masterpiece was brought to the old St. Peter's.

"The church which you will see is considered the new St. Peter's as it was built over the site were Bramante had torn down the thousand-year-old church constructed by the Roman Emperor Constantine. The Pieta's beauty brought much acclaim to the young sculptor, but not before an incident occurred which infuriated the master stone cutter. A group of art critics attributed the work to another artist. Michelangelo, standing in the shadows to hear what people said of his work, boiled with rage. When the church was closed for the night, he made his way back into St. Peter's. He carried a bag of tools. Working through the night, he carved his message so the entire world would know for all time who carved the Pieta of St. Peter's. Later, he regretted his action. He never signed any of his other works for they should speak for themselves as works of Michelangelo."

It was time for Arthur's formal presentation, so he led the class back to the Seven Holy Founders shrine. Rufus had erected a huge screen just under the fresco-like painting showing the late Pope Pius XII holding a crown over the twin spired church of Our Lady of Sorrows. This pictorially portrayed a church being elevated to the level of basilica as the crown symbolized the honor. Arthur explained that this Church received the honor for its work among the poor and the spiritual life of the faithful back in the depression days to the late 1950's.

The lights of the Basilica were turned off as Arthur ascended into the white marble pulpit. The projector was already set up. Arthur turned it on, and a photo of the Church of San Lorenzo, with its stark brick façade, filled the screen. The view made them think they could walk onto Via de Ginori, which runs between the church and Palazzo Medici both of which would have a profound impact on the young Michelangelo of Florence, Italy in 1490. With words and images Arthur brought his class back to the late fifteenth century.

Michelangelo and Granacci were walking down a pristine-looking aisle which was not exactly an aisle as there were no pews as we know them. And yet the gigantic pillars lining the sides of the narrow building gave one a sense of walking down a traditional church aisle towards the main altar. Michelangelo and Granacci were headed to that altar. Buried in front of the altar was Cosimo de' Medici, the elder, who had been proclaimed by the citizens of Florence, *Pater Patirae,* father of the country. The fifteen-year-old Michelangelo respected the Medici family even though years later he may have disagreed with their governing tactics. Now Lorenzo, *Il Magnifico*, civil leader, lover of the arts and master diplomat cast his shadow on Florence as none of his ancestors had done.

The two young men stood before the altar. Michelangelo fell to his knees to kiss the site of Cosimo's grave.

"Oh elder of a most noble family, come to my aide," he muttered.

Granacci stood in amazed silence. He bent down and touched his young friend's shoulder.

"Buonarotti, you pray to the Medici as if he were a saint."

"Francesco, the saints seemed to have turned their back on me. I have nowhere to go; only the Medici can save me now," Michelangelo replied as he looked up to the handsome Granacci, whose form was outlined in a halo of light.

A ray of sunlight struck the back of the elder young man as the younger turned to look at him. For the typically superstitious Tuscan, Granacci did appear as in a holy light. In that aura of sunlight, he reached out his hand and Michelangelo placed his hand into it as if he were touching a holy relic.

"Michelangelo, snap out of it," he called out as he jerked his friend up from his knees.

The fifteen-year-old came to his senses once again and begged for forgiveness.

"My friend I am desperate, Domenico gives me nothing to copy or work on these many weeks. Not even a second rate sketch can I get from him."

"Don't concern yourself. He's jealous of your talent that's all. Listen, I noticed a small block of marble in the *bottega* which may serve your purpose. Take a look at it and take it for your own. Bring forth its inner life, and that will prove your worth and force Ghirlandaio to recognize you," advised Granacci as they walked out of the church and paused in front of Palazzo Medici.

Michelangelo's melancholy seemed to be lifting, but his eyes showed that he still placed his hope in the Medici family. His calling had been rejected by his own father whom he loved deeply, but who did not seem to love him. Now, his master refused to give him but a crumb of work from which to learn the skills he needed if he were to become a skilled artist. He yearned for the affection of a father, an elder who would be his guide and source of encouragement.

Francesco Granacci stood slightly behind him with his hands on his hips. He knew full well that Michelangelo was in one of his self-pitying moods.

Suddenly Michelangelo gave a jump, slapped Granacci's back, and jumped on his back.

"Come dear friend enough of this. Medici or not, we have work to do."

Francesco played along and bolted like an unbroken stallion. Michelangelo ruffled his friend's golden brown, curly hair and jumping back to the walkway they both began to run back to the *bottega*.

When they arrived at the gate, huffing and puffing after running the several blocks, Domenico was standing at the entrance talking with his brother Benedetto. They were in animated conversation. Hands were waving this way and that, as if directions were being given to create some order to the disarrayed placement of art work and students in the workshop. The young men paused only to catch their breath and to stay in the shadows so they might overhear the conversation.

"Benedetto, *Il Maginifico,* himself, is on his way. He should be here any minute. Thank the saints that Davide heard of his impromptu visit or we should have been shamed," Domenico said with a sigh of relief.

There was no doubt that his nerves were frayed and he was on edge, for there was no greater patron of the arts than the leader of Florence and the Medici family fortune.

"Domenico, calm yourself. You are a master painter in your own right. *Il Magnifico* certainly recognizes that and his visit is an honor to our family," advised Benedetto. "The *bottega* is as it should be, filled with hard working apprentices honing their skills."

Michelangelo whispered to Granacci, "My prayers have been answered by the grandfather of *Il Magnifico*."

Francesco returned a smile and nod as he softly replied, "Indeed, but it will be a prayer fruitlessly answered unless we get back to our places in the *bottega* my dear friend."

Domenico seemed to be relieved by his brother's words as he looked around the workshop. He was breathing much easier now as his eyes swept from one aspiring artist to the next. Suddenly, he stopped his sweeping gaze. His eyes flashed.

"Where are those two?" Domenico yelled causing the young artists near him to jump in fright.

"What two? Who can be so important that they are missed?" inquired Benedetto.

"Buonarotti and Granacci are missing. Look. They should be at their places by that cypress tree."

"And so they're not there. So what?" his brother stated nonchalantly.

"So what? Are you mad? *Il Magnifico* is coming here and why do you think he's coming? Certainly it's not to praise my fresco work in the Duomo, of that I'm quite sure," came the answer from the raving and almost hysterical Domenico.

Benedetto took his brother by the shoulders and shook him slightly. Granacci and Michelangelo watched for a moment to slip by and fill that empty place of study to which their master was pointing. Sweat poured down Domenico's forehead. Benedetto used his sleeve to wipe it away.

"Brother, this will not do. What will Lorenzo think should he see you in this state?" asked Benedetto. He did not wait for an answer. He saw what needed to be done.

"Come into the house. Let's splash some water on your face. Should those ingrates not return prior to *Il Magnifico*'s arrival, than we shall tell that pompous Medici that they have been sent on an errand to…to the

Duomo, where they were to bring a set of your cartoons for the fresco."

"Granacci, he called Lorenzo pompous. Indeed there has never been such a leader as Lorenzo. Look how he allowed you to be sent to my father after your visit and convinced him to apprentice me to Ghirlandaio's shop," a shocked Michelangelo explained. "He could have placed me with Cosimo Rosselli, who everyone knows runs a less successful *bottega* or even Botticelli, whom I admire; but I don't understand his paintings' interpretations."

Benedetto now escorted his brother toward the small lodging building. The two teens had their chance. With the speed which would be Michelangelo's style, when carving marble, they fled to their stools. Granacci reached into his bag and pulled out a print of the Agony of St. Anthony, by the German printmaker Martin Schongauer, who was also a painter.

"Here, take a look at this. I think its presentation will please you."

The print could only be described as a gruesome and horrifying scene in which the saint was being tormented by monsters; demons to be sure. The fifteen-year-old had never seen the like.

"This is something imaginative, energetic, and frightening," he whispered. "See how they pull and tug on the holy one. Is that not what happens to us every day? Are we not tempted, in our revelry during carnival time, to be pulled into practices which would embarrass us the next day, if not having filled us with sin?"

This sensitivity towards the wild life and what, during his time many called carnal pleasures, would accentuate as the budding artist grew in age and wisdom. Coming from the mouth of a young teen, however, only resulted in a raucous laugh from Granacci.

It was a laugh short-lived and swallowed whole. As it burst forth, the sound of horses hooves clicking down on stone came to their ears. A young man dressed in fine silk leggings of blue and a tunic woven of silver and indigo threads stood at the gate. All eyes in the *bottega* turned as the gleaming figure held the gate open for another to enter. None of the students knew at the time that the one holding the gate was the eldest son of Lorenzo, *Il Magnifico*, named Piero de' Medici.

Benedetto and Domenico had just come back into the workshop courtyard as the young man appeared. They knew at once who he was and who would follow. However, instead of the father entering ceremoniously, there entered a rather plump boy, the same age as

Michelangelo. It was Giovanni de' Medici, who, interestingly, had been named a Cardinal of the Church through the diplomatic maneuvers of his father. That fact would not become common knowledge for two more years. Giovanni, the future Pope Leo X, was pulling on a hand. The hand was gloved in gold silk and belonged to Lorenzo de' Medici who entered the *bottega*. He was just a bit taller than Michelangelo, but unlike his second son, was trim and quite athletic. His hair of light brown took on a bright glow as the rays of the sun reflected off his golden chest plate.

The Ghirlandaio brothers were beside themselves, especially Domenico. They rushed to the gate, ignored the sons and bowed to *Il Magnifico*; an act which Piero, when he became head of the family and head of the Florentine Government, would never forget.

Michelangelo and Granacci watched the brothers' display of courtesy with amusement. They feigned working on their projects. Actually, Michelangelo had created a thumb nail sketch of the Agony print but with his own modifications.

Lorenzo de' Medici, genuinely gracious as usual, exchanged pleasantries and walked toward the cypress tree under which Michelangelo and Granacci sat. The teens feverishly rubbed their black chalk against the paper hanging on the easel in front of them. The eyes of all the apprentices watched the drama which they were sure would be taking place. The Ghirlandaio brothers gulped as the three Medici approached the boys pretending to be working.

Piero walked behind Granacci and peered over his shoulder. Giovanni, the same age as Michelangelo, pondered the Agony sketch. His bulky frame almost toppled Michelangelo from his stool as he insisted on watching the young artist's hand quite closely. The close scrutiny was due to poor eyesight, an inherited trait from his father, who also was myopic. The bulging eyes created a sight problem for father and son. Lorenzo also had to view the work at close proximity, but he politely excused himself first.

Michelangelo stood when he was addressed.

One would have thought that the sensitive lad would have shuddered in the presence of *Il Magnifico*. He was certainly impressed; but rather than fear or anxiety, Michelangelo felt comforted. The benign smile of the first citizen of Florence set him at ease. The ponderous son's joviality relaxed him. Only the stern eyes of Piero caused him some degree of alarm. Lorenzo de' Medici made some unintelligible sounds as he viewed the sketch and then asked to see other examples of the young artist's efforts.

From a bag leaning next to the stool, Michelangelo pulled out some other examples of chalk drawings. Lorenzo's smile became larger and was mirrored by the Ghirlandaio brothers. They were delighted at the pleasure of the great Italian leader. Michelangelo felt he had to show some type of respect to his patron; for that was what Lorenzo was and would continue to be.

After *Il Magnifico* had returned the other drawings to the teen, Michelangelo took Lorenzo's outstretched hand and kissed the ring on his finger. The act of reverence was typical of the day but usually reserved for religious leaders or kings.

Lorenzo jerked his hand. Michelangelo felt fear now but needn't have.

"My dear young man, I am not the pope. There is no need for such reverence to me," he gently said as he placed his arm over Michelangelo's shoulder and drew him close.

The hand with the ring he had kissed now rested on his shoulder. From his peripheral vision Michelangelo could see the ring. He turned his head slightly to get a better view of it, for it was a work of art. At the same time he took great pleasure in *Il Magnifico's* gesture. For the first time in his young life, Michelangelo felt comforted and supported by a father figure. He melted into the metal chest plate and relished the affection offered in friendship. That friendship, though to be short-lived due to Lorenzo's untimely death, would grow. Lorenzo would relish the time he would spend with Michelangelo.

"So, young master, you admire this ornament on my hand, do you?" asked Lorenzo as he withdrew his arm so that he could hold the hand in the sunlight to best set off the admired ring.

Michelangelo could only smile as he felt that he had been caught at something he should not have done.

"It is rather unique at that," added *Il Magnifico*.

The ponderous Giovanni de' Medici could not control himself any longer. "Young Buonarotti, my esteemed father holds great treasures from antiquity and modern art and yet it's that trifle on his hand which he would never be without. He insists it contains magic that even the wizard Leonardo da Vinci would want to master."

Piero, not at all appealing or gracious, now jumped in. "Brother, do not mock what you do not know for certain. Its power comes from antiquity and its blessing upon our father is beyond measure."

Lorenzo should have seen it coming but was too slow to react in time. Once again the elder brother and younger brother were at odds. Giovanni, now a Cardinal of the Church, saw the ring in terms of superstition and theology. Piero, on the other hand, could not be more symbolic of the people of Tuscany as far as their obsession with magic, the supernatural, and the power of wizards.

Il Magnifico was not pleased that his sons chose a public place for their clash of viewpoints and basic philosophy. It was especially irritating since they argued over the ring; which he knew was enchanted, but would not speak of it. Not long after this event he would describe his three sons thusly: "I have three sons, a decent one, (Guiliano who was a patron of the arts and wrote poetry like his father), a wise one (Giovanni who became Pope Leo X), and a crazy one (Piero who would become the leader of the family and of Florence and who would bring ruin to both)."

Il Magnifico had to get his sons under control. He waved his hand and directed they should bring forth the Ghirlandaio brothers, who all this time had stayed at a discreet distance so as not to be intrusive. The wave of the hand served notice that their father was not pleased with their confrontation. Without hesitation they made their way to the operators of the *bottega*.

"Now, young Buonarotti, I have news which I hope you, and your father, will receive with pleasure," Lorenzo began.

Michelangelo cast a quick glance to Granacci; then shifted his weight to stand more erect, as if he should do so in order to receive the good news.

Domenico and his brothers now came into thier presence. Escorted by the Medici brothers, they took a position next to the easel holding the hastily drawn sketch. Lorenzo looked at them with kindness, although he was not happy with Michelangelo's progress; neither the lad nor the Ghirlandaio brothers knew his true feelings. Lorenzo proceeded to solicit from them the conditions of the apprenticeship. He learned that Lodovico Buonarotti was receiving twenty-four florins to be paid over three years for the services of his second son.

"You are most kind, Master Domenico, to provide me with this information. As you know, I have a keen interest in the talent of Lodovico Buonarotti's son," he presented most formally. "Now then, it's only reasonable to explain the reason of my visit to your illustrious center."

Domenico bowed in appreciation to the compliment. *Il Magnifico* took little note of it and continued.

"With your cooperation, of course, I wish to have your brothers Benedetto and Davide accompany my sons to the Casa Buonarroti."

Michelangelo stood as if in a trance at his place. It was Granacci who broke the silence with a gasp.

Lorenzo smiled warmly at both of the young men.

"Master Granacci, Master Buonarotti fear not. My sons will only suggest a meeting between Lodovico and myself later this afternoon."

"Thank you, your Excellency. I am most pleased but you don't understand…well you can't possibly realize what my father may do when your sons arrive unannounced," Michelangelo tried to explain to the first citizen of Florence and one of the most renowned heads of state in Europe.

Once again Lorenzo warmly smiled. He assured the lad that all would be fine. Without any further comment, he sent his sons off with Benedetto and Davide Ghirlandaio. As for Domenico, he instructed that Michelangelo's possessions be prepared for transport to his new home in the Medici gardens. There he would come to learn his craft from the masterful works of art which the Medici family had collected for generations.

Domenico hastily obeyed. He called for two of the young artists to help Michelangelo and himself in gathering his belongings. All eyes of the apprenticed artists were now watching the unfolding events. No one pretended to be working at their craft.

Michelangelo did not move to follow Domenico. He was frozen to the ground on which he stood. Lorenzo once again placed his arm around the lad's shoulders, squeezed him lightly and with just the lightest touch directed him to follow Domenico. It was then he thawed and jumped and skipped his way to catch up to his master. All the while he thought, "My prayers have been answered. Lodovico or not, I shall leave this place."

"And now Master Granacci would you mind showing me around the *bottega*?"

Francesco Granacci, filled with pride for his young friend, bowed to *Il Magnifico* and presented him to the apprentices of the Ghirlandaio *bottega*.

Arthur Colonna, rather than turning off the projector, left the last image, that of the Medici Garden area of Florence, upon the screen. "Are there any questions?"

Jessica Caesarea, a raven-haired beauty whom his son, Richard, had once taken to prom, spoke. She stood to address Arthur who was still high above them in the pulpit, so typical in cathedral-like churches throughout Europe and those built in the nineteenth century in the United States. It was now John who looked towards her. He was admiring a beauty which would rival that of the Botticelli Venus, which they would soon be seeing in person in the Uffizi Galleries of Florence, Italy.

"Mr. C., whatever happened to that ring you briefly mentioned?"

"Ah yes, the ring. Good question and one which I will answer in detail at our next session. Don't let me forget, Jessica," Arthur answered with a grin. "For now, let me just say that it has been lost to history, like so many of Michelangelo's art pieces."

Another hand was raised and a quiet voice spoke. Patricia Hapsburg, currently attending Carroll University in Wisconsin, had a question. Before she spoke, she gave John a look that carried a particular meaning which John easily understood. They had been dating for some time prior to John's departure, last semester, for the University of Florence and then Oxford University in England. She was one of the few who did not have Arthur for a teacher, or principal, as she had met John when they were in college. She flipped her long brown hair behind her and asked Arthur her question.

"Are you saying that the ring was Michelangelo's work?"

"Heavens no, Patricia," Arthur responded. "I only meant that it has suffered a similar fate as some of the great master's works: some in marble, like the toothless Faun, of which you will hear more about next week; some in bronze, such as the statue of Pope Julius II in Bologna, Italy; and in paint, such as the lost cartoon, which is actually a chalk sketch of the Battle of Cascina. To my knowledge, Michelangelo never created a piece of jewelry, as many of the artists of his day had done. He was only admiring it for its uniqueness and perhaps creative rendering. Of course, we describe it as "unique and creative" only because Michelangelo looked at it with interest. We cannot actually say it was so, since, to my knowledge, we have no visual evidence of the ring."

Now it was the rather bombastic Ryan O'Donnell who jumped up without raising his hand. A tall lad with curly, light-red hair and blue eyes, he was exactly opposite of Danny Garcia in coloring; but just as breathtaking in his physical appearance, and he knew it. Despite that, there was a sigh or two from the girls. His toothy smile reminded Arthur of a teeny-bopper movie in which a sparkling light shone on the teeth of the hero whenever he smiled at his true love. The smile caused the normally flirtatious and hysterically funny blond, Kristin Sharp, and her friend the slim, auburn-haired Colleen Ross, to swoon and sink into their pew.

"Mr. C., how can you speak about something you can't prove existed?" He was sure he had trapped his former teacher in an error of some kind; he smugly flashed that smile and sat down.

"Gee, Ryan, how should I answer? It's really a philosophical question rather than an historical one. Let me just say, it comes down to us through oral tradition. Perhaps one day it shall be proven to have existed. After all, archeology continues to uncover many lost treasures." Arthur gave the answer as he made his way down into the shrine area to be closer to his students for the final directions.

Seeing no more hands, nor efforts to ask a question, Arthur motioned to Rufus who turned off the projector. A moment later, the lights of the basilica were on and, as dusk had now covered the sky outside, a whole new sight filled his students' eyes.

The session next week would take place at the Chicago Museum of Natural History where a traveling exhibit, *The World of Michelangelo and the Medici*, would be on display for a limited time. It would contain stunning examples of Renaissance art and memorabilia, some of which had never been seen in public.

"Dad, the surprise, you promised," called out John. His surprising outburst caused his fellow students to become all ears and rather agitated.

"Right, OK. Well here's the surprise…" began Arthur, who was noticeably embarrassed.

"Next week, the premiere of the film, *The Leprechaun King*, will be held here in Chicago."

Several students smiled and nodded their heads as if they were quite aware of their teacher's announcement. Most of them had read about the upcoming film debut in the gossip columns of the Chicago Tribune.

Arthur continued with a smile. "Thanks to the Mayor, it will take place at the historic Chicago Theater on State Street."

Some of the students were catching on, others were clueless. Arthur felt compelled to explain further though he really didn't want to; this unusual feeling of humility was being felt by his sons. Rich, Arthur's youngest son, finally jumped up in his pew to take over.

"My dad seems not to be able to talk about his accomplishments. I think he has some traits of Michelangelo, himself. Anyway, here's the real story. Our dad has written a book. Some of you know about it. Well, they turned it into a movie and he wrote the screenplay for it. Next week, at his insistence, the premiere will take place in his hometown, right here. All of you will have a special place in the audience. So I think we're supposed to dress appropriately, as Dad would say."

The applause was spontaneous and resounding. It echoed through the shrine. In no time at all, Arthur was surrounded by his students and, in a flash, Danny and Ryan had him elevated on their shoulders.

"Guys, put me down. This is a church," Arthur directed kindly.

As when they were in in grade school, they obeyed immediately; but they did hug him, anyway.

"By the way, my sons, Rich and John, created some of the scenes in the film." With that there were hugs all around. John anxiously waited for a jug from Jessica but it was given to Rich. The bubbly blond Breanne would have John as her target.

Chapter 3: Revelation in the Field Museum

Agnes la Straga was shouting her final directions as the last of the exhibits were being placed. Rather than using a wing of the Field Museum, for the traveling exhibit of *The World of Michelangelo and the Medici*, she arranged for the exhibit to be in the center of the vast lobby. This rectangular area, surrounded by majestic Roman columns, impeccable stone work, and marble accents, created an environment such as one might find in the Rome of antiquity and during the Renaissance. Agnes didn't care that this area of the museum was dominated by battling wooly mammoths and the skeletal remains of the Tyrannosaurus rex named Sue. She wanted the Medici and the master stone cutter to be surrounded by majesty and grandeur as they had been in their lifetimes.

The last crate was being unloaded and brought through the colonnade and portico at the rear of the building. The blue skies and the quiet waves of Lake Michigan, whose waters seemed to almost match that of the sky, created a peaceful feeling for the shippers. Their chore of carrying the crate up the stone stairs became an act of beauty and harmony. They entered the immense exhibition hall area. Agnes stood before them. Dressed in the retro style of 1950's Italy, in an ankle-length black dress with ample space for her curvy figure, she appeared more like a nun than the artist-historian who traveled with the exhibit as assistant curator. Besides being a mature single woman, there was no similarity between her and nuns. It was she who was responsible for the appearance of the exhibit and its authenticity. Anselmo Roselli, the curator of the exhibit, was nowhere to be seen. He knew better than to interfere with Agnes during set-up time.

All feelings of harmony ended when the unloaders stood before the tiny woman in black. Two hulking young men, whose size alone would cause pause to those who might challenge them, now faced the tiny woman in black. She was not in the best of spirits since the construction of the displays had not gone smoothly. The contents of this last crate, in particular, were very dear to her. She wanted to ensure that they were displayed with the utmost of care. She was short of time. Anselmo would soon arrive to conduct the final inspection and cut the ribbon with the Mayor of Chicago, which would officially begin the exhibit's time in Chicago, before it went on to New York.

She stood with arms folded across her ample bosom and one foot tapping on the marble floor. The echoing sound of that tap caused alarm to Pietro and Andreas. They found themselves unable to proceed, so they stood in front of her waiting for instructions.

"Ah, so finally you bring in the priceless jewels of this exhibit," she began harshly in broken English, though she needn't have spoken English since the two brothers were from Italy. Nevertheless, speaking English would help her, as well as the two standing before her, to perfect their communication skills. At least, that was her intent.

The two men began to shift their weight; the heavy crate wobbled in their arms.

Agnes was horrified. "*Idioso*, put that down before you destroy the priceless works within it."

Pietro and Andreas had been unloading the artifacts for the exhibit since they arrived in America; beginning in California at the San Francisco Museum of Art and working their way to Chicago via Denver, Colorado and Dallas, Texas. They knew every artifact which was crated and every crate which held those particular items. Though they did as she directed, they could not understand why all the fuss. In the crate which they gently lowered to the floor were some prints made of long-lost sketches, which were in the preliminary step to becoming a painting.

The prints were of Lorenzo de' Medici and his eldest son, Piero de' Medici. They were shown in their formal role as first citizen of the Florentine government. Though over 500 years old, the prints were not original works of art. In fact, they had only recently been discovered in the storage area of the convent of San Marco in Florence. They were added to the collection just before its shipment overseas. Along with the prints, the crate contained a small box with a piece of jewelry; but that too, from their understanding, was only a duplicate of a lost original piece which was supposed to have belonged to the Medici family for generations. The artifacts contained in the crate now, resting on the Field Museum floor, served to complete the story about the Medici family and their relationship with Michelangelo.

The only possible original artifact within the crate was contained in a long rectangular box. In that box were six bronze balls. These six balls were part of the coat of arms which once hung above the doorway on the Palazzo Medici in Florence. They were not perfect specimens, as one of them was damaged, but they were original pieces.

"Maybe it's the balls that attract the witch," Pietro whispered to Andreas. They both laughed out loud. The English translation of *la Strega* is 'the witch'; however, it was to her disposition that the brothers were referring, not to her name.

"*Mama mia*, but you are…are without brains," the witch named Agnes began. "See, before you is the display case of glass. Open the crate so that I may display its contents."

"*Si signora*, whatever you wish," replied an obedient Andreas. Though Agnes la Straga was unmarried, they used the respectful term *signora* in deference to her maturity and position.

With precision and care the brothers opened the crate and, one by one, handed the items to the witch. She, in turn, gently placed them in the display case. This case represented the Renaissance Medici and was unfortunately positioned under the rump of one of the fighting elephants.

Had Agnes known Roselli had deliberately positioned it there to mock her reverence for the pieces, she would have confronted him. The entire exhibit was arranged in a giant oval. As visitors walked from one display to another they walked into the Medici history and into the development of Michelangelo's art. Some of the displays were elaborate, and they depicted a wall of a famous church or the exterior of a *palazzo*. One exhibit was an original sculpture by Michelangelo. It was one of two figures created for the tomb of Pope Julius II but which were never placed on it. They were called the slaves, and until the time of the exhibit they were located in the Louvre in Paris, France. Through the remarkable efforts of Anselmo Roselli, the Louvre agreed to release one of the sculptures for the traveling exhibition. Not since Pope John XXIII allowed the great master's Pieta of St. Peter's in Rome to be displayed at the New York World's Fair had such a coup in artistic diplomacy been achieved with a work of Michelangelo. That coup is why Anselmo, and not Agnes la Straga, served as curator for the exhibit.

Across Grant Park and above its centerpiece, Buckingham Fountain, a figure took in the view from a seventh floor window of the Hilton Hotel. Overlooking Grant Park and Lake Michigan, the classical Field Museum was a spectacular sight for Arthur Colonna. Today was the opening day of the Michelangelo exhibit at the Field Museum, and he was soon to join Agnes and Anselmo to set up his presentation for the class. Tonight was the American premiere of the film, based upon his book, *The Leprechaun King*. Little wonder that his family was referring to the day as his "day of days."

As Arthur stood at the window, with all of these soon-to-be-celebrated events filling his thoughts, he was thinking of how his life had changed. The events of the last two years had altered him and his family. They now knew that once-unknown legends were historical fact; they had experienced enchanted realms as reality; and they knew the very foundation of their faith not only served to support the faithful but also needed to be supported lest it be destroyed. All this newly found knowledge flooded his thoughts.

He was almost relieved that he was conducting these sessions preparing students for the celebration of Michelangelo's life and works. The program served to keep him in the real world and dealing with ordinary teaching things; things which made him feel comfortable after three decades in education. He didn't mind at all that he was teaching on his special "day of days" and then running off to the Chicago Theater for the film's premiere. He had made sure that the class would be part of that celebration. He would arrive at the premiere on a school bus with all his students and his entire family.

None of these activities really flustered him because he was preoccupied with his meeting with Anselmo Roselli and Agnes la Straga. His serenity was interrupted when his wife, Donna, disrupted his reflective thoughts.

Donna had come from the rooms of their other three children and their families. Last-minute decisions were being made regarding how this or that color would, or would not, clash with the dress of another sibling or, heaven forbid, the Roses. The Roses referred to the women who, with Arthur and Donna, had saved the Leprechaun King two years ago in a struggle to protect the truth of the shamrock. The book Arthur eventually wrote of this adventure was considered to be fiction and fantasy. Only the family and the Roses knew otherwise. The burden of having so many people keep the real experiences secret was possibly the most difficult feat of their entire adventure in the enchanted realm. All sixteen, even the grandchildren, had kept the secret.

As a result, today would be about clothes, seating arrangements, time frames and cordial meetings scheduled with the Producer of the film, Arthur Lovell and of course the actors who portrayed the "Thorn and Roses" in the film. Needless to say that the term, Thorn, referred to Arthur and was the title given to him two years ago in Ireland by the actual King of the Leprechauns, Finbar X.

"Good grief, Arthur. I don't think I can do this," Donna began in a highly agitated voice.

Arthur turned from the window and collided with the armchair next to him. He stood speechless and let Donna continue to ramble.

Her first concern was for their youngest daughter, Kathy. Her fiancé, Alun, had not arrived. His flight from London was late.

"He'll be half dead by the time he gets here from O'Hare airport," she exclaimed, then took a breath and continued.

Her focus then went to their other daughter, Jana. It seems that Jana was concerned that the color of her gown would clash with that of Tricia, their daughter-in-law. Donna commented that their son, Ron, and son-in-law, Chris, didn't seem to have a care in the world. They had fought the forces of evil in a joust for the preservation of the Holy Grail, and now everything else was a piece of cake. They, therefore were not at all concerned that their ties were not matching their wives' dress colors when they were supposed to. As for the grandchildren, the little boys were playing their video games.

"Thank goodness, Olivia has some sense. She will look like the princess you call her," Donna concluded. She paused for a breath again and that's when Arthur jumped in.

"Woman, you look spectacular," he proclaimed with utmost truthfulness, using his pet name for Donna which she thought cute despite her daughters thinking it crude.

"Arthur Ronald Colonna, have you been listening to me?" she responded using his full name. "Oh, you nut. Do you think this really fits well? Are my... you know, are they too... well... exposed?" She needn't have asked; his eyes told her everything she wanted to know.

The silk gown covered in layers of emerald green lace flattered her figure. The emerald necklace she wore, a gift from Arthur on their twenty-fifth wedding anniversary, rested daintily on the upper portion of her bare bosom. Her flaming red hair, which lamentably was not inherited by any of their five children, shimmered brightly as the sunlight from the window reflected off its curls. She had been modeling the gown for her mother and Arthur's mother and hadn't realized she still had it on.

"So, you really like it, do you?" she asked as she came up to Arthur to snuggle.

"Goodness sakes, you know I do," he said with a kiss on her neck.

Suddenly, reality struck. He finally realized that he had to: conduct a class; meet with the Italian curators; arrive at the Chicago Theater on time; walk down the red carpet with his entire family and class; and meet with the producer, director, and various film people. He sat down on the chair he had almost knocked over. Donna pulled up the matching chair opposite him.

"I see that it's beginning to get to you," she began quietly with understanding.

He nodded slightly.

"Arthur, you have dealt with the evil of Mordred's ancestor to save the Holy Grail. You have faced hundreds of people at graduation ceremonies for three decades. You saved the kingdom of the Wee Folk. Certainly, this is but another adventure of sorts, isn't it?"

Arthur laughed. "Maybe it is. But I haven't ever done the movie thing and have never walked down a red carpet."

"True, but you have walked your daughter down the aisle and will soon do so with our Kathy," she said trying to reassure him.

"Thanks for bringing that up. As for the former, I was so nervous that I almost forgot to stop and kiss you. Our daughter had to pull my arm to remind me. As for Kathy's wedding, that will be after the Dublin premiere, which we have to attend, and before the Michelangelo tour. Perhaps we're getting too old to handle all of this commotion."

"Arthur Ronald, you will never be too old to handle anything," she insisted as she transferred to his lap.

After a moment, she jumped up and almost ran to the closet.

"Your students can barely keep up with you when you take them on trips. By the way, here's your tuxedo. It has an emerald green tie. Nice touch, don't you think? The boys are supposed to match you and me. The married and engaged ones are to match each other. Clever, don't you think?"

But all that Arthur could say was, "Tuxedo," and he sank lower into the chair.

As he did so, a knock on the door announced the arrival of Chris and Ron with John and Rich in hand.

"Mom," they dramatically began, not including their father in the salutation as they were going for drama and the response would not be the one they wanted from their father.

"These young-uns were in the bar," Ron began with flair.

"They were flirting with the help," added Chris with a chuckle.

"Indeed…well I never," responded Donna just as the older sons had hoped for.

All was soon forgotten as the boys came to her and kissed her on each cheek and complimented her on how terrific she looked.

"Don't you be giving me any of your blarney. It won't work. Now, here, take these bags with your tuxedos. Be sure to change into them after the lecture tonight and before you board the bus to pick us up," she admonished.

"Alright, Mom," they chorused together as they kissed her again, grabbed the tuxedo bags, threw them over their shoulders, and, winking to their elder brothers, pranced out of the room. Turning as they went through the doorway, they told their father that they'd meet him in the lobby and not to worry about the cab.

"It's already here waiting for us."

"Your sons will be the death of me," the exasperated mother sighed, with but the slightest of grins. "Here you go," she said as she presented Arthur with his tuxedo bag. "Now, be sure you call when you're almost here with the bus," she almost concluded, but he was already out the door.

As the cab pulled up to the rear portico of the museum, Arthur looked at the huge stone columns which created the classical temple appearance and recalled how many times he had brought his students here. It seemed strange now as he returned after several years with only his sons. What was even more difficult to grasp was how still everything was. The museum had been closed for the day so that the exhibit might be constructed and ready to open tomorrow to the public. Arthur had received permission to conduct his class here in a side room on condition that the displays were all in place. If they were, he would also be allowed to bring his students to view the exhibit.

As he and the boys entered the Exhibition Hall, Pietro and Andreas were leaving, carrying pieces of an obviously newly-opened crate. They were muttering something in Italian about a witch. Johnny chuckled; he had learned some Italian while he studied in Florence. The Italian brothers, seeing his response, waved and offered a greeting and a smile. The boys were carrying the equipment to be used for the presentation, but, nonetheless, tried to return a gesture.

Arthur was ahead of them as they had paused to take in the sight of the remarkable exhibit. There were towers and miniature temples, sections of palazzos, and a piazza with a fountain, columns and walls of stone. John and Rich appreciated the work now that they had had some experience building movie sets. While the boys admired the sets, Anselmo and Agnes greeted Arthur and led him around the exhibit. They explained how, for the first time, pieces of the Medici era and that of Michelangelo had been gathered from different locations and exhibited together so the important stages in the history of the noble family and master artist could be exhibited more authentically. Arthur could not praise them enough. Never in the history of these pieces had they been together in one place. Tonight, when Arthur talked about them and the time period in which they were created, his students would see them. The nervousness about the premiere vanished as feelings of magnificence and splendor filled him.

"Tonight," he thought, "the Stone Cutter Genius, as Arthur referred to Michelangelo, will take on life for my students."

Had he realized what would be revealed to him a little later, he might have considered himself a prophet.

The boys returned after setting up the equipment and testing it. It was a go, they reported to their father as they joined the private tour of the exhibit. Anselmo Roselli, since he was the curator, was in charge of the tour. He was describing the ribbon-cutting ceremony which would be held later in the afternoon with the Mayor of Chicago, his entourage, and now Arthur's students as well.

Arthur knew the Mayor. In fact he also knew the Mayor's father who had since passed away as his own father had by an unsuspected heart attack. In their college days Arthur and the current Mayor both attended Loyola University together. During those college days the then Mayor of

Chicago was the father of the future Mayor, who was to soon be present to cut the ribbon at the opening ceremony. Now the story went like this: One day Arthur was conducting research in the Chicago Public Library; Not the new one named after the late Mayor Harold Washington. It was the one built after the Chicago Fire on Michigan Ave., which now serves as the Chicago Cultural Center. On that day there was located on the chair next to him a baby seat in which his oldest son, Ron, rested. The Mayor and his entourage came walking through the area where Arthur had his books spread across the table. Little Ron was cooing away. This sweet sound attracted the Mayor who approached to admire the baby and compliment Arthur on how well-behaved the baby was. Introductions were made, and when graduation came around the Mayor made sure Arthur's family sat close to the first family of Chicago.

While Arthur was reminiscing, he missed Anselmo describing the artifacts. John grabbed his arm as they walked by a glass display case.

"Dad, look at these prints," John directed. Anselmo, oblivious of the pause, continued onward and was two displays away before he realized no one had followed him.

Arthur, flanked by his two sons, peered into the case. The prints were displayed in ornate wooden frames trimmed in gold filigree. There was no doubt about it. Both Lorenzo and Piero de' Medici wore it and both on their right hand. It was the ring to which he referred in last week's session.

"See, it's got to be the ring you talked about," observed Rich.

"No doubt about it, boys. And to think I almost walked right past it," Arthur said.

"Wait until Ryan sees this. He called it a figment of your imagination, didn't he?" stated John triumphantly.

This exchange between father and sons did not go unnoticed; but it was Agnes la Straga who did the noticing.

"Signore Colonna, I could not help but to hear of your interest in the…shall we say, the prints," she began quite mysteriously. She squeezed between John and Arthur as she spoke. This caused a gulp from John and uplifted eyes from Arthur as she brushed past them. Marilyn Monroe had nothing on Agnes la Straga when it came to the female figure. "Perhaps I can show you something else which may be of further interest to you."

By the time Arthur could answer, Anselmo had returned and had overheard Agnes.

"Now Signora la Straga, you are not going to tell your little tale to these nice Americans, are you?"

The now disgruntled la Straga was not about to back down.

"Curator, you know full well that it is not a tale but is based on fact, as demonstrated in these prints."

"You are speaking like a student of astrology, not a renowned archeologist and historian," the curator retorted.

Her hazel eyes were now flaring. Arthur and his sons backed away from the display case as it appeared the confrontation may become less than professional. Agnes would have none of it.

"I shall come to see you after your presentation, Signore."

She walked off in a huff, her long black skirt swaying violently with each step.

Anselmo looked pale, but kept his professional poise as best he could.

"Signore Colonna, the ring. Always the ring, that's all she can talk about. What do you think of the so-called legend?"

"Signore Roselli, I am just a teacher and author. I have heard about the ring as a symbol of the Medici family and these prints obviously prove that it existed. As a source of power, that is something of which I have no knowledge." A diplomatic Arthur responded. "If you will excuse me, my sons and I must prepare for my class."

"But of course, Signore. I shall see you at the ribbon ceremony then?" asked the curator.

Arthur, being gracious, told him he wouldn't miss it for the world. All the while, he was thinking of how he could sneak off to meet with Agnes la Straga. He hastily made his move toward the meeting room, beckoning his sons to follow. He directed Rich to go to the rear portico and wait for the bus. John, who had set up the equipment, would stand guard outside the room. Arthur sneaked around the outer rim of the display area and made his way towards a small office next to the ticket booth.

Time was short. The bus would soon be arriving with the students. After the presentation, there was the ribbon cutting ceremony and then everyone would board the bus, pick up the family at the Hilton and be off to the Chicago Theater for the movie premiere. Luckily, Anselmo had gone off to find Pietro and Andreas to check on their progress in setting up the area for the ceremony. Arthur was able to walk past the normal staff of the museum without arousing any suspicion. As he walked under the giant jaw of Sue, the dinosaur, he glanced up and thought how he might be caught in the jaws of a great controversy if he were not careful.

The opportunity to hear about the legend of the Medici ring was too tempting for Arthur to ignore, especially since he knew legends often contain elements of truth.

As he checked for any sight of Anselmo, Arthur slipped into the doorway of the small office area. A large window behind a rather modest wooden desk with a highly polished surface, a bookcase and a couple of chairs were all he noticed as he entered. Sitting behind the desk, Agnes was bent over a parchment-like paper. There was only one other object on the desk: a small metal box. As Arthur drew closer to the desk, he noticed the box had designs on its sides and cover.

Agnes, seeing a shadow crossing the desk and coming to rest over the box, suddenly rolled up the paper she was studying. She placed her hand over the box as if trying to conceal it. She stood up quickly.

"Ah, Signore Colonna, you have managed to stop by," she began cordially, without the slightest hint of acknowledging her invitation made earlier.

Arthur didn't know how to respond to her greeting, as he didn't want to say, "Hey, you're the one who asked me to come and see you." So he said nothing; he just smiled and nodded.

"Good, now come here next to me, I wish to share something with you. There take that chair and come," she directed with urgency. "That curator, Roselli, he thinks that because his ancestor was Piero Roselli he has a special insight into the life of the great master."

Arthur was taken aback as he had no idea to whom she was referring. His face must have shown his feeling.

"Well, how could you be expected to know that Piero was one of the master's assistant artists? In fact, one who had aided Michelangelo when he created the wonder of the Sistine Chapel ceiling painting," she explained to Arthur. His understanding of what she had meant could be read on his face, through his expressive eyes.

"But I always thought the Sistine was the work of his hand alone," Arthur finally said.

"Precisely my point *signore*, the master would not share his task, for none would be able to match his skill. He used Piero Roselli, Giuliano da Sangallo and even Francesco Granacci along with some boys from his workshop to undertake minimal tasks. They would... how would you say it? Ah yes...run errands. You know, fetch the paint, carry the cartoon up the scaffolding, and bring him a piece of bread for his lunch or dinner. As you must certainly know, he continued to work as he paused briefly to eat."

Arthur was glancing at his watch and Agnes noticed. She apologized and recognized that he must leave soon to conduct his presentation. And she was not ignorant of his need to be at the premiere of his movie, as she referred to the film. Arthur, on his part, tried to explain that it wasn't his movie; that he had only written the script for it.

"Nonsense," she interrupted. "It was your creative genius who came up with the story and made the book and put the words into the actors' mouths."

"I am honored by your compliment Signora la Straga. But as you say, I have a class to teach," Arthur said without further attempts to sway her opinion.

"It is but the truth. Now let us get to the point of my invitation."

And with that she unrolled the papers which she still held in her hand. This required her hand to be removed from the metal box. In doing so Arthur was now able to clearly see the designs. On the lid was a pattern of three circles intertwined. On the front panel was what looked like three crowns, on both of the side panels was a formation of three balls. The back panel, he would later note, showed a large star from which three streams of light flowed downward to a small building.

"So the box interests you, Signore Colonna?" she asked with a hint of delight in her voice.

The urgency of teaching a class began to recede as she handed Arthur the box and he turned it around to view it from every angle.

"Its delicacy is truly lovely, signora."

"It's the work of the master, Donatello," she commented. "Our curator would say it's a fake, but I know better. I can point out to you why this is, without a doubt, a work of the early master. See how this has been cast? If you compare it to his David in bronze or the pulpits in San Lorenzo church you will see similarities that could only come from his hand. Nevertheless, Roselli has decided to remove this from the display case with the prints of the Medici and their heraldic symbols."

"What a loss to those who visit, for whoever did create the piece certainly deserves recognition," concluded Arthur so as not to say the curator, or she, was in the wrong.

"*Sì*, you are right, but let us get on. I know that your time is short. I already hear the footsteps of a crowd coming across the marble floor of the museum. Hopefully, the curator will conduct a tour while they wait for you."

With that, she drew his attention to the pages she was flattening out on the desk.

By the time she had finished explaining the contents of the document and how the pages were found, Arthur was dumbfounded. When he learned that the pages had been concealed in the famous Medici Chapel within one of its carved choir stalled panels, and that those stalls had been created by Michelangelo for the chapel, he was enthralled with the revelation.

Premiere or no premiere, class or no class, he had to know more.

She told the Medici legend by pointing to those parts of the manuscript she had just rolled out which pertained to the story that she was telling.

"To help you better comprehend that which I will come to show you, I must first take you back to the origin of the ring's existence, and to do that we must travel back in time to Bethlehem of over 2000 years ago. Mary and Joseph had been able to move out of the stable and into a small house shortly after the birth of our Lord. There they were to wait for their turn to be counted in the Roman census ordered by Caesar Augustus. Only then could they make arrangements to join a caravan going back to Nazareth in the province of Galilee." And so her words brought Arthur back to Bethlehem of the first century of the Christian era.

"Dear Joseph, it's beautiful, truly a work of art," the joyous Mary told her husband.

She walked over to the cradle to admire it more closely. In her arms her infant son wiggled a bit, but made no noise of complaint.

"I'm glad that you like it Mary. It's the best I could do with the scraps of wood which I was able to find," he responded. "Do you think the babe will fit comfortably? For if he continues to grow much faster, he will surely outgrow the cradle before he gets to use it."

Mary just smiled as she placed the child into the cradle. In an instant, the infant Jesus had fallen asleep.

"Look, he takes to it. It's as if he wants you to know how much he likes his new bed."

Joseph smiled broadly as Mary tucked the thickly woven woolen covering around the sleeping infant. Just as she had finished and they stood over the cradle to admire the sleeping Jesus, as any young couple might do, there was a pounding at the door.

Joseph hastened to answer the knock at the door to prevent another banging which might wake the child. When he opened the door, there stood before him a young lad dressed in a white tunic trimmed at hem and sleeves with bands of blue. In length, the hem reached his knees. His head was bare, revealing dark hair which flowed just below the ears. His dark blue eyes met Joseph's dark brown eyes.

"Would this be the home of Joseph of Galilee?" the boy inquired.

It is indeed," replied Joseph pleasantly. "And whom do I have the pleasure of greeting?"

"I am Timothy of Syria, but that is of no importance. I am commanded by my masters to seek out a child; a child whose birth was foretold in the heavens by a wandering star which led them to this place," the lad explained.

Mary was alarmed and stood in front of the cradle to conceal it from view. The town was abuzz with news that three strangers were seeking the newborn King of the Jews. She knew only too well who her son really was. And yet she was a mother and a protective one at that.

"Is that so? I do remember seeing a bright light in the sky when Mary's son was born. But we were in a stable in the mountains at the time. I doubt that the child is the one you seek," Joseph explained. "Wouldn't you think a king would be born in a castle?"

"The will of God is not mine to question, sir," the wise lad answered.

"Well then Master Timothy, in that case, who are these masters of whom you speak?" inquired Joseph as he turned to Mary and winked. This gesture offered great relief to Mary as to the safety of her son.

"Perhaps it's best that they introduce themselves, for they approach us," and Timothy gave a low bow and moved to the side of the doorway.

Joseph could only stand amazed as the first of what would be three obviously regal personages bent below the door's top beam to enter the house.

The man was rather tall, not at all like those of Rome. His robes and headdress were threaded with gold and studded with precious gems. His pure white hair reached his shoulders and his long, well-trimmed beard matched it in color.

"I am Melchior of the eastern province of the Empire called Armenia," he announced to Joseph.

Before Joseph could but gesture a welcome to enter, the next was at the door.

This man was also regal but his garb was in the style of the Far East. In color, it was dark indigo trimmed in silver thread. In height, he was of the size of a Roman though his complexion was of dark olive not from Italy.

He bowed to Joseph. "I am Balthazar of Persia."

Just as Joseph made a sweeping low wave so as to direct where the regal Persian should go, the third arrived.

In flaming red robes which reached the floor and fastened at the waist with a golden band, he presented himself in a manner which dazzled Joseph who, in all his life had never seen or met personages of such obvious importance. Upon his head was a turban of wrapped cloth in various shades of reds and oranges laced with white pearls.

Also with a reverence to Joseph he entered. "I am Caspar of Ethiopia."

He joined the other two who now stood to the left of Mary. She was picking up the child from his new crib.

Mary sat on a wooden chair next to the new crib. Her long dress of white wool flowed down to the floor. The blue veil covering her head revealed her youthful face and the edges of her chestnut-colored hair. The child, Jesus, nestled his head into her so only his dark brown hair was seen by the three guests. She appeared as the blessed mother in Michelangelo's painting of "The Madonna of the Stairs."

Mary lifted her eyes from her son and gazed into each of the eyes of the guests. Her smile softened the hearts of all present, and the resulting feeling of warmth must have been felt by the child, Jesus, for he immediately turned his head. As the Three Magi gazed upon the divine face they fell to their knees and presented their gifts of gold, frankincense, and myrrh.

"He is the promised one. Of this there can be no doubt," uttered an enraptured Melchior.

Balthazar and Caspar joined Melchior who reached out to touch the divine son. As they did so the rings which they wore on their right hand seemed to take on a life of their own as Melchior's gold band glowed, Balthazar's silver band radiated and Caspar's copper band glistened.

Mary, Joseph, and Timothy marveled at the three rings. The child reached out and touched each of the Magi's fingers on which the rings reflected the divine presence. Tears flowed from the Magi as they felt blessed by the promised one. Each removed the band from his finger. They motioned to Timothy to take them and present them to Mary. Each placed his ring into Timothy's outstretched hand, placing them one upon the other. Timothy could see that they were simply made. On the interior of each band was engraved the name of the one who wore it. On the exterior was an astrological symbol which represented their gifts; gold, frankincense, and myrrh.

Timothy approached the Holy Family and bowed, kneeling before them. His hand was still extended. He elevated his hand towards Joseph. The Magi smiled and asked that he accept this additional token of their esteem.

Joseph looked at his wife and knew her wish without a word being spoken.

"With your permission esteemed guests. We believe the rings were intended to be returned to your servant. Let it be our gift to him in appreciation for his introducing you to us."

The Magi could not be more pleased. "Timothy, take the rings with our blessing," directed Caspar.

The lad picked up the top band, so that Balthazar might place it on his finger, only to find that the three bands were now joined together, intertwined to make one ring. Jesus, Mary, and Joseph smiled and the Magi interpreted the miracle of the rings to be a sign of favor upon the lad and any who possessed the gift of the Holy Family.

"And that, Signore Colonna," concluded Agnes la Straga, "brings me to the contents of the Donatello box."

Arthur was speechless as his thoughts were brought back to the present. In the mean time, she placed the box on top of the papers, which contained the story she just shared.

It was at that point when John entered the tiny office looking for his father.

"Dad, everyone is here. I don't think they can take much more of Mr. Roselli."

Agnes la Straga laughed at John's evaluation of the tour. She lifted up the lid of the bronze box and there it was: a ring of three intertwined bands. One was gold, one was silver, and one was copper. It was John who realized what it was.

"Dad, it's the Medici Ring," he exclaimed.

"Your son is almost correct," responded Agnes. "It is a replication of the ring of the Magi created for members of the Medici family who came to power years after Piero was killed. The original was lost shortly after Piero de Medici's death at the Battle of the Gagliano River near the abbey of Montecasino. In that battle, Piero tried to defeat forces sent against him as he attempted to regain his power in Florence. His body was taken from the river to a temporary burial site near Naples. On his right hand was the ring of the Magi bequeathed to him by *Il Magnifico*."

"Then there really was a ring of the Medici or should I say, the Magi?" Arthur asked when Agnes' revelation sank in.

"Indeed there was and is…" she began when the curator, Anselmo Roselli, burst into the office.

"Ah, Signore Colonna…I see that your son has found you. Your other son awaits you with your class as the tour has long since ended," the curator announced.

With apologies, Arthur took his leave, after he offered two invitations.

Arthur asked Signora la Straga and Curator Roselli to be his guests at the premiere and at the reception at the Chicago Hilton.

Chapter 4: The Medici Gardens

Arthur and his son couldn't wait to share the legend with Rich, but they would have to wait. There was a class to teach and a film premiere to attend before they would have time to indulge in legends. They entered the room expecting to bring the world of Michelangelo to life amidst examples of his writing and art.

Neither expected the room to look like Prom night.

His students had decked themselves out in suits, tuxedos, and gowns which dazzled the eyes. They wanted to show how much they had appreciated their teacher's invitation to participate in his "day of days." John meekly took his seat next to Rich as the only two people in the room in jeans and tee-shirts. The tee-shirts were appropriate, Rich's had the book title and a shamrock and John's had Michelangelo's David superimposed on an outline of Italy, but they felt very out of place. Their tuxedos were in plastic bags at the rear of the room; ready for them to wear after class.

Showtime, thought Arthur, as he switched on the projector and computer. The first image was the Palazzo Medici.

"You may be surprised that the family home of the Medici was a rather plain-looking building built by *Il Magnifico's* grandfather, Cosimo. It was his intent that it should be unimpressive on the outside," Arthur began, "but when they entered it, visitors were awestruck with its marble accents, fine statuary, and library of ancient manuscripts and paintings of some of the most renowned artists of the age. We shall learn more about it as we see Michelangelo living in it; for, unlike other artists invited to learn in the Medici Gardens, this would-be stone cutter was given rooms in the palace itself."

Arthur pressed the remote and the Piazza San Marco with the church of the same name came into view.

"Here is where the Medici gardens were located," Arthur continued. "Michelangelo would make his new home in a protected environment with high walls and covered workplaces so no prying eyes could disturb his development of artistic skills. Before any of that could take place, however, there was the matter of getting Lodovico's permission." Arthur narrated the class back into the fifteenth century.

The younger Ghirlandaio brothers and Medici sons, Giovanni and Piero arrived at Casa Buonarroti in early afternoon. Uncle Francesco opened the door to a loud banging. Piero, as usual, made the excessive noise. He was never to be one who would be sensitive to others or their interests or needs. It was all about him and what he wanted. On that afternoon, it was about bringing Lodovico to the Palazzo Medici to meet with his father, *Il Magnifico*. The only salvation in this initial contact was that Lodovico, as did most Florentines, respected Lorenzo de' Medici and would never have dreamed of refusing the invitation.

Piero marched past Uncle Francesco into the living room, where that last beating of Michelangelo had taken place two years earlier. There would never be such an incident again. *Il Magnifico* would see to that.

"Signore Buonarroti," Piero began as he walked into the room where Lodovico was now standing in response to such grand visitors being in his modest home.

"My father has need of your presence at the Palazzo this afternoon. What say you to his request?"

The normally vociferous Lodovico looked over the young Medici's shoulder to catch sight of Francesco. He could barely speak, let alone respond in an intelligible manner.

"Well, what is your reply?" asked Piero as he sat down in a chair with cushions normally used by Lodovico and no one else.

"Young sir, this is such a…a surprise," Lodovico stammered, then quickly added. "To be sure, it's a great honor, as well."

"Good, then I take it you shall present yourself to my father this very afternoon," Piero concluded as he rose from the chair.

His brother, Giovanni, now age fifteen and future Pope Leo X, being called the wise one, simply had to say something. He moved his plump frame to stand in front of his elder and more athletic-looking brother.

"Signore, our father would be honored to meet with you on such short notice, though if that should prove too unreasonable, he would understand."

Uncle Francesco was making his way to stand next to Michelangelo's father. He did not want him to blow up as he would often do with his second son when talking about matters of artistic endeavors. Luckily for the Buonarroti family, and especially Michelangelo, his father had sense not to overreact.

"Noble gentlemen, you do this house honor and we shall come to the Palazzo this very day," Lodovico Buonarroti answered pleasantly.

With that said, Piero immediately turned and made his way out the door before Giovanni and the artists could offer a more gracious farewell.

Giovanni and the Ghirlandaio brothers were left to chase after him with but a bow; they could already hear the horses' hooves clattering on the stone pavement as Piero prepared to depart. Their servant had barely given a foot up to Giovanni before Piero was trotting down what is now called Via Ghibelina towards the Piazza della Signoria. The news of the noble guests at the Buonarroti house spread throughout the quarter and the neighbors were hanging out of their windows and standing in their doorways so that they might see the Medici and shout greetings of praise to them. The greetings of *"Palle, Palle"* were more in honor of their father whom they respected. Such adulation would never be offered to Piero when he succeeded his father, a mere two years later in April of 1492.

Back in Casa Buonarroti the scene was fast-paced as Lodovico was quickly changing into clothes worthy of his noble ancestry as well as being presented to Lorenzo.

"So the Medici now has taken to my son," Lodovico cursed. "They seek to have this calling of his fulfilled. Our family is destined to be poor, Francesco."

"Brother, do not fret so. Imagine the possibilities should your son please the Medici," Francesco consoled.

"All I can see is my eldest, Lionardo, now talking of entering the Order of St. Dominic. When that happens, our house shall not have an heir from the eldest. Then I see my second son, nothing more than a stone cutter covered in white marble dust and for what, I ask you? For nothing more than embellishing their grand Palazzo."

"Lodovico, perhaps the Medici can place you in a position with income," Francesco offered hoping to end his lamentation. "Would that not make his apprenticeship worthwhile?"

"Now you have hit upon an idea of merit," a more opportunistic Lodovico answered.

Lodovico and Francesco arrived at the gates of the Palazzo later that afternoon. The two were escorted down a mosaic walkway to the main part of the Palazzo. Lorenzo hoped to impress Michelangelo's father with a hint of what was being offered to his son, while not overwhelming him with the opulence of the interior of the Palazzo. Statues from antiquity were scattered throughout the garden and yet they represented but a few of what would be available to Michelangelo in the Medici Gardens just a few blocks away.

Lorenzo chose to meet with Lodovico in the *Cappella dei Magi*. It was a small, intimate room, stunning in its decoration with frescoes by Benozzo Gozzoli. One day, Lodovico's son would design and create the choir stalls which stand in the chapel today. As the two men entered, *Il Magnifico* stood resplendent in a white and gold coat and tunic. Coming down from under the tunic were red leggings more closely fitted as tights. Lodovico noticed that Lorenzo's attire matched that of one of the three Magi in the fresco on the wall next to where he stood. The countenance of the youngest of the three kings was that of *Il Magnifico*, though much younger.

All of Florence, and indeed Italy, knew of the Medici attachment to the legend of the Three Magi. It is said that these three Wise Men had blessed the Medici family. The family itself believed the legend and therefore the decorations in their Palazzo reflected the theme of three. Two sets of three balls were part of their coat of arms. The three Wise Men were depicted in various artistic works throughout their Palazzo's chapel and their villa outside of Florence. The ring, which Lorenzo wore, consisted of three independent bands intertwined to make one ring. That ring was said to be blessed with the power to bestow its wearer with the gold of prosperity, the preeminence of frankincense, and the sweetness of myrrh in a peaceful death. It had come into the hands of the Medici when Lorenzo's grandfather, Cosimo received it as a gift from the antipope, John XXIII, after his abdication. It was this warrior-pirate turned-Cardinal, who tried to claim the papacy. It was also he who had stolen the ring from its shrine in Rhegium.

Lodovico was surrounded by frescos which practically confirmed the legend of the Magi and their connection to the Medici. *Il Magnifico*, himself, stood before him and extended a hand of welcome. On the index finger of that right hand was the very ring of the Magi. Lodovico bowed to kiss the ring on the hand. He felt a sense of warmth, a feeling of peace, an exhilaration of spirit, as he did so.

"Welcome, Master Buonarroti, or may I call you cousin, to our home," Lorenzo began. "You honor us by your presence."

It seems there was a family connection on Michelangelo's mother's side, and therefore, the term cousin was most appropriate.

"On the contrary, you are the one who honors me, my brother, and my entire house," Lodovico replied in a manner which seemed foreign to this usually sullen man.

As they spoke two chairs were brought in behind them. Lorenzo invited them to be seated. His son, Giovanni, brought in Michelangelo.

"And here is your son now, Master Buonarroti."

Michelangelo hoped to see a gleam of love, and if not love, perhaps an acceptance of his calling. He approached his father and bowed. Lodovico nodded his head. There was no sign either of love or the acceptance of his calling. On the other hand, at least there was no sign of anger.

"I will get right to the point. Your son has demonstrated an enormous creative talent in the Ghirlandaio *bottega*. So much talent that I feel only in the Medici Gardens could he continue to grow in skill and expression of his art. Therefore, I wish him to become a member of my household," the charming leader of the Medici family stated without his normal diplomatic jargon.

Lodovico saw a chance to back out of this proposal. Due to his family's noble connections, to be a household servant would be beneath a Buonarroti. "My Lord, our family is honored and yet my son has an ancient bloodline."

"Master Buonarroti, have I misspoken? Your son is not to be a servant of the household, but a member of my family. He is to live in the Palazzo and enjoy all that my own children enjoy in comfort, education, and artistic endeavors," the shrewd Lorenzo countered.

The young fifteen-year-old glanced at Giovanni de' Medici and smiled broadly. He could not hide feelings. Lorenzo noticed his pleasure and pursued his proposal to bring the boy into his family circle.

"Your son shall learn what my sons learn under the guidance of the Greek scholar and author, Marsilio Ficino. Your son shall dine at my table. He shall converse with poets and philosophers, such as Angelo Poliziano. What say you?"

It was Lodovico's turn to seek guidance, while showing amazement, as he glanced at Francesco. The uncle could only return a gesture of open hands pointing to Lorenzo. This was not unnoticed by *Il Magnifico*.

"By the way Lodovico, have you a position of honor in our city?" He asked, although he knew the answer.

"I am a humble man with some land, but I can read and write," the elder Buonarroti answered.

"I think I have a position which would compliment your talents. What say you?" asked Lorenzo with sugar on his tongue.

"I say, Excellency, that you do the house of Buonarroti a great honor," Lodovico replied.

It was settled. Lorenzo directed Michelangelo to take leave of his father. As the boy approached his father, he glanced at his uncle who showed no emotion whatsoever. His father rose and the boy embraced him. In return, Lodovico placed his hands on the boy's shoulders and wished him every success in upholding the family honor.

This too did not go unnoticed by *Il Magnifico*, who immediately put his arm around the boy, and with the other arm, brought his own son into the embrace. The threesome walked past Uncle Francesco and Lodovico. They were a living sign of the Medici and their heritage from the three Magi. Out of the chapel and into the palazzo, the threesome glided as if on a cloud. One was to become the greatest artist of his era; one became a pope of the Universal Church; and one was a patron of the arts and the greatest of the Medici.

The uncle and father stood looking around the *Cappella dei Magi*. Neither understood the significance of the Magi legend, but they did understand power and wealth; they were hopeful that Michelangelo might see what they saw and give up this notion to be a stone cutter.

There were others who fully understood the significance of the legend. They had been in existence since Timothy first brought the miraculous Magi ring to Italy. Many prominent and educated men of the era became members of what came to be called the Confraternity of the Tre Magi during the Medici rule of Florence.

The role of the order was simple: to tell the story of the three Wise Men. They were also to interpret the heavens for messages from God; as did the original three Wise Men when they saw the star which led them to Bethlehem. The order was not particularly secretive, but very selective of who might become members. It was this group who managed to preserve the Magi ring for centuries; until it finally came into the possession of the Medici family who revered the legend of the Three Kings as much as the confraternity did.

"The Florentines were particularly interested in the sect as they placed great trust in signs of heaven. Even the Buonarroti Family was interested in astrology for Michelangelo's biographer, Condivi, writes about it. And certainly this information came from the sculptor himself. He recorded that 'Mercury and Venus were in the second house and in a favorable aspect to Jupiter.' This message of the stars and planets on March 6, 1475, the day Michelangelo was born, indicates that the boy child would be successful but primarily in the arts such as painting, sculpture, and architecture. The alignment of the planets must have been auspicious indeed, for by the time Michelangelo would pass from this life to eternal life on February 18, 1564 writers such as Lodovico Ariosto were referring to him as being, 'more than a mortal; a divine angel...' and that was in 1516."

Arthur looked at his watch and turned off the projector. The mesmerized students suddenly found themselves back in the museum.

"I'm afraid that will be it for today. It's almost time for the ribbon cutting ceremony and then we're off to see the movie. I still have to get dressed; it wouldn't do for me to be upstaged by my elegantly-attired students."

The students giggled, laughed, smiled and shouted hurray for Mr. C. as Arthur made his way to collect the plastic bag containing his tuxedo.

By the time Arthur and the boys joined the class in the exhibit area, there was quite a gathering of glittering guests. The red ribbon had been stretched across the open space between the white marble sculpture *The Slave,* and the display case which held the prints depicting Lorenzo and Piero de' Medici wearing the Magi ring. John noticed that the box which contained the duplicated Magi ring was back in the display case despite what Anselmo Roselli directed. He tugged on his father's tuxedo coat.

"Look, she put it on display anyway."

Arthur admired the delicately designed container. He observed that it was placed next to a long rectangular box containing six bronze balls, one of which was charred as if it had been in a fire.

As he returned his attention to the ribbon, he saw Agnes on one side of the Mayor and Anselmo on the other side. She gave him a mischievous smile, as if she were saying, "The box is by Donatello and the ring does exist and deserves to be exhibited."

Anselmo must not have noticed the changes to the case, for he was all smiles and gracious to Agnes. His remarks were quite complimentary to the assistant curator, who, in her long black evening dress, reminded Arthur of a stereotypical Italian bomb shell in a 1960's movie. What came to his mind were Sophia Loren and Gina Lollobrigida, the former being a particular favorite of his. She's trying for that look, that's for sure, Arthur thought, noticing what a commanding figure she possessed.

"I declare the exhibit of Michelangelo and the World of the Medici open," proclaimed the Mayor, as he cut the ribbon and it fluttered softly to the ground. The guests began to mill about as Arthur led his class to the bus. He was sure that the family must be waiting in the lobby of the hotel by now, anxious to get to the theater.

This time, instead of the usual yellow school bus, the waiting bus was from the Chicago Bus Tours and Cruises Co. The mini motor coach was to be a surprise for Donna and the family. It was ridiculous enough to arrive at the Chicago Theater by bus, but a yellow one would have been too much, even for Arthur; his wife and daughters would never have forgiven him.

As the bus arrived at the Chicago Hilton Hotel on Michigan Avenue, the family poured out onto the expansive sidewalk. If the gathering at the Museum was glittering, then this gathering of the Colonna clan was dazzling. Arthur saw that Alun had arrived; he was arm in arm with Arthur's youngest daughter, Kathy. Alun's bushy black hair and vibrant blue eyes towered over her petite frame resplendent in a sparkly, champagne gown. Arthur and Donna's grandsons were adorable in their tuxedos: Arthur V with a red tie, Riley with a white tie, and Connor with a blue tie. Their mothers, Tricia and Jana, thought the patriotic colors would be good luck. Arthur's granddaughter, Olivia, now eleven years old, was quite a little lady in an A-line gown of royal blue. Arthur and the boys got off the bus to help the family board. Donna knew most of the students from when they were kids in Arthur's school, so it was old home week as she boarded the bus. The students wanted to tell her about the trip and about the magical ring, but the commotion of Ron and Chris helping Donna's mother, Grandma Shields; and the boys assisting Arthur's mother, Nona Colonna, onto the bus caused a distraction. Despite traveling on a bus for this day of days, the grandmothers were thrilled.

"If only my Arthur was alive and here to see this day of days for our son," declared Nona to her grandsons through eyes glistening with tears. Grandma Colonna's melancholy mood soon lifted. Once on the bus, she began to tell a story of her youth when she went to see a movie and a stage show at the Chicago Theater; the very one to which they were headed. The family and students sat enthralled listening to the tale of her meeting Frank Sinatra at the back stagedoor during those last days of World War II. She and her friend Minnie Afronto had run from the front entrance of the theater to the alley entrance to get his autograph.

The Roses, as everyone now called Anita, Marilyn, and Nancy, were the last to board. They were the people who, with the Papa and Grammy characters, were the main characters in Arthur's book, and now in the movie. They were excited about again meeting the actresses who played them on film. The Roses had participated in the casting process; perhaps that was why Marilyn's role went to an Academy Award-winning actress and retired singer; Nancy's role went to the famous character actress known for having beaten up her co-star in a movie; and Anita's role went to another Oscar winner famous for her ten minute role as England's Queen.

The producer, Arthur Lovell, had called in some favors from the studio and the result was *The Leprechaun King* would be given a formal premiere in the United States and Europe. The entire family, the Roses, and now the students were a part of the festivities. The excitement built as the bus made its way around the block to get to State Street. Arthur wanted to be on the right side of the street when they got off and he also wanted to pass by the former Marshall Fields Store, now Macy's flagship store. Everyone on the bus would be going to the famous Walnut Room located on the seventh floor of the historical store for a high tea on Saturday. The event would also allow the film's producer to speak with Arthur about a new project he had in mind while the family went off to the Field Museum to view the Michelangelo exhibition.

The evening was pleasant with a breeze, coming off Lake Michigan, bringing a refreshing coolness on a summer-like evening. The women were particularly grateful for the breeze and lack of humidity as their coiffures would not wilt. This relief was being expressed as the bus was in a line of limos and cars waiting to be unloaded. The ABC network in Chicago had the best view of the proceedings from their studio, directly across the street from the theater.

"Good grief," Arthur exclaimed. "Arthur Lovell has outdone himself."

"I'd say," Rich observed. "Look at that red carpet. It covers the whole sidewalk."

"Well Dad, now what do you think about getting off a bus on your day of days?" asked his daughter, Jana. Of all Arthur and Donna's children, she would be the most sensitive to what others thought about the family and her father.

Arthur understood her concerns; however, he didn't much care about the opinions of others. He cared more about having his family together, and the bus was the most practical way to accomplish that. Anyway, he would say, "What would a city boy raised in the west side suburb of Oak Park, Illinois want with a limo?" He was not able to even think of such a prestigious and ostentatious arrival. Luckily, his students had their arrival all planned by the time the bus got to the Chicago theater marquee area. The students and Jana took control of disembarking from the bus.

The bus drew nearer to the red carpet area. The huge marquee letters spelling CHICAGO were flashing. Huge black letters announced the name of the film: American Premiere of *The Leprechaun King*, Starring…and then the list of the actors' names in smaller letters followed. As the bus slowly approached the theater, Arthur was taken back to his youth and he started to reminisce with those present.

"How this brings me back to my youth," Arthur began. "I was about Michelanngelo's age when he entered the *Ghirlandaio botegga*. My cousin Bud and I took the EL to the Loop. We were going to our first live performance. The play starred a well-known New York actor named Cyril Ritchard. You kids probably remember him as Captain Hook in the Mary Martin version of *Peter Pan* on TV."

There was nothing but blank looks coming from the young people.

"Well, anyway, like Nona did, we ran to the rear of the theater and got to meet Captain Hook. It was quite cool for two Taylor Street boys looking for a bit of culture. We gave him an umbrella as I recall."

"Dad, are you for real? You gave a big star an umbrella?" a horrified Jana asked.

"Well it looked like rain and I thought that would be a more appropriate present for a guy," he said in defense to the weird looks from his students and family, who were hearing the tale for the first time.

He continued with his story of how the actor's assistant was so impressed by the gesture that the boys were invited into the Michael Todd

Theater dressing room to meet the Broadway star. It turned out that Cyril Ritchard was originally from Australia and had moved to London to begin his acting career. While there, his wife was killed during a World War II bombing raid. After the war, he came to New York to pursue his acting career on Broadway. And the rest, as they say, is history. Taking the umbrella with profound thanks, he asked Arthur to pray for him. Later that week, Arthur and Bud received a note of thanks from the actor. They continued to correspond, and whenever Cyril was in Chicago a set of tickets were on hold for Arthur. When Arthur married Donna, the same tradition continued. It was at a performance of *Side by Side by Sondheim* in Chicago that Arthur and Donna would speak to him again. While on stage, the actor collapsed and Arthur accompanied him to Northwestern Hospital where he stayed with him until Cyril's foster son arrived from New York. That was the last time Arthur saw him.

"Perhaps I could have told a happier memory," he now thought to himself as he looked at the saddened eyes of his students.

Luckily, the bus jerked to a stop bringing everyone's attention back to the premiere. The door of the bus opened; Danny and Ryan stood to announce the plan for disembarkation. Arthur was surprised and waited for his instructions. The students left the bus first. They formed a double line of honor between which the family would walk. Danny and Ryan were closest to the bus door to help anyone who needed it. Once the double line was formed, each little family within the clan left the bus. Kathy and Alun; Jana and Chris with their sons, Connor and Riley; Ron and Tricia with their children, Olivia and young Arthur V; The Roses; the boys, John and Rich; Nona Colonna and Gram Shields; and finally, Arthur and Donna made their way through the honor guard to the glass doors held open by Jessica and Jenny. Arthur and Donna were both teary-eyed by the students' thoughtfulness.

Arthur had not been to the Chicago Theater since he and Donna moved the family to Wisconsin when Ron was five and Jana three years old. The marble staircase and chandeliers of crystal were as he remembered them. Sculpted works of art stood in niches and alcoves throughout the lobby area and along the staircase. This was, after all, a renowned movie palace when it was built. The opulence was meant to lend elegance and legitimacy to the film industry of the 1920's. It could rival a Medici Villa.

Arthur Lovell stood on the first step of the staircase. He was waiting to greet Arthur and his family and to direct the actors and actresses to their special box seats jutting out from the end and to the sides of the mezzanine. Arthur, his family, and his students would sit in the mezzanine, which would conveniently hold the more than thirty people in his group. As everyone took their seats, Tricia and Jana made sure the little boys did not hang too far over the railing. The auditorium and gigantic stage spoke of the golden age of film. In the midst of the commotion to get settled, John and Rich waved wildly to a group seated on the main floor. Somehow the reservations were mixed up and Arthur's widowed sister, Janice, from Philadelphia and her family were directly below them. Next to them were Donna's brother, John, and his family. Everyone was waving enthusiastically to each other and mouthing the words, "see you at the hotel." Donna's mother and Arthur's mother began to cry.

"Mom," he began, "this is a happy movie, really."

"I know," replied his mother as she wiped away her tears. She handed some of her tissue over to Donna's mother.

The lights dimmed and a spotlight followed a lone figure along the stage line. It was Arthur Lovell, the film's producer. He welcomed everyone to the premiere of *The Leprechaun King* which, he added, "was the inspiration and creative work of Arthur Colonna and his sons John and Richard Colonna." Another spotlight shone on the mezzanine and the boys dragged Arthur to his feet. The three waved and sat down amidst a flood of tears from the family.

The producer introduced the actors; the director, Nolan Clancy; the assistant director, Dan Caesare; and so forth. He invited everyone in the audience to fill out a comment card after the show.

"You may place them in the boxes located throughout the lobby."

There was an applause and then darkness as the majestically trimmed curtain folded upwards to reveal the gigantic screen. The theme song began. It was the *Magic of Life* composed by two of Arthur's former students, David and Steve Mason. They were seated with their families, and parents Don and Rosemary, in the orchestra section.

As the celtic melody filled the theater, the camera swept across the west coast of Ireland. The huge screen on which the opening credits were projected absorbed the audience into its visual scenes. A tingling sensation could be felt in one's abdomen as the camera zoomed down along the cliffs of Moher and over the Torc waterfall.

As the view hovered over the falls, a rainbow shot upwards towards the audience. Members of the family actually jolted backwards in their seats as they tried to avoid being hit. John and Rich poked each other as they saw the reaction to the effect they had created. The audience was then taken over the Atlantic Ocean, ever westward with the sensation of flying still tingling in their stomachs. The names of the actors swept across images of New York City. The credits continued as the scenery took the audience away from the east coast of the United States towards the heartland of America.

One could hear some "oohs" and "aahs" as the landscape sequences of Amish farms unfolded. When the aerial view swept across Chicago and those familiar places which Arthur's family had just seen, the words "Screenplay by Arthur Colonna based on his book: *Papa and the Leprechaun King*" appeared on the huge screen.

Thunderous applause from the mezzanine and a few rows in the orchestra made Arthur slink down into his red-upholstered seat. Arthur Lovell looked over from his box to the mezzanine area, smiling. Donna pulled on Arthur to sit up straight so that he could see the producer. The rainbow crossed the Daniels dairy farm in Wisconsin, over the town of Burlington, and into a subdivision, towards a colonial-style two-story home. As the rainbow descended down towards the house, the scene dissolved into the living room and the story began.

Arthur listened intently for audience reaction. He could hear some gasps during the fight sequence on top of Dun Aengus on the cliffs of Inishmore Island. There were giggles of delight when the leprechaun king appeared and bantered with Arthur in the movie. Arthur's grandchildren, who knew the leprechaun king personally, took great delight in these scenes. During the dance sequence, he felt that the audience got into its rhythmic pattern. The Roses, themselves, took great delight in how they were being portrayed.

All of this reaction paled in comparison to the reaction when the real Thorn and Roses made their cameo appearance in the Blarney Castle scene, and when Arthur and Donna's children and grandchildren, as extras, made their appearance. The students, and family in the orchestra, went wild. Mercifully, those scenes were short and the uproar did not detract from the film. And so it went, the audience continued to be thrilled with the chase scene and they were in awe during the breathtaking sequences of Glenedalough and the Aran Islands. They seemed to enjoy the movie immensely, especially the ending sequence where those portraying Arthur's characters entered the Hollywood – or, rather London -- version of the Wee Folk Realm, filmed at Pinewood Studios. As the musical crescendo of the ending celebration unfolded, the students, family and the audience were tapping their feet. The scene dissolved back into the living room where the film's adventure had begun. A gold coin was twirling in the air. The characters of Arthur and Donna kissed as their grandchildren, who played themselves, slept on the sofa and floor.

THE END came onto the screen. The ending credits rolled as the audience applauded rather modestly, in Arthur's opinion. That's when John and Rich's names, The Roses, and the names of all family members who were extras appeared in the credits. Not one person on the mezzanine moved until the house lights were turned on.

It was over. Arthur was breathing regularly once more. If those opinion cards were decent, perhaps the film would pay for itself, he thought. He knew that there were movie reviewers in the audience. Even he and Jana wrote a review column for the local Milwaukee newspaper. The great grandmothers were hugging Olivia and the little boys and still crying when Arthur began to issue directions to meet in the lobby for the ride back to the hotel.

"We'll meet there and discuss what we thought about the movie then," he had said. "Perhaps the producer will bring some of those opinion cards as well."

It was a simple plan. Meet in the lobby; wait for the bus under the marquee; go to the Hilton Hotel ballroom for the reception. Then, talk about the movie.

As the old adage says…so goes the best laid plans. Having over 2,000 people leaving a theater at the same time presented a challenge. Each of the Roses had her family present, and added to Arthur and Donna's family, that presented another problem. It would be impossible to casually walk to the exit doors and wait for the bus. Countless members of the audience stopped various members of the family to express their opinions. People were jammed everywhere as they tried to get to the State Street exits. The Hollywood people exited by other doors not seen by the public. Since Arthur had so many people with him, and more in the audience, they had to use the front doors. It was 9:00 p.m. before they boarded the bus. As Arthur was boarding the bus, Agnes la Straga and Anselmo Roselli came out of the theater. Seeing them, he waved.

"*Molte bene, Signore Colonna*," Agnes called out.

"*Si*, it was a pleasure to watch," added Anselmo. "You must tell me how those little people scenes were accomplished."

Arthur knew, but was not about to share the truth, that the images of the wee folk were not computer-generated. "You'll have to speak with my sons. They created the magic."

"*Va bene*, this I shall do. See you at the hotel," and Anselmo walked on. Agnes paused, pulled on Arthur's sleeve as he stepped onto the bus. Arthur bent down and she whispered in his ear, "We shall talk at the hotel, yes?"

Arthur nodded in a most emphatic manner as he boarded the bus. His thoughts were far beyond the reception at this point. He was already thinking of a Doris Day song, "What will be, will be,…*Que sera, sera*" as far as the movie was concerned. The legend of the Magi ring would be the focus of that meeting with Agnes.

Chapter 5: The Ring of the Magi

Arthur had arranged with Earl Colaianni, the bus driver, for a more scenic ride back to the hotel so the group might again get off the bus on the correct side of the street. Earl drove up State Street and past Holy Name Cathedral. The students and family hardly noticed the building, let alone it being designed and constructed in a similar style and material as the Water Tower. The chatter was all about the movie. Had Arthur realized the film would have made such an impression, he would not have arranged for this scenic ride. Only Arthur relished the ride down Michigan Avenue on that night ending his day of days. When the bus passed the Tribune Tower, and Arthur pointed out that it was his favorite building in Chicago, only his grandchildren paid any attention to his explanation.

"Look closely as we pass it kids. See the rocks and stones cemented right into the building. Now that's a rock collection which Papa really would like to have."

Embedded in those gothic walls, with buttresses and stone arches reminiscent of the Middle Ages, were stones from famous places all over the world. There was a stone from the White House in Washington D.C. and St. Peter's in Rome. There was a rock from the Great Wall of China and the Tower of London. Over the years more stones were added representing historical and cultural sites of significant value to the civilizations of the world.

"And that's why Papa likes this building best of all," he concluded to no one, as the grandchildren ran to the front of the bus to sit by their Uncles Rich and John. The grandchildren wanted to hear the tale of how the leprechaun scenes were created.

As the bus rolled over the bridge where Fort Dearborn had once stood and across the Chicago River, Arthur was alone with his thoughts of Agnes and their upcoming meeting. Images of the Donatello bronze box, the Bethlehem story and the duplicated ring filled his thoughts.

The bus was filled with the chatter of what scene was whose favorite; how well done were those scenes which the boys had created; and the excitement of seeing themselves on the screen. The students, of course, only saw the movie as a Hollywood-type film and were impressed because their teacher and his family were part of it. The family and the Roses, who actually experienced the story, tried to stay with the movie-critic approach since they could hardly reveal the secret.

The bus came to a smooth stop and the students formed a double line to the hotel's doors. The group entered an already-filled Grand Ballroom since most people hadn't taken the scenic route from the theater to the hotel. John and Rich were asked to take the students and introduce them to the actors. The Roses split up to find their families and get reports on the film from audience members. Arthur and Donna escorted their mothers, their children, and grandchildren to join up with the rest of the family who had attended the premiere. The little cousins were soon off on an adventure talking about leprechauns. After some chitchat and promises for a longer conversation later, Arthur excused himself. He instructed his children to make sure they greeted Arthur Lovell, and Nolan Clancy some time during the evening. They and their adult cousins nodded agreement as they left to collect autographs.

Arthur looked around for Agnes la Straga. The gentle light from the giant crystal chandeliers and the multi-storied, white Romanesque columns around the room made him nostalgic. The last time he had been in this ballroom he had brought the Student Council from his school to meet the now-Blessed Mother Teresa of Calcutta. Some of those students were with him again in this Michelangelo class and tour. He made his way up the grand staircase to the balcony overlooking the ballroom.

On his way, he bumped into Arthur Lovell. "Oh, I beg your pardon," Arthur began, not noticing into whom he bumped.

"Arthur, I'm glad we bumped into each other," the film producer said. "Are we still on for tomorrow's meeting to discuss a project I have in mind?"

"Lovell, I didn't see you. This is so, well, it's all overwhelming. You certainly have outdone yourself," exclaimed Arthur.

"Good, and thank you, but you had a lot to do with this event," the producer explained.

"I did? Lovell, all I did was show up at the theater with a bus load of family and students."

"Well yes, the bus thing was rather…shall I say unusual," Arthur Lovell laughingly said. "But really, were it not for *The World of Michelangelo and the Medici* exhibition and the Mayor showing up for both events because you were involved in them, I don't think we'd have gotten such a soiree."

"I'm flattered that you think so," Arthur humbly replied. "As for that meeting, I'm taking everyone to the Walunt Room tomorrow for tea. Perhaps we could meet afterwards before we head back to Wisconsin."

"Wisconsin," the now shocked producer uttered. "Don't you have other classes to teach before you're off on that Italy tour thing?"

"But it's only a little over an hour's drive from the city. I can handle it."

"Well perhaps, but I don't think I can. You Yanks drive on the wrong side of the road," the producer protested.

Arthur laughed. "Oh, I understand now. It was okay for me to learn to drive on the left side of the road in Ireland and in London traffic, which makes Chicago rush hour traffic look like a walk in the park; but you can't handle an hour to Wisconsin."

"Ok, you have me there. All kidding aside, there are a lot of important studio people here tonight. They'll be caught up in all of this, but they want to meet with you tomorrow, too. And should our little get together go well…" the Producer stopped himself. "Besides they want to meet your sons."

"That's a horse of a different color, I'd say. When do I meet them? I mean… when may I introduce them to my sons?" Arthur enthusiastically asked. "Oh, by the way, this place is expensive so I'll have to look for more reasonable lodging."

"Where is your wife when I need her? Arthur, I hear that your book is selling pretty well, isn't it?"

"I would say modestly well, yes. But what has that got to do with it?" asked a confused Arthur.

"It has everything to do with the matter at hand as you would call it," the producer answered. "Anyway, you're not paying for this, the studio is. You needn't worry about the cost, which in any case you can now afford, Michelangelo."

Now Arthur was taken aback. "Why are you calling me Michelangelo?"

"You don't know? You, who are teaching about the great artist, must know."

Arthur looked at him blankly.

"Good grief, Arthur. He was cheap, always calling himself poor even after he had achieved success," the producer finally explained to the now-embarrassed Arthur.

"I…I…I don't know what to say," was all that Arthur could get out.

"Just say that you'll stay put for a couple of days."

"Indeed, Arthur, no problem. I'll see you right here and my sons will be here also," the flustered Arthur replied as the red in his cheeks began to subside.

Arthur Lovell slapped him on the back and told him how pleased he was. "See you tomorrow around 4 p.m. shall we say?"

"Yes, of course, 4 p.m.," Arthur replied still surprised to have been called, cheap. *I'm not cheap*, he thought to himself. *And neither was Michelangelo; he just saved his money to take care of his family, and that's what I hope to do now that there is some money coming in..* With a shrug, he was off, to find Agnes la Straga.

Arthur made his way up the remaining stairs to the balcony. He searched the floor below hoping to spot that black dress and the black hair pulled back into a bun not unlike that worn in the 19th Century. Placing his hands on the railing and leaning over, he spotted the Roses talking with their respective families. He focused on Arthur Lovell again, who had one arm around Rich and the other around John, and facing Donna and the grandmothers. As he pondered the scene with a bit of pride for his youngest sons, a hand touched his shoulder.

Moving quietly from behind the pillar next to which he stood, came Agnes. She had kept herself hidden from view from the floor. Arthur turned and was about to say something but Agnes placed her finger in front of her mouth to silence him. She motioned him to follow as she walked toward a huge mahogany table holding an oversized vase with fresh flowers. She stood behind that vase to conceal her presence. *Why can't she be seen speaking with me?* he asked himself. From the table, she walked through a lounge area and through a door into a small meeting room.

Arthur felt he was acting as if he were some kind of spy on a clandestine mission. He picked up a bottle of water from the bar in the lounge, watching her walk into the meeting room. He walked, seemingly nonchalantly, through the lounge while sipping the water. As he neared the meeting room door, he paused, checking for anyone who might be watching him. The space was disappointingly empty. He entered the meeting room and closed the door behind him, almost out of breath from this anxiety-filled short walk from the balcony.

Agnes was sitting at a long banquet table on the opposite side of the room next to a large window with long draperies. A soft light from lampposts outside illuminated her and the papers she held. Arthur approached her, "Signora, why all this secrecy?"

"*Mi dispiace, Signore Colonna.* I'm truly sorry for all of this," Agnes started to explain. "However, I hope that what I tell you now will help you to understand why I must do what I do in this manner." She separated the pages, placing one next to the other.

"*Non importa, Signora la Straga,* I assure you," he replied, now consumed with desire to hear her version of the Medici legend.

"*Grazie,* now shall we begin?"

"*Si,* by all means. And please call me Arthur," answered Arthur as he pulled up a chair so that he could face her and read the pages. He soon realized they were very old and mostly hand-written in Italian and Latin.

"*Certamente, Arturo*…ah, Arthur," she attempted successfully. "Now as we begin, I ask you this. Do you understand the meaning of my name?"

Arthur was taken aback. He certainly did know its meaning, but not what possible relation its root meaning had to the Medici. "*Si* signora, I do indeed." Then he hesitated for he didn't want to insult her; he only knew its meaning through an Italian Christmas legend.

"You pause, why?"

"I…I don't mean to hurt your feelings, "Arthur said with utmost honesty.

"*Mille grazie,* but if you know please tell me," Agnes gently directed.

So with a deep breath, Arthur explained his understanding. The Italian Christmas legend, he went on to retell, is a story of an old woman who refused hospitality to the Three Kings who had come to her home seeking the Christ child. When she learned of their true identity, she went to seek them out but it was too late. They had gone far away. So each year at Christmastime she would go out to seek the Three Magi. To the children of the homes she visited seeking that same Christ child as the Magi, she left a gift. In time, she became known as *La Strega Nona Natale,* the Grandma Witch of Christmas or La Befana.

"*Si, buon,* you have learned the story quite well," Agnes la Straga complimented. "And of course you now know the meaning of my name."

"I know that it's a fairy tale, like Cinderella or Pinocchio," Arthur answered, still trying not to be insulting to her family name.

"I believe that I overheard your son, John, say that in legends there is an element of truth," she countered. "Is that not true?"

"Why yes, it is. But what has that got to do with your name?" the now-uneasy Arthur asked.

"Signore, the name means 'the witch' when literally translated and spelled with the Italian "e" instead of the anglo "a" which my family now uses. Let us not play games any more," she finally said with a smile.

Arthur was relieved that it had finally been said. Now they could get to the reason for the secretive meeting.

Agnes la Straga went on to tell a story of how her family name came to be. It seems the Christmas legend grew out of the activities of the Order of the Magi, two millennia ago. The legend originally rose from their own ranks to deflect attention to their group. As the centuries passed, however, rumors of their existence spread and soon the followers were called witches or sorcerers. This was still true when Galileo, in the sixteenth century, who himself was called such names, endeavored to bring truth to the study of the heavenly bodies. "And remember Leonardo da Vinci was also called a wizard before he was called the master artist," she added, almost as a postscript.

"One way to distract attention from the order was to adopt the very names used to refer to them. I am born of the descendents of a family who, centuries ago, adopted a variation of the old woman of the legend, *la Straga,* as their family name. They always connect it to the Christmas legend and not to its true origin," she explained.

There was illumination in Arthur's eyes as he connected the meaning she was trying to present. "Then what you're saying is that you are a descendent of someone in the Order of the Magi?

"*Si, Arturo,* you are correct in part."

Oh no! Arthur yelled in his head. *Not again! This cannot be another half truth!*

This, of course, was a brief reference to how he came to learn the secret legend of the Shamrock almost two years earlier.

He looked into her eyes with dismay. He knew what was coming, but didn't want it to be said.

"I see, you already know what I am about to say," Agnes observed calmly as beads of sweat appeared on his brow.

"*Si*, I know…at least I think I know," Arthur hesitantly confirmed. "You are part of what is now called the Order of the Magi, right?" He sat back in his chair to wipe his forehead with his handkerchief. All the while, he was thinking. "It's happening again. The legend is real and something is occurring, or eventually will happen, which needs to be solved or saved or something like that. What am I, a magnet for the supernatural and enchanted realms of the world?"

He answered his own question without saying a word. He was exactly that. He had been called to be the chosen leader when he and the Roses fulfilled the Clonmacnoise quest. Just last year, his entire family was called on to save not only the truth of the legend of King Arthur and the Knights of the Round Table but the divine message of faith, hope, and love. No one said that once those quests were fulfilled there would never be another one. And yet, he had hoped to enjoy an ordinary tour of Italy, tracing the steps of Michelangelo, the master stone cutter.

He pondered his call to lead the Clonmacnoise quest and combat the dark forces of Morgan le Fay, still alive and well in the twenty-first century through her followers. They sought, as she did, to destroy the truth of the divine message. He lifted his head, which he had held cupped in his hands as he dwelt upon these experiences and what may yet lie ahead. He resolved to take upon himself whatever challenge the signora was to put forward.

"Ok, Signora, I'm ready now," Arthur said with resignation and wonderment. "What are these pages?"

Agnes picked up one of the pages. "This one has just recently been found. This is a translation of an encrypted message concerning the assassination attempt on Lorenzo de Medici's life in 1478. In that attempt his brother, Giuliano, was murdered right in the Duomo of Florence, the Cathedral of Santa Maria del Fiore, while attending mass. The plot by the Pazzi family, in league with Pope Sixtus IV, and led by his nephew Count

Riarro and other minor co-conspirators, is now well known. However, there is a line within this letter which is of interest to us."

Arthur interrupted to note that Michelangelo would have only been three years old at the time of the plot. He had intended to ask a question about how the plot would have any effect on what they were attempting to discover, but Agnes continued before he could present the question.

"True, Arturo...Arthur," she began. "The plot to kill both Medici brothers at the same time serves only as a reference point for what Lorenzo would do later."

She went on to the contents of the next yellowing parchment. This page was once part of a journal kept by Michelangelo. It was found lining the bottom of a sealed box on the night the artist died, Feb 19, 1564. In that box was a considerable amount of money. Some say the amount was 7,000 gold florins. Others place the number at 8,000. In either case it was quite a sum of money to have lying about the house. It would also dispel the thought that Michelangelo was poor when he died at age 89. On the page he had written some of his thoughts about carving the "Giant" as he termed the marble statue of David.

She laid it beside the Pazzi plot page and picked up the next sheet of paper. The handwriting on this page was that of Frate Girolamo Savonarola. He became the conscience of Florence and eventually its dictator when he became the de-facto leader of Florence after Piero de' Medici, the son of Lorenzo, was driven out of Florence in 1494.

During his influence over the next four years, Savonarola would seek to destroy all that Michelangelo would come to elevate as in the image of God. Everything the young artist learned, in the Garden of the Medici and at Lorenzo's table in the Palazzo, would come in conflict with this Dominican friar, in whose order Michelangelo's older brother, Lionardo, had entered.

After she lay Savonarola's writing down, she took into her hand several sheets of paper. "These," she said with pride, "will finally prove that the Order of the Magi existed and that the legend of the Medici, more correctly called Magi ring, was historical fact."

She explained that the pages were written by one of the teachers of Michelangelo at *Il Magnifico's* table. He was a priest and an astrologer. He was devout and a philosopher. His name was Marsilio Ficino and he wrote these pages which prove his involvement with the Medici legend and the Order of the Magi.

A spark began to shimmer in Arthur's eye. He reached out to touch the pages as if by merely holding them he would learn of the legend's truth. He was hooked, no doubt about it. He had to know more about the Medici legend and the power of the ring of the Magi.

That glimmer of curiosity and attraction in his eyes did not escape Agnes la Straga, as she studied his face intently. "Arturo, am I correct in saying that you are interested in my story?"

"Most assuredly, Signora," Arthur answered.

"Ah, then I shall begin, as you say here in America, in the beginning, with the Pazzi conspiracy," she began.

Arthur was truly surprised. *What could the assassination plot against the Medici brothers have to do with legends and the Magi?* he wondered but did not ask.

"Once again I see light in your eyes Signore Colonna…ah, Arturo, but also confusion. But I assure you, once you hear the beginning you will better understand what is to follow." And with that explanation she began to tell her tale. "We begin at the gates of Jerusalem during the first Crusade to save the Holy Land. Pazzo "the Madman" Pizzi is climbing the walls of the city during the long siege. The year is 1099 A.D."

She went on to tell how his heroism helped free Jerusalem for occupation by crusaders from the United Kingdoms of Europe. So impressed were Pazzo's commanders that he was given a gift of three sacred stones from the Holy Sepulcher, where Jesus had been buried and rose from the dead. It was this hero of the first crusade who founded the Pazzi family, and whose descendents were in bitter conflict with the Medici family of Florence four hundred years later. The rivalry was most apparent every year on Holy Saturday. That was the day that the Pazzi family lit the Easter fire from which all fires in Florence were rekindled. This holy fire was kindled from sparks made by the three stones of the Holy Sepulcher.

"This rivalry goes back some thousand years?" asked Arthur.

"Not quite," she replied. "For you see, the Medici cannot trace their roots further back than the year 1360 A.D. They are a young family compared to the Pazzi, and this fact contributed to the animosity existing between the families."

As she went on with the tale, Agnes jumped over 250 years to the time of Giovanni "Big Change" di Bicci. It was he who would begin the Medici line and its fame in the banking industry. "Only, how shall I say it? I believe you Americans call it laundering of money."

"You mean the Medici founder was a crook?" questioned an astounded Arthur.

"Well in terms of today, perhaps you are correct. But back then it was do the laundering or lose your life," Agnes tried to explain. "And so it came to pass that Giovanni was the banker for the infamous pirate of the day, Baldasarre Cossa. And that, Arturo, is why you must hear how the Medici and Pazzi began their families."

"But what does piracy have to do with the legend?"

"Oh it's not the piracy which is important, but what the pirate Cossa did for Big Change di Bicci, the first of the Medici," Agnes continued. "For it was the gift of Baldesarre Cossa, who became Pope John XXIII, the antipope, which would change the life of Giovanni di Bicci and his family forever."

"Good grief, the founder of the Medici helped to finance a pirate to become a pope?"

"An antipope, signore, and there's no proof that Medici money helped, as Cossa had plenty of his own."

She continued with the complex story of how Cossa left the military service which served as his cover for pirating; then about his success in studying law at Bologna which enabled him to become the financial administrator of the papal lands. For that success, he was made a Cardinal. Eventually, he became a powerful Cardinal at the First Council of Pisa, where he was instrumental in breaking away from Pope Gregory XII and having Alexander V elected pope in 1409. Then, she pointed out, Cossa was elected pope at a gathering of Cardinals in 1410.

"So you see the Church had multiple popes all under the influence of kings and princes who sought to control the Church for their own growth in power. And don't forget, there was still antipope Benedict XIII who claimed to be pope until 1417."

Even though Arthur was a student of history and understood this battle for the Papacy in the late middle ages, he still couldn't connect Cossa's becoming one of the antipopes to the Medici legend.

"Signora, all of this is interesting from the perspective of an historian. However, what did Cossa's becoming an antipope have to do with the Medici?"

"Actually, there are two points which connect Cossa, the antipope, to the Medici and the legend," she answered.

Agnes explained the first point was Cossa. Upon giving Giovanni di Bicci de Medici some of his plunder to transform into gold, Cossa had found a unique ring among the goods. He told Giovanni he had found it on the island of Sicily, in the ruins of an ancient temple. In reality, he had stolen it from a small shrine where Christians revered it as a symbol of the three Magi. Therefore, the ring itself became a heralding symbol proclaiming the coming of the Messiah. Cossa had shown the piece to Giovanni but decided not to seek gold for it.

That led to her second point. When Cossa gave up his life of pirating and entered the Church, that ring became important to him. For now, he too was a herald of sorts. When he rebelled against Pope Gregory XII and had himself elected as John XXIII, that ring stayed with him always as a symbol of his authority, which he really didn't have. When the Council of Constance was called by King Sigismund on behalf of Cossa, the antipope went to Florence on his way to the City of Constance. There he once again met with Giovanni and was introduced to the banker's son, Cosimo de Medici.

The lad accompanied Cossa, antipope John XXIII, to Constance. In that city, after two years of haggling, all three popes abdicated. Gregory XII being the only legitimate one did so to preserve the succession from Peter. He thought that the election of a new pope would end the schism in the western Church. When the Council eventually elected Martin V, the schism was healed and the Roman line of popes remained unbroken. Cosimo de Medici, only in his twenties, now found himself allied to an ex-pope. Cossa was held as a virtual prisoner by King Sigismund of Germany. Martin V gave him a title of bishop and Cosimo Medici got him back to Florence where he died on Nov. 22, 1419.

Before Cossa died, he gave the triple-band ring to Giovanni de Medici for Cosimo as a token of his esteem for bringing him back to freedom. Cosimo, in turn, gave it to his eldest grandson, Lorenzo, called *Il Maginifico.*

"And that, Arthur, is how the ring of the Magi became part of the Medici possessions and their legend," she said ending her instruction.

"Then the ring is real and what is shown in the prints proves it. Why is Roselli so against displaying it?" asked Arthur.

"His objection has some validity. The ring in the Donatello box is a copy of the original. How that came to be, I shall explain. What you should know is that Roselli has other reasons to suppress knowledge of it," she explained. "Roselli is a descendent of a family, one of whom wrote extensively about what happened at Lorenzo's death. To produce the ring of the Magi would refute what was written and establish the power which the ring possessed. This would of course..."

She hadn't time to finish her statement as the meeting room door opened and Roselli himself appeared in the glow of the lights from the crystal chandeliers lining the walls of the hallway. "Signora la Straga, there you are and who is that with you?"

Arthur rose and turned to face him, concealing Agnes folding the papers.

"Why it's Signore Colonna. I have found the prize of the evening," Roselli sweetly stated. "The entire body of guests are wondering what on earth had happened to you. Why, even your own wife and those two sons, John and Richard, had no idea where you had gone off to."

"And now you've found us, how lucky you are," Arthur pleasantly replied, ignoring most of what Roselli said. "And the signora and I had thought we had found an out-of-the-way spot to chat about the exhibit and my trip to Italy with my students and two sons."

"Indeed, I must be very lucky."

"Well Agnes, we've been found, so there's nothing we can do but return to the party," Arthur said dramatically as he held out his arm for her to slip her arm into. "Do come along Signore Roselli, we shouldn't keep the guests waiting any longer."

Agnes la Straga of the Order of the Magi slipped the papers into her bag and joined Arthur, arm in arm, to brush past Roselli and into the bright lights of the ballroom. Roselli followed on their heels after glancing about the meeting room.

"We need to meet again," she whispered.

"Oh yes indeed, we should carry on our conversation. There's so much I need to know about Italy, and where my students should visit, and where we should eat, and so forth," Arthur loudly stated so Roselli could hear every word. "I know, next week I'll be holding the class at St. Giles Church in Oak Park. Perhaps, after the exhibit closes, you would like to speak to my students about the fun parts of an Italian visit and those which are profoundly important to civilization."

Agnes caught on quickly. "Why how charming Signore Colonna, *mi piacere.*

"Oh, Signore Roselli, do catch up. Would you like to come as well?" Arthur asked to the horrified look of Agnes. "You must have something which you could contribute to my students' preparation for the pilgrimage."

Chapter 6: Murder in the Duomo

"Mom, can you believe it? *The Leprechaun King* is barely out and people are already talking about a sequel," an excited John shouted as he came running into the living room of their Wisconsin home.

"Oh, Johnny, I'm so proud of you and Richie," she replied with a kiss on his cheek. She turned to Rich, who was coming in on John's heels. "Now Richie," she began, with a kiss for him as well. "You did explain that you cannot do anything about this new movie until after your sister's wedding, right?"

The boys quickly exchanged a glance; one which did not go down well with their mother. "Mom, it's just talk. You know, from the cards in the opinion boxes," Rich quickly explained.

"Right," added John. "You know… just talk from when we met all those folks in the Walnut Room at Macy's the other day."

Donna wasn't quite convinced. "Where is your father?" she asked with apprehension.

"Dad…well he's still outside with Arthur Lovell," Rich hesitantly answered, knowing full well what the reaction of his mother would be.

"The movie producer is here, outside, right now? I thought all that movie business was over when they met in the Walnut Room." their mother exclaimed in horror. "Anyway, your father could have at least given me a warning. I haven't a thing in the house. Quick! Clear the table and put the newspaper in the garage will you Johnny?"

"Mom, Mr. Lovell just wanted to stop in before returning to Dublin to get the premiere ready over there," John tried to explain. "You don't have to fuss."

"Fuss? Not a scone in the house and you call that fussing?" Donna was on a roll as she began to give a series of orders for preparing the dining room table for tea. "Luckily, Kathy is upstairs looking at Grandma Colonna's wedding gown with Jana and Tricia. I think it will have to be adjusted. And she wants to add lace to it."

"Mom, why didn't you tell us that the girls were here? Where are Ronnie, Chris, and Alun?" asked Rich as he began to run upstairs.

"Richard James, don't get her all upset if that gown isn't fitting just right," Donna ordered. She knew Rich had a crushingly honest and opinionated persona and it wasn't what Kathy needed right now.

John was now looking out the sliding doors leading onto the deck as he called to Rich.

"Rich, the guys are in the backyard playing bocci ball with the kids. I'll meet you out there."

"Bocci ball, that's it," Donna exclaimed. "Richie, go tell your father and Mr. Lovell that they're invited to play. That will give me time to get tea set up here." As he moved down the stairs, she added, "but first, be a dear and tell the girls what disaster has befallen us. I'll need their help."

Rich ran up the stairs; this time he wasn't going to be stopped.

Meanwhile, John ran around the house and caught his father and the producer as they were walking to the front door. "Dad, Mr. Lovell, how about joining the guys for a game of bocci ball? Mom says she...well she says you could sit on the deck if you don't want to play."

"Good idea John." And with that he directed the producer around to the back of the house. "Donna must need time to prepare something, so we had best give her the time."

"Arthur, you didn't tell Donna I was coming?" asked the producer.

A mildly-embarrassed Arthur had to admit that with the wedding plans, writing the movie-review column, and preparing for the class, he had forgotten. He omitted mentioning the legend which had preoccupied his mind since hearing of it from Agnes la Straga. "But don't worry Arthur. She loves company. Besides, all the kids are here to help her."

Arthur Lovell laughed, knowing only too well that the so-called help from the kids was no help at all.

When Rich entered his parents' room, Kathy was in Nona's white-satin wedding gown. Jana was fussing with the ten-foot-long train. Tricia was holding a crown-like headpiece in front of Kathy, who was deciding how the veil netting would connect to it.

Rich was awestruck at this vision. "Ah...Mom needs your help. Mr.

Lovell has come for a visit." He was afraid to say anything else.

"Well, Richie, what do you think?" asked Jana.

"I…I don't think. I'm not supposed to say anything, Mom said so."

"Rich, I think you can offer an opinion," observed Tricia.

"Ok, but don't tell Mom," Rich stated while making sure no one but they heard him.

"I think that you'll make a beautiful bride," he said as he made a hasty retreat downstairs and outside to join the bocci ball game.

Kathy was crying. Her baby brother liked what he saw and that meant the world to her.

Jana, the practical one, hurried her out of the gown. "We had best get downstairs to help Mom. My guess is that Dad didn't tell her that Mr. Lovell was coming to visit."

A short time later, Donna walked onto the deck to greet Arthur Lovell and cast a "wait until he leaves" glare to her husband.

"Mr. Lovell, what a surprise. I hope that you don't mind a simple tea."

The producer rose and greeted Donna with a kiss on the cheek and some words of flattery which ended in truth. "Donna, if what you are serving comes from your hands, then anything would do. Anyway, that husband of yours probably didn't warn you of my coming over."

Donna smiled and called out over the deck railing for the guys to bring in the children for a treat.

The children were seated at the kitchen table with their treats, and the family gathered around the dining room table, all eager to hear what the producer had to say. The oak table around which they sat could seat twelve comfortably and fourteen if everyone squeezed in a bit. Donna had a place setting for eleven for today's gathering. On placemats depicting scenes of ancient Ireland, alternating with scenes of quaint Irish cottages, she had placed her Royal Tara white china, trimmed with sprays of shamrocks and encircled in gold. The cups and saucers matched the dishes. Her complaint of having no scones really meant that she had only frozen ones along with some Welsh cakes. The Welsh cakes, of course, had been made by Marilyn Griffiths, who was one of the Roses. She had dropped some off on her last visit. Donna quickly heated them while the water boiled for the tea. On a separate platter was an assortment of biscotti. Donna had baked these Italian cookies based on Cookie-Grandma's recipe. Arthur's grandmother was called by that name because her cookies had delighted the family for many years during her 102 years of life.

Jana had removed the live shamrock plant which usually sat in the center of the table. She knew that her mother did not like obstructions between the guests. Only the Waterford crystal candlesticks were allowed to remain on the Irish-linen runner along the center of the table.

Arthur Lovell did not have to flatter any longer. "Donna, you needn't have done all of this for me. I didn't mean to inconvenience you, really." Then, picking up one of the cookies he added, "These look scrumptious."

"Nonsense, it was no bother," Donna fibbed in reply. "Have you ever had biscotti? They are made from an old recipe in Arthur's family."

Alun, in the meantime, was whispering to Kathy that the Welsh cakes not only looked, but tasted, as good as those his mother makes.

"I'll have to tell Mrs. Griffiths. She'll be delighted to hear that her cakes were a hit with a true Welshman," she commented back.

The table talk didn't last long. Everyone was waiting to hear why the producer had come to visit. Arthur Lovell didn't want to drag it on and create unnecessary suspense.

"You are all wondering why I have come up to Wisconsin when we just met in Chicago a few days ago," he began. "After lunch at the Walnut Room, I met with the studio representatives. We discussed the movie's future in terms of a successful box office. They told me that it had taken in $22 million dollars in that opening week-end."

There were audible gasps of disbelief around the table. One didn't throw around figures like that in the Colonna household.

Arthur Lovell realized that the family was being overwhelmed, though Arthur himself remained silent during the announcement of the gross income.

"I know all this seems to be rather unbelievable but trust me, that figure is not as great as some films, and obviously better than many others. Yet telling you of the film's box office take is not the primary reason for my being here today."

Eyes began to dart about the table, each pair coming to rest briefly on one of the family and then rapidly moving on to another. Everyone's question was unanimous; *what other reason does he have?*

Arthur had no choice but to try and calm the situation. "Our guest, I believe, has a bit more to tell if I'm not wrong."

The family settled down, uttering no more than a murmur.

"Thank you, I would like to share what I think will be good news for all of you. The studio reps believe that if the opening comments and income are any indication of the future for the film, then it will be a successful film. Therefore, they have decided to make a sequel based on your father's new book, *The Shamrock Crown and the Legend of Excalibur*," the film producer proudly announced.

Cheers broke out as they jumped from their chairs to hug their father and shake the hand of the producer; the joy was almost raucous. Donna sat quietly, crying and holding onto her youngest sons, who were a special part of this movie which would now have a sequel. She could feel that they too wanted to jump for joy and go to their father. She kissed them both and released them. They didn't have far to go, for Arthur had come to Donna to kiss her and hug his sons.

The producer interrupted and everyone froze to listen. All eyes turned to him. Arthur was standing behind Donna; the boys stood on either side of him. All the others had stopped on their way back to their chairs.

"There's just a bit more, if I may," he began.

"We're sorry, Mr. Lovell," answered Donna. "You know, it's not every day an entire family is involved in making a movie and then hears about prospects for another one."

The producer smiled with understanding. "I quite agree Donna, but I really do have a bit more."

They all quietly went to their seats expecting to hear about actors or which director would be taking on the sequel. Instead, Arthur Lovell told them that John and Rich would be asked to work on the sequel and that their father had been asked to write the script.

The entire family erupted in cheers and heaped their affection on the boys, who were so thrilled that they were speechless. The grandchildren ran in from the kitchen and climbed on their uncles, giggling and laughing. Arthur now sat quietly watching his family reacting to each other with love and joy. Of all thoughts rushing through his mind at that moment, it was the words of Lorenzo de' Medici which rang out:

"He who wishes to be happy let him be so, for of tomorrow there is no knowing."

By the end of the week, the excitement had settled to a dull roar and was somewhat under control. There was a wedding to celebrate and a tour to take before there could be any thought given to a sequel, no matter how great an honor it was. Donna established the priorities for the

Colonna clan and turned her attention to the wedding. Arthur was off with the boys to Oak Park to present the last class before leaving for Europe.

Donna was also off to Chicago, only she was going to Carmella Ferrara's shop. Carmella had designed Donna's wedding gown and now her daughter, Marcella, had taken over the business. Marcella would alter Grandma Colonna's gown to fit Kathy, and then it would then be sent to Ireland where the Irish lace would be added by Kathleen Gaffey, the drapery lady of Clonmacnoise. Having had a special connection with the family, the drapery lady, as she was fondly called, was thrilled to be part of the wedding preparations.

Donna and Kathy were accompanied by Jana, Tricia, and Olivia in Jana's van. The men were in charge of the little boys and were taking them, by train, to Chicago so that they could see *The World of Michelangelo and the Medici* exhibit at the museum. At the end of the day, everyone was to meet at Buckingham Fountain for the light display. Arthur and the boys would join them at the fountain.

As Arthur drove the Chevy Uplander down tree-lined Augusta Boulevard, he pulled up in front of a four-flat apartment building at the corner.

"This building is where Aunty Jan and I grew up. We lived in that apartment on the first floor to your right," Arthur pointed out. "In fact, your mother and I lived here after we got married. We were on the second floor, above Grandma and Grandpa Colonna. Ronnie and Jana were babies here."

The boys, who had been born in Wisconsin six years after Ronnie, Jana, and Kathy, had been born in Evanston, Illinois, were what Donna termed surprise blessings from God. They knew that their father was getting into a sentimental mode, and they needed to bring him back to the matter at hand.

"This is great Dad. How far is St. Giles from here?" asked Rich.

Arthur, realizing that he had been gazing at the building as if it were some kind of shrine, became focused once again.

"Oh, it's about eight blocks up the street and then a few more up Columbia Avenue," he said as he moved the car into traffic.

"Dad, what do you really think about the sequel?" inquired John. "I mean, have you told Mom that they expect us to get going on the project soon?"

"I have not and neither shall you," Arthur emphatically replied. "The schedule won't be set until we get to Dublin for the premiere. That should give us plenty of time to worry about when you must start your job. As for the screenplay, the basic treatment is almost done."

By the time they had decided to keep Donna in the dark for a little longer, they had pulled up in front of St. Giles Church.

"Here we are, boys. This is where your mother and I were married and where Ron and Jana were baptized," announced Arthur. "We're going to meet the class in front of the church, then walk through it. Then we'll cross the courtyard and enter the old convent building for the presentation."

The boys were still on the baptism. "Where was Kathy baptized?"

Arthur explained she had been christened at St. Francis Xavier in Brighton, Wisconsin, as they had been. She had been born in Illinois because their mother did not want to find a new doctor when they moved to Wisconsin.

"Let's unload the van and set up so that we'll be ready for everyone's arrival."

The parish complex was in a U-shape. The church stood on the right along the side of another street. The rectory faced Columbia Avenue. In front of it was a grass-covered court with a statue of Jesus. To the left was the old convent building now housing parish offices and a meeting area. The façade of the entire complex was constructed of tan-colored stone; the roofs were of reddish tile. To the untrained eye, the complex appeared to be Spanish Mission style, similar to what one might see in the southwest United States and California. Because of the stone's color and the fact that the stonework was really *Mankato* stone, however, the architecture is considered northern Italian. Arthur chose this site not only because it was a sentimental connection, but because it reflected, in his mind, many Renaissance buildings, with their straight horizontal and vertical lines, plain exterior, and richly-decorated interior using a variety of marbles and colors.

As they unloaded their supplies, Arthur had the distinct feeling he was being watched. He looked around and saw a single car in the parking lot across the street. It was a red Ford Escape and in it sat a person behind the steering wheel. Thinking that perhaps the person was waiting for a meeting of some sort at the parish, Arthur continued to hand off items to his sons. After a few minutes, it was apparent no other cars were joining the one in the lot. Arthur glanced over to the lot again. The window on the driver's side lowered and a hand came out. There was no wave, but more of a motion to come over to the car. As no one was around, Arthur realized he was being summoned. As he meandered across the street, he could now see who was in the car.

"Signora la Straga, what on earth are you doing here?"

"Signore Colonna, did not we make a plan to meet at your next presentation site?" Agnes la Straga asked.

"Yes of course, but I thought you'd come after the presentation. The students should be arriving any time now," Arthur apologetically said.

Agnes ignored Arthur's concern and zeroed in on the coming of the students. "*Va bene,* then this wonderful voice in the device on the dashboard did get me here in time for the students' arrival."

"Yes, indeed, but as I said, there is no time to talk now," Arthur attempted to explain.

"Ah, but Signore Colonna… ah, Arturo…er, Arthur I have come to sit in on your presentation. I was hoping you would allow me to add a little to it," she stated.

"Good grief Signora, I cannot have my students hearing about the legend of the Medici ring. They could not possibly understand the…shall I say, complexities of its story."

"*Mama mia, Arturo,* you don't think I would tell them such a tale as I shared with you?" Agnes cried out in shock. "But I could add some historical perspectives, which you may not have, to your next session, which, I believe, involves the death of Lorenzo and Michelangelo's later teenage years."

Arthur was relieved and graciously accepted her offer. His students, after all, already knew her from their tour of the exhibit. They strolled across the street and walked into the parish office building where they found John and Rich connecting the projector to the laptop. Soon the yellow school bus arrived and the students, back in their jeans, khakis, and tee-shirts, piled out of the bus. John and Rich went out to greet them and guide them to the meeting hall. Arthur decided the church would be viewed after the presentation. He wanted to make sure that he got to Buckingham Fountain in time to meet the rest of the family.

Ryan, impeccably dressed in neatly-pressed, off-white khakis and a pale blue Ralph Lauren shirt, lead the group with Amanda and Breanne flanking him. These girls were cousins. In appearance and personality they were not like the lovely Botticelli Venus, Jessica, nor like the flaming red-haired lass of Italian heritage, Jenny. These two girls were engaged in conversation with Tom Collins and Michael Dumbrowski. At least Jessica thought she was in conversation with Tom and Mike. In reality, John had managed to separate her from Tom and Mike on the pretense of discussing Florence, where he had attended the University for a semester. He had always been interested in Jessica, though it was Rich who had taken her to the prom. Back then, it was Patricia Hapsburg who was John's steady. Her presence in this course was not a problem as she and John had maintained a cordial friendship after they went their separate ways. Bringing up the rear of the group were Danny Garcia, Joseph Bloomberg, Dena Settefratti, Kristin Sharp, and Mary Beth Burns.

It didn't take long for Arthur to introduce Agnes la Straga, the Assistant Curator of the Medici Exhibit. The class, duly impressed with her credentials, was told that she would be adding highlights to the evening's session. Arthur asked if there were any questions before the session began. The words had hardly left his lips before Ryan stood up in his obviously new apparel, which he wanted to show off. The girls gave him the look he desired and the guys looked aggrieved. Just like junior high school again, Arthur thought to himself.

"Mr. C.," Ryan started to say, "last week you told us about the Medici ring. Now that we have seen it as part of the Medici prints, could you tell us more about it?"

Arthur had no intention of getting into the legend of the Medici ring tonight, or any other night. Before he could put Ryan off, however, his own son jumped up to make a comment.

"Ryan, I see that you're now a believer in the ring," John stated sarcastically.

Ryan was taken aback as he hadn't expected to be attacked. But he was not about to shy away from the challenge. "It seems to me that a ring did exist, I'd have to admit that, John. However, I am not convinced that it was anything more than ornamentation, a piece of jewelry favored by the Medici."

John now had to uphold his image as son of the teacher as well as champion of the round table, though the latter was only known to his family. Ryan could not be allowed to get away with his cocky assumption that legends are simply myths. "I am sure that Signora la Straga has insight into the legend as history. Ask her. And another thing, according to my

Dad's notes, there was this guy called Baldasarre Casso who became the antipope John XXIII. Ask about him too."

In ten seconds, John, in his effort to put down Ryan, had revealed almost the entire truth of the legend known only to a handful of people. Arthur, not to mention Agnes, stood paralyzed with disbelief. John should know better, Arthur was thinking. Agnes la Straga, bewildered, could only look to Arthur for guidance.

"So what's a pope got to do with the ring, John? It's only a story anyway."

John was turning red. In someone who was normally the most mild-mannered person one could possibly meet, this was a sign he was losing control. Rich recognized the signs and interrupted the exchange. Rich was in the dark about the legend and his attempts to calm the situation only resulted in the class asking more questions about the legend, the ring, and the Medici's use of it.

Agnes rose from behind the table and walked around it so that her curvy figure would dominate the scene. "*Studenti,*" she began. By the time she finished presenting the historical evidence of how Baldasarre was a pirate who became a student of law, a Cardinal of the Church, and then falsely elected a pope, the class sat with their mouths open and Ryan had sunk, stunned, into his chair. She had managed, however, to reveal nothing of the legend, or the power of the ring, during all she presented to the class.

"Thus when the antipope John XXIII abdicated his claim to be pope, he returned to Florence and to the Medici home where he died. He gave the ring, which we see in the prints at the exhibit, to Cosimo de Medici who had accompanied him to the Council of Constance. When Cosimo became head of the family, and leader of Florence, he would have a magnificent monument tomb built in honor of Baldasarre Casso. In due course, Cosimo would give the ring to his eldest grandson, Lorenzo. It would be he who was later called *Il Magnifico.*"

A sea of hands jutted up into the air. The students bombarded Agnes and Arthur with question after question. Some were logical ones flowing from the historical narrative.

"Then Lorenzo passed the ring onto his son, Piero, right?" asked Jessica.

When Agnes la Straga affirmed Jessica's conclusion, the now-sullen Ryan dared to speak again. "So what's so important about the ring?"

Arthur was about to have apoplexy when Agnes began to answer the question.

"Signore Ryan, we may never know of its true importance, but obviously, it had significance or it would not have been passed on from father to son. But important as it was, just how precious it had become to the family is best illustrated by the events leading up to and including the assassination attempt on the lives of Lorenzo and his brother, Giuliano."

She then set the scene for that plot in 1478. In no time at all, the students were envisioning the Papal Palace of Pope Sixtus IV in Rome.

A captain of the apostolic guard, named Giovan Battista, stood at the gates of the Vatican Palace. Inside the immense fortress waited Pope Sixtus IV, the very one who would build the chapel called Sistine in his honor. It would be that chapel which would make Michelangelo's fame immortal. The pope's nephew, Count Girolamo Riarro; the Archbishop of Pisa, Francesco Salviati; Bernardo Baroncelli; and Francesco de Pazzi waited to be admitted. Having been properly identified, Battista ordered the gates to be opened and he escorted the agitated group into the papal presence. Each man approached the papal throne, and knelt and kissed the ring of the pope. Forming a semi- circle facing the pope, they laid out their plans.

"I am told that you have finalized a plan to remove the Medici from Florence once and for all," Pope Sixtus IV stated with a hint of pleasure.

His nephew, the Count Riarro, answered. "Your Holiness, our plan cannot fail, and once accomplished, the whole of central Italy will be open to your benevolence."

Francesco de Pazzi, stood seething. The Pope could not but notice the rage within Pazzi.

"Signore Pazzi, what say you to the plan?" asked Sixtus IV.

"I say, good riddance and may the Medici heads be stuck on poles in the Piazza Signoria."

Captain Battista was horrified. He had no idea that murder would be part of the removal plan. His thought had been to bring liberty from the Medici power by an overthrow of the government; not by assassination. "Your Holiness, are you condoning this plot to kill the Medici brothers?"

"The pope cannot approve of murder. There shall be no death," was the pope's first reply.

Francesco's rage burst forth as he stepped toward the pope. Captain Battista jumped in front of him to protect the pope from what he saw as an uninvited approach into the papal space.

"Your Holiness, this is an outrage. Tell this guard to stand down," Pazzi exclaimed in horror and anger.

The pope waved his arm, being assured that Pazzi's movement was not meant to encroach upon the papal well being. Battista moved aside and allowed Pazzi to continue.

"You tell us now, after months of planning, that death cannot be a part of the plan?" Francesco Pazzi asked with immense control of his temper. "How are we to succeed?"

"You shall succeed by doing what is necessary to accomplish the removal of the Medici brothers, Lorenzo and Giuliano," replied the pope very calmly. "And now I think I have heard enough. You may leave my presence and report back to me when the deed is accomplished."

The heavy oak door opened and Battisti escorted the pope down the marble-lined hall decorated with gold and paintings of the early masters. Once he had gone, the captain returned to the men who now were shouting. It was all he could do to bring order to the flaring tempers.

"We cannot kill the brothers," insisted Captain Battista. "The Holy Father has said; thus cease your arguing as to who should thrust the knife."

"My dear Captain, you are mistaken," Count Riarro said in a tone of authority. "What my uncle, the pope, said was, 'do what you must to accomplish the deed.'"

The captain backed down, for what the count said was indeed true, though he also said that no killing should be part of the plot. The Archbishop of Pisa quieted the captain's anxiety.

"My son, the liberty of Florence is the real issue here. Shall we continue to live under the Medici rule, or seek our fortunes through free choice?"

Words like liberty and freedom were then being shouted in response to the question. In the end, the captain agreed to participate in the overthrow, but no killing. The others would accept the responsibility of doing what had to be done to achieve the deed. And so, messages were sent to the other plotters as to when the act should take place. After several false attempts they decided upon April 16. The year was 1478.

An invitation had been sent to another nephew of the pope. Raffaele

Sanoni was the Cardinal of San Girogio. He was invited to come to Florence. Francesco de Pazzi had enough influence with the Florentine Council to achieve the invitation being sent.

It was a gesture to bring peace to central Italy. At least that is what Lorenzo thought it to be. And so a great feast and reception was planned for the cardinal as he would be present for the celebration of Easter. The Pazzi family would once again light the Holy Easter fire on Saturday. The light of the fire would be paraded throughout the city to kindle the fires of the hearths of Florence. On Easter all would attend High Mass at the Duomo. The troops being brought to Florence under the guise of protecting the visiting cardinal was well-accepted protocol. What Lorenzo wasn't told was that Jacopo de Pazzi, son of Francesco, had troops hidden outside the city and ready to enter the city when the deed was done.

The majestic procession on Easter morning began at the Medici Palazzo and wound its way through several blocks to the Duomo with its green marble façade. Accompanying the cardinal were two priests, Antonio Maffei and Stefano da Bagone. They walked on either side of the horse on which sat the red-robed cardinal as they made their way to the cathedral. Lorenzo and his brother, Giuliano, were astride horses decked out with silk coverings of silver, gold, and purple. They wore silk tunics of brilliant colors, Lorenzo once again in white and gold and Giuliano in silver and blue. Their leggings matched the blue and white of the tunic. Upon their heads were large round hats with plumes on the side. Each was studded with jewels. In addition to the three-banded Medici ring, the gift of Cosimo to his grandson Lorenzo, he wore on his left hand several rings encrusted with precious stones.

The Medici brothers, themselves, escorted the cardinal into the Duomo for Easter Sunday services. Stefano and Maffei followed behind the cardinal. Friends of the Medici brothers were nearby, but only Francesco Nori was within a distance to come to the aide of the brothers should trouble start. The fear of violence was always part of any excursion by people of power, even one as popular as Lorenzo de' Medici. The entourage stood throughout Mass only kneeling at the consecration of the bread and wine. The festive nature of the Easter triumph filled the cathedral, immersing those in attendance with a sense of heavenly grace.

The priest sang, "*Ite missa est, alleluia*, go, the mass is ended, alleluia."

Bernardo Bandeni Baroncelli, one of those who met with Sixtus IV made his move. He ran up to Giuliano de Medici.

"Here, traitor," he shouted as he thrust his dagger into the unsuspecting Giuliano who staggered right into Francesco de Pazzi's arms.

Pazzi, in a series of savage blows, thrust his dagger time and again into every part of Giuliano's body. Blood spurted out into the assassin's eyes. He thrust so hard that he penetrated Giuliano's body and stabbed his own upper thigh, thus crippling him as he tried to escape. Giuliano fell to the floor, dead.

Then Cardinal Riarro, so full of fear, ran to the altar and hid behind it fearing for his own life. He was later brought into the old sacristy for his own protection.

Lorenzo turned to the screams and saw Stefano and Maffei coming towards him with daggers pointed. A dear friend, Francesco Nori, jumped between the would-be assassins and *Il Maginifico*. It was he who would feel the blades thrust into his abdomen.

Baroncelli however did manage to reach Lorenzo and wounded him in his neck.

As Nori fell, the two priests fled, Baroncelli with them.

Antonio Ridolfi grabbed his friend and led the shocked Lorenzo over the wooden communion railing towards the west sacristy. As Lorenzo jumped over the railing, Ridolfi held his hand with such force that the triple banded ring flew off his finger and bounced off the railing, onto the marble stairs.

Lorenzo broke away from Ridolfi, bolted back over the railing and chased the ring which rolled to a stop in the blood of his brother. Ridolfi shouted for the bells to be sounded. Lorenzo grabbed the ring, clutched it in his hand, and ran to the west sacristy with Ridolfi. Once inside, they bolted the door and Tornabioni, Mortelli and Angelo Poliziano, the poet and future teacher of Michelangelo, guarded the door to the sacristy. Lorenzo walked to the wooden wardrobe where the vestments where placed. He opened a small drawer and took out a purificator used to clean the chalice once mass was over. He placed the ring with the blood of his brother on it and wept silently as he wiped it clean. Ridolfi, in the meantime, climbed into the organ loft and peered out over its wall. He saw the body of Giuliano lying motionless in a pool of blood on the floor of the now-desecrated cathedral.

By now, the cathedral bells were sounding the alert and calling the citizens of Florence to come to its aid. Hearing the alarm being sounded,

Ridolfi returned to Lorenzo and saw to his wound.

Running down the street towards the Palazzo Pazzi were Fracesco de Pazzi, the two priests, and Baroncelli. Pazzi could bearly walk due to the wound he had given himself while killing Giuliano. The others had to hold him up and carry him. The bells were echoing in their ears when they reached the palace and barricaded the doors behind them. Crowds were pouring into the streets.

On the other side of the city, the Archbishop of Pisa, Salviati, approached the Palazzo Signoria or what is now called the Palazzo Vecchio, the seat of government for the City of Florence. It was his job to enable the troops, led by Jacopo de Pazzi, to take the governmental palace. The archbishop entered the palazzo and sought out the Galfalonier of Justice, whose name was Cesare Petrucci. With the archbishop was Jacopo Braccilini.

"What do you wish here, your Excellency?" Petrucci asked, hearing the sounding of the bells.

The archbishop could not respond at first. Then he said, "I have come to talk about the situation in our beloved city."

He broke down, could not speak, and ran from the room. As he did so Braccilini drew his sword and moved to slay Petrucci. In a quick move Petrucci overpowered the swordsman and threw him to the floor. He called for the guards who stopped the archbishop as he fled down the stairs. It was over. The archbishop surrendered and the palazzo was made safe. When Jacopo de Pazzi came with his troops they found the palazzo barred and were unable to enter. So he ran through the streets of Florence yelling, "People" and "Liberty."

The people did not respond to his call, but to the bells calling them to help save their city and their beloved leader. Crowds screaming *"Palle, Palle"* rushed to the Palazzo Pazzi and crashed down its doors. They found Francesco Pazzi naked on a couch having his wound tended to by the others who fled with him. Giving him no dignity to dress, the crowd dragged him through the streets and to the Palazzo della Signoria with the others. Pazzi was brought to the top of the tower where he was thrown out the window falling to the stone piazza below. The archbishop and Braccilini were questioned and they, too, met their death in the same fashion as Francesco Pazzi. All the others were arrested. They, however, were tried by the Florentine High Court of Eight. Thus they joined their fellow assassins in death at a later date.

The news spread throughout Italy and was brought to Pope Sixtus IV. He flew into a rage as he learned that Lorenzo survived and that his cardinal nephew was still held in Florence. He excommunicated Lorenzo de Medici and placed an interdict on the entire city so that no celebration of the Eucharist or sacraments could be held.

When that news came from Rome and was announced in the council chamber, Lorenzo de Medici stood to make an offer to save his beloved city.

"I shall place myself before the pope, to suffer exile or death, putting the common good above my own life."

The signoria wept as he spoke and refused his offer. "Did we not release his cardinal nephew to the pope and did he not prove to be untrustworthy anyway?" they cried out.

"No, you shall not give yourself up to the pope."

Lorenzo would not give up his efforts to save his city. He insisted on going alone to the King of Naples who was an ally of the pope and to him he would place himself at his mercy. For three months he would be a prisoner, but in the end, the king sided with Lorenzo.

The pope, seeing that success was now impossible, lifted the interdict, and Lorenzo returned to Florence triumphantly. Florence was saved and Italy, so prone to being constantly fought over, was saved from bloodshed, at least for a while.

As the final image of the Palazzo della Signoria faded from the screen and Rich turned on the lights, the class sat in silence. Agnes had delivered a history lesson unlike any they had ever heard. The bells of the Duomo were still ringing in their ears. The screams of *"Palle, Palle"* and "Liberty and Freedom" were echoing in their heads.

The horror of the murder in the Duomo and bodies being thrown from the palazzo tower still created vivid scenes in their minds' eyes.

Arthur regretted breaking their reflective and stunned silence.

"Let us offer our thanks to Signora la Straga. If you have any questions you may present them now."

After the applause subsided, Jenny raised her hand rather meekly. She was dying to know, but didn't want to resurrect the argument of the ring again. Arthur noted the hesitation and guessed what was coming. Nonetheless, he called upon her to ask the question.

Chapter 7: The Ship Wreck

Arthur was correct. Jenny rose, though with hesitation.

"Signora la Straga," she softly asked. "Whatever happened to that ring which fell off Lorenzo de Medici's hand?"

The room became as still as a field of wheat on a windless day. Each waited for the assistant curator's response with excited anticipation.

Agnes pulled from her bag the Donatello box, which contained the duplicated Medici ring. Though a copy, she made it clear that such a ring did exist and was an important symbol of the Medici power and family heritage. Lorenzo had passed the original ring onto his eldest son, Piero, for it appears in the print which everyone saw in the exhibit.

"After Piero, there is no mention of the ring in history until the Medici family came back into power in the second decade of the 1500's. And then it was this duplicated ring, which was worn." She held up the box and took out the ring.

"The original was gone," she concluded. "If you look closely you will see these are just three plain bands of gold, silver, and copper. The symbolic engravings, which were on the original, are not present."

A relieved Arthur thanked the assistant curator again. While he was giving final instructions to the group, he heard the outer door of the former convent close very loudly. He paused, but since no one entered their room, he decided someone must have left the building. He walked to the window to glance outside while still talking. A tall, dark, shadowy figure could be seen briskly walking past the statue in the plaza. As the shadow came near the statue, a spotlight lighted the moving figure. It was a man dressed in dark pants and a white shirt. He wore no jacket and had dark wavy hair. Only the back of his head could be seen. Arthur was suspicious, though he couldn't figure out why.

"Our next session will be in London, England," he began to say as the students erupted into loud cheers and applause. "When you arrive there, my sons and I will meet you. After a couple of days we shall fly onto Italy."

The day they had longed for had almost arrived. In an effort to keep the focus on the sessions, Arthur had deliberately not shared the itinerary of the trip with his students until that night. The excitement from the announcement proved to him he had been correct. He smiled, and lifted his arms to calm the group.

"We shall all meet in London in two weeks. The exhibit you have seen here in Chicago will have begun in London. Signora la Straga has accepted my invitation to join our tour after the exhibit closes in London."

The students applauded politely as Arthur continued.

"Since I'll be in Dublin for the premiere of the movie, and unable to fly with you to London, you will need a guide, a leader whom your parents trust. I have a surprise for you."

The students once again sat in stunned silence, glancing at each other and trying to guess who that person could be. Arthur let the silence grow and the questioning looks build excitement before he spoke.

"I am pleased to announce that Mrs. Maura Kennedy will be the co-leader of the tour and escort you to London to meet me and my sons."

Almost everyone seated in the room knew Mrs. Kennedy and loved her. She had been Arthur's administrative assistant when he was principal. More than that, she served as the school's music teacher.

Had it not been for her talents, Arthur could never have created the upscale school musicals which became the envy of the district. Arthur brought an experience of fine arts to life on stage as perhaps the master himself strove to bring life out of the stone he sculpted. He served as the play's director while Maura served as the musical director. Together, they became a team which enabled many of the students seated before him to demonstrate talents they had never dreamed they possessed. Seated before him were students who had performed roles which would at best be called "uncool;" and they did so in a school which had almost no history of performing arts. By graduation time, those students would be as proud of their accomplishments and drama awards as they were of their sports trophies.

As Arthur heard the gleeful shouts, he saw his Tin Man, Scarecrow, Lion, and Dorothy in those seats. He was remembering the flight of his Peter Pan as the cables lifted a singing Danny off the stage floor and swung him out over the audience, and how Mary Beth, as a flying Wendy, was shot down by the arrow of a lost boy. They were young men and women now, in college, but they still remembered those days and that made Arthur proud.

"Next week, you and your parents shall meet with Mrs. Kennedy to review the details of the trip. That meeting will be on Friday at 8 p.m. at St. Mary of the Lake University Seminary in Mundelein. Please take the packet which John and Rich are handing out and discuss its contents with your families."

With final directions in mind and packets in hand, the students departed for the waiting bus. Arthur stood at the doorway listening to them chattering and laughing about how great this trip was going to be now that Mrs. Kennedy was part of it. That's when he noticed a black car pulling out of the lot where Agnes la Straga had parked.

The boys were taking down the equipment as they told Signora la Straga how much they had enjoyed her version of the murder in the Duomo and the Pazzi conspiracy.

"Will you have other neat stories like that?" asked John, always looking for the gore and intrigue in a story. Rich's questions dealt more with the factual details in the tale.

"You can never tell Giovanni. The Renaissance era is full of such thrilling scenes which might have changed the course of history," she replied as Arthur reentered the room. "Ah, Arturo you have returned. Your sons, Ricardo and Giovanni, have expressed much interest in my story."

"I'm sure they have, Signora. You did tell quite a thrilling tale."

"*Grazie*, but now I have a favor to ask of you," Agnes went on to say. "Given that darkness is falling and I am not how do you say…knowing of the way of the roads back to the museum, would you mind driving with me?"

The boys said they could handle driving the van back downtown without a problem.

"OK, boys. Park in the lot by Van Buren and Wabash. You'll have an easy walk to Buckingham Fountain. I'll meet you and the family there."

Off John and Rich went with armloads of equipment and their own packets with the trip itinerary.

"Now Arturo," Agnes started to say. "You are no doubt wondering as to why I should want to speak with you, given that I have that lovely lady's voice telling me where to turn and which street to take at any given moment."

Arthur smiled and nodded agreement. Then he paused to let Agnes finish her explanation.

"But first I'm sure you saw what I saw out the window tonight, no?"

"If you mean that guy in the courtyard, yes I did see him."

"That's exactly who I mean. There's no doubt about it. It is him," she continued.

"Him? Who's him?" asked Arthur.

"Why Roselli of course; who else?"

"Signora, you mean to tell me that he followed you here? But why?" inquired Arthur.

Agnes went on to explain that Roselli may discount the Magi ring legend but he knows it to be true. "Why else would he follow me but to hear what I had to say about it. To find out something which he may not know himself. Hah, and all he heard is what any historian could tell him," concluded a delighted Agnes la Straga. "And that is why I have asked you to ride with me back to downtown."

"So there's more to the story, I take it," Arthur said as they approached her car and waved to John and Rich as they drove off.

"Not so much of what happened during the murder plot but of what Lorenzo did afterwards and then years later," she clarified.

As they drove off towards North Avenue and turned east, Agnes began to explain what she meant. She did this by taking him back to the time when Lorenzo de Medici traveled to see Ferdinand I, the King of Naples, and an ally of Pope Sixtus IV. With only a companion servant and no guards, he took the perilous journey to Naples.

"Knowing how dangerous it would have been to travel through Papal lands, he decided to sail to Naples. Once there, Lorenzo surrendered himself to the king who, in turn, kept him hostage. Part of those months when he was held, Lorenzo was sent to the Isle of Capri. The island was as it is today, a beautiful site to behold. Its mountainous form jutted out of the sea and was crowned by the ruins of the palace of the Emperor Tiberius. Its harbor was filled with fishing vessels and the homes of those fishermen dotted the cliffsides. Being on the small island just outside the harbor of Naples allowed Lorenzo some freedom, and yet he was totally isolated from the rest of Italy. The king needed time away from the gifted and loquacious Lorenzo while he considered what Lorenzo had told him about the pope's desire to expand his lands, thus threatening the Kingdom of Naples as well."

"Ah this is but a summary of the end of the tale you told in the session earlier," Arthur observed, "except for the Capri part," he noted.

"Exactly Arturo, and it's that small addition which makes a world of difference in the telling of the tale."

While on Capri, Lorenzo heard a part of the legend of the ring of the Magi which he hadn't known before. It seems that the servant of the Magi, Timothy, to whom the ring was made a gift, decided to travel to the heart of the Roman Empire to tell the story of Bethlehem and the birth of the promised one. With the blessing and support of the three Magi, this young man, who had probably not seen sixteen years, traveled to Jerusalem. There he offered a sacrifice in the Temple and prayed for a blessed journey.

He joined a caravan traveling through the province of Judah into Samaria. Once there, he booked passage on a ship sailing from Caesarea on the coast of Samaria. The trading vessel was to stop at ports in Crete, Malta, and Sicily before it reached its destination at Rhegium. This final port was located on the boot tip of the Italian peninsula. From Rhegium, Timothy planned to travel up Italy to Rome using the famous Roman roads which led to the capital city, home of the emperor, Augustus Caesar.

As the ship left the Island of Malta and headed toward Sicily, a violent storm swept across the Mediterranean Sea. The small trading ship was tossed off course and instead of traveling to the eastern side of Sicily, they were blown around to the northwestern side of the island and into what is now called the Bay of Naples. The ship crashed onto the rocks surrounding the Isle of Capri. One group of those stacks of limestone rocks can be seen today jutting out of the sea and forming a giant natural arch of stone.

A portion of the ship lay wedged within that formation, which today are called the Fraglioni. Timothy and some crew members clung to broken timbers hoping they would not be washed away and lost forever. Unfortunately for Timothy, the piece of mast to which he clung, and had tied himself to with rope, broke away. The three crew members tried to reach him, but to no avail. Timothy was washed away, trapped by the ropes which had earlier saved him. Wave after wave tossed him toward the white stone cliffs soaring above him. Little did he know at the time that at the summit of those cliffs was the emperor's palace. The emperor used this palace as a retreat to get away from the cares of governance. It was Tiberius who was emperor when the tiny ship was crushed on the rocks surrounding Capri. Tiberius would spend long periods of time on Capri and govern from its fortified position safe from assassins.

The broken mast finally hit solid rock and splintered. Timothy, barely conscious at this point, was released from the ropes by the breaking timber. He was washed into the mouth of a tall, narrow cave, coming to rest at the bottom of a staircase formed from the rock. His white tunic, torn to shreds, clung to his limp body. The curly black hair, matted with salt water, was void of all lusters. The leather belt around his waist still held a small leather pouch in which coins were clanking as waves pushed his body up and unto the stone stairs. On his finger glistened the gold, silver and copper bands of the Magi ring.

As he revived and crawled up the stairs to distance himself from the water, which he now feared, he came to a crevice about three feet in height and just as wide. A bluish light shined through the opening bouncing off the white rock formation. Pausing to catch some dripping water in his cupped hands, he moistened his parched lips and lapped the remaining water from his hand.

Breathing heavily, he pulled his battered body through the hole and onto a ledge bordering a vast cavern. His barely-opened eyes took in the beauty of the clear turquoise waters reflecting their color throughout the cavern. His ears picked up shouts of laughter, so he pulled himself to the ledge's edge and peered downward. On the opposite wall of the cavern he entered was a long, precisely-cut, staircase descending down to the stone surface. This stone platform bordered the clear blue waters of a lagoon surrounded by stone walls. The ledge was only three or four feet wide. To Timothy's right was a narrow opening at water level. This narrow opening leading to the sea was so low anyone riding in a small boat would have to bend over and lay flat to go through.

Timothy folded his tired arms and laid his head on them. As he watched three men in the water, another four young men ran down the stairs opposite him, tearing off their tunics and jumping into the water.

What Timothy didn't notice were the Roman guards surrounding the cavern and standing on the ledge on which he now lay. The guards were dressed in short white tunics trimmed in red, covered with chest plates, metal arm protectors and silver helmets with short cropped red plumes. In their right hands they each held a long spear with its bottom resting on the stony ledge. At their sides were short-bladed swords in leather sheaths held by wide brown leather belts.

Timothy was exhausted from the shipwreck and from being tossed about on a piece of wreckage. He only noticed the blue colors bouncing off the cavern's walls, reflections from the clear waters below, which were hypnotizing him with a sense of peace. Even the playful splashing of those in the grotto below seemed a dull sound to his now mesmerized being.

Suddenly a rough hand grabbed the back of his tunic and pulled him up. He twisted to try and see who had grabbed him.

"You there, who are you? What are you doing here in the emperor's grotto?" the enormous guard asked gruffly.

Timothy could hardly speak. Not only was he battered and bruised from the shipwreck and now being choked by the guard, but he wasn't fluent in spoken Latin.

"I…I am Timothy of Syria," he gasped out. "My ship lies crushed on the rocks of this island."

"We'll see about that. Come with me," the guard now said, softening his tone. Claudius, the guard, now helped Timothy to his feet. Seeing his torn tunic, bleeding arms and legs and weakened condition, he believed the lad's story.

He walked, and then carried, Timothy, to the next guard's station.

"Fabius, this lad says that his ship lies wrecked out on the rocks and he found his way here through a crevice at the top of a cave."

Claudius placed the limp body of Timothy on a stone slab. Fabius looked the lad over, turning him around. He grabbed the pouch hanging from the belt and bounced it in his hand.

"Well, perhaps the lad is telling the truth. He seems to be a person of means."

They revived Timothy and led him around the ledge taking him to the stairs from which those four young men had jumped into the grotto's pool. Still not steady on his legs, Timothy was held up by Claudius. As they approached the bottom of the staircase, two of the men pulled themselves onto the rocky surface. They ignored the three and went directly to a long white toga trimmed in purple. Then two others pulled themselves out of the pool and then knelt to assist an older man out of the crystalline waters.

Timothy's eyes were focused on the purple trim. Only the emperor wore such trim, he was thinking. "Who would dare have such a trim?" he thought aloud. The guards hushed him immediately.

The older man stood with his arms raised as the two young men draped the toga around him. Only after he had been arrayed did they don their own knee-length tunics. The older man, with black hair streaked with silver and wearing his purple-trimmed tunic, turned his attention to the guards.

The guards saluted the man with a fist banging against their chest plate. "Hail, Caesar," they shouted out.

Timothy was shaking and fell to his knees. It was the emperor himself, though he thought it was Augustus.

"And what do we have here disturbing the recreation of Tiberius of Rome?" asked Tiberius.

"Caesar, this lad claims to have been shipwrecked on the rocks beyond the blue grotto's walls," answered Claudius.

"Well then, you are my protectors; do you believe him?" questioned the emperor.

Claudius answered affirmatively much to Fabius' regret as he eyed the pouch of coins.

"Of course, your story can be proven easily enough," the emperor responded as he turned to his companions. "Justin, you and Metallus take some guards and seek out evidence of the shipwreck. Come to me with your report."

The two men bowed and left immediately, running up the stairs.

"As for you lad, I wish you to accompany me. It seems that a little food and some wine might help you gain some strength after your supposed ordeal. Guards, bring him to the palace."

With that, he ascended the stairs followed by the remaining companions. Behind them, Fabius and Claudius escorted Timothy. When they came out of the hole at the summit, it was protected by a dome held by four pillars. As Timothy looked around he saw the Italian mainland in the distance and the turquoise waters of the Mediterranean. To the left of them stood the white marble palace with a portico held up by a series of Corinthian columns. Not since the Temple in Jerusalem had Timothy seen such a wondrous sight.

The guards brought the lad to their barracks where he was attended to and made presentable for the emperor. He was bathed and his wounds were dressed. Timothy was furnished with a fresh tunic and allowed to keep his own belt with pouch of coins. A pair of brown leather sandals was placed on his bare feet. Now he was ready to be brought into the imperial presence.

The glistening white pillars towered over him as the guards escorted him to the emperor.

Walking through the portico and through iron doors fifteen feet in height, he noticed the paintings on the walls. Brightly colored renditions of stories from mythology lined the corridor surrounding the main part of the palace. In the interior was an open courtyard with a fountain in the center. At each corner of the fountain pool was a statue of the gods Apollo, Mars, Minerva, and Juno. In the center rose a statue of Neptune with trident in hand. Beyond the courtyard, the dining hall was being prepared for dinner as they entered. At the head of the low-standing table was placed the reclining couch of the emperor. Other couches of simpler style bordered the table. These would be used by the guests, of which Timothy was considered one. The others would be filled by the swimming companions.

Timothy stood next to the couch at the head of the table until he received the sign for him to recline at his couch located next to that of Emperor Tiberius. The dinner was not a court occasion, though Timothy would have ranked it as being fit for a king. Emperor Tiberius had entered with his companions in conversation. The only formality had been that of waiting for Tiberius to recline. First he walked up to Timothy and greeted him once again.

"It seems that your story is correct. Other survivors have been found and some wreckage as well. Don't worry. They are being attended to on the mainland."

Tiberius took his place at the table and so did the others. Timothy had to be instructed on how to dine Roman style.

"Now then," began Tiberius. "You must tell me all about this city called Bethlehem in Judea."

Timothy told the story of his life in Syria and how it was changed by the three Magi. Tiberius' eyes widened so as to make them pools of blue; as blue as the grotto below. By the story's end, the Emperor had made a decision.

"I wish you to remain with me, Timothy of Syria. I wish to learn more about those events in Bethlehem and where I might find these Magi of whom you speak."

Timothy became agitated. His mission was to share the story, but not to reveal the Magi's whereabouts. And yet, how could he refuse the emperor in his own palace. His young mind spun with scenarios as to what he might do, but the reality was that there was no way to leave Capri unless Tiberius willed it so.

"Caesar does me great honor," Timothy replied. "I come from the desert. The only water I have ever seen until these last few weeks has been the River Jordan. Now you offer me joy beyond all measure."

And yet in all his flattery and revelation of his life, the lad never betrayed the whereabouts of Caspar, Melchior, and Balthazar.

Tiberius smiled and placed his hand on Timothy's shoulder, shaking it ever so slightly.

"We shall talk again, but for now I must make preparations to return to Rome. When I return, we shall begin where we have ended this day."

With that, the Emperor rose, as did all present, and calling for his guard, left the dining room.

Timothy went to the docks on the rocky shore far below the palace summit the next day. With great ceremony the Roman ships hoisted their square sails of red and purple and made ready to receive Tiberius. Along with the emperor's swimming companions, Timothy watched as the ships' sails caught the wind and moved into the Gulf of Gaeta. No sooner were the ships gone than Timothy made his way around the island, exploring for an area where he might slip off so that he might begin his mission. After several days of fruitless exploration, during which he encountered patrols of imperial guards, Timothy felt his flight would never take place. One day, the emperor's companions invited Timothy to take a swim with them in the grotto. Although the grotto was the emperor's private pool, they would use it as they wished while he wasn't on the island. A day of frolic was planned. Near the imperial docks a small village housed those who served the imperial household. Fishing boats were allowed to dock as they would bring their catch for the imperial table. The lad watched their fishing routes from atop the summit and made his plans of escape.

Claudius and Fabius were off duty the next day and were to join Justin, Metallus, and the others for a carefree day. They brought along Timothy since he was assigned to their barracks.

"Hail, Timothy of Syria!" they shouted as they approached his quarters.

"I'll be right there Claudius," Timothy shouted back and then appeared in the doorway, fully dressed.

"Lad, we go to use the grotto not dine at the palace," remarked Fabius.

"I know but if you will forgive me, I come from a far land where one doesn't walk around in his loincloth," Timothy said shyly, so they would ignore his traveling clothes.

The guards laughed and clapped him on his back, as they joked that he would certainly drown wearing that pouch of coins on his belt. The lad laughed as well. They climbed down onto the stairs which led to the grotto. Timothy left his tunic and cape, belt and coin pouch on the ledge where he had first walked with Claudius and Fabius. He was delighted to see that when the emperor wasn't around, there were no guards. After several jumps into the grotto's waters and attempts to stay afloat, he feigned tiredness and excused himself to rest. He first laid upon the rocky platform at the water's edge, breathing heavily. He then inched backwards to the stairs. As the guards and the companions frolicked, Timothy slowly made his way up to the level of the ledge. He quickly grabbed his clothes and made his way to the opening where he had first come in. As he crawled along the ledge, he could see the guards and their friends in the grotto pool and heard their echoing voices.

"Claudius, where did the Syrian lad go?" asked Metallus with concern in his voice.

"Metallus, he's right on the stairs there, resting. What concerns you about him?"

"You know as well as I that when the emperor invites you to stay, you have only two choices. Stay and enjoy his hospitality or leave and meet your end before you can take one foot off this island," replied Metallus. "And as I look at the stairs, I see no one."

Fabius confirmed that he could see no one on the stairs. He and Metallus soon swam towards the rock apron at the bottom of the stairs and jumped out. Timothy was only a short distance from the crevice which led to the sea, but was now in a panic as the men were running up the stairs shouting that he was nowhere to be seen. He took a risk and stood, so that he could move faster. It was a bad move. Claudius and Justin spotted him as he made his move to get to the crevice in the rock wall, through which he could get to the far side of the island. The companions in the grotto basin were running up the stairs to the ledge as Timothy ran for the crevice. Fabius and Metallus were only a few feet from him as he crawled through the opening and tumbled downward toward the cave entrance. He found the piece of mast which had saved his life days ago. The guards had squirmed their way through the crevice and were shouting at the lad.

"Timothy, don't be a fool. You cannot defy the emperor," cried out Fabius.

The lad made no response. He was too busy tossing the piece of mast back out onto the sea and plunging towards it. Once out beyond the crashing waves, he clung to it and kicked his way out where the water was quite calm. There, to his delight, he saw what he had hoped to see. A fishing boat was coming around the outer rocks. He waved frantically to get their attention and they heaved him on board. His woolen cloak was so heavily saturated that it had almost drowned him.

As he placed a coin from his pouch into the captain's hand, he caught a glimpse of Metallus and Fabius shouting from the cave opening. No one noticed that he rubbed the ring of the Magi and offered a prayer of thanksgiving for being saved. Now he could begin his mission to announce the good news which occurred at Bethlehem.

Agnes, having finished her narrative of how the Magi ring got to Italy, silently watched for a response from Arthur.

"So that's it, signora? That's how the ring got to Italy?" asked Arthur.

"I don't get it. What does this story have to do with Lorenzo de Medici?"

"Only everything, Arturo. Only everything," responded Agnes. "Timothy traveled up and down Italy with the story. It is said that from those travels grew the roots nourishing the legend of the Christmas witch. More than that, as the lad matured, he married a Jewish girl and settled in Pompeii, where a cult developed around the ring of the Magi. This cult existed until Mount Vesuvius erupted in 79 A.D. Almost all of Pompeii's residents were caught in the lava flow and smothered in volcanic ash. Several of the Order of the Magi escaped the devastation. One of them was Timothy's son. He and the other members made their way to Rhegium where the ring became the centerpiece of a shrine honoring the Bethlehem story. It was at Rhegium where the soldier-pirate Cossa confiscated the ring which he later gave to Cosimo de' Medici for his kindness at the Council of Constance, where Cossa abdicated as the antipope John XXIII."

"Good grief signora, then Lorenzo really did have the miraculous Magi ring."

"Indeed so, Arturo. When Lorenzo was confined on the Isle of Capri he, too, entered the blue grotto, once the private pool of the emperors of Rome. He found, within the cavern with its shimmering pool, that he was able to mourn the loss of his brother and friend," she revealed. "He also discovered the story of Timothy, told by some local members of the Order of the Magi. The members would meet in the blue grotto to retell the tale and seek ways to regain the ring."

"I'm beginning to understand, signora. Lorenzo, who was a virtual prisoner on the island and also the most famous leader of Italy, fell into their midst. Am I right?" an excited Arthur asked.

"You are most correct," Agnes answered. "We know Lorenzo meditated in the grotto. We know that the Order met there as well. We know that something transpired between the Order and Lorenzo because of what would later happen at Lorenzo's death... but I get ahead of myself."

As she drove down Harlem Avenue towards the Eisenhower Expressway, she shared the rest of the tale.

"It was in the heat of the summer, July of 1478 when Lorenzo explored the ruins of the imperial palace on the summit overlooking Capri," Agnes started to say as once again, Arthur could virtually see the blue grotto she described.

Lorenzo found the staircase which only the emperors, and those whom they chose, could use to enter the grotto. As he descended the worn stairs, littered with centuries of destructive residue caused by nature and humans, he felt a refreshing coolness. He descended to where the waters of the grotto basin lapped the rocks gently and he encountered people in small boats. These boats were formed in a circle and the people in them held lighted candles. They were chanting a hymn which sang of the Magi and how they read the signs of heavenly light.

> The kings of the universe bring tribute to the Lord, alleluia.
> The mountains shall yield peace for the people and the hills justice.
> He shall defend the afflicted among the people,
> Save the children of the poor,
> And crush the oppressor.

Lorenzo stood on the stone apron stretching from the stairs. He was astonished at the sight and elevated in spirit by the chants of those in the boats. The small cave opening allowed light into the grotto to reflect its heavenly blue light off the water and onto the rocks. Lorenzo, at first, thought he was a witness to spirits gathering in the human realm. His first thought dissolved as his presence became known to those in the boats. Not realizing why this sudden attention was directed to him, Lorenzo, *Il Magnifico*, hardly felt magnificent. Rather, he was frightened as he noticed what brought the occupants' attention toward him. The reflecting light had struck his triple-banded ring. So dazzling was the light streaming from the ring's three bands that its brilliance was as if a star from the heavens had entered the grotto. The people in the boats stopped their chanting and turned to the source of the starlight.

Lorenzo stood in shock as the ring was now tugging on his finger, as if wiggling its way off his hand. He held out his hand for those in the boats to see. The members of the Order broke their circle and paddled their little boats in a semi-circle near the stone platform where Lorenzo was standing. The light from their candles was being absorbed by the ring, which finally slipped off Lorenzo's finger and floated between him and the people in the boats. Streams of light, like ribbons of glowing phosphorus particles, ran from the ring to each candle. As the ring settled over Lorenzo, he became surrounded by these glowing particles. One boat came closer to where *Il Magnifico* stood and a tall man, dressed as the others in an ankle-length indigo robe, stepped out of the boat and onto the stone platform. He bowed to Lorenzo de Medici, who bowed back.

"There can be no doubt; you have brought us the blessed ring of the Magi," the blue-robed man stated reverently.

Lorenzo made it clear he had no idea what the gentleman was talking about. Matteus de Pompeii, leader of the Order of the Magi, chose to ignore his statement.

"Many centuries of time have passed since the ring was lost in the destruction of Pompeii. Then a ring was revealed in Rhegium and revered as a holy object until the pirates stole it in a raid on the city. We were not entirely sure the ring at Rhegium was real, for it gave no hint of what we are seeing this day," explained Matteus.

Even though he was in awe of the radiant light, Matteus knew who the finely dressed man standing before him was. He quickly explained how Timothy of Syria first brought the miraculous ring to Italy with the good news of Christ's birth.

"And there's more to the story," he continued. "If this is the authentic ring, then Timothy's spirit may be called forth to claim the gift the Holy Family gave to him."

"By all means, call forth this spirit; for I wish to know if this gift to my family might preserve and protect us," Lorenzo responded with urgency.

There was no hesitation on Lorenzo's part, as Tuscans are firm believers in spirits and their world.

With that permission, Matteus began to lead a chant. "Servant of the Magi, Bearer of the gift of Bethlehem, Timothy of Syria, return to us in spirit."

Over and over, they repeated the petition until there was rumbling in the grotto and loosened rocks fell from its ceiling, splashing into the clear blue water. Despite the rocks and the exploding splashes of water, those in the boats continued to chant. Most of the rocks splashed into the basin, however, some fell thundering onto the stone platform. In the midst of the melodic chant and thunderous splashes and crashes, a bright light appeared at the cave's opening. It was not the source of light which caused the blue hues reflecting throughout the cavernous grotto. This light had the form of an athletic young man dressed in a simple white tunic. It flew above the heads of those in the boats. The members of the Order fell to their knees at the sight, despite the rocking boats. The spirit hovered at the water's edge facing Matteus and Lorenzo.

Though he was the leader of the Order of the Magi, Matteus was also a practical man. He had come to believe in the source of the legend, but never truly thought there would ever be a chance to call forth a spirit until the light coming from Lorenzo's ring filled him with conviction. Now, he stood in stunned reverence before a spirit he was certain was of heavenly origin

Lorenzo, on the other hand, was from Tuscany where spirits, wizardry, and superstition were part of the fabric of life. Though humbled by the apparition, he was not frightened, but welcomed its presence.

"My Lord Timothy of Syria, is it truly you?" he asked respectfully, while keeping an eye on the ring, still elevated and gleaming brightly.

"I am he who accompanied the three Wise Men to Bethlehem. I am he who received the gift of the ring from the Holy Family to whom we came to pay homage. I am the witness of the miracle of the ring. I am the one who brought the ring of the Magi to Italy with the good news from Bethlehem. I am Timothy of Syria," proclaimed the spirit.

Then the spirit moved to grasp the ring floating before him.

Lorenzo could not risk losing what he was now certain was a source of power and protection for the Medici family. He raised the hand which bore the ring for so many years and cupped the floating ring in his hand. Immediately, the rays of light were extinguished and the ring rested on his open palm. He held it before the spirit as Matteus and those in the boats gasped in horror.

"My Lord Timothy," he began. "I am Lorenzo de Medici who has worn this gift of the Magi these many years. I came to your dwelling place, here in this grotto, to pray for protection for my family. Now I ask of you to safeguard those I love."

"What you ask I cannot grant," replied the spirit.

"Do you then come not from heaven but from the depths of hell?" inquired Lorenzo.

"I came from Bethlehem to Italy as I have told you. I came to announce the good news, not to perform evil deeds. I have dwelt in this grotto since my life ended in Pompeii, but never was it possible to be called forth as the ring had been lost. Until such time that the bearer of the ring commands such, I may not go to meet the Messiah whom I saw in Bethlehem," explained Timothy.

The members of the order could hardly believe their ears. Lorenzo seemed to be questioning the very nature of the spirit. Even more appalling to them, the spirit was actually explaining his condition of being caught between heaven and hell.

Timothy continued as the others watched in shock. "You bear the ring, will you release me?"

Lorenzo, ever the diplomat, saw a chance to save his family and end this war between Florence and the pope and his ally the King of Naples.

"I would be most pleased to release you my Lord Timothy…"

Before he could finish, the spirit and the members of the Order began to rejoice. Their reaction was premature; Lorenzo had not concluded his thought.

"As I was saying, my Lord, I would be pleased to do so, however, I am a prisoner here in Naples and my city lies in a state of siege. I must use all power available to help my fellow citizens."

And so Lorenzo de Medici manipulated the spirit into becoming one with the ring and bring blessings to him and his family. At the end of Lorenzo's life, the spirit was to be given his freedom. Timothy agreed to the conditions, but explained that the protection could only be to the actual bearer of the ring. The Florentine leader and the spirit were in agreement. The spirit was absorbed into the ring with a flash of light so bright that those present had to shield their eyes.

The bright lights of oncoming cars brought Arthur out of the grotto and back to Chicago. The car was traveling down Congress Parkway towards Columbus Drive and approaching Buckingham Fountain, pouring out its illuminated waters. Soon, lights having the colors of the rainbow would make those waters dazzling streams when the light and water show began.

"And that is how the ring came to protect Lorenzo de Medici," concluded Agnes la Straga, as she pulled up to the curb of Grant Park on Columbus Drive.

"Signora la Straga, I can only say that I'm intrigued by your story," an exhausted Arthur said as he got out. "However, I still don't understand how all this pertains to me."

"Just this Arturo; the ring I have is an old copy, but the original must exist somewhere. After all, Piero de Medici, Lorenzo's son, did wear it. Though to be honest he wore…shall I say, an empty ring. Tradition records that upon Lorenzo's death, a spirit was released from the ring he wore, and afterwards, great trauma occurred throughout Florence."

"I am aware of the spirit story. It's part of my presentation for the class when we talk about Lorenzo and Michelangelo as friends as well as having a father and son relationship," responded Arthur. "But I still don't understand why you have told me the story."

"Arturo, I have reason to believe that the ring still resides in the area around Naples and I need your help to explore and find it. Your trip with the students is the concealment we would need so others would not grow concerned about our traveling together and visiting the sites where the ring was last known to have been seen," explained Agnes.

By the look on Arthur's face, she knew he had some grave concerns, not the least of which was the safety of his students as they pursued a lost miraculous ring. Agnes assured him that the students would be perfectly safe. "What better cover could there be than the innocence of true tourists?" she asked and then answered. "All will be well for them. I would accompany you as a professional guide and historian and they would enjoy the sites, history, and legends of Italy as you planned."

She went on to confirm their meeting in London in two weeks time. There Arthur would meet his students after his daughter's wedding. From there, they would begin the *Walking in the Footsteps of Michelangelo* tour.

No sooner had Arthur confirmed the plan than a tap at the car window startled them. Agnes lowered the window to greet the curator of the exhibit, Roselli.

"Signora la Straga, I thought this car was the one you drove. How nice to see you and is that Signore Colonna with you?" he asked charmingly.

"Si, Signore Roselli, it is indeed Arturo Colonna. We have just come back from the class presentation," she rambled on.

"Yes, I know…I mean…I thought you might be returning as you mentioned you were going to the class to help out," Roselli said with that syrupy tone. "I was just on my way to the museum, to ensure that Andreas and Pietro had things under way, when I spotted your car."

"What do you mean under way, Curator?" a frazzled Agnes asked without waiting for an answer. "I was under the impression that we were not to dismantle the exhibit until tomorrow."

Arthur was now rather unnerved as he felt himself caught up in two professionals getting ready to do battle. Feeling how upset Agnes had become, he decided to enter the fray. "Signore Roselli, your assistant gave a most thorough presentation this evening to my students. I must commend her to you. She really knows her stuff, as we say here in America."

"Indeed, I'm sure Signora la Straga was most competent, Signore Colonna. However, now we must get to work on the exhibit. We must be off to New York tomorrow."

"Well then, I had better get out and let you two get on with your work. Signora, I wish to thank you again for your help tonight. Here's my card so that you might contact me if I can ever be of any help to you. See you in Italy in a couple of weeks." And with that, Arthur was out of the car waving good-bye to Agnes and Roselli.

Turning to Agnes as Arthur walked away, Roselli asked his assistant if he heard correctly. "You are to meet the American in Italy then?"

Agnes was noticeably anxious. She didn't wish Roselli to have any idea that she and Arthur would be meeting again in London, and so she dwelt on what he heard concerning the meeting in Italy.

"*Si*, the Signore has asked that I conduct a lesson once again with his students. Naturally I agreed since the exhibit would be ended by the time he is on tour."

"I see, Signora. Perhaps you might tell me all about it when we get to the museum. I shall see you there now," Roselli said with authority as he returned to his car and then drove off down Columbus Drive with Agnes la Straga following.

Meanwhile, Arthur had reached Buckingham Fountain just as its color display was hitting its high point. The center stream of water was shooting upwards into the sky. A mist from the falling water sprinkled those standing on the south side of the fountain. Naturally, his young grandsons were standing right there with Uncle John and Uncle Rich. His granddaughter, Olivia, would never dream of running around in such a fashion. She was much too grown up; so she watched with just the slightest wish that she was young again so that she, too, might run through the mist. The entire family, catching a glimpse of Arthur's approach, waved and shouted a greeting to him. Arthur waved back and then trotted towards the south side of the fountain. Grabbing Olivia's hand as he ran past, he playfully tugged her along into the spray of the falling water. Protesting, but enjoying every moment, Olivia suddenly was running ahead of him. The little boys ran up to them and circled them.

"Look, Papa, the water is green just like in the wee folk's house," exclaimed Connor.

"Maybe the king is here," added little Arthur.

"Shh, boys, no one is to know the secret, remember?" Arthur responded.

"Oh we forgot," the two eight-year-olds quietly replied, just as the third grandson came into the mix singing the leprechaun song they had learned last year. Immediately, Arthur V and Connor hushed him. "Riley, it's a secret remember?"

Riley responded with a sheepish grin. With that, the three chased Olivia into the mist, as she screamed her delight covered in a tone of protest.

Arthur motioned to John and Rich to join him as he walked towards the rest of the family.

Once they all were gathered, and the roar of the water with its colorful display was taking up the attention of those around them, Arthur quickly informed them of what had happened at the presentation at St. Giles parish center.

"There's no doubt about it; that Roselli guy is up to something, but what that might be is the question. We must be on guard, boys, when we get to England and meet Signora la Straga."

Now it was his wife's turn to express two concerns.

"I thought this was to be a normal tour, no magical or supernatural events. And what's this about that woman meeting you?" Donna said first with a tone of utmost concern which changed to one of feminine inquisition as she focused on Agnes la Straga.

The entire family roared in laughter.

"Mom, she lives there," their eldest, Ron, tried to explain in vain.

"Good grief, Mom, I think Dad could do better. I mean if that was his intent," the ever-observant Jana, their eldest daughter, said as the rest of their children and their spouses once again broke into laughter as Donna blushed.

But their youngest daughter, Kathy, asked the really important question. "Will this new adventure affect my wedding plans?"

"Oh dear, the wedding," Donna exclaimed as she wrapped her arms around Kathy. "No dear, nothing will interfere with the wedding in Wales. Will it Arthur?"

"Everything will go off as planned. Now, if everyone can get a grip, I think that we should get back to the hotel where we can better plan for what's to take place next. John, Rich, and I will make a stop at the

Museum first. I want to make sure *that woman* is still in good health," Arthur grinned. Kissing Donna, he left with John and Rich.

By the time the three reached the steps of the Museum, Arthur had retold the story he heard from Agnes.

"Now you understand why we must ensure that Agnes is okay. Meeting her in England and then in Italy is of paramount importance if we are to help her and prevent Roselli from learning of the ring's reality."

Chapter 8: The Mayday Carnival

Arthur and his sons ran up the rear stairs of the museum. The truck transporting the exhibit's artifacts could be clearly seen at the dock area. On its sides was the iconic hand of God touching the fingers of Adam as seen in the master's painting on the Sistine Chapel ceiling. Under the image were the words, *The World of Michelangelo and the Medici.*

"Boys, I'll keep an eye on the dock while you check the doors," directed Arthur.

"Okay, Dad," they responded as they ran to the doors. "Dad, they're locked," shouted John.

"Quietly, please," Arthur responded. "We'll have to enter through the loading dock; follow me."

The three made their way in darkness to the loading dock. Pausing at a clump of bushes at the corner of the museum, they stooped to watch for Pietro and Andreas. They were nowhere in sight. Creeping along the side of the building, they made their way to the truck itself. When they reached the truck, they could clearly see the dock doors.

"Good, it's open," Arthur whispered. "All we have to do is get inside unnoticed."

"Oh, is that all?" Rich sarcastically asked. "What if those big guys are there? Then what are we going to do?"

"Rich, I think we can handle those guys," John said with conviction. "Anyway, I've picked up this stone which might come in handy."

"Let's not get too excited and, by the way, drop the stone, John. What we don't need is a commotion which might place Agnes in greater danger than she might be in right now," Arthur told his sons.

"We just want to make sure Roselli hasn't found out anything which may jeopardize her position with the exhibit or in helping us on the tour."

He waved at them to follow behind him as he crept alongside the truck. Just as they reached the lip of the dock, Pietro and Andreas wheeled out a large crate. The boys ducked under the truck behind the rear wheel, while Arthur flattened himself against wall beneath the dock hoping the shadows would conceal him.

Speaking in Italian, the young men seemed agitated. Arthur could pick up some of what they said.

"What's with Roselli? He calls us to load the truck at night, why?" an angry Pietro was asking his brother.

"Who knows? These artistic people are all the same. They care nothing for time of day or for what others are doing. It's all about the exhibit," Andreas responded irritably. "Oh well, at least I got the girl's phone number before we left the bar."

There was laughter regarding the latter part of his statement as Pietro pushed out the now empty cart. The two men stood on the dock. "Speaking of women, la Straga won't be seeing that American teacher again. Her heart is probably broken," mocked Andreas. "It was probably her last chance at getting a man."

"Ah, she'll be lucky to get through this exhibit season in one piece as far as I'm concerned. If she gives me one more order, I'll…well I'll tell Roselli that we won't help him," Pietro added.

"Quiet, stupid one," cautioned Andreas as he looked around and out over the dock's edge directly above Arthur. "Roselli is paying us well to keep an eye on the witch, so just continue to obey her every command like a sheep."

"Alright, but I still don't know what's so important about her," answered Pietro as they pushed the empty cart back into the museum.

Arthur popped his head up into the light and waved to his sons. As they approached, he asked them if they had heard.

"We heard about her broken heart," John laughingly said. "But seriously, you were right."

"The signora is in trouble and may not know it," added Rich.

"Exactly, so let's get a move on," Arthur directed as John gave him a foot up and he climbed over the dock's edge. "And don't you be telling your mother about any broken heart. There's no such ailment, I assure you."

"Dad, for once I agree with Jana," John smirked. "You can't do better than Mom."

"How right you are, Johnny," Arthur smilingly responded as Rich gave John a foot up and Arthur pulled his son onto the dock.

After pulling up Rich, they entered the museum. Arthur took out a map of the museum from his jacket pocket. It was the same one given to visitors, but it did show the loading dock and its relationship to the main atrium where the exhibit was set up.

They made their way along the corridor quickly. Beyond the doors in front of them would be the main reception hall where the elephants and Sue, the dinosaur, watched over the works of Michelangelo. The doors began to open. Arthur and his sons darted into a doorway leading into a storage area which contained crates for the next exhibit.

As Arthur peered out around the corner, he could see Andreas fixing the doors so they stayed opened as Pietro wheeled a cart, with another crate on it, through them.

Ducking back into the storage room, they waited until the two pushed the cart out onto the dock. Then they made a beeline through the open doors and into the exhibit area.

"We'll check her office first. John, you stay in the rear since you know where it is. Rich, you stay behind me," ordered Arthur.

Staying behind the dismantled displays, out of the main lighted area, they arrived at the small office in short order. The door to the office was slamming shut as they came near it. Quickly, they hid behind the fake façade of the Medici chapel wall, which was part of the traveling exhibit. The three sets of wide cocoa-brown eyes rose above the top of the wall just in time to see Anselmo Roselli walking off in a fit of controlled anger.

As he disappeared across the hall, the three ran into the office. They softly closed the door behind them and leaned against it, short of breath. It was as if they had run the mile.

Heavily breathing from the adrenalin flow, they scanned the small room. No one seemed to be about.

"Where's the signora?" asked Rich quietly.

Arthur shrugged his answer. They slipped away from the doorway crawling along the carpeted floor so as not to be seen through the large window behind the desk. As they came alongside the desk they could hear a voice.

"Such a *gavone* does not exist in all of Italy," mumbled Agnes la Straga as she gathered up the papers from the floor behind her desk.

Arthur, John, and Rich peered around the corner of the simple wooden desk.

"Signora," Arthur called out in a whisper.

Agnes bolted, clutching those collected papers firmly in her hands. She was now sitting on the floor as her eyes darted about to see who was speaking.

"Signora, it's me, Arthur Colonna. I'm here with my sons."

Agnes crawled to the voice as if she knew not to stand up. Arthur did the same with his sons crawling right behind him. Soon they were almost nose to nose. Agnes' eyes widened, "Arturo, what are you doing here?"

Arthur rapidly backed off and crashed into Richie who was directly behind him. As they untangled, he responded that they had come to ensure that she was safe.

The sight of Arthur tangled in a heap with his son brought a smile to her face, once filled with distress.

"I am most appreciative, *grazie*. For the moment I am fine, though that…that curator should descend into the depths of Dante's inferno."

"But he looked so angry when we saw him leave your office," Arthur noted.

"Buon, I am glad of it," she replied. "Arturo, you and your sons are in grave danger being here. You must go."

"Don't be ridiculous, Signora. We'll stay right here on this floor if necessary until you tell us what you mean about being in danger," Arthur stubbornly responded.

"*Va bene*, okay, but your sons, do you not care for their safety?" she asked trying a different tactic.

"Signora, don't worry about us. We can handle Pietro and Andreas," John answered for his father.

"Right," added Rich though not quite with the level of confidence that John had displayed.

"So you see Signora. We are in agreement," Arthur said. "Now what has happened?"

As they continued to sit on the floor, Agnes la Straga explained that when she arrived at the museum Roselli had already put Pietro and Andreas to work dismantling the exhibit. She had asked what the urgency was but instead of answering, Roselli had insisted on learning more about the American. He wanted to know about their relationship and what she told him concerning the legend of the Magi ring. Naturally, she had stuck to the plan and said only that she was to help with the instruction of the class. He, of course, did not believe her explanation. That's when he saw the papers, the very ones shown to Arthur at the Hilton on the night of the movie premiere reception. Agnes had been in the process of mixing them with other notes and research regarding the Michelangelo exhibit.

Her panic was evident as he grabbed some of the pages on the desk. It was with relief that he had only grasped actual notes and not the ancient translations which she had shared with Arthur. Presuming that all the pages were like those he held, he swept the pages off the desk in anger. That was why she had been on the floor gathering them up.

"So you see, I am safe for now," she concluded. "But I admit that Roselli is suspicious."

"Exactly, Signora, and that is why we are here."

"Then shall we get off the floor?" she said smiling. "I will meet you back at the hotel. There I can tell you about our departure schedule tomorrow and our stay in New York City next week, *va bene?*"

"*Sì,* that will be fine," answered Arthur. "Then we'll see you in an hour or so."

Agnes agreed and Arthur left with his sons. They took the precaution to stay behind the exhibits. This time, however, they were not so lucky. When they came to the display holding the prints of Lorenzo and Piero de' Medici and the bronze balls, Pietro and Andreas arrived. They had nowhere to go, so they had to be seen in a way that would not create suspicion.

Arthur backed off to the sculpture called *The Slave* and whispered to his sons to play along.

"This is the piece called *The Slave*. It was one of the sculptures which Michelangelo intended to have placed on the tomb of Pope Julius II."

"Hey, you there, what do you think you're doing here?" shouted Pietro as he spotted Arthur and the boys standing at the marble statue.

"Oh, hi…*buona serra*. Which one are you, Andreas or Pietro?" asked Arthur nonchalantly.

"I'm Pietro…and who are you? Can't you see that the exhibit is over?"

"Well of course I can see, Pietro. Don't you and Andreas remember me from the class I conducted here?" asked Arthur.

Andreas thought hard and then recalled seeing Arthur in the meeting room with students.

"Si, I know you. You are the teacher, *il professore*, right?"

"That's absolutely correct Andreas. You are a smart lad with a good memory. These are my sons. I just wanted them to see the famous sculpture one more time before you take it away." Arthur replied cordially. "We'll be going now, thank you for letting us see the masterpiece one more time."

"*Mille grazie, Signore professore*, is there anything else that you wish to see?" asked Andreas.

Footsteps could be heard on the marble floor, getting louder by the second. The boys began to fidget and tug on their father's arm. Arthur heard the noise and got their message.

"Well, I think not. We should get going, *arrivaderci* and *grazie*," Arthur hastily answered as he and the boys started for the dock door.

The two brothers offered their farewell and began dismantling the display case with the bronze balls and the prints. Andreas was handing the bronze balls one by one to Pietro when Anselmo Roselli came up to them.

"I thought I heard voices. Who were you talking with?" he asked the brothers.

"No one. Just that American teacher," answered Pietro.

"What? You idiots, where did they go?" Anselmo screamed back.

The shout from the curator so upset Pietro that he dropped the bronze ball which was being handed to him. This upset the curator even more as it banged on the marble flooring and rolled towards the sculpture. Andreas chased after it, picked it up and rubbed it against his shirt to make sure that it was not damaged. Anselmo grabbed it from him, checked it over and began shouting again.

"Now listen to me. We must find the American right now."

The brothers stood at attention and nodded affirmatively as they handed the curator the other bronze balls and ran off to find Arthur and his sons. The shouting had been clearly heard, however, so Arthur and the boys were already jumping off the dock and running across the parking lot to their car. When Pietro and Andreas arrived at the loading dock all they could see was the empty parking lot and a car zooming out of the driveway.

"The curator will not be happy with us, Andreas," Pietro stated nervously.

They could do no more than return to another tongue lashing by the curator who was now searching for several of the bronze balls which he had dropped when the brothers ran off.

It was well past eleven o'clock when Arthur and his sons returned to the hotel. When they entered the lobby Agnes was already there. She had climbed out her office window to avoid seeing Roselli and his henchmen.

In her hands she held a folder with the papers she had been collecting off the floor.

"Signora la Straga, how did you get here so fast?" asked the boys in unison.

"I heard the yelling so I thought it best to leave by another way. Here, Signore Colonna, are the papers which I showed you. I think that it's best they stay with you, *va bene?*"

Arthur accepted the folder, but wondered if it was wise to entrust them to him. They walked to a less conspicuous location by the empty ballroom as they discussed what needed to be done.

"So you can see that if Roselli gets his hands on these pages, he may arrive at the same conclusion. And we do not want him to know of the truth within the legend and of the ring's possible existence," Agnes was saying as they took their seats near the railing.

It was nearly midnight now as she asked Arthur to remove one of the pages from the folder.

"It's the one labeled Lorenzo's death," she said.

Arthur thumbed through the pages and found it.

"I think this is it, Signora," he commented as he handed it over to her.

Agnes la Straga glanced at it. "*Si*, that's the one. Now read the translation please, but first notice that it seems to be a page from a larger body of work. Note too the condition of the original copied on the back."

The boys saw it first.

"There are burned edges on the page," noted John.

"Exactly, Giovanni, someone attempted to burn this page and probably the larger work from which it comes," confirmed Agnes. "Now what else do you see?"

Rich noted that there was a date on the upper right corner of the page.

"It says April 8, 1492," he observed. "Is that important?"

"Si, *molto importante*, Ricardo," Agnes answered. "Now Arthur, please read the entry."

Arthur took out his reading glasses and held the page to catch the light from a distant chandelier, since the ballroom itself was dark. Faint light from the street outside the huge windows was the only other source.

Today I was summoned by the servant of Lorenzo de'
Medici to come to his bedside at Villa Medici in Careggi. When
I entered the room where he lay all was quiet. Many stood
around the one called *Il Magnifico*. The women and men were
weeping. It was clear that the man was dying and yet he could
speak to me clearly.

All were told to leave the room save one. Marsilio Ficino
remained with his friend.

He stood to one side of the bed as I came to the other side
to hear the man's request.

I was asked to absolve Lorenzo de' Medici before he died.
At first I hesitated, but then I took his hand as he was
suffering. When I did this, I saw a ring of three bands on his
finger. In touching it I felt a sensation of warmth. There was
no doubt in my mind that the ring must be a magical relic of
sorts, but I feared that it was not from heaven. I dropped his
hand and refused to give him absolution.

I told him to reject this evil practice of his to follow the
way of wizards and witches. Marsilio protested but Lorenzo
silenced him. I told him that his house was doomed and that
he would die soon. He told me that he was dead already. With
that he fell silent. Marsilio ordered me from the room and the
others entered again. One who entered was called Angelo
Poliziano. I knew him as he was a prominent poet and teacher
who often worked with the students of art in the gardens
across from my priory in San Marco Church.

The poet held in his hands a silver cup. He told Marsilio
that the contents within was a blend of gold, frankincense, and
myrrh. He was told that it would have miraculous healing
powers. At that moment, I knew that I was right to refuse him
absolution. Though the medicine was formed from gifts of the
Magi, it was a magical potion; of that I was sure. And so they
shut the door behind me as I watched Marsilio, the Greek
scholar, pour the liquid into the mouth of the Medici.

By the time I reached San Marco back in Firenze the next
day, Lorenzo de' Medici was indeed dead.

Girolamo Savonarola

Arthur lowered the page; his eyes, and those of his sons, were all focused on Agnes la Straga. Each set of eyes was questioning the meaning of what was obviously a journal entry.

"So I see the writing on this page interests you," Agnes began, trying to hide her excitement.

"Signora, if this page is authentic, you have made a notable find to solve one of the mysteries of history," Arthur virtually proclaimed, as his sons still looked rather bewildered.

"Oh it is most certainly real, Arturo," Agnes stated confidently.

Rich now turned to his brother, John. "Arturo?" he asked with raised eyebrows.

John whispered back that she couldn't quite get the habit of saying Arthur. "You know like when she calls you Ricardo and me, Giovanni. Anyway, she's Italian. Everything sounds musical and romantic when they speak, so give it up."

This satisfied Rich, who of course was protecting his mother's interests, and they refocused on what Agnes had begun to explain.

Their little conversation had not been lost on Agnes, who caught their words. Of course Arthur was oblivious to it all as he was now consumed with learning about the historic page which he held. Deliberately calling them Ricardo and Giovanni in a very audible manner and with a smile directed at Rich, Agnes drew their attention back to the matter at hand. Rich returned a tiny smile as his cheeks reddened and John laughed out loud.

The laugh brought Arthur into the mix of what was going on, but only to direct his sons to pay close attention to the signora.

"Now, as I was saying," she began again. "Though the hour is late, and my time is short, as I will leave tomorrow to bring the exhibit to New York, I would like to share with you the story which came before the page was written. Then, when we meet again, we may have more time to discuss what we might do with the information on this page and on the others which you now have."

Agnes began where she had left off when she introduced the lesson detailing how Michelangelo was accepted into the Medici family and its garden for artists.

"The year was 1491. The young stone cutter was now sixteen and enjoying life in the Palazzo in the evening and honing his creative talents in the Medici gardens during the day. It was on just such a day that Michelangelo had completed one of his first sculptures which he called *the Faun*."

"Michelangelo, I like it. It brings the mythological figure alive," said the admiring Granacci. "Has *Il Magnifico* seen it?"

"No, Francesco, of course he hasn't. He's much too busy to look at this miserable attempt at sculpting," replied the young stone cutter. "But enough of this talk. How goes your design for the carnival costumes?"

"First of all your faun is not miserable; you are too modest. Secondly, that's why I've dropped by. I'd like you to take a look at the costume designs and the chariots I've created," Granacci said with excitement.

Michelangelo did not hesitate to reply that he'd love to see his work. The carnival time was a high point of Florentine life and the Medici created such an event as to make all involved forget their troubles and enjoy the music, dance, jousts, and races for days on end. To think that his closest friend was one of the artists who created the art and costumes for the celebration was quite thrilling. The young stone cutter's enthusiasm for his friend's accomplishments was not lost on Granacci.

"Now it's not true art my friend, like your faun, but it brings in some money so one might live," the excited Granacci explained. "Can you leave the gardens to come with me?"

"That shouldn't be a problem. I have no real master over me here. There's no Domenico Ghirlandaio here," answered Michelangelo. "I'll just cover this stone head and off we'll go."

Michelangelo ran off to fetch a cloth with which to cover his work. While he did, so Granacci waited and examined the head of the faun more closely.

He ran his fingers across its pointed ears and through his open and laughing mouth feeling its full range of teeth. His fingers crossed the wrinkles in the brow and around the eyes; for this faun was an aged being. As he was enjoying feeling the life his friend had put into the stone, he heard a commotion from across the garden. Granacci glanced up from the white marble and saw *Il Magnifico* coming towards Michelangelo's work area. He was with Ficino and Poliziano, the latter having been one who helped to save his life in that murder attempt in the Duomo. The garden was alive with the buzzing of the Medici presence spreading from artist to artist. Each vied to display his work to its best advantage. Lorenzo de'

Medici, though polite in his comments, had his focus elsewhere. Granacci caught the eye of *Il Magnifico*, who waved him to come forward. He knew Granacci, as it was he who would first have seen the costumes the young man designed for the carnival.

"Francesco, where is that friend of yours? Does he not work today?" asked Lorenzo de' Medici.

"My Lord, he indeed is working. Come let me show you his latest effort," Granacci exclaimed as he bowed and pointed to the sculpture of the faun.

The three men gave their thanks and moved where Granacci had pointed. They came upon the carving seated upon its pedestal. Each circled it several times and, as Granacci had done, Lorenzo ran his fingers across the life-like face.

As this was taking place, Michelangelo ran back holding a large canvas cloth.

He was muttering that one would think that in the Medici gardens there would be ample supplies for the artists. Totally unaware of who stood next to his sculpture, he was unfolding the cloth so as to throw it over his work and go off with his friend, Francesco. Only when Granacci, hearing his unflattering words, stepped in his path did Michelangelo take notice of who stood at his work. Granacci grabbed the cloth and pushed Michelangelo towards his statue.

"Ah there you are, young Buonarroti," Lorenzo began, as the lad stood frozen before him.

To be frozen before Lorenzo, however, was quite unusual for him. He dined, almost nightly, with his substitute father (that is how much he revered Lorenzo) and the very men with him. At dinner, however, he just absorbed the talk of art and music, philosophy and religion, government and politics. Never did he ever open his mouth to offer his opinion on the topic being discussed. In fact, he would guard his opinions on such matters, especially politics, most closely even in his mature years. But now Michelangelo stood frozen before Lorenzo and his esteemed mentors and friends.

"I'm sorry that I wasn't here for you, my Lord," the lad began. "I was…well I was looking for supplies."

"My boy, don't fret so," Lorenzo began. "Marsilio, Angelo, and I were just out for a stroll and we thought we'd stop to see how our young master was doing."

"You honor me, all of you. Unfortunately, all I have to show you is this head of the faun."

"That's all you say," chimed in Marsilio Ficino. "I'd say your efforts are commendable."

"Indeed so, Michelangelo," added Lorenzo. "The head has life, it laughs, so as even to show its teeth."

"The marble lives," continued Poliziano.

The lad was thrilled, but remained humble. For the three men now walked around the head of the faun to take in its intricate characteristics. Michelangelo weaved back and forth to catch Granacci's eye as he stood away from these evaluators of his work. When finally their eyes met, all Granacci could do was wave his hands in a motion which pointed to the sculpture. In other words, he was trying to say in gesture that Michelangelo should give his fullest attention to *Il Magnifico*.

Lorenzo stopped and folded his hands. He bent down and came very close to the face of the Faun.

"Master Buonarroti, the figure seems to have acquired quite an age as seen in the lines on his face and wrinkles at the corners of his eyes."

The lad mustered up all the courage he had to discuss what he had attempted to demonstrate.

"My Lord, you are very astute in your observation. The faun is, indeed, an older man and yet filled with the exuberance of a youth."

"Ah so, see Marsilio, how the lines give expression around the eyes, and yet still betray his age."

"Most assuredly a remarkable effort for one of such a tender age," Marsilio Ficino replied.

"It's a beautiful piece of work my boy," continued Lorenzo. "And yet I have to offer one more observation. If indeed the faun is an old man, then how does he come to have such a perfect set of teeth?"

The other two men bent down to take a closer look at the Faun's mouth. They too ran their fingers inside the mouth and up and down the teeth within. As they did so, they too nodded their consent to Lorenzo's observation. Through all of this Michelangelo stood rigidly silent. This did not go unnoticed by *Il Magnifico*. He clapped the lad on his back and congratulated him once again, smiling as he did so. Then he took Michelangelo's hands into his own. The one hand touched that now much admired three banded ring. A feeling of warmth filled Michelangelo's body and he was able to speak once again. However, before he could do so, Lorenzo raised the lad's hands and placed a kiss on each.

"These hands shall create works the world has never seen, or will ever see again," he proclaimed. "What say you to that my boy."

"I…I…I don't quite know what to say my Lord. But I will say that by dinner tonight you shall see an old faun."

Lorenzo laughed and beckoned his friends to join him as they bade farewell and continued their stroll.

As the Medici leader and the scholars left the gardens, Michelangelo immediately picked up his tools and approached the head of the faun. Forgetting about Granacci, he began chipping away and filing down the marble teeth.

"Michelangelo, what on earth are you doing?" Granacci questioned as he approached his friend. "They loved your work."

"Francesco, they may have loved it but it didn't convey what I hoped it would. And so I shall make it an old man so everyone might know what I meant."

Thus did the young stone cutter chisel and file until the perfect set of teeth within the faun's head were imperfect as befitting an old man, even one who was mythological. Granacci stood in awe of his young friend. The marble chips flew with such speed that his skill amazed the other artisans in the garden. The young stone cutter's strength and innate ability to know exactly where to stop his tool before the marble became irreparably damaged was mind boggling. Finally, what would have taken other sculptors many hours, if not an entire day, had been accomplished. The toothy smile was now irregular. In fact, some teeth were missing entirely.

"Now, Francesco, we may go. The faun is the old man, which I had intended him to be," said Michelangelo standing before his adjusted work with hardly a hint of sweat on his brow. "Of course he was just that before these changes which only added human age to him rather than mystical age as befitting a being of mythology."

Granacci stood in speechless admiration, for his friend could even add a philosophical interpretation to his work. Little did he know that within four years his friend would also offer a theological opinion to a work which is perhaps the most famous scene of Christian faith ever sculpted. *The Pieta* of St. Peter's in Rome depicts a serene Mary holding her dead son across her lap. Her true age as a mother of a thirty-three year old is forever hidden within the marble for it certainly is not betrayed in the peaceful composure, youthful countenance and smooth skin of her face and hands which one sees when viewing the masterpiece.

Granacci helped Michelangelo cover his faun and then the two made their way out of the garden and across the street to San Marco church. Why were they headed for San Marco and not the area around the Piazza Signoria was what Granacci was thinking as his friend clarified the detour without Granacci ever asking. Michelangelo explained that his brother Lionardo had told him about a new Dominican friar who had recently come to San Marco. He was to be in charge of the friary. He was said to be a powerful speaker and to possess the gift of prophecy. Since it was almost time for vespers, he thought they should attend and listen to this new preacher. Granacci agreed that praying would not hurt them in the least, especially since Carnival time was nearing and they would probably have to ask for a lot of forgiveness when it was all over.

"Maybe I can get in a good word for myself ahead of time."

"Granacci, you astound me," Michelangelo laughingly said. "You already know that you are going to sin and hope to get forgiven ahead of time. I don't think it works that way."

"Well my young friend who now seems to also be a theologian as well, one does not understand the ways of the Lord. Thus, what I offer in prayer now can't hurt, can it?"

"Francesco, if God doesn't hear you and smile upon your stupidity, then he is not the God of mercy. Now hurry, the bells are already ringing for the friars to enter."

As they passed through the doors of San Marco, they were shocked to see the church filled. This mass of humanity had come out on a week-day evening. The two artists wiggled their way through the crowd so they might position themselves closer to the pulpit from which Frate Girolamo Savonarola was to preach.

The incense rose and filled the air with its sweet scent as the Dominican brothers chanted an evening song. Though sung in Latin, the words rang clear in the ears of Michelangelo, Francesco, and most in attendance. He may not be able to write in Latin to any great degree but hearing it so often in church and through lectures of the scholars, Michelangelo understood each chanted syllable.

Christ, you are the savior of the world and the king of the
new creation,

Direct our hearts to your kingdom, where you sit at the
right hand of the Father.
You are the light that never darkens, even as the day draws
to a close…

The art of Fra Angelico filled the church of this convent complex. The brilliance of his colors, touched with gold highlights, dazzled the young artists. The saints, walking up to the heavenly kingdom to be judged on the last day, seemed to be floating in clouds; but not of paint, rather those created by the smoke of the incense. It would be years later that Michelangelo himself would be asked to create a Last Judgment scene in paint. His version would be so different from Fra Angelico's almost serene depiction that it would astound all who would view it. They would see the souls of the judged writhing in pain and agony or lifted up to heaven by angels to be bathed in the light of Christ's presence.

As the two pondered the meaning of the painting and how skillfully the medieval artist rendered it, the music stopped and the scripture was read.

"You are a chosen race, a royal priesthood, a holy nation, a people
God claims for his own to proclaim the glorious works of the One who
called you from darkness to marvelous light." (1 Peter 2, 9-10)

All was silent as the new preacher from Ferarra ascended the stairs of the pulpit in his white and black robes. With its black hood pulled over his head, all anyone could see of his features were his protruding nose and chin. When he reached the top and stepped into the preaching enclosure, he slid off his hood to reveal long dark hair and gray eyes like burning coal. His deep, powerful voice thundered across the assembly bouncing off the church walls and vibrating through the ears, head, and finally, entire body of those listening.

"Our Lord Jesus Christ cries out from the cross once more," Savonarola began. "Our sins once more drive the nails through his hands and his feet."

Men and women wept and clutched each other as he continued his thunderous and vivid, though dark, message of how the evil ways of the populace tortured the Savior. His voice would lower, then crescendo, and the assembly would cry and shake and embrace in horror of what judgment would befall them. There would be no message of hope, or love, or enlightenment, this night. The frate, instead, would use as his example of evil ways, the Carnival of Firenze with its costumed youth and women, several hundred in number. He orally painted the scene of the Florentines as they gathered in the Piazza Signoria, with their songs of disgusting verses. The youths would praise the naked beauty of man. They would revel in the freedom to indulge in drinking to excess, dancing in the streets, and playing pagan games.

"We embrace the paganism of the ancient days too much. We cast down what is holy and elevate the human body as the glorious symbol of creation," he bellowed.

His eyes suddenly focused on the young artists as if he knew them. He stretched out his right arm, one finger extended from his closed hand. He twirled it in a circle and then shoved it forward as the assembly gasped. It was pointed directly at Granacci. The young artist trembled and hung onto Michelangelo's arm so hard that both of them shook.

Frate Savonarola glared at Granacci, his eyes burning into those of the petrified artist

"And you Francesco Granacci; you design those costumes for the women and young men to glorify the pagans of ancient days. You go too far in your esteem for the Greeks and Romans."

As the assembly froze in silence, Granacci quivered violently and collapsed into Michelangelo's arms.

He looked up into the teen's eyes saying, "He has cursed me. Why did you bring me here Buonarroti? Why?" He pulled himself up on his friend's arm and looked into those vibrant brown eyes with his own filled with tears. "Am I to be damned Michelangelo?"

He ran through the congregation to the sole doorway at the back of the church. A bright light streamed into the incense clouds from outside. It was as if spirits floated throughout the entire interior of this house of worship. Worshipers now watched dumbstruck as the young man fled with his friend close on his heels. As he passed through the door, the setting sun's rays, struck his face. Holding up his hands as if he was receiving the curse still echoing in his ears, he blocked the glare.

He ran into the Medici gardens across from the Piazza where he fell to his knees before a statue of Christ as the Good Shepherd.

Michelangelo came up behind him and placed his hand on his shoulder. He could feel the tremors still vibrating within his friend's body.

"Francesco, I am so sorry. Please forgive me."

The now red-eyed Granacci looked up to those large cocoa brown eyes with specks of yellow and blue. He saw sorrow and concern in them.

"My friend, you did not force me. I wanted to ask for forgiveness for my future sins, remember? But alas, you were right. I should not have tried to trick our Lord."

"Granacci, God doesn't work that way. He knows you're foolish; that's not a sin. He knows you're working to create art and that is good even if your subject matter is…shall I say, less than inspiring."

A smile broke across Granacci's face as he righted himself off the ground and embraced his friend.

"You always seem to know what to say Buonarroti." He regained his composure, stating quite emphatically, "Well, this fool needs to eat and if I am to eat then I must complete the Carnival art, so let's be off."

"Speaking of eating, Francesco, there is a scholar named Marsilio Ficino who sits at the Medici dinner table most nights. He teaches that the science and philosophy of the ancients do not contradict Christian theology. But that's not what Frate Savonarola just preached at all."

"Are you saying that what I do is Christian?" a more hopeful Granacci asked.

"No foolish one. That's not what I'm saying."

Melancholy immediately spread across Granacci's face once again. "So then I am damned?"

Michelangelo shook his head and then shook his friend by his shoulders. He explained that the wisdom of the ancients, the art of the ancients, and the science of the ancients can be used to express our understanding of life and salvation. Although Michelangelo would come to believe this, he, like Granacci, would be haunted all his life by the words of Savonarola. How they would affect his work would never be fully known, for shortly before his death Michelangelo destroyed much of his unfinished and finished drawings and thoughts. Many began to presume that they may have had as their subject matter those very scenes which the Frate had condemned. Even though Savonarola would be put to death in 1498, long before the artist's own death, his words would continue to haunt him.

It was well known that his followers were still active in the Florentine community even after the death of the Frate Savonarola. And yet, despite this conflict within himself, the art of Michelangelo would reflect the themes of the classical period as well as those of his deeply rooted faith. They would extol the beauty of the human form. His sculptures and paintings would depict what Renaissance artistic thought considered to be the final test of mastery in art: *"Un bel corpo ignudo"* (a beautiful nude body), says biographer Symonds in his *Life of Michelangelo.*

But that sad day, shortly before his death, when the master stone cutter would destroy his work, was many years away. Today, the almost seventeen-year-old Michelangelo laughed with his friend Francesco Granacci. They pushed the sermon of the frate far back into their minds and frolicked along the Via Cavour admiring Granacci's contribution to the glory of the Florentine Carnival.

Several days later the frate's words were remembered with a lessened mood of damnation. Michelangelo and Granacci had entered the Piazza San Giovanni, which spreads out before the bronze doors of the Duomo, to join other youths. Those thundering words of Frate Savonarola seemed to have been spoken years ago rather than just a week earlier. As they lounged with their friends, they saw Poliziano. Scholar, poet, and friend of *Il Magnifico*, he was one of the main coordinators of the Carnival, so hated by Frate Savonarola. That connection to the Carnival would come to haunt the poet and his priest friend, Greek scholar, Marsilio Ficino. These two would witness the frate's refusal to absolve Lorenzo de Medici on his deathbed, not more than a year after the celebration of this Carnival of 1491.

The young stone cutter and the designer of carnival art joined the youths sprawled across the steps of the Duomo. The youths they joined were also in costumes designed by Granacci. Among them was Piero Torrigiano. As soon as Michelangelo saw who was among them he lunged for the youth even though Piero was significantly larger than he.

"Michelangelo, do not trouble yourself with such scum," yelled Granacci, as he grabbed his friend's arms to hold him back. With a wave of his arm he signaled the other youths who then pushed Piero away from Michelangelo's path. As Piero left, he laughed and pointed to his nose.

The young Michelangelo reeled around and shouted into Granacci's face, "How can I forget what he did to me. I will carry this nose all my life because of him."

Francesco tried to add some humor and commented that the nose was now noble in appearance and a reminder of the ancient Romans whom he admired so much. A slight smile crossed the stone cutter's lips but soon disappeared as a group of youths returned to the Piazza having gotten rid of Piero.

"See, he's gone. Let us enjoy the company of our friends," Granacci requested earnestly. "So noble men of Firenze, did you throw the beast into the River Arno?"

"Ah, Francesco would that have been a choice, but alas, the beast ran off down Via della Calzauoli. Some of our number told him of the women soon to be singing in the Piazza Santo Trinita."

"Santo Trinita," shouted Michelangelo. "Then that's where I shall go and return to him the gift of a broken nose as he once gave me."

In a flash of lightening speed the youthful stone cutter, now full of revenge, ran towards the Arno River on the banks of which stood the church of the Holy Trinity. Granacci rushed after him, yelling that he should use his brain.

"Buonarroti, did you not learn from the pain of that broken nose Piero gave you?"

"I learned this much; that no-talent beast who could not take a joke about his incompetent drawing shall suffer the same as he gave me," Michelangelo shouted back.

The scene from three years past, when he and the Piero youth were but thirteen years old, flashed through his mind as it had not done for almost a year. Many of the would-be young artists of the Medici garden had been sent to the Brancacci chapel on the Carmine. They were to study its artwork and prepare some sketches. As they bantered among each other, as they often did while lounging on the steps of the Duomo, Piero Torrigiano took particular offense to Michelangelo's comments concerning his talent, or lack of it, as was the case in that day's bantering. With a rapid swing from a height which towered over the young stone cutter, his fist connected with the bridge of Michelangelo's nose pushing the cartilage so hard that it collapsed. Piero would later brag about the nose which would carry his mark for all time.

"It fell like a biscuit," he would tell any who would listen.

The very thought of that comment enraged Michelangelo so that his face was now red with the building fury. At last they reached the Arno and ran along its bank towards the crowds at the Piazza Santo Trinita. With his usual lack of grace when angered so, the young stone cutter thrashed his way through the crowds surrounding the Piazza. Granacci offered apologies, as they plowed through the gathering.

"*Permesso*, just a spirited lad who can't wait to see the ladies," he lied to them.

The sixteen-year-old at last reached the outer edge of the crowd. Out of breath, he paused and surveyed the ring of people surrounding the Piazza. Francesco was grateful for the pause, and he breathed deeply with the hope that Piero would never be found and Michelangelo may not end up in the tower of the Palazzo Signoria. Their eyes became filled with the very scene which had attracted the crowd: three hundred and fifty young women dressed in Granacci's costumes were dancing and singing around the Piazza.

"Gather ye roses while ye may. Cast your prudence to the winds. Obey your instincts," they sang as they marched through the crowds weaving their way along the streets of Florence on their way to the chariot races.

The furious red face now became the rose color of a blushing youth. Michelangelo could hardly believe his eyes. Never before had he seen such a site as young ladies dancing in such a fashion and singing such words.

"Perhaps Francesco was right in the first place. We should have asked for mercy from the Lord ahead of time."

The thought had little chance to be reflected upon. Francesco Granacci took hold of Michelangelo's arm and dragged him into the crowds following the singing women to the chariot races. Piero was soon a distant memory as the teen entered the festivities, as youths usually do, with little thinking and much jubilation.

Chapter 9: Releasing Lorenzo's Spirit

It was well past midnight when Agnes la Straga glanced at her watch in the darkened balcony overlooking the Hilton Hotel's Grand Ballroom. "*Mama mia*," she exclaimed. "Arturo, I had no idea it was so late."

"Not at all Signora, my sons and I find your story most intriguing. Right guys?"

The boys were still wide eyed as Agnes had laid out this life-changing encounter between Michelangelo and the Frate Savonarola.

"Is there more Signora?" asked Rich.

"Like what happened after the Carnival? Did Michelangelo ever get his chance to return a punch back at that Piero guy?" questioned John.

Agnes gave the boys a smile of satisfaction. She had succeeded in stimulating their interest and hopefully they would aide their father in what would eventually have to be done once they got to Italy.

"*Allora mi amici*, indeed there is much more but the hour is late, no?"

"NO," they countered as they looked at their father.

Arthur, who was just as wide eyed and alert, was quietly gauging how much she would tell of the legend of the Magi ring. "Well, Signora, if the boys are willing then, so am I. Perhaps, just a little more of the tale, if you don't mind?"

"*Sì*, just a little more then, *va bene*?" she answered.

The stillness of the hotel became even more apparent as the conversation ceased and all ears perked to hear her tale and all eyes focused on her with new intensity. She adjusted her position in the chair and leaned forward slightly. Moving her eyes so that she could gaze directly into those of Arthur and his sons, one after another, she began in a hushed tone.

No one noticed the three men enter the Chicago Hilton lobby at this late hour. Two of them were rather brawny. Their well-developed arms and upper body bulged underneath their tight-fitting polo shirts; one a midnight blue and the other a sunset red. On the upper right of the shirt an embroidered insignia of gold thread read, *The World of Michelangelo and the Medici Exhibit*. The third man was dressed in black dress pants and white shirt with a tie of blue and gold depicting various works of Michelangelo. It was he who would do all the talking when they reached the reservation counter.

"*Por Favore, signorina,*" he began.

The girl at the check in counter raised her head and flashed him a smile. "Yes sir, may I help you?"

"Ah, most assuredly, Signorina. I believe that you have a guest registered here by the name of Arthur Colonna, no?" asked the charming Anselmo Roselli.

"I'm afraid that I cannot give out that information sir," answered Elizabeth quite professionally.

"Of course you can't. However, here is my card. As you can see, I am the curator of the Renaissance exhibit which just closed at the Museum of Natural History. Perhaps I could leave a message for Signore Colonna?" Anselmo asked politely.

"Certainly you may. Here's a card for your convenience."

Roselli took the card and began to fill it out as Andreas and Pietro took positions on each end of the counter. Having written the note, he then handed it to the young woman who graciously accepted it and placed it in a basket on the shelf below the counter top.

"*Grazie, signorina,*" Roselli said and off he walked toward the staircase which led to the bar off the ballroom. As he did so, he made a slight wave of his hand. Pietro walked away towards the elevator, while Andreas picked up a travel brochure at the counter. He thumbed through, never losing sight of the basket containing the note.

After a minute or two the clerk looked around and, seeing only Andreas reading his brochure, picked up the basket and took out several note cards. She placed each of them in a small cubby hole with corresponding room numbers on brass plates. One was placed into 520, another into 729 and the final one into 1023. Andreas noted the room numbers and went quickly up the staircase. He quickly found Roselli seated at a small table on which rested a house phone.

"Andreas, did you get the room number?" he asked calmly as he rose from his chair.

"I got three numbers. They are 520, 729 and 1023," he told Roselli.

"*Molte bene*. Now all we have to do is to go to each of those rooms and try to listen for my assistant's voice. Tomorrow, before we leave, I shall call the rooms and ask for Colonna. Once we have him on the phone, I can invite him to meet with me to discuss his tour of Italy and how I might also be able to help. Once that's accomplished we can keep an eye on that la Straga woman. Heaven knows what she will have confided to Colonna, but we shall find out."

Roselli directed Andreas to find his brother and bring him back. After Andreas left, Roselli heard a woman's voice, a rather dramatic one. It was speaking English, but there was no doubt it was not her native language. It had a pronounced Italian accent. Roselli rose and very quietly moved towards the sound of the voice.

Agnes la Straga continued her story, not with the Carnival, but with Frate Savonarola's refusal to absolve Lorenzo de Medici on his deathbed. She could hardly keep her voice quiet as the events she described were so earth-shaking that it caused her to interpret the events dramatically for Arthur and his sons. They, in turn, literally sat on the edges of their seats listening to every word with eyes and, for the boys, mouths wide open.

"Gigantic storms thundered across Tuscany for days during that first week of April in 1492. You recall those six bronze balls which were part of the exhibit no doubt," she questioned in a statement.

The three nodded. Arthur even described how one of them was damaged as if it had been in a fire.

"Exactly right, Arturo. Horrible lightening storms streaked across Florence. Bolts of blinding light struck the bell tower of the Duomo, causing part of its marble to crash to the piazza below. It was a miracle no one was killed."

Roselli could now see four figures seated near the railing of the balcony overlooking the ballroom. He changed his direction towards the bank of elevators where the table with its large vase of flowers filled the corridor. He crouched behind the table. The four could be seen and heard from this angle, so he stayed and listened to the story.

"Another bolt struck the coat of arms on the Palazzo Medici, blistering the metal of one of the six balls over the doorway. Poliziano himself saw the strike as he returned to retrieve the necessary ingredients for the potion derived from the gifts of the Magi. He hastened directly back to Villa Medici in Careggi, narrowly missing being hit himself by a thunder bolt. His horse galloped wildly through the city streets and across the Ponte Vecchio which spans the River Arno. Everywhere screams of terror were heard as one building after another was struck."

Her words dramatically painted the scene on that April day of 1492.

John and Rich were mesmerized as they listened to this unbelievable story which seemed to be taken from the Dark Ages rather than the Renaissance.

"Signora, you mean they actually did make that concoction?" asked Rich.

"Si, Ricardo. They did make the potion and Lorenzo did drink of it, as I said the other day."

"And these storms, Signora, are these just fanciful tales or can they be proven?" questioned John.

"Giovanni, the reports of the storms and damage can all be verified in historical reports of eye witnesses of that time."

"Boys, let Signora la Straga finish her story, if you please," directed Arthur.

Agnes la Straga continued her fantastic tale. She related how Angelo Poliziano jumped off his horse just as that lightning bolt struck the Medici coat of arms damaging the bronze ball, with the lily of France on it. Most of that Lily symbol was burned off by the lightning strike. As the rain poured down, Poliziano pounded on the door. Michelangelo opened the door. His classics teacher entered, exhausted and soaking wet. Michelangelo's teacher was filled with fear and worry for his dear friend back at Careggi on the outskirts of the Florentine City limits. Upon entering, Poliziano placed his hand on Michelangelo's shoulder and shook his head. Tears welled up in the lad's eyes as he knew what that nod meant. The two sets of tear-filled eyes met. He made no pause but signaled the lad to follow him to his room.

"Master Poliziano, how bad is *Il Magnifico's* illness?" the lad inquired.

"Alas, young Buonarroti, bad enough that his wife, Clarice, is there with six of their children. Only Giovanni, who is in Rome, could not make it," replied Angelo Poliziano.

He went directly to a large bookcase and pulled from it an ancient text. Fingering down through the pages he stopped, creased the page open and turned to a small cabinet. From it he removed a black chest with brass trim forming a lock mechanism. Slipping a key off a cord which he pulled from underneath his traveling cloak, Poliziano unlocked the chest as the wide-eyed youth watched. He untied his cloak and let it fall to the floor as he removed three glass cylinders from the chest. One contained gold dust, one contained frankincense pieces, and the final one contained the resin of myrrh. Naturally, the youth offered his assistance to carry the ingredients, book, and supplies to the kitchen.

The storm howled outside. While gathering their supplies, violent winds pushed open the doors adjoining the balcony. They banged loudly, but the glass in them did not shatter. Michelangelo, fearing that this wind was a sign of bad tidings, slammed the doors shut. He clutched the ancient text to his chest, breathing heavily. A servant came running into the room screaming that the tower of the Church of Santa Reparata had been struck by lightning, causing it to fragment. Poliziano ordered the servant away. He saw the fear in young Michelangelo's eyes as his world was about to be destroyed just like the bell tower of the church had been.

"Come Michelangelo, I have much to do and little time. Then I must get back to Careggi before it's too late."

They ran to the kitchen where they could create the potion to cure Lorenzo. Michelangelo stood in a corner of the large room watching every move made and every herb used. The main three ingredients were melted and mixed together, then blended with herbs and water to make a more palatable drink. After hours of mixing, melting, and blending, Poliziano poured the mixture into a metal vial. He instructed Michelangelo to go to the chapel of the Magi to pray for his master's soul. The lad reluctantly left, knowing that the happiest time of his life was about to end.

Placing the vial into a leather pouch hanging at his side, Poliziano let his servant place his still-soaked cloak over him, as he almost ran towards the front door where he had left Lorenzo's horse, Morello. Lorenzo had insisted that Angelo Poliziano use his own horse for his secret journey. No one in the city was to know how gravely ill Lorenzo really was, not until he had received the remedy.

Hours later he galloped onto the villa's grounds. The storm was subsiding and the moon peeked through the clouds before the next wave of rain, wind, and lightening rolled through. The servants, seeing Morello, ran to aid its rider. They had hoped the horse would be carrying their master, Lorenzo de Medici, though in fact they knew better.

Agnes repeated how Poliziano entered the room where Marsilio Ficino and Frate Savonarola stood. He carried what he thought would be a miraculous cure for his friend who, at age forty-three, lay dying at the pinnacle of his success and fame.

"And the rest you know. The Frate Savonarola left, refusing to absolve *Il Magnifico*. This he did as Poliziano entered with the remedy. Lorenzo de Medici did drink the mixture containing gold, frankincense, and myrrh," she confirmed. "However, it did nothing to help heal him."

"This can't be all," stated an enthralled John. "The ring, what happened to the ring of the Magi?"

"Ah, si, Giovanni…the ring," she replied almost absentmindedly. "There is one more part to this story."

She painted the scene in the Villa with words.

"The family gathered about Lorenzo's bedside. Clarice and the six children stood to one side and Ficino and Poliziano were at the other side of the bed. Lorenzo was still conscious and lucid. He asked for news of the city. Poliziano related the stories of the horrific storm which swept through as he entered the Palazzo. He told *Il Magnifico* of the bolt which struck the tower of the Duomo and Santa Reparato and then of the coat of arms being damaged at the Palazzo." Arthur and his sons seemed to be standing at the bedside of Lorenzo de Medici as Agnes continued her story.

"I am dead," Lorenzo de Medici responded to the news just related.

A howl of weeping ensued as Clarice threw herself over the weak body of her husband. Piero, the eldest, pulled her from his father's body. He deposited her into the arms of his sisters for consolation.

"Perhaps it would be best if you would take some food and drink. It's been a trying day," advised Ficino.

Piero agreed to escort his mother, brother, and sisters to a room next door where they would wait until summoned for the final moments.

Lorenzo placed his hand on each of his children's heads as they said their farewells. He kissed the hand of his Clarice. He said nothing until they had left the room. As the door closed behind the family, Lorenzo turned his head towards his friends.

"The time has come for me to fulfill my promise."

Marsilio and Angelo looked at their friend and master with a questioning gaze.

"My dear Lorenzo," began Angelo Poliziano. "What is this promise?"

"Angelo, Marsilio think back to the Capelli de Magi in our beloved Firenze," he whispered. "You know of the legend of the Magi and the Medici."

Both men knew of the family's link to the Magi as did all of Florence. Now they learned of the blue grotto and the spirit of Timothy of Syria. They heard how Timothy had saved him back in 1478 in Capri when he was a prisoner of the King of Naples after the failed assassination attempt by the Pazzi family.

"Lorenzo, let this Timothy's spirit save you now," cried out Ficino.

"No, dear Marsilio, a promise is a promise and I am a man of my word," the dying Medici leader softly spoke.

"It is time, dear friends, farewell." And with that he pulled the ring of the Magi from his finger and held it up above his chest. "You are free Timothy."

A great burst of light exploded from the ring. Ficino and Poliziano shielded their eyes as the presence of a young man formed out of the rays of light pouring from the ring. His flowing white robes glowed and fell in folds to his ankles. On his face was a smile. The two friends saw in Lorenzo's face that the spirit was speaking to him.

"I leave you one more gift. The ring will bring a troubled soul freedom as you have given to me."

Lorenzo thought he meant Piero, who would become the family leader, to be so blessed and thus he sent for his family. As the door swung open, the spirit swirled about the room creating a halo of light and then flew through the window into the moonlit night. Family and friends fell to their knees around *Il Magnifico's* bed. Lorenzo with the last of his strength placed the ring of the Magi onto Piero's finger.

"Lead well, my son."

He turned his head, smiling at his wife and children as he did so.

"Dear friends, watch over the Buonarroti boy. He has a genius which will astound the world."

"Lorenzo de Medici closed his eyes and passed to his eternal reward on April 8, 1492," Agnes concluded.

Arthur and the boys sat in awed silence as if they had just attended a funeral. Suddenly, the reverent silence was broken by an elevator bell. Agnes and Arthur hardly noticed the bell-like sound. The boys, however, looked up and turned their heads briefly towards the elevator corridor. They never noticed Roselli crouched behind the table with its large vase of fresh flowers. An elevator's doors opened and Pietro and Andreas stumbled out. The latter tripped over the crouching Roselli and crashed to the floor. Pietro stumbled over his brother and soon the two brothers were crushing the breath out of the curator, who was now flattened below their two huge frames.

"*Idiosi*," Roselli screamed, though it was so muffled that it was barely audible.

The commotion drew Arthur and Agnes' attention. Rich and John jumped up. They could all see from their vantage point several pairs of legs jutting out from behind the ornate table. The vase upon it was wobbling back and forth. Several petals fell from the delicately arranged floral piece, silently falling onto the gleaming table top.

John bent over to his father. "Dad, I think I see some guys on the floor behind that table with the flowers."

Rich nodded his agreement as Arthur placed his finger to his lips to indicate that all should remain quiet. He eased himself out of the chair motioning, as he did so, that Agnes should stay in her chair and remain unseen. She understood and slouched into its large cushions, as Rich stepped between the chair and the view of the table.

In the meantime, another clunk and a loud scream echoed across the balcony area as the table rocked violently: Pietro had tried to push himself off the other two men only to have hit his head the edge of the table. His now bleeding head throbbed. It was no use; they would certainly be found out; Roselli had to think quickly.

"Andreas, act like a drunkard, *capisce*?" he ordered.

"Si, curator," Andreas responded as he pushed his brother, Pietro, off him and back into the table which wobbled so violently that the vase tipped over, spilling its contents right over Roselli's head. There was another muffled profanity as the water dripped onto his face. Lilies and hydrangea blossoms lay strewn in the puddles across the table. One of them landed on the curator.

Roselli grabbed at the purple blossom and threw it at Andreas, who caught it and threw it at Pietro. He, in turn, brushed it aside and pulled Andreas up from the floor by his shirt collar. Pietro yanked so roughly, he ripped Andreas' shirt. Andreas nodded at Roselli as he took a swing at his brother, who blocked the shot and swung back. Pietro hit Andreas so hard that he was thrown back over the table. He rolled across the table top, through the flowers and into the toppled vase. There was a loud crash as the enormous vase was smashed on the marble floor.

John and Rich couldn't stand idly by. They ran from the mezzanine, where they had been listening to the final moments of Lorenzo de Medici's life, to the elevators, to create a diversion. In an instant they were beside the curator, who was, once again, on the floor beneath Andreas who had been knocked down and had fallen onto the curator when he had rolled across the table. During the scuffle, Arthur escorted Agnes la Straga from the mezzanine. The last thing he wanted was for Roselli to see his assistant talking to him and his sons.

While their dad took Agnes safely out of sight, the boys kept the curator's attention focused on them.

"Signore Roselli, good grief, is that you under…" began John.

"… you under this man?" concluded Rich. "Oh, pardon me, Andreas, I didn't realize it was you."

The flustered Andreas grunted at Rich's recognition as he pushed himself off his ruffled boss. Lending him a hand, he pulled the curator to his feet. Roselli was embarrassed and astounded to see Arthur's sons so late at night.

"Ah, the Colonna boys," he began with a slight cough and glare towards Andreas and Pietro, who stood before a mirror tending to his wounded head.

Regaining his composure, he became quite professional as if nothing had happened.

"It would seem our paths cross at the most unlikely times. Where would your esteemed father be, may I ask?"

Johnny was not going to let the haughty tone of this question go by without some kind of retort, for which he was most famous in the family circle and beyond. Dripping sarcasm, John replied that his esteemed and beloved father had probably gone to sleep hours ago.

"Indeed, Giovanni. Then you and your brother often sit in the darkness of grand ballrooms chatting about the day's events, I presume."

Rich's cheeks were turning crimson as his blood rose in response to the curator's arrogance. He poked John to do something.

"Well it so happens, Signore Roselli that we were in a deep discussion and guess what… it was all about your wonderful exhibit which has made a lasting impression on us."

John had accomplished what the usually clever Richard would ordinarily achieve. Roselli had become quite contrite and flattered. Rich added to the tale.

"Johnny, you're so right. To think we have gotten to see, close up, what thousands only wish they could see. Signore Roselli, you are a genius for having been so clever to arrange such an historic and enriching exhibit."

"*Molto grazie Ricardo,*" Roselli responded. "You give me too much honor."

Rich certainly had, since he knew that Agnes la Straga had achieved a *coup d'état* in bringing together the great works of the Stone Cutter Genius, Michelangelo, with the artifacts of the Medici Family for the world tour. Now that Rich had softened up the curator, he thrust his own knife-like words into the conversation.

"And so Signore Roselli, what brings you and your assistants to the Hilton so late at night?"

Roselli still feigning embarrassment from the compliment managed to mutter "assistants indeed" as he shot a fiery glance towards Pietro and Andreas. The latter was now applying a compress to his brother's head wound. Both brothers ignored the glaring stare and comment.

"Now then, in answer to your question, Ricardo, I had rewarded my assistants with one of those famous ice cream drinks which they make so well in the Hilton bar. They had worked so diligently in taking down our exhibit that I felt it was the least I could do. And you---ah boys or shall I say *amici…* seemed to have had a similar idea, hadn't you?"

John jumped in with the reply. "So it seems, minus the ice cream drinks of course."

"Right, just a couple of Cokes for us," added Rich. Then turning his attention to the Giuliano brothers, he went on with his wry remarks. "Those ice cream concoctions must really have a kick, Pietro. How's your head?"

"*Bene, grazie,*" he answered with the slightest of smiles.

"*Si amici*, my good deed has become a disaster and we have to leave early tomorrow for New York," interjected Roselli. "So if you'll excuse me, I'll just help take my wounded assistant back to his room."

"Then you're staying here as well, Signore Roselli?" asked John.

"Oh no, not here but across the street at the Blackstone Renaissance Hotel," he responded. "And we had best be on our way."

"But of course. How did you term the word friend? Ah, si, *amico* that's it? And so *amico* do have a wonderful trip to New York," John said sarcastically as he grabbed Rich by the arm to lead him away from Roselli.

Roselli however, had another thought to share. "*Ciao Giovanni e Ricardo,* but wait, I have just had an idea."

The boys turned to face the curator, thinking that their father must have had enough time to get Agnes out of the hotel. They were certain that Signora la Straga would be staying in the same hotel as the curator. Their father had probably taken her to the Blackstone Hotel.

"We'll walk with you and avoid the elevator which seems to have ill effects on my assistants," Roselli began, as he took each of the boys by an arm with him in between.

Andreas and Pietro sullenly walked behind the trio. They made their way towards the staircase down which Arthur had taken Agnes la Straga. While they walked, the curator unfolded his thought.

"I understand that you and your family are traveling to Italia soon, no?" he asked.

With apprehension, the boys affirmed they would be touring Italy with a group of their father's students. They felt it was obvious that Roselli already had this information. They told the curator they were excited to see where Michelangelo and the Medici family had elevated the world of art and Italian culture.

"*Si,* you shall have a marvelous time to be sure," commented Roselli. "And that is what my idea is all about." The boys glanced questioningly at each other as the curator continued. "Now, if I'm not mistaken, your *Italia* tour really begins in London, correct?"

How did he have that kind of information? they were asking themselves. To him, they uttered a simple "yes."

"*Va bene amici,* now we're getting somewhere," Roselli continued. "I believe that I can be of great service to your father."

The boys were all ears as he laid out how his vast knowledge could enhance the tour in ways impossible for the typical tour guide; he had access to sites not normally open to tours and his knowledge, of course, was extensive.

The curator was well informed about the upcoming tour as he pinpointed how the Michelangelo exhibit would be ending its London run just as their father and his students would be embarking from London to Milan.

"I would be delighted to take you to one of the most renowned sites in Milan and tell your group a tale of Leonardo da Vinci that few know."

The boys were taken aback. "Da Vinci? What has he got to do with Michelangelo?" asked Rich.

"Exactly, I thought the two never got along," added John.

"Ah *mi amici*, so you do know some history," a beaming Roselli remarked. "What you don't know is what I can add to your experience. I'm sure your father wouldn't want to have his students miss out on that insight."

"Well I don't know, Signore Roselli," began John. "Dad has a pretty packed tour. Something every day and almost every hour."

"Right, if you know anything about our father, it's that he doesn't waste a minute of time," interjected Rich, who was still not thrilled about being called *amici* by Roselli.

Friends indeed, he thought. The only reason he'd want to be with the tour is to find out more about the tale his assistant curator just shared with them. It was not an offer presented to *friends*, that's for sure.

Both boys knew that their father would not want to pass up a chance to experience more of the tale of Michelangelo. The two looked at each other, communicating without words, as Roselli rambled on about his Milan connections.

Dad would want to keep a close eye on an adversary, they were saying to each other. Keep your enemies close, as Lorenzo de Medici did when he placed himself in the hands of the King of Naples and ended up with the ring of the Magi in the process.

"You've got us convinced Signore Roselli," John finally stated as Rich's mouth dropped open. John tapped Rich's chin lightly to close his mouth, and smiled. Rich returned an expression of what-have-you-committed-us-to?

"Ah, then the prospect of my accompanying the tour would be to your father's liking, *si*?"

"Well, let's just say that Dad may enjoy having you present a lesson in Milan where you say you have connections," replied John. "As for the rest of the trip, let's just leave that to you and my dad when we meet in London next month."

The small group had arrived in the hotel lobby and was walking past the desk clerk who had taken Roselli's message for Arthur.

"Oh, sir," she called out as they passed. All of them stopped and turned to her. She took a piece of paper from the message basket and came from behind the registration desk to hand it to Roselli. "Mr.

Colonna has left a message for you. I had mentioned that you had been looking for him when he came by a few moments ago."

The boys' hearts sank. They were caught in their own lie. They stood frozen unable to make a comment of any kind.

Luckily, Roselli began the conversation as he took the paper from the receptionist, opened it carefully and slowly read through its hand written script that many of Arthur's confidants would find difficult at best to decipher, let alone one whose primary language was not English.

"*Mille grazie,*" Signore Roselli said as he read the note. The boys became interested in the marble beneath their feet. He glanced at the boys as he said, "So it seems your father is either sleepwalking or out for a late night, or should I say an early morning stroll."

John and Rich grinned and shrugged their shoulders.

"Well, that's Dad for you isn't it? Rich finally got out.

"Yep, just when you'd think he would be resting, he's up and about probably figuring out another brilliant plan," added John. "Drives Mom a bit crazy, doesn't it Richie?"

A quick nod of Rich's head gave the sign that they were coming to their senses.

"Ah, *si,* your *Mama*…I suppose that it would be quite challenging to live with such a spontaneous man," observed Roselli, going along with their explanation even knowing it was not the truth. "Speaking of your charming *Mama,* I would think she's worrying about you two right now."

"Oh, they have a different room," Rich blurted out.

John was not pleased with Rich having let it be known their mother would be alone. Luckily, Pietro and Andreas were with them so that eased his concern.

John wanted to know what was in the note, so he redirected the idle chatter. "Well, Signore Roselli, what did Dad have to say?"

"Well it seems that he has read my thoughts, *amici.* He has invited me to contact him at the Abbey Court Hotel in London when you arrive. Now isn't that most convenient as we will be at the Westpoint Hotel which is right next door."

"Really," a surprised Rich said. "Then I guess we will see you again, so if you don't mind…"

"To be sure," Roselli replied. "It is quite late, or early depending on how you look at it, I suppose." He laughed at his own observation, then gave each of the boys a hug and, motioning to his assistants, walked to the revolving doors. Turning toward the boys he gave a wave, "*Arrivaderci amici*," and spun out the door.

As soon as they disappeared into the street lighted avenue, the boys sought out their father. They ran towards the same doors Roselli had used, almost running into their father.

Screeching to a halt, they exclaimed, "Dad?"

"Good grief, I thought they'd never leave you," Arthur responded.

"Neither did we," an exhausted Rich said. "But what goes with you?"

"Yeah, why did you tell Roselli where we'd be staying in London of all places?" asked John.

Arthur took his sons by the arms and walked to the elevators. As they passed the check-in desk, Elizabeth beamed a radiant smile at them. Arthur returned it graciously.

"If it were not for her diligence, I would not have known that Roselli had been looking for us all night," he whispered as they strode past the desk.

Once in the elevator, Arthur explained that Agnes la Straga had told him where they would be lodged while conducting the London exhibit. Since it was next door, it seemed prudent to let Roselli know since he would probably find out anyway. It would be difficult to be discreet with a tour group of students.

"Anyway, it's best that one keep those he mistrusts close by," he concluded.

"Why that's just what we thought," exclaimed Rich.

"I see the tale of Lorenzo de Medici taught you something." Arthur smiled. He was pleased that his sons had learned something from the Medici over 500 years later.

"Then you won't mind learning that we had already told him what you did in that note," a relieved John said.

"It seems, boys, great minds think alike. You had to do what you did as I had to respond in the manner in which I did," Arthur replied. "It seems that after our stop in Ireland we will have an important meeting in London. I'll get on the phone with Maura Kennedy tomorrow and inform her that for a short time she'll have to entertain our group of students. In the meantime, don't get your mother upset with any of this. She will have enough to worry about getting all of us ready for the movie premiere in Dublin and getting to Grace and Sean's wedding, not to mention your sister's wedding the following week."

The boys agreed and Arthur, making sure all was well with them, returned to the elevator and pressed number seven. As he strode to room 729, he felt proud of how his sons handled Anselmo and his henchmen.

Chapter 10: Gifts of the King

With Agnes la Straga and Roselli off to New York, life had returned to almost normal as the family prepared for their trip to Ireland for the European premiere of Arthur's movie. Arthur's wife Donna was in a frenzy, finalizing the last-minute packing for their trip. In her mind, the premiere was not the most important aspect of this venture across the Atlantic Ocean. They were celebrating two weddings; one of those was of their younger daughter, Kathleen Mary, to Alun of Wales. Like most mothers of the bride, Donna wanted that celebration to be flawless, joyous, and filled with family love.

With all these preparations, it was not a normal day at the Colonna home as Donna phoned her sister.

"Nancy, have you made sure that Mom and Arthur's mom have all they need for the trip?"

Nancy assured her that Arthur's sister, Janice, had everything under control. Wanda would be accompanied by Janice and her children to London and then on to Wales in time for the wedding. As for their mother, Ruth, she would be brought over by Donna's brother Jack and his family. Nancy would be going with Anita and Marilyn so that they would be at Donna's disposal for all the last minute details once they got to Britain.

"Why that husband of mine scheduled a tour of Italy at this time is beyond my understanding, but that's Arthur. He thinks everything will just fall in place as if by magic," Donna continued after being reassured of the travel arrangements.

"Well, there is a chance for that after all Donna, wouldn't you say?" asked Nancy.

Donna feigned a laugh but made it quite clear that there was to be no magic involved in this wedding. As she emphasized the point, the boys popped into the room to collect the luggage. The distraction turned Donna's attention to this new matter at hand.

"Johnny," she called out. "Where is your father?"

Hearing her sister shout from the phone she had laid down, she realized that she was still on the phone.

"Nancy, I'll call you back later." She turned her attention to her second youngest son once again.

"He's in his den getting some last minute things attended to," John replied after his mother ended the call.

Donna hadn't been married to Arthur for so many years not to realize that last minute things could spell trouble.

"And what, pray tell, would that be?"

John explained that Arthur was placing his gold coin, given to him by King Finbar X, into a velvet pouch.

"Oh, by the way," Rich added. "Dad thinks that you and the other Roses should bring your coins with you as well. 'Just in case' is how he put it."

"I knew it, there's something afoot," Donna exclaimed. "Boys, go tell your father that we'll have no magic at your sister's wedding."

"He said you would tell us that," began John.

"So he told us to tell you that it was just a precautionary move. After all, the leprechauns will be at the wedding, too," added Rich.

"I give up," Donna said as she picked up the phone to call the other Roses.

The boys ran from the bedroom down the stairs to their father's den. Jumping down several steps at a time, they quickly arrived at their destination.

"Dad," they called out.

Arthur looked up from his backpack in which he had placed his lap top and the velvet pouch.

"Mom is upset with you but is calling the Roses," John began to say.

Arthur was relieved to hear the news and smiled at his sons.

"Good, now we're ready to get going."

"I still don't understand why you haven't told Mom about Roselli and those thugs," Rich stated.

John cast his younger brother a look of *are you for real?* as his father answered.

"Rich, would you say your mother could take on another problem as she tries to finalize the wedding arrangements for Kathy and Alun from across an ocean?"

Rich returned a sheepish grin and nod indicating that what his mom didn't need right now was another issue to contend with.

They heard their mother call from above to let them know the luggage was ready for them to take to the front door to be ready to be loaded onto the limo when it arrived. The boys ran from the den to retrieve the bags. As soon as the last one was brought down, the limo pulled up, filled with the rest of the family.

Arthur appeared at the doorway with his backpack strapped on. His grandchildren yelled a greeting as he made his way to the vehicle. One could feel the energy of the young ones spilling out as their parents tried to keep them in check. As Arthur stood at the open door of the limo, John and Rich came out with Donna holding her Disney World backpack containing a very special gold coin and the folder of all the details for Kathy's wedding in Wales. In an instant, they were off to O'Hare Airport where the rest of the Roses would be waiting for them.

Seven and a half hours later the conversation was still focused on that wedding folder, now spread out across their snack trays on the Aer Lingus jet. The family had easily filled the entire center row and side seats of the plane's cabin.

Arthur sat in an aisle seat with John and Rich flanking him. It was their job to make sure the family's part of the Dublin premiere of *The Leprechaun King* unfolded smoothly. The three also needed to discuss what problems might have been created by involving both Agnes la Straga and Anselmo Roselli in the tour of Italy. Arthur was concerned how the two would react to each other's presence.

Roselli must not suspect that Agnes was involved as anything more than an advisor. However, Arthur had to be realistic. Roselli had been in the Hilton Hotel lurking nearby when Agnes was relating the long-lost historical details surrounding the death of Lorenzo de Medici. Roselli was probably already suspicious of Agnes' involvement. Arthur and his sons decided the boys would have to deter Roselli whenever he tried to garner more of what Signora la Straga had shared with them.

As soon as that had been agreed upon the flight crew announced the plane would be landing soon. Donna gathered her volumes of papers and she and Jana placed them back into the folder. Kathy decided to take Jana's approach to wedding planning. Let Mom and Dad plan it. She would show up and look pretty for her groom. That attitude had been the joke of the family for years now, though it had resulted in a stress-free wedding day for Jana, perhaps the happiest bride ever to walk down the St. Charles Church aisle back home in Burlington.

Nancy, Anita, and Marilyn, collectively the Roses, were congratulating their fellow Rose on the wonderfully thorough plans Donna had presented. The wheels touched the landing strip as their words of praise were acknowledged. The slight jerk caused the new generation of boys to giggle and bounce exaggeratedly. Granddaughter Olivia, ever the little lady, cast them a look of disdain.

As the Colonna clan left the terminal building of Dublin International Airport a slight mist kissed their faces. It was a lovely, soft, Irish day which greeted them and they felt right at home. Arthur announced they were to find a bus marked CIE Tours. They would be met by Jack Connolly, one of the CIE driver-cum-guides. Arthur was excited that Jack would be their guide. He had been their guide on a previous trip and was quite hospitable and humorous. It wasn't but a few seconds of leading the formidable clan — Arthur and Donna, Ron and his wife Tricia, Jana and her husband Chris, Kathleen, John and Rich, the four grandchildren and the Roses — before they came across Jack who was standing in their path, beaming.

After a reunion with hugs, giggles, back pounding and so forth, in the wink of a leprechaun's eye, all were boarded and luggage stowed. Off they drove to Dublin city center with a metropolitan population similar to Chicago or Rome. It's a bustling town with typical traffic challenges. When they arrived at the area of Dublin called Clontarf, they were delighted to see the Castle Hotel gates.

As they entered through the glass doors surrounded by the thousand-year-old arches of the original castle keep, Arthur looked around the fondly-remembered hotel. To the left was the huge fireplace and gigantic mantle, which he dreamed of decorating for Christmas. On the ancient wall were long, woven banners depicting the heritage of the castle. Surrounding the hearth were comfortably upholstered, wooden-armed chairs arranged in conversation groupings. The grandchildren made a beeline for one such grouping with their parents quickly following.

Directly in front of them was the registration desk tucked between the elevators and staircase to the mezzanine. Arthur looked at the mezzanine and shuddered, remembering Anselmo Roselli, Pietro, and Andreas in a similar area at the Hilton in Chicago. He decided to take the elevator and avoid the balcony. He needed to take the elevator, for Arthur Lovell had arranged for him and Donna to be lodged in the King's Royal Suite.

Lavish was an understatement when describing the suite. Donna and Arthur could not believe their eyes. Both Donna and Arthur came from modest, working-class backgrounds. Both their fathers died at young ages before reaching any high plateau in their careers. Arthur grew up in a four-flat brick apartment building in Oak Park, Illinois. Donna lived in a small brick home on the northwest side of Chicago, called Norridge. Neither had ever experienced the luxury of anything remotely royal until meeting the king of the leprechauns thrust them into a world beyond their imagination.

Once again, they found themselves awed by the environment they had just entered. The heavy oak door closed behind them with a click. Without warning Arthur took a running leap and jumped onto the four-poster bed without using the convenient step stool. He bounced on it like one of his grandchildren as Donna stood ready to reprimand him. She thought better of it as he thrust out his hand to her and pulled her up onto the bed. The long flight was a distant memory as they collapsed into the red and gold decorative pillows accenting the bed covering and canopy.

"So King Arthur, what shall we do now?" asked the laughing Donna.

"Well, my Queen, I suggest a tussle to see who shall get under these covers first," Arthur teased as he winked.

Pounding on the door cut their romp short. They poked their heads out from under the pillows and Arthur called out in a strong tone, "Who's there?"

The unusually meek voice of their daughter, whom Arthur continued to call Kathy though she preferred the full name of Kathleen, answered. "It's me, Dad."

Arthur jumped out of the bed and combed his hair with his fingers as Donna slid to the edge with her legs dangling over the edge. When he opened the door, there stood a smiling Kathy with her intended, Alun.

"He had come from Wales to surprise me," she began to explain as they walked into the room.

Seeing her mother sitting on the bed and adjusting the pillows brought a smile to her lips and a blush to Alun's cheeks.

"Oh, well, we were just…well we were having a pillow fight, and that's that," Arthur bellowed out.

The four of them broke into laughter and the blush from Alun spread to the other three as well.

Kathy waved an ivory-colored envelope in her free hand, while Alun held the other. The envelope caught Arthur's eye.

"Kathy, what's that?" he inquired.

"Oh, that's what I came to show you. I mean that's the other reason I came," she corrected herself as she explained. "Take a look at it. I'm sure there's one here for you as well."

As Arthur took the envelope a series of knocks rapped upon the suite's door.

"Good grief, I think we're in Grand Central Station," Arthur commented as Alun opened the door.

In flowed the rest of his children and the grandchildren, who seeing their Grammy on the bed, made a flying leap to her. At least the little boys leapt; Olivia was much too grown up, at age eleven, for such behavior. She took the step stool, climbed aboard the bed, and seated herself next to her Grammy. The bed chamber was quite crowded, so Arthur directed the adults into the sitting room where there were two couches and several arm chairs circling a fire place. To the rear of the room was an ell containing a long mahogany table with eight high-back cushioned chairs. Windows encircled this arm of the room. They offered a spectacular view of Dublin with its many building cranes clearly visible. Arthur had been told that they symbolized a vibrant and thriving city.

"There now, is everyone comfy?" asked Arthur.

Before anyone answered Donna was answering the door again. Anita, Marilyn, and Nancy, her fellow Roses had come with envelopes in hand. She directed them to the sitting room. Each blew a kiss at little Arthur, Connor, Riley, and Olivia as they passed.

"The children have elected to stay on the bed. I turned on TV for them. I think they'll be fine as they're rather tired after the flight." Donna said as she took a seat next to Arthur.

Arthur, Jana, and Tricia pulled out gilded folded cards from their envelopes. Chris noticed an ivory envelope up on the mantle. Ron, seeing it also, took it down and handed the envelope to his mother, Donna. John and Rich held onto their envelopes waiting to hear what Arthur was about to read.

"The Irish Film Board, Dublin Films and Arthur Lovell cordially invite you to a Celebration of the European Premiere of the film *The Leprechaun King* based on the novel by Arthur Colonna. Dinner and Cocktails will begin at 8:00 p.m. in the Grand Ballroom of the Castle Hotel of Dublin on June 18th," Arthur read. "Good grief Donna, they've scheduled the party on Chris and John's birthday."

His son-in-law and Johnny were assuring Arthur that it didn't matter. They considered it an honor to have the premiere on their birthday. The conversation quickly turned to what would be worn for the premiere. The women decided they would wear the gowns given to them by the wee folk at the joust at Warwick Castle last year. They could hardly enjoy their beautiful gowns then; the joust with Medraut and his thugs against their husbands and brothers was so intense that nothing else mattered. Now they could enjoy them fully at the premiere and at Grace and Sean's wedding. For a moment, it seemed strange to think they would be wearing those gowns to Grace and Sean's wedding; Sean had been one of those against whom the Colonna boys fought; Grace was a direct descendent of Morgan le Fay and had led adherents of the dark side of magic until her conversion to the message of faith, hope, and love before the Holy Grail and the spirit of King Arthur of Camelot. Love had saved Grace and Sean and was shared between them and the Colonna clan.

"After all," Jana stated oblivious to the symbolism of the gowns. "No one at the premiere or the wedding would have seen them."

If Jana, the daughter who was most consumed with fashion attire and appropriateness of dress, saw no problem with wearing the gowns twice, then certainly none of the others would object. Just as Arthur was about to suggest that everyone get some rest, Jana continued.

"As for you guys," she began. "Since the wedding will be an old-fashioned Irish one in Saul Church in Downpatrick where St. Patrick himself first preached the message, I think it best that you dress in tuxedo kilts."

"Are you crazy Jana?" shouted John. "They don't wear anything under them do they?"

"We'll catch a death of cold," added Rich.

"I'd rather wear my armor from the joust than a skirt," cried out Ron.

"My knees are too boney for a kilt," Chris said in a manner trying to focus on how he would look. After all, Jana being his wife might better appreciate that type of objection.

Tricia and Kathy came to Jana's aide and soon the men were defeated; except for Alun who, coming from Wales, saw no problem with wearing a kilt.

"Good, I'm glad that you have that settled," Arthur chimed in. "Now can we get some rest?"

"Not quite," continued Jana. "The little boys should wear kilts too."

"That would be darling," agreed Kathy. "Can they wear them for my wedding too?"

"Why sure," Tricia and Jana exclaimed together.

"But not us," cried out their husbands and brothers.

"We'll see about that later," concluded Kathy as she got up, pulled up Alun and set out for the door.

"Just a minute," Donna called out. "What about your father?"

"Me? What about me?" Arthur stammered out.

Donna explained it would be fitting if he too would wear a kilt to the weddings. Arthur became indignant.

"Woman, are you serious? Me in a kilt would be like putting …well I'm no Prince Charles and let's leave it at that."

"Well, I think that your legs are just as good looking as those of His Royal Highness the Prince of Wales," Donna retorted.

Arthur could see her eyes flashing. His children were about to gang up on him as well.

"Okay, okay, but if I catch a cold it will be on all your heads."

Now everyone was up and laughing. Alun walked up to his future father-in-law.

"I'll give you a few hints on how to wear the kilt quite modestly and, shall I say, cozily."

Arthur gave him a half smile as Kathy tugged on Alun's arm to lead him out.

Upon entering the bed chamber they found all four children asleep. The parents picked up the children and carried them away. Soon it was quiet. Arthur was standing with the premiere invitation in hand. He shook it at Donna.

"So, you little devil, think you've won? I have not yet begun to fight."

"Well put your cannons down John Paul Jones, or whoever said that, and let's be off to plan your daughter's wedding day," a smiling Donna answered.

Arthur wasn't about to give up. He mumbled about the wedding and how inconvenient it was to expect half the family to travel to Britain for it. As usual, Donna was ready for his newest concern. She pointed out that most of those who would have come to Wisconsin from Philadelphia, Boston, or Florida had planned a special vacation this year. Even on this issue, it seemed Arthur had lost the battle.

There was nothing to do but settle down to deciding who would be sitting at what table, which of the three little boys would actually hold the pillow with the rings and whether or not their granddaughter, Olivia, would walk alone as a junior bridesmaid or be escorted. As they focused on these pressing issues, Arthur's mind was not always on the matter at hand. Donna, delighting in the details, saw him wandering in thought as she pressed for a decision on who would carry the ring pillow.

He had answered, "Oh yes, that would be fine."

And that had almost caused another battle.

"Arthur Ronald," Donna chided. "You are not paying the least bit of attention to your own daughter's wedding day."

Arthur snapped back to the matter at hand. He forced himself to turn from his thoughts of how people in Europe would receive the film, and what would take place in London when they met up with his students, Mrs. Kennedy and Agnes la Straga. In the mix of his mind's wanderings was also the suggestion that Grace Morgan, might be alerted to the possible confrontation with the exhibit's curator, Anselmo Roselli. After all, Grace was a sorceress of sorts, though having come into the light last year, she would only work for the spreading of the good news.

"And yet wouldn't the legend of the Magi ring be part of the message?" he was asking himself as Donna brought him back to focus.

"This time you did bite off more than you can chew, didn't you?" Donna asked with her hands on her hips.

"Well..." Arthur hesitatingly said.

"Well nothing," she continued. "You will have yourself worn to a frazzle and not even be able to enjoy your daughter's wedding day."

"Nonsense, we'll just bring my students over to St. David's city and they can enjoy the wedding too," said a now enlightened Arthur restoring himself to his usual coolness and clarity of thought.

"What?" she exclaimed, though in her heart she knew that it was too late to question the idea. When her husband thought of a brilliantly conceived plan there would be no thwarting him. She sighed as she made her last attempt to bring logic to the situation.

"Arthur, be realistic," she began. "You are talking about twenty more people coming to the wedding, when we had originally thought that your Italy trip would be over before the wedding day arrived."

"You're absolutely right," he replied as a smile crossed her face.

"Could my husband, the Peter Pan of the twenty-first century, actually be seeing my point?" she was thinking while beginning to be pleased with herself.

Then the other shoe dropped and the smile became a gaping mouth unable to utter any intelligible words.

"Of course the number of additional people is more likely to be around 40 to 45," he smiled as he gently placed his fingers under her drooped chin and lifted it back into its rightful place while moving closer to plant a little kiss on her now closed lips.

"Arthur, don't try to distract me," she began. "Well maybe a little distraction would ease the situation…absolutely not. Now you've done it. How can we possibly add more guests? And who are these guests anyway?"

Arthur, who had stretched across the table around which the family had been seated now eased himself back into the high back Queen Anne chair.

"So I haven't lost my touch even after all these years and five kids later?" he asked with a smirk.

"You're impossible," she retorted but couldn't help to break a little smile in spite of herself. "But the matter at hand is still before us."

"Yes it is, no doubt about it, so I guess I'll have to explain."

"That would make for a wonderful beginning," she agreed.

Arthur Lovell, the producer, had been in contact with Arthur regarding the premiere in Dublin. During the planning of the Dublin event, Arthur explained that the premiere had to coincide with his daughter's wedding in Wales shortly after the premiere. It would be far more economical to bring over the family if they had their fares paid for by the movie event budget, Arthur explained to the producer.

The producer responded that Arthur was sounding like Michelangelo again, ever so frugal as to be in denial of his capability to pay for the slightest essential. Once again Arthur became ruffled over the comparison. He much rather thought of himself as saving his family from double expenses, which they truly could not afford.

In the end, the producer agreed to pay for the family's airfares and housing out of the film's premiere budget…as long as Arthur agreed to invite some of the actors to the wedding. Many of the film's actors and actresses and several of the crew had come to know Arthur and his family, particularly his daughter Kathy, her fiancé, Alun, and granddaughter Olivia. After all, the producer reminded Arthur, it was on the Rock of Cashel set that Kathy and Alun first met. They met in a scene during which Kathy, who had a small acting part, literally tumbled into Alun's arms while Olivia stood stunned, witnessing the romantic nature of her Aunt's fall.

Arthur was honored that such accomplished people would deem a family event so appealing. He happily invited them to cross the Irish Sea with them and attend the wedding. The producer agreed and thought about twenty would make the trip. Arthur hadn't realized that he hadn't shared with Donna the conversation he had had with the producer.

By the time Arthur had finished his story, Donna's attitude had changed.

"You mean, herself, the one who won the Oscar, is coming to our daughter's wedding?" Donna gleefully asked.

"Well yes, I do, but there will be quite a few others," Arthur replied.

Donna was excited, forgetting about her husband's students completely, and wondering where she would seat the movie stars.

"I'll need to speak with Kathy and the girls right away. We'll have to plan the seating so no one is offended."

"Oh, I see, and my students have just become chopped liver, I suppose," Arthur quipped. "Anyway, it's been much too much of a day. Let's get some rest and figure this out tomorrow."

Donna, however, was on a mission. Though she agreed not to disturb the girls, she already had found the seating chart for the wedding. She pulled it out of a small suitcase and spread it across the table. She opened the drapes and began to move little pieces of paper around on the chart.

Arthur left her to her chore and slipped from the sitting room to make two phone calls. The first call was to Mrs. Kennedy to make sure they would arrive in London, in a week's time, on time to meet the bus.

All was fine with the time table for his class. His students and Maura would arrive in London on the Friday before his daughter's wedding. That day, they would tour Windsor Castle, the largest and oldest working castle in England and the home of the Royal Family of the United Kingdom. Following 900 years of tradition by previous monarchs, the Royal Family lived and worked at Windsor Castle when not at Buckingham Palace in London proper. The next day the class would travel to St. David's in Wales with a stop at Cheptsow Castle along the way. Barring any unforeseen incidents they should be at the cathedral for the wedding service with plenty of time to spare.

The second call was to the producer to tell him everything was just fine as long as he didn't mind some star-struck behavior from his family. Arthur thought bringing over so many well-known actors and actresses was surely going to create quite a stir in the smallest city in the United Kingdom. Luckily, the producer, Arthur Lovell, had taken care of the transportation needs of the prestigious group which would turn St. David's into a mini Oscar night event by their presence. Arthur Colonna could only pray that their attendance did not detract from the wedding, not after all his family had been through to make sure that it would be a flawless event. The father of the bride informed Lovell that he had reserved the Glan Y Mor Guest House on the bay for the actors and actresses. Given its secluded position overlooking the sea, it afforded basic comforts and privacy. He had reserved the Warpool Court Hotel for his own family and the remaining Hollywood entourage. The arrangment ensured they would enjoy the same lovely view of St. Brides Bay, yet be within a five minute walk of the town where the wedding ceremony would take place in its one-thousand-year-old cathedral. Arthur was feeling quite proud of himself having performed his fatherly duties to ensure the guests were housed in truly Welsh-style inns.

The Warpool Court was at one time the Cathedral Choir School and had outstanding gardens surrounding it. The lovely summertime flowers and vine-covered trellis would provide an ideal setting for the family wedding photo which would become the insert for the family Christmas card. All of that would have to wait until next week. There was a premiere to worry about in Dublin and the wedding of Sean and Grace on the following day. That ceremony was to take place in Saul Church near Downpatrick, where St. Patrick himself had first preached the good news.

It was with a bounce in his step that he returned to the sitting room expecting to find his wife diligently arranging seating chart cards. Instead, he found her, Kathy, Jana, Tricia, and the Roses unzipping long garment bags from which they were pulling out gowns.

He paused in the archway and watched the delighted women holding up their dresses so that sunlight filtering in from the windows highlighted sparkling crystals in the material of their jousting attire. He was remembering the joust at Warwick Castle in England last year when the wee folk had surprised the women of the family with those magically glistening gowns designed especially for them using the colors of the rainbow on which he and the boys had walked to enter the Tower of London. It had been a dangerous mission to recover the sword, Excalibur, spirited deep within the tower's rocky foundation by the legendary wizard Merlin. It was Merlin who, centuries before, made sure King Arthur's weapon would lay in a realm soon forgotten. The sword was there, under the ruins of a Roman fortress over which William the Conqueror built the White Tower for his home. Succeeding kings of England would call it their home. Later the enlarged fortress, the Tower of London, served as a prison housing such famed personages as Sir Thomas More, and Mary, Queen of Scots. Now of course it's also the home of the Crown Jewels of Britain.

None of this mattered as he watched his wife and daughters twirl their gowns in the sunlight, creating waves of color which bounced around the room, filling it with the red of a cardinal, the yellow of a sunflower, the green of a shamrock, the blue of the sea, and the deep purple of an amethyst.

The women were enjoying their gowns so much more this day before the premiere than on that fateful day last year at Warwick Castle. On that day, their loved-ones fought to preserve the very foundation of civilization. The joy of their success paled the vibrant colors of the gifts of the wee folk. On this day, before another day of days, they were taking full delight in the gowns.

It was Jana who first noticed her father standing under the highly polished wooden arch, his eyes aglow and misty. Her twirl came to an abrupt halt as she ran to him.

"Look, Dad, the room is filled with a rainbow."

She grabbed his arm and dragged him into the room of twirling women, encircling him. They stopped suddenly still holding up the gowns in front of them.

"Do you think we'll out-dazzle those Hollywood people?" asked a grinning Donna.

"Without a doubt," Arthur responded. "No one will even notice the red carpet once all of you are on it."

On the day of the premiere, as the sun shone its setting rays over

O'Connell Street, the women stepped out of their horse-drawn carriages as they had done at the joust. This time Arthur, and his sons, and his soon-to-be son, were dressed in tuxedo kilts intead of armor. The Savoy Theater, built in the late 1920's, took the place of the thousand-year old castle. The grand cinema shined as it had when it was the foremost theater in Ireland; where all the new films took their first bow. Lovell had pulled off another coup for the film. This premiere was kicking off the recently-created Dublin Film Festival. Though not in the same league as the Venice or Cannes film festivals, its promoters had great aspirations for this Irish counterpart. Red carpets lined O'Connell Street. On its edges, velvet ropes kept back crowds who came to see their favorite stars being interviewed on their way into the theater. When the carriages arrived with the Colonna clan, it was natural that the crowds went wild with expectation. As the Roses and the girls were helped out of the carriages in their glistening crystal-encrusted gowns the excitement built to a crescendo. Young people hoping to see Hollywood stars screamed wildly as older folks cheered the family, though not one of them probably ever heard of Arthur, the writer of the screenplay and certainly not of any of the family.

It was so different from the Chicago premiere where the Colonna family had passed unnoticed into an equally majestic theater of the 1920's. When the little boys jumped out of the carriage in their kilt tuxedos, the crowd gasped when the boy's kilts flared up. The little boys didn't notice; they were totally at ease with themselves as they helped the beautifully-dressed Olivia down from the carriage step. She seemed to float in her royal purple silk and lace gown shimmering with amethyst crystals. The crowd was enthralled with the young ones and oohed and aahed over the Colonna women's gowns. Not that the Colonna men were unnoticed as they appeared in their kilt tuxedos of hunter green with black jackets and white shirt and ties. Only John and Rich had difficulty keeping their kilts modestly at their knees as a gust of wind flipped the edges of the plaids. The boys became flustered, making the issue more obvious and delighting the giggling teenage girls they passed.

"I told you that purse thing should have been worn in front," chided Rich to his brother.

"I know. You're always right; but I didn't want a purse hanging on my front," replied John.

"Well it's not a purse anyway as I told you. It's called a sporran."

"Well whatever it's called, it felt uncomfortable leaning against…well you know," John tried to explain unsatisfactorily.

"You're unreal Johnny. Now look at us as a result of the decision. We look like two girls in school uniforms," a sarcastic Rich retorted referring to the Irish National Tartan they were wearing.

"We'll just have to walk slowly so the wind doesn't shoot up the skirt. Deal with it," John ordered.

They walked in slow motion, delighting the girls even more as they did cut a fine figure in their Irish National Tartan, black jacket, white shirt and tie. Soon they were laughing at themselves and flipping the kilt now and then in good fun.

Little did the locals realize that they were being impressed by the enchanted work of their very own wee folk. The lucky locals who got into the theater, with the guests of honor from the Hollywood and European film industry, witnessed true enchantment filling the screen as *The Leprechaun King* made its European debut.

On that evening, magic seemed to leap off the screen whenever a sequence occurred involving the wee folk. Had the audience any idea of who was causing the thunderous applause during each of the leprechaun scenes, the whole realm of legend may have been revealed. Luckily, the audience never caught on that the wee folk were hiding throughout the balcony high above the human folk. Most of the audience attributed the clamor to overly zealous fans, and that was just fine with Arthur. He and his family did lift their eyes toward the gilded ornamentation each time the cheers erupted. Only once did they catch a glimpse of Finbar Finnegan X, King of the Leprechauns, as he revealed himself to let the family know it was his people making all the noise during those scenes.

The evening became more memorable when everyone returned to the hotel for the reception. Jana interviewed actors for the column she and her father wrote for the newspaper back in the states. Much of the chatter in that lavishly decorated room centered on the liveliness of the audience and how they must have really enjoyed the film.

During the evening's festivities, Arthur slipped out of the Grand Ballroom of the Dublin Castle Hotel and walked in the garden. The premiere, the talk of making a sequel, Grace and Sean's wedding the next day, his daughter's wedding, and looking forward to events in London in a week's time began to overwhelm Arthur. A breath of fresh air was just what he needed. Much of what was happening to him and his family was quite new and unusual. It seemed, however, that Donna had everything under control and his children and grandchildren took to this new notoriety with ease and grace. He flipped the gold coin over and over again as he meandered along the garden's gravel paths.

"Ah, Finbar Finnegan, if only I could do magic and make everything just right," he spoke softly as he caught the coin once more. It was the very coin given to him by the actual King of the Leprechauns when the Clonmacnoise Quest was successfully fulfilled back in Ireland some two yers ago.

From a flash of green sparkling dust, out popped the king. He stood on a stone bench like the one at Clonmacnoise where the drapery lady Kathleen had first introduced Arthur to the legend of the wee folk.

"Ah, my dear Thorn," the King began, using his pet name for Arthur. "You seem perplexed."

"Your majesty, how nice to see you," Arthur courteously responded without any excitement. His mind was preoccupied with the Cathedral of St. David where his daughter's wedding would happen. He had been proud of his hotel arrangements for the Hollywood guests and his students, but now he was having second thoughts. Maybe he ought to have helped more; after all, Donna couldn't be expected to do everything.

The king, being quite intuitive of human feelings, invited his friend to sit with him and have a chat. Soon Arthur found himself explaining all the activity with his daughter's wedding and the tour of Italy, shadowed with the mystery of the Magi ring.

"All I've done is make some hotel reservations," Arthur concluded.

The king tried to lighten the mood.

"Well, I think you've done more than that," he began. "After all, aren't I bringing the mead for the wedding toast?"

Arthur grinned, a little.

"Ah ha, mi boy, so 'tis your old self I'd be seeing beneath that grin, to be sure. Now let us talk of the wedding your lovely wife has planned...oops, I mean that ye both have arranged."

Arthur's grin faded, but erupted into a laugh.

"Mead, indeed, and it was all my wife's doing; so you needn't make out that it wasn't. I just needed to hear that it was okay, your Majesty."

"But lad, it is as you call it, okay," the king tried to explain. "Is your wife happy with the planning?"

"Yes, I think so. Every time she arranges the seating chart with our daughters she seems to be in her element."

"So you see, my dear Thorn, you are worrying yourself into frenzy over nothing. By the way, it's not the seating chart which is her element, it's the fact that she has her girls about her choosing this color or that, seating Aunt Sally here and Uncle Joe there, choosing the chicken or the beef or hopefully some Irish stew."

Arthur jumped to his feet as he proclaimed the little king a genius. His soul had been freed from the burden. No matter how much Donna protested in his lack of presence, that was all part of the wedding game. All she needed was his occasional involvement, but not too much, for it was her vision which was being painted in those long discussions with Kathy, Jana, and Tricia. A pop in from Arthur now and then to share a smile of his agreement was her delight. The Roses, Marilyn, Nancy and Anita, fussing about the cut of the gowns or their colors were really the input she needed. Taking care of hotel rooms was just fine for the father of the bride. With a bow, and a promise to talk more later, Arthur scampered to the party.

As he made his way back, he jumped over a low hedge and right into Rich and John's arms.

"Dad, what on earth are you doing?" they shouted as they all collapsed onto the grassy border of the gravel path.

"Well if you must know, I was having a heart to heart chat with the king," he started to explain.

The boys jumped to their feet, hardly noticing that their father still remained on the grass.

"The king," yelled John.

"The king is here right now," Rich shouted as Arthur nodded affirmatively.

"Quick Rich, we need to get his view on the movie before he puffs away," and John jumped over the hedge and spotted the king still standing on the stone bench scratching his head over the yelling and sound of colliding bodies.

"If you don't mind, Richie," Arthur said holding his hand up for a lift.

Rich grabbed his father's hand and brought him to his feet. "There, Dad, now you're sure you're okay?"

"Yes Richie I am more than okay. Go and visit with his majesty. I can already hear the blarney talk."

With that, Richie jumped over the hedge without a tumble.

"And tell his majesty to keep it down to a roar lest we have all of Hollywood out here to meet the wee folk."

Arthur walked spryly toward the hotel's garden doors thinking as he did so.

"And this is my element, making sure that all the plans being made would be fulfilled. Now where are those other sons of mine? We have some toasts to plan to go along with that Bunratty mead being delivered by his majesty."

Chapter 11: The Manchester Madonna and the Snowman

The Ryan Air jet landed at Gatwick Airport on time. The Colonna clan and Roses were a bit tired after Sean and Grace's wedding celebration, and the conversation focused on Grace's beauty as she was escorted down the aisle by Sean's jaunty cart driver partner, Bobby.

Grace lost her parents when she was quite young and Bobby had become a father figure to her. Sean's huge Irish family caused Saul Church of Downpatrick to be filled to capacity. If the Colonna family had not sat on the bride's side, Grace would have had very few guests besides Jim and Mary Coffey of Kate Kearney's cottage in Killarney. Jim and Mary had raised Grace. They saw that she was educated and gave her a position in the cottage restaurant while she was attending college. Also in attendance, much to Arthur's delight, was Professor Harold Cornwall and his wife Sarah. They too, had been a part of the Excalibur quest last year and had been on the side of Medraut's forces. He, being a scholar on Arthurian legend, was indispensable to Medraut and Grace as they plotted to steal Excalibur and destroy the Holy Grail once it was found.

At the height of the confrontation beneath the stone ring of Avebury, the professor's wife had pleaded with him not to throw away years of work and study for selfish reasons. Her love won out and they joined with Arthur and his family to save the holy vessel.

Arthur now had a chance to speak with him about a very different legend: the relationship between the Magi, the Medici, and Michelangelo. He wanted that discussion to take place before his daughter's wedding even though Cornwall would be attending.

Arthur met with the Professor outside Saul Church where St. Patrick had first established Christianity in Ireland. Arthur wanted the professor's view concerning the Manchester Madonna before he went to see it in London. In the painting, though an unfinished one, are two elements of particular importance to Agnes la Straga. Since Harold Cornwall was an expert in legends and artisitic renditions of legends, Arthur wanted his opinion.

"Harold, I am so pleased that we could meet before Kathy's wedding."

"As I am, to be sure, Arthur," the Professor replied as he embraced Arthur heartily. "Grace was a vision fit for a Botticelli painting wasn't she?"

"Or perhaps a Michelangelo?" questioned Arthur.

"Oh yes, I see what you mean. However, may I say that what Michelangelo did to elevate the male figure, I believe his friend Botticelli did for the female figure."

"I see where you're coming from Harold. Indeed, the *Birth of Venus* in the Uffizi and Botticelli's *Venus and Mars* in the National Gallery in London would support your view of the sublime beauty of the female form. Nevertheless, when I look upon the serene face of the Virgin of the St. Peter's *Pieta* I can imagine nothing more lovely."

"To be sure, my friend," the Professor replied. "You will find that same serenity in the face of the Virgin Mary of the Manchester Madonna. Since both works were begun around the same time, I believe Michelangelo may have used the same model for both works."

"Or perhaps he simply held the same theological opinion whenever he depicted the Mother of Christ. After all, didn't he counter criticisms of his *Pieta* regarding the youthfulness of his Mary with the argument that her sereneness and eternal youthful beauty came from the blessing of her motherhood to the Savior? In any case I've never seen the Manchester Madonna so I'll let you know what I think when we meet again."

It wasn't the countenance given to Mary which was the burning issue for Arthur; it was the two elements in the painting which he had never seen. He pressed the professor for his knowledge of the Magi legend and its possible connection with the Manchester Madonna.

Harold made it clear that any serious student of legend and history would be aware of the reverence in which the Magi were held in the Medici family. As for the two elements, -the book held by Mary, and the scroll held by the angels, -the Professor could add little to the typical conjecture of scholars. The book, held by Mary and towards which the child Jesus reaches, is said to contain the prophecy of his sacrifice. Mary does not want the child to see its contents at such a tender age. The scroll held by the angels is said to proclaim, *Ecce Agnus Dei* or, behold the Lamb of God. That proclamation would be announced by John the Baptist years later at the River Jordan where he baptized Jesus. Though traditionally accepted, there is no proof of either interpretation. The master had not left any notes pertaining to the work. Arthur thanked the professor for his insight and promised to keep him informed after he arrived in London and met with Agnes.

"Harold, if this mystery of the book and scroll is what Agnes wants to discuss with me, I think I may need your help and connections."

"I will be delighted to help in any way that I can, Arthur," the professor promised.

Now, five days later, the family was being dropped off at the Abbey Court Hotel in London. He and the boys transferred into a cab and rode to the National Gallery to meet with Agnes La Straga. He had no intention of wasting time. Though Donna was not pleased he was taking off on one of his secret jaunts, she also knew it was hopeless to deter him when he was on a mission. She made the call to the gallery informing Agnes that Arthur was on his way.

Leaving the hotel, the driver took a route along Oxford Street to Charing Cross Road and turned right. Within a few blocks they passed Trafalgar Square with its famed column depicting Admiral Lord Nelson.

The cab pulled up to St. Martin-in-the-Fields Church which had its own fame as an oustanding concert venue. Directly across the street was the National Portrait Gallery, which adjoined the National Gallery, where the exhibit was to open the next day.

Arthur and the boys decided to stroll across Trafalgar Square and walk up to the main entrance of the gallery where they were to meet Agnes. The traffic, as usual in London, was horrific and their decision proved to be a good one as they walked around the fountain in the square and directly up to the center portico with its stone columns between which now hung twenty-foot-long red banners announcing the new exhibit: *The World of Michelangelo and the Medici*. Directly under one of those banners stood the assistant curator; she was wearing her usual black dress accented with a gold brooch. The boys jumped up to the edge of the fountain's basin and waved to the tiny figure under the banner. They were sure the woman in black was Agnes. When the figure waved a black and gold scarf back and forth, their opinion was confirmed and they jumped off the fountain and ran across the square and up the stone stairs towards her. Arthur, lagging behind, arrived huffing and puffing as Agnes was hugging the boys.

"*Ah, Signore Colonna...Arturo, buon giorno,*" she exclaimed with a smile.

"*Buon giorno, Signora La Straga,*" he gasped out. "Give me *un momento por favore.*"

"*Si,* but of course," she replied. "But do follow me into the gallery when you are ready. I think you'll like how we set up the exhibit."

"We Signora?" asked the boys.

"You mean Signore Roselli and his guys are here, right now?" questioned Rich.

"Unfortunately, Andreas and Pietro are still connecting the fountain in the piazza set, so when you come through be...how do you say it...kind?"

"*Si,* whatever you say," answered John.

"Sure, we'll be the most polite guys you'd ever want to meet," added Rich.

"Boys, we cannot endanger the signora so don't get cocky with them," chimed in Arthur.

"*Si papa...*er... Dad, we know," the boys responded.

"Anyway, we'd need Ronnie, Chris, and Alun here to take care of them like they should be taken care of," reflected Rich.

Arthur chose not to respond to the threatening language of his youngest son and gave his full attention to Agnes.

"What about Roselli, where is he right now?"

"In that regard we have *molto fortuna...*luck. He is with Signore Nicholas, the director of the gallery. They are discussing the opening event. Of course you and your family will come, no?"

"Why *si,* of course, we'd be delighted. That is if you think it won't create a problem with Roselli."

Agnes assured them it would not create a problem. With their lodgings right next door to the Colonna clan's hotel, it would be impossible to escape being noticed. Arthur had also accepted Roselli's offer to conduct a class with his students when they arrived in Milan. Like Lorenzo de Medici used to say, "keep your enemies close to you." Arthur felt that five-hundred-year-old piece of advice was just as fresh and relevant today.

As Agnes and the Colonna men arrived at the exhibit area, the fountain in the center of the piazza, which served as the center of the exhibit, sprang to life. Water bubbled out of the sea shells held by cherubs. The streams of water gently cascaded down into the pool beneath the ledge on which the four little angels sat. Pietro walked out from behind a partially constructed wall and announced the fountain was in good working order. Andreas poked his head up from behind the half wall and smiled. They took no notice of the group entering the exhibit but, instead, walked away from the piazza and disappeared beyond the columns.

The boys did not wait for the Giuliano brothers to get out of sight. They hunted out the glass case holding the drawings of Lorenzo and his eldest son, Piero.

As in the Chicago exhibit, they found it at the beginning of the circular route visitors would follow to each display.

"So Signora," called out John. "I see that the Donatello box and the ring are in the display case this time."

"*Si Giovanni*," she answered. "Roselli finally agreed it was noteworthy, though a fake."

"Speaking of something that is a fake," added Arthur. "Where did you place the Manchester Madonna?"

Agnes smiled and led them to an area displaying Michelangelo's early work, when he first arrived in Rome around 1496. She paused at an oblong, clear-plastic display case, which was about seven feet tall. It was about three feet wide and deep. Inside the display case stood an empty gilded easel. The boys walked around the case looking for something to magically appear, and Arthur stood before it looking perplexed. Agnes explained the Manchester Madonna was no longer considered a fake or the work of another artist of Michelangelo's time. It had been considered so in the nineteenth and twentieth centuries but has since been verified as an unfinished work of the master himself.

"Because of that staus change is the reason I needed to see you. I left it to be the last piece to be set out. Please follow me and we shall see his work close up."

Like ducklings following their mother, the Colonna brothers and their father followed Agnes beyond the columns where Pietro and Andreas had disappeared. As in the Field Museum in Chicago, she had a small office. It did not have a window, but what it did have, resting on a plain wooden easel, was the Manchester Madonna. Agnes walked up to one side of the painting and, with outstretched hands, introduced her ducklings to the

Manchester Madonna.

Arthur walked up to the painting and looked into the face of the Madonna.

"It's true. The professor was right," he muttered aloud.

Rich and John looked over their father's shoulder but didn't understand what he was talking about.

"What's true, Dad?" asked John.

Arthur turned and told them of his conversation with Professor Cornwall.

"Signora, you have seen the *Pieta* in Rome, right?" Arthur asked Agnes.

"*Si*, many times," she answered. "And I have been closer to it than most people can get since the attack on the statue. There is now protective glass between the piece and the public who come to revere the masterpiece."

"Okay then, do you see what I see in the face of this Madonna?"

His sons, not having seen anything but pictures of the famed sculpture, hadn't a clue as to why their father was asking the question. Agnes leaned into the painting and in a moment her mouth opened and she looked up to Arthur.

"*Arturo, il face'*, the face...the look upon the face...the," she began to exclaim.

"The serenity of the mother's face," Arthur said finishing her thought.

"*Si*, that's it Arturo. *La Madonna*...she is serene and beautiful. Her skin is smooth and flawless as the master said it should be, given her blessed state. Your friend, this professor, he noticed this too?"

"He discovered it, I would say," answered Arthur. "But I am taking you away from the reason of our visit, Signora."

The boys were relieved that this artistic interpretation of the mind of Michelangelo had ceased. Though John, being in the arts, was fascinated by the comparison of the works, now was the time to uncover more of the mystery of the legend of the Magi and the Medici. Their young thoughts were focused on the adventure and challenges which they believed would meet them when they got to Italy.

"Not at all Arturo; I find this most interesting."

"*Grazie*, however I'm fairly certain that what you have to tell us may help us understand the master's mind when it comes to the legend," Arthur offered gratefully.

"You are most kind. *Alloro*, then, let us begin. Our story takes us to 1494. Lorenzo was dead around two years and Michelangelo had returned to his father's house in Florence…"

The house on Via Ghibellini was quiet. Lodovico was gone on an errand. Why he had chosen to go out on foot on such a bitterly cold day, which brought a snowfall so deep carriages were unable to make their way through the frosty layer, was unknown to anyone. Michelangelo was deep in thought as he sketched an idea. He jumped up from his chair in response to a powerful knock on the door, overturning the ink bottle as he did so. When he jumped to his feet he nearly toppled the table at which he sat. The loud pounding on the door persisted as the young artist sat back down and attempted to ignore the noise.

In Renaissance Florence one did not just drop by without making arrangements ahead of time. The young artist had no intention of finding out who was at the door. The person, whoever it was, would not give up. The pounding continued and, finally, Michelangelo threw his chalk pieces down on the table and left his room; bounding down the stairs in one of his terrible rages, to discover who could be so ignorant to disturb a noble family such as his.

He swung open the heavy wooden door so roughly it slammed against the wall, loosening the snow which had collected on the eve of the house. Before the stone cutter could utter his profanity, a huge clump of snow fell upon the young man standing in the doorway. He was covered in the rare white substance, looking like a snowman. The profanity yelled out was his; not Michelangelo's. Granacci looked so ridiculous Michelangelo could not help but laugh at his snow-covered friend.

"I do not find this at all amusing Buonarroti," he shouted while brushing himself off.

Michelangelo had little to laugh about since Lorenzo's death and sight of his dearest friend in such a state was just what he needed to lift his declining spirit.

"Let me help you, Francesco," Michelangelo said as he tried to help remove the snow.

"Watch where you're brushing Buonarroti or I won't even tell you the purpose of my visit," the irritated Granacci said as Michelangelo roughly brushed away the melting snow.

"Well pardon me your highness, but it was you who came to disturb my peace," the young stone cutter retorted.

"PEACE?! What peace do you speak of? Could it be the peace of your father's gentle voice telling you how the family fortune is cursed, or maybe it's his calling your profession worthless," Granacci mocked.

Michelangelo flung his arm around his oldest friend and gently pushed him past the doorway and into the sitting room where he had first been invited to enter the Medici Palazzo to study art.

"Stand here by the fire. It will help dry you. And now my *rex di amici* what brings you to my peaceful house?"

Francesco Granacci smirked, then laughed aloud. "Peaceful indeed. Buonarroti, I will never understand you. Why do you put up with this…this place you call peaceful?"

"Not all of us can live by designing carnival costumes, my friend. What have I been able to do since *Il Magnifico's* death? Nothing. Nothing is what I have done. Drawing after drawing, chip of marble here and a chip there but no form, no life within the stone."

"Then *mi amico*, may I brighten your melancholy mood? I have an invitation for you from the luckless one himself."

"Francesco, you wouldn't be playing with my emotions would you? Is it really Piero de Medici of whom you speak?" asked a hopeful Michelangelo.

Granacci dropped his cloak to the floor and threw his hat across the room.

"Look into my eyes you wretch. Would I, your dearest friend, deceive you?"

"I am most contrite Francesco, of course not. Your eyes are true as your friendship to me is. But two years have gone by and not a word from the Medici. Two years of being here with the father I love most deeply but who cannot understand love. All he speaks of is money and land."

Granacci took the teenage artist's hands into his own and kissed them.

"These instruments of genius, as Lorenzo called them, will no longer do nothing. Our luckless leader, Piero de Medici, calls for you this very day."

Light returned to the brown eyes with yellow and blue specks. A smile crossed his lips and a feeling of worth once more crept into his being. The eighteen-year-old embraced his friend with all his might. Granacci cringed under the pressure of those mighty arms, which could bring life to a block of stone as no other could do. He only smiled back until he could bear the pressure no longer.

"You squeeze the life out of me, Buonarroti. Let me breathe," Granacci gasped.

The young artist immediately released his hold and jumped backwards as if he had harmed a work of art.

"My dear friend, are you in pain? I didn't mean to…I mean I'm just so pleased with your news."

"*Certemente*, do not be alarmed," Granacci softly spoke. "I may not be able to carve the stone of Carrara but I am still a mighty man. Look at these arms my friend."

And they both laughed until they could only gasp out a squeal.

Relieved now, Michelangelo asked for the details. There were none to give however, other than Piero Medici, leader of Florence, wanted to see him immediately. Off they strode together on foot through the deep snow to the Medici Palazzo. As they were admitted to the marble-lined hall, Michelangelo felt at home once again; especially when Marsilio Ficino appeared at the top of the staircase.

"Young Buonarroti, it is you. Come greet your tutor," the priest-scholar beckoned. "You have returned to us then?"

"I don't know. All Francesco knew was that His Excellency wanted to see me promptly."

"Then by all means go. Granacci come up here and bring the lad to the chapel. I presume that's where the meeting is to take place." Ficino directed. "We shall talk when your audience is concluded."

The Greek scholar who taught Michelangelo the Platonic lessons on love, art, and life descended the staircase. He turned his head and gave a smile of good luck to his young protégé. Perhaps this time the eldest son of *Il Magnifico* would show compassion and understanding to the fragile youth who so loved his father. Unfortunately, the scholar-priest knew Piero was often so arrogant that even his earnest intentions were seen as condescending. Fincino made the sign of the cross and offered a prayer that all would go well for the artist whom Lorenzo had proclaimed to be a gifted genius whose works would bring glory to the world.

A servant stood at the chapel door and opened it upon seeing Granacci.

When they entered the small chapel dedicated to the Three Kings, as the Magi were now called, there stood Piero. He was studying the painting on the wall, the very one which Michelangelo knew so well. It depicted the Medici as the Magi. He was dressed in warm clothing of earth tone wool. There were no flashy colors or silk embroidered courtly dress on this day. The practicality of staying warm took precedence over all else. Piero had his right hand raised up to the painting. He seemed to be tracing, or perhaps pointing to, each of the Magi as if he was trying to identify them. The kingly person robed in Renaissance style clothing of white and gold had the countenance of his father, Lorenzo. On the index finger of the elevated hand was the legendary ring of the Magi. He heard the lads enter but chose to continue his study of the fresco.

Michelangelo and Granacci said nothing. They had to wait to be recognized. The youths were impatient to hear of Piero's plan for the younger of the two and the time seemed to drag on and on. Finally, while they shifted from leg to leg once more, Piero turned.

"Ah, I see you have arrived," he began with feigned surprise.

The two youths exchanged a quick glance at each other and nodded yes with a smile.

"Good, now then, Granacci you may leave us," Piero continued with a wave of his right hand in such a way as to have light from outside reflect off the Magi ring.

There would be no point in asking to stay with his friend. All Granacci could do was shrug his shoulders to Michelangelo, tap him on the shoulder, and bow to Piero as he left.

"Now then young Buonarroti, we can talk." Piero took a seat in a gilded chair. He motioned to the lad to come and sit across from him in a wooden chair with no arms, obviously placed with purpose in that position.

Michelangelo said nothing but, as he approached the chair, he first knelt before Piero de Medici, removed his hat and kissed the Magi ring. A sense of warmth filled his body. The chill of the unusual day had left him entirely. Only then did he take his seat as directed.

"Master Buonarroti, my father had great admiration for you, as of course do I. It's been much too long a time since you lived with us in our home."

Piero went on to greet him again and rambled on about the time which had passed and the genius of Michelangelo's potential. All that the young artist could do was occasionally offer a smile of gratitude. Even this gesture was a strain on his impatient nature.

Better if the luckless one would get to the point. Would there be a commission to create life out of stone? he thought to himself.

Piero had returned to talking about the weather as Michelangelo's mind began to wander. In particular, he spoke again of the snow which blanketed his beloved city.

"Yes, Your Excellency, the snow is quite deep, limiting movement in the city." This he said as his feet were lightly stomping the marble floor in a back and forth motion.

"Indeed, as you say the snow is very deep and that brings me to the point of my invitation to you," the Florentine leader nonchalantly said. "I wish to offer you a very special commission."

"Your Excellency honors me. Shall it be a work from the Classic myths or a reverent work illustrating the divine message?"

Piero had the young artist where he wanted him. He puffed out his chest now realizing the lad was desperate for work. He smiled benignly as he spoke.

"Oh the subject may be to your choosing, whatever your creative mind wishes to bring forth."

"I shall reflect on various ideas that I have been working on," Michelangelo replied. "When do I leave to choose the marble?"

"Oh my dear Michelangelo you will not be using marble on this project."

The artist was obviously disappointed but he said, "Then this is to be a project in paint?"

"Perhaps another time, but not for now, it will be neither paint nor marble." Piero could see the blood drain from the lad's face. "Michelangelo, you shall create the most outstanding work of art ever created in a sculpture made of snow.

"SNOW!" exclaimed Michelangelo as he jumped to his feet, without realizing that he was shouting at the leader of Florence.

Piero rose and placed his hand on the artist's shoulder guiding him to the window across the room. He opened it so that below them the snow-covered street and buildings could be seen glistening all around them.

"You see a new world of opportunity which lies before you. By the end of the week we shall hold a great feast and the guests shall walk among your snow sculptures. To help you I have invited the apprentices of the Medici garden and Ghirlandaio *bottega*."

The blood-drained face became red with rage barely under control. Michelangelo offered his gratitude, for if this was not to be done then no other possible work would ever come his way. That's how Piero wielded his power. Thus he could do nothing but excuse himself so that he might begin the project.

"*Scusi*, Excellency, but I will need the artists gathered in your courtyard by tomorrow morning with tools with which to shape the snow. Now, I beg your leave." The words dripped without color or feeling from the teen's lips as his whole body vibrated with rage.

"I thought you would see my vision, Master Buonarroti. Go now and do what you must do."

Piero turned to take in the view once again as Michelangelo crossed the room with such haste that he had to come back to get the hat he had left at his chair. This only further aggravated him. He swung open the door startling the guard and Granacci who waited, sitting on the stairs. Granacci saw the fire in his friend's eyes. His friend hardly noticed his presence as he swung his cloak about him and jumped from step to step skipping quite a few in the process.

Granacci ran down after him. "Michelangelo, what happened?"

"Snow! This genius who can bring life from stone, as he himself said, is to sculpt snow."

Michelangelo did not wait for the servant to open the door. He flung it open and it was all that Granacci could do to ensure it did not strike the servant. Kicking the snow piles, he stormed down the Via Martelli. Each of his violent steps caused the snow to leap into a spray of mist which struck his face and Granacci's.

"Michelangelo, do stop. I cannot keep up and my face is soaking wet."

The eighteen-year-old turned to face his twenty-four-year-old friend. He took the hem of his cloak and wiped the melting snow from Francesco's face.

"You needn't do that. I didn't mean that you had to be a servant to me."

Michelangelo looked into his friend's eyes and water, though not of melting snow, flowed from his eyes. They stood in the Piazza de San Giovanni at the famous Baptistery of Santa Maria del Fiore. The Duomo seemed to look particularly grand with its green marble shining as it contrasted against the pure white snow clinging to the marble high above them. Francesco Granacci pulled his friend by his arm and led him up the stairs in front of the cathedral. He swung Michelangelo around so that the Piazza in its white, glistening state appeared before him like the clouds of heaven itself.

"And is this sight not worthy of an artist my friend?" he asked.

"It is a scene from the writing of Dante himself to be sure. It's not this snow which is so upsetting, but how the great Medici expected me to take the task with fervor and without question," Michelangelo spoke gently to his friend.

Ever the practical one in regards to artistic work, Granacci pointed out that his work for the carnival was destroyed each year. Thus his work melted from the Florentine scene never to be seen again. Michelangelo's work will be absorbed into the very earth of our beloved city and bring life to it in the spring.

"Francesco, I had no idea that you could be so... so eloquent." Michelangelo brushed aside the heavenly clouds of snow so that they may sit, as they often did in the summertime, on the stairs of the Duomo.

"Francesco, I shall create a scene of the story of Bethlehem with the Magi coming to the newborn king. You shall help me. We shall get help from the *bottega* and from the San Marco gardens. Then shall this great leader wish that I had been given a commission to bring to life the story of Bethlehem and his beloved Magi from the Carrara stone. He shall see which better reflects the sun with more brilliance, represents the clouds of heaven more majestically, and gives lasting glory to the creator of both the frozen water and the hardened stone."

"You outdo yourself. Talk about eloquence, I'd say you're far beyond my meager abilities. You should write poetry and sonnets my dear friend," a breathless Francesco, who was now full of awe for his younger friend, spoke with admiration.

The cold on his rump brought him back from his euphoric state.

"And now my friend, can we leave this wonderland and take a hot drink to thaw my frozen *cuolo*?"

The laughing duo strode out of the Piazza and made their way towards San Marco and its gardens. As they did so, Francesco remarked about the time they had heard the Frate Savonarola preach at San Marco. He did not relish approaching the Frate's domain, for he still stung from being told that his work was virtually that of the devil. Michelangelo comforted him, asserting that the Frate would certainly appreciate the snow sculptures of the Nativity. He also knew, because of his brother being a member of the

Dominican priory over which Savonarola presided, that the power of the Frate was growing with each day.

"The Medici, like the snow sculptures, would soon be gone," he confided to Francesco though very quietly. "And before that happens, I shall depart my beloved city and my friend whom I owe so much to," a once again melancholy Michelangelo went on to say.

"...And shortly after the snow sculpture was completed he left for Venice and then Bologna. For the better part of 1494 Michelangelo wandered, returning to Florence near the end of the year. The Frate, Savonarola, who was now the powerful leader of Florence, gave him no commissions nor was he recognized in any fashion. Another Medici, a cousin of the deposed Piero, who now fought with the French to regain his power in Florence, took the young artist under his wing. Lorenzo di Pierfrancesco 'de Medici was the name of this cousin, and for him the young master stone cutter would create two sculptures. One would be that of St. John the Baptist as a child and the other, that of a sleeping cupid. The latter piece would attract the attention of Cardinal Raffaele Riario in Rome who invited the young artist to Rome. The year was 1496," concluded Agnes.

The boys and their father sat dumbfounded. How can one person know so much and also possess the ability to bring the story to life?

"Signora, your portrayal of Michelangelo is moving and profound. But what has it got to do with the legend of the Magi ring?" asked Arthur.

"I see your point Arturo, I may still call you by your given name, no?" Agnes replied meekly.

"*Si, certemente Signora*, by all means...ah Agnes, if I may?"

"*Grazie*, now where was I? *Ah, Giovanni e Ricardo* do you have questions?"

The boys were still reeling from their father's now informal address to the assistant curator. "Agnes indeed," they were thinking to themselves. Her question, however, brought them into focus.

"No, Signora la Straga," answered John with emphasis on her family name and with a glance towards his father.

"But do go on. What happens next, Signora la Straga?" added Rich, who then gave a look of appreciation towards his brother.

Arthur laughed aloud and thumped his sons on their back whispering, "Your mother would be proud of you."

Soon all three were giggling while the signora looked at them and wondered what she had said which was so amusing.

"*Scusi*, Agnes *mi figlii*, my sons, are just ensuring that their mother's interest is protected. If you know what I mean?" Arthur said with a wink.

"Papoo," exclaimed the boys as they covered their mouths in surprise. They had said their pet name for their father even though it was supposed to be used only in a family setting.

Agnes was still bewildered by the term "papoo" but decided to proceed rather than asking for further explanation. She chalked it up to her misunderstanding of the American way of speaking.

"It is June of 1496, the twenty-year-old master artist is preparing to leave for Rome having accepted the invitation from Cardinal Riario…" Agnes continued her story.

The shutters were open and the breeze, on a lovely early summer day, swept across the room. The young man's hair gently lifted and fell onto his forehead as the gentle wind reached him in his final moments of deep sleep. Wearing his long cotton bed shirt and boots he twisted and turned, his covering having been thrown off sometime during the night. There was a yearning deep within his heart not to wake up and to face the new day. That yearning was touching his very being, thus he twisted his way into the pillow to prevent the inevitable.

"Michelangelo," Lodovico bellowed from the lower floor. "Francesco has arrived. Are you ready?"

The young man threw the pillow onto the floor and jumped from his bed. He called down to his father, "Tell Francesco to come up, I am almost ready."

Francesco was relieved to get away from the dour elder Buonarroti who always made him feel inferior. He took the stairs two at a time and barged through the door as if being chased by a vandal. Michelangelo had thrown off his night shirt and stood only in his boots before a basin of water. He was splashing the cold water into his face to revive himself for the inevitable morning which he did not want to dawn.

"Buonarroti, you said that you were almost ready and all I see is your dainty *cuolo* and those worn old boots."

"And the former is one which would look good carved into the stone, jealous one," he jokingly replied. "And as for these boots, they will never leave my feet until they fall naturally from them in pieces."

"And this is how you are to meet the cardinal?" asked the stunned Granacci.

The younger of the two responded with a laugh. He explained that his feet would be of no interest to the eminent prelate, rather, it would be his hands and mind. He pulled up his leggings and threw on a cotton tunic rather than his usual wool one. Buckling the leather belt he asked if he looked presentable.

"Perhaps if you were visiting your brother on the farm," Francesco mocked. "You're going to Rome, Michelangelo; The Eternal City. You'll go to Palazzos and maybe into the presence of the Holy Father himself."

Michelangelo remained unimpressed. After all, he dined at the table of *Il Magnifico*, no greater experience could he have even in Rome. He casually placed the bed shirt into a small leather trunk, which he had pulled onto the bed, then started to tie it shut.

"See that's what I mean," Francesco Granacci said as he pushed the lad aside.

The young artist looked at Granacci with bewilderment, not having a clue what he meant. The older lad saw that confusion in his eyes. His heart sank, thinking that the friend he valued more than any other would be ridiculed by the high and mighty of Roman society. He grabbed the leather trunk and opened it. Taking out the bed shirt he went to the window where the breeze still filtered in softly. He shook it over the ledge and held it briefly with his outstretched arms so that it hung over the street below.

"Oh I see that's really a gentile thing to do. Now the whole world can see my underwear," laughed Michelangelo.

"Indeed, but at least it will smell fresh." Granacci answered with a smile as he folded it meticulously and arranged the other garments in the trunk with similar preciseness. "Besides, were the ladies of the Carnivale Chorus passing by they would stop and sing an ode to Michelangelo's bed shirt even if you weren't in it."

Michelangelo laughed, but inside his very being was moved. He understood what his dearest friend was attempting to do. Water began to fill his eyes but he would not allow a drop to fall from them. He ran to the window pushing Granacci aside in the process.

Hanging over the ledge he yelled back, "Where are these ladies of the Carnivale when we need them? I see only a few of our comrades from the Duomo steps."

Granacci, having fallen onto Michelangelo's bed, smiled devilishly.

"Depending on which ones you are seeing, they too might sing a sonnet of joy."

Suddenly, a pall of darkness and fear filled the room. The sun was still as bright as ever and the day so clear that from his window the steeple of Santa Croce Church was visible.

Michelangelo walked slowly from the window, casting a last glance towards Santa Croce, and sat on the edge of his bed next to his friend.

"Francesco, you are never to joke that way; not with the Frate Savonarola in power. Even Botticelli has destroyed his works and drawings because they were deemed to be glorifying paganism and therefore erotic. The magnificence of the human form made in God's image is no longer a thing of beauty in our beloved city."

Francesco understood only too well how Florence had changed now that the Medici were thrown out. The Florentines had given up a strong hand of governing for an even stronger one which squeezed the creativity and joy from the life of the city. It seemed that balance simply was an unattainable goal for the citizens of Florence. The artist of the now defunct Carnivale would not let his friend know of his feelings, so he picked up the pillow and threw it at Michelangelo to chase away the melancholy.

"Ah my dour friend, the Frate's days are numbered. So off you go to the grand City of Light with a smile. Now don't forget, you must smile even if you're angry like when you had to sculpt snow for Piero," Granacci counseled.

Michelangelo returned a wide exaggerated grin, fluffed up the pillow in his hands and threw it into Francesco's face.

"And they would think me a dim-witted fool should I follow your advice."

"Michelangelo," bellowed Lodovico. "What takes you so long? The cart has arrived and the cost of it increases with each moment."

The two stopped their wrestling which followed the pillow attack. Michelangelo jumped to his feet. His boots thumped on the oak floor boards.

"We come Father," he yelled back. "Well friend, it's time. There is no delaying now or my father will cancel the cart and I would be walking to Rome."

"*Ciao amico,*" was all that could come from Francesco Granacci's lips, as he picked up the leather trunk and flung it over his back.

"You shall write Francesco and tell me what is happening here in our city?"

"Of course, now let's get going before your father sends your cart away."

"So then, this is how friends say *arrivederci*?" Michelangelo walked towards the door of his room.

Tears streamed down Francesco's cheeks, cleanly shaven for the farewell meeting.

"Are we to bid farewell like two Carnivale girls then? Would that make you happier?"

Michelangelo turned and stood as rigid as the stone he carved.

"At least it would show that we are alive and have hearts not made of stone."

Francesco lowered the trunk onto the bed. A good six inches taller than Michelangelo, he took him by the shoulders, tears still streaming down his face and looked into those big brown eyes with yellow and blue specks.

"And do you say that I have no heart?" he sputtered emotionally.

Michelangelo could feel the control Francesco was exerting to keep from openly sobbing.

"No my friend; I can feel that you have a heart," replied Michelangelo as he placed his hand on Francesco's chest to feel the rapidly beating heart.

With a hug to beat all hugs that Italians take joy in exchanging, a proper farewell was made. He abruptly broke the hold and ran down the stairs to his impatiently waiting father.

"By June 25, 1496 with reins in his hands, the soon-to-be master stone cutter traveled to the Eternal City and by July 4th, he celebrated his independence from his father's rule by beginning his first work in marble in Rome. It was to be a life-sized rendition of the ancient Roman god Bacchus." Agnes paused in her story as the Colonna boys exchanged a glance between themselves while totally ignoring the latter part of the story just shared.

"Giovanni, I see a questioning look on your face, no?" she commented.

John and Rich were a bit embarrassed with her question for they really didn't want to have to answer it. Their father, unlike Lodovico towards Michelangelo, knew quite well their plight.

"So boys, what did you think of the story? Have you ever experienced such a depth of friendship?" their father asked.

Finally, John had to say it. "So did Francesco and Michelangelo have a thing for each other?"

Rich, though thinking the same thing, would never have said it aloud.

Arthur flashed his cow like eyes towards Agnes who smiled and nodded with understanding. She explained that their question could never be answered.

"In all the historical evidence which has been preserved, and in the case of Michelangelo that was quite an amount, despite his destroying of much of his unfinished works shortly before he died, there is none which would... how you say... indicate a thing between Francesco Granacci and Michelangelo Buonarroti."

The boys' faces flushed red, but they said nothing.

Agnes further explained that in Renaissance Italy the scope of love was far broader and used as a description between friends, family, lovers, men and women, husband and wives. Scholars of the period tell us that its use did not automatically mean that there was a physical relationship though there could have been.

"Oh, I see. They were a huggy kind of people, like Cookie Grandma was, right Dad?" John asked referring to his great-grandmother who had passed away several years ago.

"That's a good analogy. Your great-grandmother was indeed a huggy kind of person."

Feeling a bit more comfortable with their sexuality again, the boys sat back in their chairs.

"So what happened in Rome, Signora?" Rich asked with a sense of relief.

"That Ricardo, is why I have told you this part of the story, for what happened to Michelangelo while on his first residency in Rome is important to our search for the ring of the Magi."

Rich and John both leaned over so that they might focus on her words.

"As I have said, Michelangelo received a commission from Cardinal Riario. Now the cardinal knew full well what the artist's choice was for the block of white marble he had purchased. The block was set up in a house

Michelangelo bought for himself; a short walk from the Roman Forum. In that building there were living areas and working areas and even rooms for his apprentices. These helpers served both in the studio courtyard and in the house fulfilling the ordinary duties it takes to run a household. His fame was growing from the sculpture of the sleeping cupid which created a sensation when it was first offered as a found sculpture from antiquity. Pier Francesco Medici had deceived Michelangelo and suggested that it be created to look ancient. Even when the scam was found out, the cardinal was so impressed by the work he offered the invitation to come to Rome. Thus, the artist had become a celebrity before he even entered the city," Agnes went on to explain.

Marble chips flew to every corner of the covered courtyard as Michelangelo worked through the hot Roman summer days. And yet barely a sweat was broken, so when his apprentice insisted that he take a drink of water, the artist was displeased with the interruption. As he would during the midst of any of his extended works, he lived and breathed the subject on which he worked as he tirelessly strove to complete it.

"Why do you disturb my work?" an irritated Michelangelo screamed at his apprentice.

Shaking from head to toe the young lad almost dropped the tray with the piece of bread and a cup of wine on it. "Master Buonarroti, you must eat something," the lad Paulo replied.

The easily irritated and temperamental artist saw the lad's hands barely able to hold onto the tray and spoke gently.

"Mille grazie, Paulo. Just place it there on the table. I promise to get to it."

As he walked past the Bacchus, the lad looked up at its form rising from the marble. "Master Buonarroti, he appears to be lifting himself from the stone."

"And he is, my good fellow, he is. All I am doing is releasing what is contained within the marble; chipping away what is unnecessary so that the life within may come forth."

Michelangelo stepped down from his stool to sip from the cup and take a bite from the bread. As he did so he gave Paulo a smile but what he was saying inside his head was, "There, now I have drunk and eaten. Go and leave me at peace."

Paulo understood and made his way back into the house from the courtyard.

Holding the cup of wine he toasted his work, "To you Bacchus, that we may bring joy to the beholder." He took a drink from the cup. "But not too much lest I become like you, unable to stand straight and be full of nonsense."

He walked around the block now revealing parts of a human body being hewn from the stone. The head with curly hair was wreathed with grape tendrils; Bacchus' eyes rolling back from too much drink; the elevated hand held a cup of wine as if returning a toast to his creator; the muscular upper arm and chest were so well-defined that its ribs seemed to move from breathing. This work was to be one which should be seen from all sides. As he passed the workbench on which the sketches of the arms, hands, chest and abdomen, and head lay, he ruffled through them.

"Paulo ...Paulo where are you when I need you?"

The lad ran in panting. "Master Buonarroti, what has happened?"

The artist pointed to the drawings on the table.

"I need a good pair of legs Paulo and I have none."

The lad carefully went through each sketch, placing one to the side as he looked for the legs in question. "Master, there are no legs here."

"Then we must be off to find a good pair of legs for our Bacchus," Michelangelo responded as he grabbed his tunic, slipped it over his head and headed for the gate leading to the street beyond. "I shall return when I have found what I'm looking for, Paulo."

Off he went to look for just the right pair of legs. Michelangelo often used a variety of models, taking from each what he thought best to bring forth the creation he carved out of the stone. He would sketch them to save the appearance he wished. He used sitting models for both his drawings, which would often become painted works, and his sculpting.

"How easy it was to make the muscle tissue seem visible under the skin," he thought to himself.

It was not always that way. There was a time when he thought he would never master the art of human dynamics; that which makes the body move this way or that way, to writhe in anguish, to look placid and calm.

As he walked up toward the Palatine Hill, through the ruins of the Roman Forum, his thoughts flashed back to the Medici gardens where he had worked with Francesco Granacci. How he missed those days working for *Il Magnifico*. How he missed Francesco and their adventures. Were it not for him the now nearly twenty-one-year-old artist would never have learned about human anatomy.

More than that, it was not easy for Michelangelo to make friends because of his short temper. It didn't help that his perfectionism, his sometimes arrogant personality which flared when he felt the person viewing his work to be stupid and ignorant, often hampered forming close relationships.

Now he needed a pair of legs to immortalize in his first life-size work. He decided he needed a young man's legs before they became distorted with disease and age. His Bacchus was to be youthful and vibrant and a little tipsy. How very many legs, torsos, arms and heads with closed eyes he had seen in the hospital morgue of Santo Spirito near the Arno River in Florence. It was difficult to remember the number of times he cut into the bodies to study muscle tissue, connections of tissue to bone, internal organs and the external areas of the masculine form. He had been allowed to view only male bodies out of respect for women.

His thoughts brought him back to those days of his teen years. It was a day much like any other in springtime in the Medici gardens when the lessons began. It was after *Carnivale* time and after the work on his faun.

Granacci came running through the gates. He had been absent from his work area all day.

"Michelangelo, it's been arranged. We are to be there within the hour," he called out to his sixteen-year-old friend.

"Calm yourself, Francesco. Where are we to go?"

"I told you that my family knew the Prior of Santo Spirito did I not? Well, I have talked with him and he is allowing us to enter the morgue beneath the hospital," an excited Granacci relayed.

"You mean we'll be able to view real people?" a thrilled Michelangelo asked.

"Buonarroti, they're dead," was the reply.

The teen artist just rolled his eyes. "I know that, *idioso*. Come, we have no time to lose if we're to get there within the hour."

The artist threw a variety of knives, probe sticks, paper and chalk into a heavy cloth sack and headed for the gate. He ran down the streets with Francesco barely able to keep up with him. Not a moment's pause did he make until he reached the Piazza della Signoria next to the Palazzo Vecchio where the Florentine seat of government was located.

Michelangelo took a sweeping look around the Piazza, which served as the major gathering place for Florentines over the centuries. At the far end was the Loggia dei Lanzi, built in the 1300s. It served to house the bodyguards of Cosimo I, but soon became a staging area for civic events and to display great works of art.

"One day, Francesco, you and I may have our work displayed here."

"There is no doubt that you shall glorify the piazza my friend." And off they ran towards the Ponte Vecchio, a bridge which has spanned the Arno River for centuries. About half way across the bridge, Francesco paused.

"Buonarroti, let's take in the breeze for a moment. I think that you'll appreciate the freshness of the air before we enter the tomb of death."

At last they stood before the rather plain façade of Santo Spirito Basilica. It was the work of the famous architect Fillippo Brunelleschi and was completed when Michelangelo was but nine years old. Next to it was the thirteenth century Augustinian monastery with its hospital where the young men were headed. A monk greeted them as they entered the gates and led them to the courtyard. The prior waited for them.

"Ah, Francesco and this must be the lad of whom you spoke so highly." Then turning he continued. "So, Michelangelo Buonarroti, you strive to be a master stone cutter, I understand."

Michelangelo hated the term stone cutter, but wisely held his temper, something of an accomplishment for the lad. "Yes, your eminence, I hope to be a sculptor."

"Then perhaps I can help. Mind you, this is not to be discussed with anyone, is that clear?"

"Yes, Eminence, we understand," they answered together.

Through the white-washed walls of the hospital corridors they walked until they reached a door which brought them into a gray stairway leading downward. Only a torch and slits in the walls brought light into the damp and cool room into which they now walked. The stench was strong as many of the bodies lying on the stone slabs had been there for some time waiting for arrangements for burial. Many had no family or identities and no one to take charge of them. The monks would see that they were given a Christian burial.

"There will be no one down here today Francesco so you and your friend may take your time. When you have had enough of dealing with death you may leave as we entered, but do not come back through the courtyard. Leave from the hospital doors. May God guide your hand, young sir." And with that, they would never again be escorted by the prior as they would come and go through the hospital, usually in the evening.

The two stood and took in the sight of body after body lying around them. Each was covered in a white cotton cloth so that only a hint of their features was detectible. Granacci took the lead and pulled the cloth from the body which rested before them. It was that of a younger man cut down in his prime. He had a sword wound through his side.

"Okay, Buonarroti, he's all yours."

Michelangelo made the sign of the cross over himself, and took out a sketch pad. He felt the arm cold and stiff. He lifted the arm then the leg with some difficulty. He drew them quickly onto his pad. This he did with every part of the body until he reached the wounded area. By then the smells of the morgue had filled his nostrils so potently that his eyes watered and his stomach began to churn with revulsion.

"Francesco, I think I'm about to vomit. Quick, get a bucket or something." He doubled over, holding his abdomen as if he were in excruciating pain.

Francesco found several buckets used to carry away the internal organs when they were removed. Unfortunately they, too, smelled to high heaven, but they served the purpose.

"Michelangelo, you are not well. Let's get out of here back into the fresh air."

"No, I must learn. I must know so that my work reflects what is real."

Wiping his mouth with the edge of the cloth which had covered the fallen soldier, he entered the body cavity with his hands. That would be the scenario on each visit. Michelangelo would get sick and Francesco would get the bucket.

"Hey you, watch where you're going, *idioso*," a gruff voice yelled, causing the daydreaming artist to come back to the Forum in which he was walking.

"I beg your pardon; I was distracted," the artist replied.

Then he saw before him one who was not much younger than he. The man was dressed in a tunic of antiquity. Accompanying him was a band of fellow actors who were using the Forum to portray a work from Virgil. Their legs were bare as was the style of youths in ancient Rome.

The artist introduced himself. Before he could continue, one of the lads exclaimed. "Not the Florentine who carves the Bacchus?"

"The very one, but how do you know of my work?"

"Does not all of Rome know of your work Master Buonarroti? The city awaits the unveiling of your work with great anticipation. My brother is on the staff of His Eminence, Cardinal Riario and that's all the prelate can talk about."

Michelangelo went on to thank the lad for the honor of his comments. Looking at the lad's legs, he had a thought which would require a bit of acting.

"Alas...what did you say your name was?"

"It's Giorgio, sir."

"Alas Giorgio, the work may never come to completion."

"But why, sir?" asked the young actor.

"I need a pair of legs to complete the work," a slightly grinning Michelangelo said.

There was a collective exclamation of "WHAT?" from the lads and Giorgio.

The artist asked the youths to gather around him for a quick lesson in art. They were only too happy to be taught by the great visiting artist from Florence. By the time Michelangelo was done telling his story of how he gathered his material to create a work of art, each lad was offering his legs to the artist to draw for the Bacchus.

The effervescent artist thanked them profusely and chose Giorgio as the model. He sketched the legs on his pad with red chalk while all the lads watched in wonder.

"You will need to pose as well, does that suit you Giorgio?"

After the lad enthusiastically said yes, an appointment was made and the legs became those of the Bacchus.

"As the work on the Bacchus continued, patrons submitted commission offers for a variety of works. Soon Michelangelo found himself preparing two paintings of the Madonna with child and St. John the Baptist. One of those is known today as the Manchester Madonna," concluded Agnes La Straga.

"But what happened to the Bacchus?" an excited John asked.

"Giovanni, it's not important to what I have to tell," she then paused. "But I shall tell you. The Cardinal came to view the statue. With great pomp and circumstance was the unveiling done. What do you suppose happened?"

"Michelangelo became wealthy with what he got paid for the statue," the still enthralled John answered.

"Not quite Giovanni. The Cardinal hated the piece. He said it was not a Roman god but a drunken youth. He refused to pay and the statue was left without an owner until finally a Roman banker by the name of Jacopo Galli bought it for his garden collection of ancient statues."

"Wow, Michelangelo was rejected," the awed Rich commented. "So how did he live?"

"As I have said, Ricardo, he had other works in progress and that brings me to the point of this meeting."

Agnes directed them to take a good look at an obviously aged paper lying on the small desk behind which she sat. Arthur knew immediately that it was like those which she had shown him in Chicago and which he brought with him in his bag hanging from his shoulder. She explained that the paper had a sketch drawn on it with red chalk.

"Like the legs of the Bacchus," interrupted John.

"Yes just so, but this is a design for St. Peter's Dome in Rome, which of course in his later years Michelangelo was asked to create. The document was found in the Vatican Archives on Dec. 7, 2007. How it escaped the master's frenzy in the last days before he died one does not know. Somehow it wasn't burned, as were so many of the great artist's incomplete or so-called imperfect works. This sketch was made in 1564, shortly before his death. What is remarkable is that it was copied on a paper already used by Michelangelo. Possibly it was used to make notes which he was to share with Ascanio Condivi, his biographer, a decade earlier. Given Michelangelo's proclivity for frugality it is not surprising he should save paper, which he would probably plan to destroy later anyway," Agnes explained.

She pointed out that how it was saved was unimportant. What was important were the notes on the back of the sheet. The notes referred to his first beginning his work in Rome on July 4, 1496."

"Signora, you mean that no one knew about this... this drawing until 2007?" a shocked Rich asked.

"Si, Ricardo and no one would have dreamed that the faded script on the back was from the hand of the master himself."

Agnes turned the paper gently towards the boys who now leaned over it trying to see the note without much success.

"Giovanni, take this magnifying glass. It will help you see the script," she directed as Arthur joined his sons trying to see the writing.

"Er, it's in Italian, I think," John remarked though he could hardly see it even with the glass.

"Si, perhaps this translation will help." And she handed Arthur the translation which stated:

> Bacchus, rejected by the buffoon
> Pieta, too bad I signed it.
> Frate Savonarola, my brother has worries
> The Madonna, child reaches for Magi book.

Arthur's naturally large brown eyes became even more pronounced as he read the last line. "Signora, then the master, himself, knew of the Magi legend?"

"There is no doubt he knew of the legend… after all he had lived in the Medici Palazzo since he was thirteen years old. What it tells us is that the master intended to authenticate the legend in his art," Agnes replied.

"How did you come by this?" asked Arthur.

"I was lucky to be involved, in that as a local art historian, I was invited to view the find by a dear friend of my family," Agnes explained.

"How many people know of this drawing, Signora?" inquired Arthur, whose thoughts were immediately focused on Roselli.

Agnes knew what he was driving at and said that as far as she knew only the drawing of the Dome was made known to a hand full of scholars. She went on to say that the exhibit's curator, Roselli, was not part of that group as the drawing appeared to have nothing in common with the Magi Legend and the Medici family.

"In any case," she continued, "our friend Roselli was not there. As for the others who were present at the discovery, they would have no idea of what the script on the back of the Dome drawing said. It was not until later that this friend saw the smudge on the back of the paper was more than chalk marks. I was with him when he translated the deciphered writing."

"This is great news Agnes and, with Roselli not in the picture, much in our favor," commented Arthur. "Where do we go from here?"

Agnes felt they should proceed as planned. After Kathy and Alun's wedding, Arthur and his youngest sons would travel with the students to Milan. Once there, Roselli would conduct his class for Arthur's students. After that, it would be Agnes who would be assisting with the tour. The search for the Magi Ring could be conducted simultaneously.

Arthur felt that the plan was a sound one. He addressed an issue which Donna had given to him.

"Speaking of weddings, my wife and I would be pleased if you could join us at our daughter's wedding at St. David's Cathedral in Wales."

He handed an invitation to Signora la Straga.

The boys were shocked as they turned to each other and blurted out, "From MOM?"

"Arturo, you do me a great honor to be part of your family. Inform your lovely wife, who told me of the invitation when she called, that I shall accept and be there."

"And of course, since you'll be with us, should anything else develop you won't have far to go to inform me."

"*Va bene,*" she answered. "And now until that day we must say *arriverderci.*"

With a smile and a hug for her Giovanni, Ricardo, and Arturo, she bade them farewell.

As the boys desended the stairs back into Trafalgar Square, their whispered comments were not of the discovery but of how long the hug given to their father by Agnes lasted compared to the ones given to them. Their youthful minds concluded that it was not a Cookie Gram type of hug.

Chapter 12: Rainbows in the Cathedral

As the sun rose over Pembrokeshire, the Cathedral of St. David shone as if they had used pink marble rather than the gray stone of Caerbwi Bay when it was re-consecrated in 1181 A.D. Almost six hundred years later the destruction ravaged upon the Cathedral by Oliver Cromwell's forces two hundred years earlier was finally countered by a major reconstruction and restoration effort. Luckily for Arthur and his family, the refectory's restoration had been recently completed making it available for the wedding reception.

The waters of St. Brides Bay seemed particularly turquoise when yet another day of days dawned. Gentle waves lapped the shoreline, sending up sounds of the sea as a soft wake-up call. The Hollywood crowd at Clan Y Mor guest house and the family at the Warpool Court Hotel could not have asked for a more enchanting new day.

The rooms of the Colonna clan were buzzing with activity as Donna and the Roses were already organizing the wedding breakfast. Kathy, being a late sleeper, was still in bed when the door to her room suddenly thundered with the banging of her sister's not-so-gentle knocking.

"Kathleen Mary, are you up?" called out Jana.

Kathy rubbed her still-closed eyes vigorously as if to force them to open. Only on a work day would she ever see such an early awakening. She looked at the travel clock sitting on the bedside table.

"Good grief Jana, it's only eight o'clock, come back in an hour," she called out.

"Are you crazy? Open this door. Tricia and I have a lot to do for you to get you ready," insisted Jana.

"All right but shouldn't you two be getting the kids ready or something more useful?"

Kathy threw off her covers and grabbed the violet-colored robe hanging over the chair. As she tied the belt around her waist she looked up and out the window overlooking the sea.

"Wow, it's beautiful," she exclaimed silently. Then she opened the door.

Tricia and Jana, all aflutter, rushed in.

"Mom is getting breakfast ready for the whole crowd," announced Tricia.

"So we're here to help you get ready," added Jana.

Kathy rolled her eyes, but it was a poor imitation of the talent Jana inherited from Arthur and he in turn from his grandmother. Nevertheless it was a good try. Kathy, ever the practical one and certainly not into pomp and circumstance, looked at her sister and sister-in-law with cool and calm half-shut eyes.

"Okay, let's get to it," she began to say to the other girls' short-lived delight. "First of all, I am not going down to breakfast with a whole gang of people. It's bad luck for them to see the bride ahead of time," Kathy announced.

Jana and Tricia could feel what was coming. Jana attempted to counter by saying that the tradition of not seeing the bride before the ceremony was only for the groom. Her attempt didn't work.

"So Tricia, if you would be so kind as to sneak an English muffin and some tea up here, I'd be eternally grateful. Jana, my lovely Matron of Honor, if you would ensure that my dress is ready, I'll go shower; and then maybe, I'll be ready to face this day."

"Well, if that's what you want. Mom said we have to do what you want today," replied Jana. "But don't dawdle. You have no idea how fast time will fly and then it's time and then we'll be rushing like crazy people and then only God can help us."

"And that's why she's a great mom; she always knows just what her children need," grinned Kathy. "And I think God is on Mom's side."

Tricia left to obtain a secreted breakfast and Jana went to her parent's room where the wedding gown was kept. Just as Jana reached up to knock on the door of her parents' room it opened and out strolled Arthur.

"Dad, you're up and ready and everything?" the shocked Jana said.

"Well, I have been ordered to chat with the family and guests as they come down for breakfast. What are your orders?"

"Actually my orders come from Kathy. Mom said Tricia and I have to do what she wants today and not what we think should be done. So I'm checking out the gown and Tricia is getting breakfast for her. She doesn't want to come down," a disheartened Jana explained.

Arthur recognized that his eldest daughter wanted to make sure everything was perfect for her little sister, but Kathy wanted it kept simple. This simplicity was contrary to Arthur's and Jana's tendencies, leaving both of them in a dilemma. Finally, he found words to speak.

"Jana, do you remember the day you and Chris got married? You placed all the planning and staging of events into your mother's and my hands. That resulted in a stress-free day for you, didn't it?"

Jana smiled; she knew what her father spoke was absolutely true.

He explained that Kathy also wanted a stress-free day and for her that meant the least amount of fuss possible before the big event. She knew that with Arthur in charge of the ceremony and Donna in charge of the reception that a big fuss was inevitable. To save herself from undue nervousness, she wanted a quiet and uneventful morning.

"And that's why your mother is tending to breakfast and I am to chat with the guests. The last thing your sister needs right now is all the relatives fawning over her."

"Well, as they say, Father knows best."

"In this case it's Mom knows best," he corrected. "By the way, Jana, what could be more important than getting the symbol of the day ready for your sister?" Having said that, he kissed her on the cheek and made his way down the hall.

Jana stood for a long moment holding her cheek.

"Dad never spontaneously kisses anyone," she thought.

Then she smiled, knowing how much he wanted to comfort her, and focused on her orders. Entering her parents' room she walked to the bay window, opened to a view of the sea beyond and the gardens below. She heard the chatter of the family gathering on the terrace. The warm rays of the sun bathed the room in a bright glow as she opened the wardrobe allowing the rays to strike the wedding gown inside. It became a dazzling raiment as in Scripture symbolizing all that is holy and beautiful in love.

She stepped back to absorb the sight. Since Jana had chosen to wear their mother's gown of silk and Italian lace, Kathy had decided to ask Grandma Colonna if she could wear her wedding gown. Grandma naturally was thrilled and honored. The satin gown had been handed over to Kathy back in Wisconsin and then sent to Ballydangan, Ireland, specifically to Kathleen Gaffey, the drapery lady of Clonmacnoise. Being a master seamstress she transformed it into a gown fitted to Kathy's petite figure. She also created an overlay of Irish lace with Celtic designs. The veil was trimmed in lace and attached to Donna's wedding crown of white crystal.

Only Jana, Tricia, Kathy, and their mother knew how the final design looked as they took Kathy for the final fitting after the film's premiere in Dublin.

"So I guess there is nothing more important than this," she spoke aloud.

Just as she took the gown from the wardrobe closet, Tricia walked in.

"I left the breakfast on the table in Kathy's room. She was still in the shower, so I came to see if I could help."

"Well, what do you think? Didn't the drapery lady do a magnificent job?" asked Jana.

"It's spectacular and stunning. Kathy will look like a princess. Wait until Olivia sees this," and she picked up the headpiece.

After spending some time admiring the drapery lady's handiwork, the girls decided to give Kathy a little more time and went off to breakfast. They would bring her the gown afterwards.

Kathy wrapped herself in her fluffy violet robe once again and wrapped her hair in a white towel. It was her practice to sit and air out after a shower and that routine was not to be changed. Finding the breakfast Tricia left on the table by the doors opening onto a small balcony, she pulled up a chair and poured herself a bit of tea.

She had kicked off her slippers and was rubbing her feet together when she heard a rapping noise on the window. Looking up, with tea cup in hand, she saw Alun. So startled was she to see her betrothed that she dropped her tea, which then splashed on her causing her to jump up and fall backwards. During the fall she knocked over the chair and fell to the carpeted floor with a thump which caused her robe to fly open and the towel on her head to unravel.

Alun was scared to death that she was injured and it would be his fault. He tugged on the door and luckily it flung open. Running toward Kathy, who quickly wrapped herself in the robe whilst still on the floor, he bent down to help her up. She was trying to adjust the towel around her head but gave up on it, throwing it to the floor.

"What on earth are you doing here, Alun? Jana will have a heart attack that you've seen me before the wedding.?"

"Jana? As in your sister?"

"Well me too. You're not supposed to be here," Kathy directed.

Alun picked up the chair setting it exactly where Kathy had it when she toppled over.

"I had to see you before the ceremony Kathleen."

Alun knew she wanted to use her complete name and always tried to address her so.

"Good heavens, what could be so important that it couldn't wait?" she impatiently asked. "What if my mother comes up; then we'll have a lot of explaining to do."

The pacing groom-to-be didn't know how to answer or what to do.

"Alun, have you gotten cold feet or something?"

He took her in his arms and gently placed her onto the chair. The sunlight shimmered through her auburn hair. She looked into his crystal blue eyes with her cocoa brown ones questioning his motives.

"No I haven't got cold feet, but you may get them when I'm finished telling you what I must tell you," he tenderly but nervously said.

He stopped, unable to go on.

"You mean, you're divorced, or a criminal of some kind, or maybe I'm not good enough for you? Is that it? Well why did you wait until our wedding day to tell me?" Kathy, now thinking the worst, asked the increasingly flustered would-be groom.

Alun took hold of himself, breathed heavily, and gently spoke while holding his hands gently on her shoulders.

"No my love it's not you who may not be worthy but me for having kept it from you."

"Oh my God and all the angels and saints, you are a criminal then," Kathy exclaimed in disbelief as she grabbed his arms and removed them from her shoulders. The forlorn Alun looked at his hands, not knowing what to do with them.

"I am perhaps a liar or at least one who did not reveal the whole truth, but I'm not any of those things you are thinking and I do love you more than, well, more than my title."

"Your what?"

"My title," Alun softly, almost with a whisper, said. "You see, I will one day be the last Earl of Ramsey."

Kathy looked into his eyes and saw that they were bloodshot. He must have been up all night trying to think of a way to tell me, she thought. Now she began to shake with the news just heard and filtering into her consciousness.

"Is that something like Prince William?"

Alun was able to smile. "No my love not quite so grand but it's a title nonetheless. I am a Peer of the Realm. Is that okay with you?"

"I love you, not your peerness. Is that okay with you?"

Alun plopped down on the edge of the bed across from Kathy. Relieved and smiling, but not willing to take a chance to hold her once more.

"Oh that's very okay with me. That's why I never told you in the first place. But then I knew the bishop would have to call you by your new title and then I'd be placing on your finger the Rose of Ramsey diamond which is quite a gaudy thing really but you don't have to wear it all the time."

Kathy walked over to him and sat beside him on the bed. They said nothing for a moment, just looked out the window to the island beyond, where seals come to play on a day such as this. Finally, Kathy just had to ask a question.

"If you're a peer of the realm, why do you run a pub in a small town?"

"Well love, it's like this…"

Alun went on to say he wanted to prove himself on his own without his father's money or title influencing anyone. That's how he ended up with the Goat St. Pub. As for being a small town, he explained that it's really the smallest city in the United Kingdom and that it's part of his family's earldom.

Pointing out the balcony doors he added, "That island out there is Ramsey Island. A gift to my country by my family for allowing us to accept the gift of Henry VII whose father, Edmond Tudor, is buried right under where we will take our vows this afternoon."

Kathy was finding it difficult to understand the scope of what Alun was telling her. So she focused on something which she could relate to with ease.

"Won't my nephews and Olivia be thrilled when they hear that their aunt is… by the way what will I become?"

"You will one day become the Countess of Ramsey, your Ladyship. Does that please you?"

"Only if it pleases you," Kathy responded.

"Oh, believe me, it does," Alun answered with relief, taking her into his arms. Then with newly found courage he placed a gentle kiss on her soft lips.

"Your Lordship," she exclaimed as she pushed him off causing him to fall off the bed's edge. She stood over him laughing. "You take liberties with the Countess of Ramsey before the vows, now be off before my father sees you. And by the way, diamonds are a girl's best friend, so don't worry your little head over how gaudy it is."

"Aye, your Ladyship, I don't want to have to face your father," and with a bow he threw open the glass doors and jumped on top of the balcony's stone railing blowing kisses.

"You idiot, stop that, I want to be the Countess, or whatever," she called out.

Alun paused and pretended to lose his balance as Kathy looked on with a mixture of shock and mirth as he righted himself and jumped again down to the balcony.

"Alun, you really must leave now," Kathy insisted.

"I know, love, but your mention of diamonds being a girl's best friend has reminded me of something my mother gave me to present to you."

Kathy sat on the edge of the bed and watched him approach. Alun was removing something from his pocket.

"Thank God it's too small to be a crown, I don't think I could handle being that royal," she joked nervously.

Alun smiled gently at her attempt at humor while holding a small, rectangular, velvet-covered box. He sat himself next to Kathy and opened the lid revealing a gold twelve-pointed-star brooch. Each point was encrusted with diamonds. In the middle was a smooth piece of white Carrara marble in the shape of a trapezoid, surrounded by pearls. He lifted it gently from its silver silk-lined place and placed it into Kathy trembling hands.

While holding her hands, he told her that his mother would be most honored if she were to wear it on her wedding dress. Kathy smiled and told him that it would be an honor and after all she did need something borrowed.

"Oh no love, not something borrowed, perhaps something old, for this is a gift from Mother to her new daughter."

"Her daughter…well I'm honored. And I do need something old as well. How old is the brooch Alun?"

"According to father it was made in the sixteenth century by Michelangelo for the only woman he ever loved, Vittoria Colonna…

Kathy screamed out… "WHAT?"

"I know love, the name is like your own family name. Perhaps you are a descendant of that old Italian family."

"I doubt it. We're just Americans from the mid-west."

"Trust me, I would not want it any other way. Perhaps your father would find the history of this brooch interesting. Is he not teaching about Michelangelo and taking his class to Italy?"

Kathy calmed herself and told him that her father would wish to hear all about it but that he dare not try it on their wedding day or her mom would be most upset. Alun understood. He kissed the hand holding the Michelangelo star called "Caput Mondi," the Head of the World, ran out onto the balcony and began his descent.

As he dropped out of sight, she flung herself backwards onto the bed.

Kathy's head felt like it swirled round and round. Only the knocking at the door brought her back to the moment. She jumped up and quickly placed the brooch into her robe pocket.

"Kathy, what's going on?" yelled Jana through the door.

Kathy skipped to the door and pulled it open "Oh nothing at all dear sisters, nothing at all. Now I'm ready; what comes next?"

Jana and Tricia stared at the bright smiling face of their sister. They entered and went to work on her hair and make-up. Through it all Kathy smiled and joked about what kind of life she would have with Alun running a pub.

By the time the clock struck noon, all was ready. Kathy appeared at the door of her parents' room. Jana and Tricia stood behind her beaming with the success of their efforts. She stepped through the doorway in her grandma's gown and mother's crown. Arthur and Donna were stunned as they came to hug her.

Tears were steaming down Donna's face. "You look like a princess, Kathleen."

"Thanks, but I think a countess will have to do," she laughingly said. "Mom, would you pin this brooch on me? It's the something old I needed and supplied by Alun's mother."

"It's quite lovely dear," Donna said as she attached the pin onto her gown. "It has an antique quality about it, wouldn't you say Arthur?"

"And just wait until you hear about its history, Dad," a smiling Kathy added.

Her parents looked at each other; they chose not to question, but rather enjoy the final moments with their baby daughter. Arthur finally said that it was time. Tricia and Jana, leading the little entourage to the stairs, were dressed in yellow gowns just a shade different than the daffodils which they carried. Daffodils are the national flower of Wales and especially grown at this time of year in honor of the country. Donna and Arthur escorted Kathy down the stairs to her waiting siblings, niece and nephews. They were speechless as she descended the stairs like a radiant light; her crown shooting off rainbow colors as the sun's rays passed through the crystals. Through all the fuss she remained serene and calm, now and then touching the beautiful brooch.

Arthur had made arrangements to transport the rest of the family to the cathedral earlier so his sister and Donna's brother could welcome the Hollywood guests, Arthur's students and Alun's family. This was not to be an ordinary wedding ceremony. The presence of the Bishop of the Diocese of St. David and the Archbishop of Chicago, who was a friend of Arthur's and had received permission to co-preside at the ceremony, certainly made that quite clear. When the parents of Alun arrived it became obvious. The Earl of Ramsey was dressed in the garb of the Order of the Garter which represented the knighthood bestowed upon him by the Queen.

Three carriages pulled up in front of the hotel. Kathy had always wanted a castle wedding at Disney World, so Arthur at least wanted to provide a carriage ride. Kathy entered the first horse-drawn carriage with her parents. On the seat lay her wedding bouquet of white roses. Into the next carriage entered Jana as Matron of Honor with Chris and their sons Connor and Riley. Into the third carriage rode Ron and Tricia with their children Arthur V and Olivia. Kathy looked around and waved at her family. She didn't see John and Rich until she turned back and realized that they were driving the carriage in their kilt tuxedos.

The glistening brooch caught their eye. "So you already have a new piece of jewelry…" they chimed.

She laughed and changed the subject by telling them that she hoped they wouldn't catch a draft. Within five minutes they had arrived at the front of the cathedral.

As the trumpets sounded, a series of sparkling green clouds exploded along the Irish oak beams supporting the ceiling. King Finbar X had arrived with some of the leprechaun clans. So enthralled were the guests at the sight of Alun being escorted by his royally-robed parents, that no one noticed the wee folk's arrival.

The trumpets sounded once more. John and Rich escorted their mother down the aisle to the first pew where her mother and Arthur's mother were seated. They were already in tears and the service had just begun. Donna paused as she reached the pew to extend a greeting to Alun's parents. Alun was in place and next to him was Professor Harold Cornwall whom he asked to be his best man. His local friends served as ushers seating the guests as they arrived.

The trumpets sounded a final time. Jana hastily fluffed up Kathy's veil and train ensuring it lay perfectly. Then the newly-restored organ sounded its mighty pipes as Purcell's *Trumpet Voluntary* rang out through the walls of the ancient shrine. Arthur chose that musical piece to compliment Alun since he had not become a Knight of the Round Table, as his sons had, during the quest of the previous year. Alun had not been part of the ceremony of the joust pledge in Trinity Church of Stratford-upon-Avon when that very piece had been played. Little did Arthur realize that another title was the last thing Alun needed.

The procession began. Connor and Arthur V flanked each side of Riley who held the ring pillow upon which lay the Rose of Ramsey ring and a wedding band of gold engraved with a design said to be a symbol of Michelangelo's family. Once again, they were dressed in their tuxedo kilts and once again, the little boys were handling it better than the adults. Regardless, Jana was worried that Riley might trip or drop the Ramsey family heirloom. Olivia followed the little boys. Her golden gown and long black hair crowned with a wreath of baby's breath created a striking image. Rich, then, John, escorting Alun's cousins followed. By now they were pros at wearing kilts and strode masterfully down the aisle wearing their sporrans this time, just in case. Tricia and Ron followed; then Chris and Jana. Both of the men wore their investiture sash as Knights of the Round Table across their kilt tux. No one except the family knew exactly what the symbol signified. Just as Kathy stepped into the door frame the rays of the sun shifted and shone behind her so it appeared as if she was an angel coming down from heaven. Arthur took his daughter's arm as Alun's eyes bulged and his smile grew. His lady entered every bit a princess. As she processed golden flakes showered her from the beams above, seeming to dissolve before they reached the floor. The wee folk simply had to add a touch to the occasion and Kathy looked up and winked at King Finbar X.

The choir sang beautifully as the bishops entered to begin the service. Ron read from Corinthians II: "Love is kind, love is gentle…"

The words rang true as they had never been heard before. There were so many in that cathedral who knew first hand how powerful the divine gift of love was. As the words were proclaimed Sarah Cornwall looked into the professor's eyes as did Alun into Kathy's, Sean into Grace's and Donna into Arthur's.

The moment came for the exchange of vows. The Bishop of St. David's began:

"Do you Alun Arthur, Viscount of Ramsey, take unto yourself Kathleen Mary Colonna to be your wedded wife; to have and to hold in sickness and in health, in plenty and in want, with honor and with love all the days of your life 'til death do you part?"

As Alun answered boldly his "I do" Arthur almost tumbled off his seat as he grabbed onto Donna. "Viscount of Ramsey! And I was worried that he wasn't knighted. And he's an Arthur also."

Donna answered calmly, "It will be fine Arthur. You will always be my knight in shining armor."

The vows having been concluded with Kathy's resounding "I do," the Archbishop of Chicago called forth Riley, who brought the priceless Rose of Ramsey and the simple gold band which had belonged to Kathy's grandpa Colonna. Alun placed the diamond onto Kathy's finger, "with this ring I thee wed and pledge my love in the name of the Father, and of the Son, and of the Holy Spirit." The sun caught the diamond and it radiated its brilliance. Kathy took the golden band and placed it onto Alun's finger. "With this ring I thee wed and pledge my love and devotion…"

It was done. The bishops proclaimed them husband and wife and gave them permission to kiss while the organ and trumpets sounded and the choir broke into a favorite hymn of both families, *How Great Thou Art*. At its conclusion the bishops introduced the couple.

"My Lord and Lady Ramsey, Lord and Lady Colonna and Honorable guests we present to you for the first time, Lord and Lady Ramsey."

Kathy had insisted the honorary title bestowed on her parents by the king of the leprechauns be used, much to the surprise of all, especially the wee folk who were overjoyed upon hearing it. In thanksgiving to having their realm recognized, the King waved his shillelagh. The light gently filtering through the gigantic rose window at the rear of the nave suddenly burst forth brilliantly and fused one color with another. The nave was illuminated with a spectrum of colors forming arches over the aisle down which Kathy and Alun walked. All in attendance were awed and could not get over how the beauty of the stained glass could create such magnificent light effects. The Colonna Clan, the professor, Sean and Grace, and the drapery lady, Kathleen of Clonmacnoise, knew better, but said nothing.

After the obligatory family photo sessions, the Ramsey and Colonna families were able to join their guests in the refectory or in the tents amongst the ruins of the prelate's palace which Alun's family arranged to have set up. Mercifully, it was a balmy and pleasant evening as the celebration began in earnest. Kathy and Alun, along with their parents, were still standing under the stone arch of the restored ancient monastery refectory. They were greeting the last of the arriving guests.

The hall was buzzing as the Hollywood crowd entered. They were most gracious by allowing Ron and Chris to introduce them to their grandmothers and the rest of their families. Arthur Lovell, the film producer, made a point of speaking with John and Rich about their duties for the upcoming film production so the boys were thrilled beyond words. No matter how truly excited they were, in deference to their sister, they made no mention of it to the family. When the actors, talked to John and Rich, the actors were as excited as the boys, but for a different reason. They were dying to know how the special effects of the falling golden flakes and rainbow arches were created during the service. Much blarney spilled forth from John's mouth in particular as both tried to explain the unexplainable.

The little boys were running about checking out each nook and cranny of the ancient edifice. The children of Arthur's niece and nephew, Samantha, Ashley and Matthew, joined the little boys in the fun. Madison never left Olivia's side, and she would never dream of running about the hall in such a fashion. As the six children ran into an alcove just behind where the cake was displayed, they ran through a cloud of sparkling green smoke.

Arthur V, Connor and Riley came to a dead stop causing Samantha and Matthew to knock them over, kilts and all flying about.

"I don't think we should be here," a very calm Connor announced.

"Right," added young Arthur V as he adjusted the sporran on his kilt. They helped the others up from the floor and quickly left, knowing very well they had stumbled upon the hiding place of Finbar X, King of the Leprechauns. Not a word did they say for they knew how to keep an important secret.

Riley poked his head back into the alcove after all had exited.

"It's okay now, your Majesty. We'll make sure no one else comes in here."

"Thanks lad," came his reply as the glistening shimmer of the Shamrock Crown became visible again.

Finally, the last of the guests arrived. It was Agnes la Straga. Arthur was delighted she made it. As usual, she was dressed in black, this time it was a lovely gown just off the shoulders. About her neck Donna noticed an amulet, one she thought she had seen in the exhibit back in Chicago and on her daughter's gown. When she made mention of its beauty, Agnes verified its historic nature.

"It is lovely isn't it? And it's the only piece of jewelry that we know Michelangelo himself designed for the only woman he ever felt love for."

Arthur's eyes brightened. "Another story in the making to be sure," he was thinking as he introduced her to Kathy and Alun.

Just as Agnes took Kathy's hand she noticed the brooch shimmering on the wedding gown.

"My dear, pardon my stare, but your brooch; it's exactly the same design as the amulet I am wearing."

Alun knew not to explain its origins, not with his new mother-in-law right there, so he just smiled. Kathy however spilled the beans.

"Oh do you like it? It's a gift from Alun's mom. It really fulfilled the something old part of what I should wear. You know- something old, something new, something borrowed, something blue."

"Indeed it does if it's what I think it is, *vero*?"

Kathy leaned into Agnes and whispered that the brooch connections with Michelangelo, but she's not supposed to talk about it now. Then she said aloud, "Perhaps we can chat later this evening after dinner."

"Most assuredly my dear," Agnes responded while turning toward an uneasy Arthur and a wide-eyed Donna. "I am most excited to hear about the tale behind that piece."

"Yes I'm sure we are all interested, but for now let us celebrate," said a controlled Donna through her teeth.

"*Va bene*, see you later Arturo."

Arthur returned an uneasy smile and nod.

Agnes took her place at what Arthur called the Irish connection table. Seated there were Anne Marie and Patrick Ryan of Cranberry Cottage, the Coffeys of Kate Kearny's cottage, the drapery lady of Clonmacnoise, and Bobby, Sean, and Grace.

A blast of trumpets sounded. Those seated at the head table, members of the bridal party, stood. The guests stood. The grandmothers, at the table directly in front of the head table, stood with hankies at the ready as did the Roses. The vicar of the cathedral announced the bishops. They entered in crimson robes and stood at the end of the head table. Alun's parents were announced to a great ovation. Arthur and Donna were introduced to a more American hoot-and-holler reception.

Finally, it was Kathy and Alun's turn. The trumpets flourish resounded as Lord Alun and Lady Kathleen Ramsey were introduced to the accompanying clamor of American hoots and British hip hip hoorays. Once they were seated all others sat.

Kathy leaned over and whispered into Alun's ear.

"Thank goodness, we can eat now. Thanks to your visit this morning I've only had a sip of tea."

Alun smiled saying, "And what a charming visit it was, my rump still hurts from the fall. By the way, my mother is most pleased that you wore the brooch."

Alun's father, the Earl of Ramsay, cleared his throat. The toasts were about to begin. At each place setting was a small crystal goblet filled with golden mead. Each glass was engraved with a large "R" in the center and a smaller "A" and "K" on either side of it. These were the gifts of the wee folk, for weren't those streaks of rainbow light dancing within the goblets?

Kathy noticed an empty chair at their table. It was between Alun's father and her brother Johnny. Just as she was about to ask who was missing, the trumpets flourished once more.

The Earl stood. "Ladies and Gentlemen, His Royal Highness, Prince Harry."

Everyone gasped, including Alun who was totally shocked by the announcement. Arthur Ramsey leaned over and whispered.

"Just a little surprise, son. The Prince, upon hearing of you taking the vows, wanted to drop by to offer the best wishes of the family."

Kathy grabbed onto Alun's arm tightly. "Your dad does mean the Royal Family, of course?"

"Yes, love, but don't worry; it's just Prince Harry who's dropped by."

Kathy gulped, "Right, just Prince Harry."

The applause, as the prince proceeded through the guests, drowned out the whispered conversation. He paused behind Kathy and Alun who turned to face him. Kathy curtsied remarkably well and Alun gave a nod of his head. The prince congratulated them, gave Kathy a peck on the cheek and hugged Alun, whom he knew from attending the same school as children. After taking his seat along with the others the toasts began.

The earl talked about hands reaching across an ocean to bring together two families now bound with a common love for their children. Arthur rose and spoke about a little girl who cried each time she had to leave home to go to class. The Rose, Marilyn, smiled and cried for she knew how true a statement that was. Donna would be distraught over Kathy's tears until she entered the doors of the school where Arthur was principal and Marilyn was the first grade teacher. Then Kathy would become the happiest person on earth, full of smiles and joyful to have in the classroom.

"So now it's our turn to cry as she leaves the family who loves her and yet be happy as well as our Kathleen joins Alun on a new journey."

After the toasts, the pheasant and roast potatoes were served. During the meal the Prince turned to John and Rich.

"You're Kathy's brothers aren't you?" he asked.

"Yes, we are, Your Highness," John replied, suspecting he may have overused the royal title but distracted by what was probably coming next.

"But we've met before. I'm sure of it," continued the Prince. "Now where was that? After all you're from the states."

"Well actually it was right here in Britain, sir."

"Indeed, but where pray tell?"

"Last year I was in the joust at Warwick Castle. You were in the Royal Box…"

"Holy….then that was you who crashed into the box, I remember now," the Prince said as he finished John's explanation. "By Jove that was a great performance, John. And here we are again at your sister's wedding to my pal."

John smiled and thanked the Prince but wanted the subject dropped for he knew that being such a sportsman Prince Harry would continue to question him about weapons used and armor and so forth. He wasn't about to give the true details and had to play along with the tournament as a performance. He decided to change the subject and chatted about the film he and Rich had just finished with their father.

"Truly that's you also. The whole lot of us just finished seeing your movie with my grandmother, the Queen. She thought it was quite amusing."

"My family and I are honored." Then John turned to his younger brother. "Richie, the Prince liked the movie."

Prince Harry bent over and gave a wave to Rich which ended in a thumbs up gesture.

After dinner, the Prince bade farewell. He personally greeted everyone at the head table and then went to each guest table to extend a greeting.

When he arrived at the tables where Arthur's students were seated the girls became jittery and bubbled with excitement.

"Jessica he's coming our way! What should we do?" a flustered Kristin asked.

"Just smile but I think we all need to stand and curtsy like John and Rich's sister did."

To the relief of all, the Prince had asked that everyone remain seated so that he could better circle the table to offer the bests wishes of his family. As the glasses were refilled with mead and the dessert was served, the Prince slipped out into the night.

Now it was Kathy and Alun's turn to greet the guests again as well as Arthur and Donna and Alun's parents. Donna headed for the Irish connection table to chat with Agnes. Arthur first went to visit with Maura Kennedy and his students. Since they just arrived the night before, he expected them to still be jet-lagged but found them quite chipper and ready for the flight to Italy. It was difficult to discuss the itinerary; the students were still buzzing about the Prince and the wedding and the movie stars. Never in their wildest dreams did they ever expect to attend a wedding in an ancient cathedral, let alone meet Hollywood stars and authentic royalty. Anything that would happen in Italy would be anticlimactic, they thought.

Arthur had given up trying to establish firm plans other than confirming the departure time from Cardiff airport. The dancing started and soon everyone was filing out into the moonlight and walking over to the tent where the band had set up.

Alun and Kathy were radiant in their first dance together as Alun demonstrated his sense of rhythm. They floated across the dance floor. Soon each of Kathy's brothers took their turn and her sisters did the same with Alun. Then the parents had their turn. When it was Arthur's turn, one could hear Kathy's grandmothers crying in the background.

"Dad, this is so wonderful," Kathy began as Arthur smiled and choked back his emotions.

"Oh by the way, Alun and I have been talking with Sean and Grace. They postponed their honeymoon so that they could attend our wedding. Now they're off to Italy like us. We're going to meet up in Capri. Isn't that great?"

"I guess so. What do Alun and Sean think about it?"

"Oh they're all for it. We're not teenagers Dad; we'll have plenty of time to be together."

Arthur was fine with their plans until she dropped the other shoe.

"We thought it would be great to end our trip with a family gathering before we all have to go home." Kathy now began to choke up. "You know… you and Mom back to America, the boys to London, me to Wales."

Arthur hadn't even thought of the prospect that Kathy would be staying in Wales and now stopped dead in the middle of the dance floor.

"Dad, keep dancing. Everyone is looking," she whispered while tugging on his arm.

"I hadn't…I mean your mother and I had no idea that you would make your home in Britain."

"I know, but he's a peer. He has to be here some time, doesn't he?"

"I have no clue about the responsibility of a peer. Have you told your mother yet?"

"Oh yes. We both did. She's already planning Christmas in Wisconsin and you guys are coming here for the summer. Anyway, you and the boys will be here quite a bit with the movie making and all won't you? Rich and John haven't said anything to me but that producer fellow was talking with them for a long time. Didn't you notice?"

They took a couple of more twirls to the delight of the crowd but Arthur's heart was not in it. His little girl was going to live an ocean away from them. His head now spun and not because of the dips and turns either. The news that the boys would be starting so soon, as there could be no other reason for such a lengthy conversation right now, was sinking in as well. To relay his true feelings about her residing in the UK, and losing Rich and John to the studio, he decided to get back to the Capri gathering idea.

"You're right." He said. "We should be here a lot over the next year. Now what about this meeting in Capri? What were you saying?"

Kathy reiterated. Since they were meeting Sean and Grace in Capri it would be a great chance, since Arthur would already be in Italy with the boys, to come down for a visit before everyone had to get back.

"Well, you know" Kathy said. "get back to their regular lives, jobs, school, making movies, whatever."

Mercifully, the song about kisses, butterflies, fathers and daughters had ended and the grandmothers and Donna were crying once more. Arthur didn't notice any of this. He had already begun to plan this final family gathering. He escorted Kathy off the floor smiling to his students, bantering with the Hollywood crowd about his lack of grace and so forth.

"Kathy, please get Alun. I'll get your mother, brothers and sisters, and meet you at the cake table. Everyone will think we're there to cut the cake."

Kathy looked at her father with puzzlement, kissed him on the cheek and scanned the room for her new husband.

"Okay we'll meet you by the cake. This is just like a mystery movie isn't it?"

Off she went, and she was stopped at every step by Alun's family or her own to say a word or two about her future or how beautifully the ceremony was conducted and so forth.

A mystery indeed, Arthur was thinking as he searched for Donna. If Kathy only knew what kind of mystery adventure he was already involved with, this Capri meeting plan would seem like a walk in the park.

"Ah, there you are Donna," he said as he slipped her arm into his as if they were about to go down the aisle again. "Helen, how wonderful to see you again. I hope you don't mind if I steal my wife away for a moment; we have a cake to cut, I'm told. Oh and by the way Lovell, I'd like to speak with you later about what you discussed with my sons."

"Great, I never dreamed you would have the time," answered Arthur Lovell, the film producer.

As Arthur and Donna made their way to the cake table, they gathered their children. Soon they made a small semi circle from the alcove to the cake table.

Arthur explained Kathy's idea about meeting at Capri.

"So as long as the boys and I will already be in Italy, it only seems natural that the rest of the family should come to Capri as well. After all, your mother needs a little rest after all of this is over."

The family, as usual when first hearing a brilliantly conceived plan by their father, stood motionless and silent. Eyes rapidly met other sets of eyes as each watched for a reaction from one of their siblings. It was, however, Alun who first spoke.

"Dad, that's a great idea. We're to meet Grace and Sean in Capri anyway. Listen, my folks share a little place in Tuscany with a group of their friends. I'm sure they wouldn't mind if I offered it to you for your gathering until the end of our…well you know…"

Alun began to stumble over his words as he spoke of the honeymoon in front of Kathy's parents. Calling his father-in-law Dad had already caused quite a silent stir in the group.

John came to his rescue in his usual blunt and forthright manner. "Alun, you can say it, come on you can do it…say honeymoon."

The blushing Alun cracked a smile and soon everyone in the circle broke into laughter. He turned to John and gave him a hug.

"Thanks Johnny."

Alun winked at Kathy and got down to business. He explained that the getaway was located near a small town named Ponte Buggianese in central Tuscany and very convenient to Florence, Siena and Pisa if they'd like to do some sightseeing.

"Then by the time our HONEYMOON is near its end you could make your way down to Sorrento and ferry across to Capri. There's a lovely hotel in Sorrento and we would have a great celebration before we said our good-byes."

The plan excited everyone until the part about it really being a time to say good-bye was mentioned. Of all people it was Donna who ignored the true reason for the gathering and got to other practical aspects of such a plan.

"Alun, dear, we're a big family. Do you think this getaway place will fit everyone?" Then to Ron and Chris she asked when they would have to get back to their jobs.

Her eldest answered that he had rolled all his vacation time together as had Tricia so they had the rest of the month off. Chris echoed that he and Jana had done the same.

"Well then, it seems work is not an issue. Now Alun, about the accommodation size..." Donna continued.

"It seems to me that the villa can hold upwards of twenty people as I remember it. And Dad and the boys won't be there nor will Kathy and I. But I've only been there one time. I'll ask my parents to be sure."

"Did you say villa, Alun?" asked Jana.

"Well yes but it's just a big house really, nothing fancy. It has a pool and gardens and vineyards. Oh great. I'm sounding pompous aren't I?"

"Just a trifle, but don't worry about it. I think we can get use to it," Jana answered with a grin. "Anyway, the pool will occupy the kids and the gardens will be a wonderful place to walk and reminisce about this wonderful day."

As Alun was offering contrition, Donna was doing the math. She determined that indeed the family would only number nine. Then almost coyly she approached Alun and took him by the hands.

"Since this getaway could hold twenty do you think we could invite my sister, Marilyn, and Anita?"

"Oh, you mean the Roses? That shouldn't be a problem at all."

Planting a kiss on Alun's cheek and patting it, Donna turned and sashayed back to Arthur who took the opportunity to get in a few words of his own. He pointed out that Ponte, as his family referred to the town near which the villa was located, is the ancestral home of the Naninni branch of the family on his mother's side. It was actually to be part of the tour and would be visited by his students. He suggested that everyone might come to the site when they got there. Then he talked about Capri. It was to be a side trip after the excursion to Pompeii and just before the students' departure from Rome. He suggested that everyone plan to be in Capri when they were there.

"We could do the Blue Grotto visit together. Then after I drop off the students at Rome's Da Vinci Airport, I would return to the family."

The plans were made, and overhearing all of this were one little king and the Chieftain, Lord Schaughnessy.

The newlyweds left the circle to retrieve Alun's parents and when they returned, the cake was really cut by Viscount Alun and Lady Kathy Ramsey. After the ceremonial cutting Arthur took Alun and Kathy aside.

"Alun, you said that you had a story to tell about the brooch Kathy is wearing. Would you be willing to meet with me and Agnes la Straga outside of the Bishop Palace ruins?

"Why certainly…Dad, but what's so important about a piece of jewelry?" Alun asked.

"I'm not sure, but if Agnes is correct about its origins then that shiny piece of gold may be able to help us quite a bit," Arthur answered without really explaining a thing.

Kathy voiced her concern that Mom would be upset with solving mysteries during the wedding, but she also felt that if the brooch could help in whatever her father was up to, then the meeting should take place. Arthur went to find Agnes while the bride and groom discretely made their way outside to the ruins.

Arthur and Agnes were standing at the crumbling wall of the ancient building illuminated by one of the torches set about so that the guests might easily make their way from the reception to the dancing tent. As Kathy and Alun came up to them, Agnes expressed her profound regrets that they had been asked to leave their reception.

"But you do understand that what you are wearing may be invaluable to what your father and I are working on," Agnes said.

Kathy had no idea of what that *thing* was but her father assured her that Alun's family story about the jewelry would help with the exhibit's goal to present the work of Michelangelo while demonstrating his connection to the Medici family.

"Then my dear may I take a closer look at the brooch?" asked Agnes.

As Kathy took off the brooch Alun was asked to tell his story. The story Alun told was more than a history lesson; it substantiated the connection between Michelangelo and the Medici family.

Chapter 13: Burning of the Vanities

The small jet was sitting on the tarmac of Cardiff International Airport. Neither the students nor his assistant Maura Kennedy, the chaperone, had ever walked out onto a tarmac. Arthur, was the exception. It was quite the experience as the engines roared and they climbed the metal staircase into the cabin. The student group almost filled the cabin area as they boarded.

While Arthur was off to Italy, Donna and the Roses began their own tour, taking the family to the locations in Arthur's new book about the Thorn and Roses' adventure in the Excalibur quest the previous year. Kathy, Alun, Grace, and Sean were on their way to London. After visiting the exhibit they would begin their separate honeymoons in Italy. The four would come together on the Isle of Capri along with the entire Colonna clan for their farewell celebration.

As the plane skirted the coast of France, Arthur and Maura Kennedy were discussing the details of the tour and whether the kids would want to visit the Duomo first or go to the famous shopping galleria across the Piazza from the cathedral. They were fairly certain that the indoor multi-storied mall would be the choice, so they planned on lunch there and then go off to the Duomo. After shopping, they felt the students would be ready for Roselli's presentation in the shadow of Da Vinci's famous painting of the Last Supper before their own supper.

Arthur was arranging several maps and guide brochures on the tray in front of him when a hand reached over and tapped him on the shoulder. So intensely was he reviewing the maps with Maura that it startled him. He jerked around so quickly to see who it was that he knocked several brochures into the aisle.

Scusi Arturo," an apologetic Agnes said as she leaned into the aisle at the same time Arthur did to help pick up the brochures. Their heads collided with a bang.

"*Santa Maria degli Angeli*, that hurt!" cried out Arthur, who, catching himself using Italian holy names in an almost profane manner, quickly started to rub his head and apologize.

It was too late. His sons had witnessed the entire incident and were now craning their necks to see what that Italian woman was doing with their father.

All they could see were pamphlets in the aisle and Arthur vigorously rubbing his head.

"It's Agnes again," commented John.

"Yeah, what is she doing traveling with us anyway?" questioned Rich as if he never heard of the plan change in which she would accompany the group from this point on.

John gave him one of those brotherly looks of "Get real. She's supposed to be here."

The facial expression registered and Rich made an effort to justify his remark by cloaking it in his concern that she was flirting again, a bit too much even for an Italian.

"Rich, you're an idiot. Dad is a big boy and can handle himself even if what you infer is true which, by the way, is quite off base."

"You may think so, but if Mom were here I wonder how she'd see that tap on the shoulder and clashing of heads and the oh-so-sweet *Scusi, Arturo* bit." This of course was performed with great melodrama.

"You're full of it…hey look, there's the Matterhorn," John exclaimed.

With that the two boys leaned into the window to catch a spectacular view of the Alps as they flew over Switzerland.

In Rich's mind that Agnes la Straga woman, who tried to be too much of a young Sophia Loren and therefore a threat to his mother, was worth keeping an eye on.

If they had stopped for a moment more perhaps John would have changed his viewpoint. Agnes was now dabbing Arthur's head with a wet napkin which she had dipped into her water glass. Maura sat trapped by the window on one side and Arthur on the other, unable to help.

"I am so sorry Arturo. You are bleeding no?"

"Just a little. You know, you have a hard head," Arthur kidded.

"So Roselli tells me almost daily," she commented back with a sheepish smile. "Would you like me to moisten the napkin again?"

Arthur said, "No, I think I might live to see another day."

They laughed aloud. This time both of the boys exchanged questioning glances as they looked away from the Alps to the view of the two leaning into the aisle and laughing.

"For this I am glad, Arturo. I just thought perhaps we should review the lesson Roselli will probably present in Milan and what to do for the rest of the day there. Also I think we should review the information which Alun gave us regarding the family brooch which your daughter Kathy wore at their wedding. He saw merit in her proposal and excused himself. Arthur crossed the aisle and sat next to Agnes.

Arthur opened his shoulder briefcase bag. In the bag were the documents Agnes had given to him as well as the translated copy of the St. Peter's Dome drawing with Michelangelo's hand-written notes on the back. Before Arthur would pursue the legend of the Magi ring or follow up on Alun's revelation, he needed to ensure the tourist part of the trip was in place without a flaw. Having reviewed the itinerary and confirming the Galleria, Cathedral and Da Vinci's *Last Supper* Painting stops in Milan he turned to Agnes.

Agnes and Arthur focused their attention on the documents, Agnes' notes from Alun's story, and the photos of the brooch. Arthur spread out the journal page of Marsilio Ficino. The page dealt with the aftermath of Piero's expulsion from Florence and the rise of Frate Savonarola as a political and spiritual leader who would lock horns the Pope Alexander VI, infamous member of the Borgia family. As they discussed the dark events after Piero Medici was expelled from Florence, a pall of dark clouds spread across the Lombardy plains below as the plane began its approach into Milan's air space. Turbulence caused the captain to turn on the seat belt sign. As the plane began a circular holding pattern, only John and Rich seemed to notice the same cloud formations and distant mountain peaks being passed over and over again.

The students exhausted by the wedding and meeting Hollywood movie stars were now talking about the swimming time Mr. C had promised them in the Adriatic Sea and Mediterranean Sea. They realized that these coastal visits would not be for several days, but that didn't matter.

Arthur and Agnes were absorbed with Ficino's journal writings on the Savonarola takeover of Florence's government which, after Piero Medici's departure, became dysfunctional and incapable of governing.

Within six months the Frate had stepped into the void and assumed the role of political and spiritual leader. The art world and that of teachers and writers like me were now in panic. The poet Angelo Poliziano had left the Palazzo Medici for the last time shortly after Piero's fall from power along with mine. We rented a small house near the Duomo and not far from where Sandro Botticelli and Francesco Granacci live on the same street. –Marsilio Ficino.

"Marsilio, you are still sitting where I left you," an agitated Angelo Poliziano said running into the upstairs apartment and gasping for air as if he were to collapse at any moment. At forty years old he would soon leave his friends and enter eternal life.

"Angelo, why the panic in your voice today?" Marsilio calmly asked. "Has Piero returned with an army?"

"Hardly. We just said our good-byes to Emperor Charles and now we have to warm up to that fanatic from Ferrara. As if that wasn't cause enough for any scholar or artist to panic, I have just learned of a calamitous plan that our beloved Savonarola has devised."

"Keep your voice down," cautioned Ficino. "You visit the marketplace too often and hear too much gossip, my friend."

"This is not gossip. Granacci himself told me of the plan."

Marsilio jumped up from his chair. "What, Francesco has joined the likes of that…that friar who is bent on purifying not only the church but all of Florence for the image he wants created?"

Angelo calmed his friend, who normally was the picture of control. He explained that their friend and colleague, while not in league with the Frate, was forced to take on a job or be ousted from Florentine artistic life. Marsilio asked him what kind of job an artist could take with the friar and not be in league with him. The poet, still shaking, revealed Granacci's role as he himself had explained it.

"Marsilio, our friend is tormented and emotionally drained. He was beside himself as he relayed his story of what he had to do for Savonarola in order to be saved from damnation."

"Angelo, for heaven sake! Get on with what he said. What is his job?"

"Savonarola's plan was to end the Carnivale of the Medici, which was no surprise. But a new celebration was to take its place, one which would be solemn and moral and cleansing. Granacci was to create the decorations for the celebration which will end with the Burning of the Vanities."

Marsilio's heart was caught in his throat as he asked what Angelo meant by the term, Burning of the Vanities. He felt that he already knew what it meant.

Angelo explained that the friars were organizing bands of children and youths. These bands would scour the city for unneeded, immoral, inappropriate and profane works of art, poems, and books. No one would be safe. The youths have the right to enter any school, hospital, church property, artist's studios, citizens' homes and business or governmental offices. If the owner refused to give up the sinful or vain item, they would be listed and later taken away by force.

"Ultimately, these given or confiscated books, manuscripts, poems, and works of art would be thrown on a pyre and purified in flames of destruction," the exhausted and now weeping poet concluded.

"And he uses youths and children to make such abominable decisions," Marsilio said through tears of his own.

Taking hold of the situation he threw on his cloak and went for the door. He was off to warn their friends. When he got to Sandro Botticelli's studio, it was in shambles. The aged artist himself was throwing his drawings and unfinished works into a pile. Already a recognized accomplished painter, his works such as the *Birth of Venus* and *Springtime* had been acclaimed works demonstrating the blending of Christian and Classical thought. None of that mattered now; not with the bands of youths scouring the city.

Marsilio grabbed his friend, trembling from head to toe. He looked at the pile on the floor.

"God of mercy and love, dear friend. These are masterpieces you throw onto this pile."

"They are an abomination to God and man, Marsilio. The Frate has said so and he is of God and does God's work."

"Sandro Botticelli, get a hold of yourself," the defiant scholar shouted. "Just because some over-zealous friar deems classical art immoral does not make it so. Do you think our friend Michelangelo believes in such nonsense as burning works of art and scholarly books?"

Were Marsilio to truly understand the torment of Michelangelo's soul he would have learned that the one who would soon be called *Il Divino,* the divine one, constantly struggled to bring to life the truth in reverent works and classical thought.

Botticelli fell to the floor. In his hands he held sketches showing a work similar to his mythological themes from earlier years.

Marsilio took the sketches gently from his friend's hands as he slumped in a trance-like state staring at his life's works in a heap on the stone floor.

"Sandro, what Michelangelo has done to bring dignity and grace to masculinity, you have done with the female form. It is a thing of beauty, not a sinful act."

Botticelli sprung to life.

"Michelangelo, we must send a letter to him and warn him not to return to Florence. He is safer in Rome."

He immediately went to his workbench, took out paper and quill, and began to write.

"Here take this and send it with all speed. You know how defiant our friend can be. His temper will destroy him here. He must know that even the lovely nudes of what they call the Botticelli angels and cherubs is considered obscene."

Marsilio understood the aging artist's concern. He took the note and advised Botticelli to take but a few of his works to the pyre in the Piazza de Signoria and hide the rest. He departed to see to his other friends and Angelo. The famous poet never lived to see the first Burning of the Vanities which took place in 1497. As grief-stricken as Marsilio was, he gave thanks that his friend Poliziano hadn't witnessed the abomination and that Michelangelo heeded their advice and stayed in Rome.

There was a sudden jolt and the plane dropped and leveled again causing all aboard to experience their stomachs in a manner usually reserved for the plunge down the roller coaster of a theme park. It was only that feeling which could have brought Arthur back from his thoughts of Renaissance Italy.

"Agnes, that's the year Michelangelo finished the *Bacchus* which was rejected by the Cardinal. Could Cardinal Riarrio have been influenced by Savonarola? After all, were not the Frate's thoughts along the lines that those who participated in what he thought to be sexual excesses, or even gambling, should be burned at the stake?"

Agnes felt it was the artist rather than the prelate who was most affected by the Frate Savonarola's teaching. She pointed out it was at this point that he took commissions to paint two Madonnas, one, the Manchester Madonna, they had seen at the National Gallery in London a short time ago. More importantly it was during this year that he accepted the commission to sculpt from white Carrara marble what would become known as the most famous religious work in marble, probably in history, *The Pieta* of St. Peter's in Rome.

They discussed how the events leading to the burning of the vanities connected with the legend of the Magi ring. Adding to that discussion, Agnes laid across the tray her photos of the Ramsey brooch.

"The question is," she began. "How does this piece of jewelry link Michelangelo to the legend?

"Good question Agnes," commented Arthur. "The fact that it came to the Ramsey family by way of Mary, Queen of Scots who in turn received it from her mother-in-law, Catherine de Medici, Queen of France, might hold the answer."

Agnes was reflecting on Arthur's premise when the plane's announcement bell interrupted their discussion. The captain announced that their flight had been diverted due to an unexpected weather front.

They would be landing in Florence instead of Milan. A loud moan of disappointment from the students swelled throughout the cabin. Arthur heard the girls crying out that they would never see the fashion capital and the guys were just complaining about having to be on the small plane even longer.

"Agnes, you will have to excuse me. I must get with Maura. We'll need to find lodging for these kids and decide what to do about Milan."

"*Certemente Arturo*, I understand. But one other point must I make. Roselli…what about Anselmo?"

Arthur threw up his hands as he sat down. Whatever Roselli planned to present could probably be done elsewhere should they not be able to return to Milan. He would call the curator when they landed and decide then. The most important issue was getting the students lodged somewhere.

"Then we'll be able to delve into Alun's history lesson and figure out where Roselli fits."

Off he went to meet with Maura, stopping on the way to speak with his sons about helping to quiet the students' concerns, especially regarding shopping.

"Perhaps you can spread the word that Florence is the capital of leather goods and gold jewelry."

"We'll get right on it, Dad" they replied and in a flash they started to work the cabin.

In no time at all the bumpy ride smoothed out along with the concerns of the students. The least of their issues was lodging so they weren't bothered as the plane flew over the vineyards of Tuscany. The rerouting had become an adventure for them.

They left the pall of clouds over Lombardy and entered the sunshine of the land of Michelangelo and the Medici. The plane landed at Aero Porto di Peretola without further incidents. Once again, they would walk across the tarmac in the open and make their way to the terminal where Arthur anticipated contacting Roselli and CIE International Tours. Through their connections he hoped to find the extra days of lodging he needed in Florence. The attendant opened the cabin door and the staircase was wheeled up to the doorway. Once again apologies were made prior to leaving the plane about the rerouting and directions were given to the help counter in the terminal.

The wafting in of the warm Italian summer air gave those aboard their first hint that sweaters would not be needed in Florence. The cool breezes of the United Kingdom would eventually be missed as the days became warmer and even hot, but for now it was a welcome feeling. Sweaters and jackets were quickly stowed in backpacks as all made ready to disembark. It would be Rich and John who would lead the group off the plane as John had had the experience of being at the airport before when he arrived to begin his studies at the University of Florence the semester before joining Rich at Oxford.

The boys tried to keep the students, many who were of their age, in control so as not to have them running about the tarmac as they rejoiced in being free and on land once more.

Ryan was beyond their control as he romped about the girls pulling them this way and that way. He laughed and skipped and joked about how the girls should watch out for those Italian men.

"You know they haven't come into political correctness as yet," warned Ryan. "They will come up to you girls and suddenly you will feel a pinch."

The girls were appalled at his attempt to demonstrate. Jessica made it clear to him that since he was not Italian and was a boy of the twenty-first century he should know better. Put in his place, Ryan joined the group as they followed John to the terminal. Turning to Danny, John confided that he was delighted Ryan had gotten heat from the girls who normally fawned over him. Danny, who himself vied for such attention, was most pleased with such a development.

Getting through customs was accomplished without incident and that was a good omen as far as Arthur was concerned. He and Donna had a horrific security experience upon leaving Wales a few years ago. Going through a security check still conjured up that memory. The original security trauma began in Wales. Marilyn, Anita, and Nancy had passed through the security point and were seated on the other side watching the process they had just gone through. Arthur and Donna placed their carryon bags on the belt to be screened and inspected.

Suddenly, the security person alerted others to look at the screen. Arthur and Donna were told to wait on the opposite side of the screen. One of the guards questioned them about attempting to carry weapons on board a plane. They denied any such attempt and asked what such talk had to do with them. The guard insisted that they tell the truth and in doing so things would go easier for them. On the fifty-degree day, sweat poured down Arthur's forehead. Donna was close to panic. The other Roses were stunned with disbelief as their friends were threatened with being taken to an interrogation room.

One of the guards asked why they had brought a sword in their carry-on bag. Arthur told them the only swords they had were wooden ones for their grandsons and these had been placed in the checked baggage. The guard would not relent. Donna was holding back tears. Arthur was horrified with the possibility of being arrested. Finally, an idea popped into his head. He asked Donna where she had packed Johnny's souvenir, a miniature Excalibur sword stuck in a stone. She said she didn't pack it at all. Knowing that he hadn't packed it either, he told the guard the story of the paper weight. The guards, and the Roses, were greatly relieved. The souvenir was taken out of the carry-on bag. Arthur ran it down to the check-in area where their bags were being processed and placed it in the checked baggage. By the time he got back, Donna was being consoled by the Roses and they were about to board.

Avoiding a similar experience at Italian customs gave Arthur a sense of relief as they walked into the main lobby. To add to that relief, Arthur saw a uniformed driver holding a card. It read, "CIE Tours Colonna

Group." God bless Mary Pat, Arthur petitioned. CIE Tours had been told of the rerouting and had come to their rescue. The driver, who would be their guide as well, invited Arthur to follow him to the bus. His name was Ambrogio Camadoli. Arthur found his English to be fluent with a touch of the poetic rhythm Italians blend into English as they speak it. Ambrogio's Italian-English brought back another memory.

He remembered his college Italian language professor advising his students to practice the language by having a conversation with someone who could speak Italian. Arthur asked his grandmother if she would help him. She was pleased to do so. However, whenever he would read an article in Italian or try to converse, she would laugh. To her, it was funny to hear Italian spoken with an American accent.

Camadoli told Arthur about the hotel he reserved for them. Since summer is the height of the tourist season, there were few hotels left with enough empty rooms to accommodate a group the size of Arthur's. The reserved hotel was smaller than what he may be used to. On the other hand, he explained, it was within walking distance to all the famous sites of Florence, including the Uffizi Gallery along the Arno River and Ponte Vecchio with its many jewelry shops. Arthur thanked him profusely for saving them. He was certain the hotel would be fine for their needs.

Having made his assurances, Arthur got his brood aboard the bus and Ambrogio sped off down the A11. It would lead them directly into Florence and become the Viale Francesco Redi. As they made their way into the city, Arthur had a moment to call Anselmo Roselli. Agnes, sitting next to him, was interested in hearing how Anselmo would react to the news. Maura sat across the aisle from them. The students were congregated in the back, marveling at the sites seen through the windows. There was no answer, so he and Agnes began to plan the day. Looking at his watch, he determined the day would be totally unsuccessful until they fed the troops.

Informing Ambrogio of the need to feed his students, the driver took a turn onto Viale Fratelli Rosselli. This, he informed Arthur, would lead them into Viale Filippo Strozzi. "Once past the ancient Fortress da Basso, it would be a short distance into center city where there is a very good restaurant across the street from the Duomo of Santa Maria del Fiore."

Arthur barely heard anything about the restaurant. He was focused on the name of the street called Viale Rosselli.

"Good grief Agnes, we can't even get away from Roselli when we drive down a street."

Agnes laughed and pointed out that the street name had two S's in its name.

"Not that this would matter," she added. "Names often change over the centuries for a variety of reasons as they are adapted to fit the times."

"You offer no comfort whatsoever, Signora."

"*Mi dispiacere, Arturo.* However, may I suggest that you look to your right? That is San Lorenzo, the church where Cosimo Medici is buried and to your left is the Palazzo Medici."

Arthur quickly took to the microphone and called upon his students to look out their windows.

"Tomorrow, we begin to actually walk in Michelangelo's footsteps, but first to lunch."

The cheers were deafening.

Those cheers had hardly subsided when the bus pulled up alongside the Duomo. Even though Ambrogio drove a mini-bus, he deemed it prudent to get off at the Duomo and walk down the very narrow Via Ricasoli to the restaurant. Hunger pangs or not, here they were at the very spot were the Medici brothers, Lorenzo, and Giuliano were attacked. The latter was murdered within its walls on that April day of 1478. Here is the shrine where the Ghirlandaio brothers, who operated the *bottega*, demonstrated their gift for painting. Here the famed Donatello's bronze doors still gleamed on the *Battistero de San Giovanni,* the Baptistery of St. John the Baptist, Patron Saint of Florence.

After a short stroll down the street they arrived at their destination where they saw a line forming from an alley-like walkway running along the building. Through the window facing the street, they saw people enjoying what Italians call "slow food."

Slow food is a movement to bring back traditional dining during which people talk with each other and enjoy what they are eating. For those waiting for the dining experience, it could be a staggeringly long wait.

Agnes offered to make herself useful. She explained in fluent Italian to the hostess that the students had just arrived after a harrowing flight from London. The hostess assured her a long table to fit the entire group would soon be available. In such a situation, it was natural for Arthur to create a teachable moment. He reminded his students that the street on which they stood saw the likes of Michelangelo, the Medici brothers, Granacci,

Botticelli and so many others walking on its pavement some five hundred years ago.

"Try to imagine them walking from the Duomo, where we disembarked, to eat at a place like this. This inn has been here for centuries and the building even longer than that," he began. "Wouldn't it be interesting to know if this was the street on which was located the shed in which the *David* was carved?"

The question went unanswered as they were called to enter.

It was Johnny's turn to shine as he had dined in many Florentine restaurants during his months of study in the city. This place, however, had not been one of them. Though not excessively expensive, it was beyond a student's budget. This meal was included in the tour price and Arthur was prepared to cover *il conte*, the bill.

John explained the various dishes listed, calamari in particular. He explained that the dish was squid prepared in olive oil, garlic and breading. It was his favorite snack food in Italy. A platter of calamari to share was ordered, along with a variety of pasta dishes and Tuscan minestrone soup. It was a feast. It would be served, course by course, in traditional style. There was no anxiety to turn over the tables to the next group.

When the calamari was brought out however, rather than being breaded it had been steamed or boiled, perhaps marinated before hand. The tiny tentacle creatures looked like the small squid they were. There was a gasp of horror as the students saw the dish. Johnny jumped in to counter the revulsion with humor before any of Arthur's students became ill. He picked up one of the creatures from the appetizer platter. It was pliable and rubbery to the touch.

In an instant, it had become a talking creature of the sea inviting those around the table to have a taste of his relatives.

"Better to taste and enjoy than live with them," that's what he had the creature saying.

It worked. The girls and Ryan squealed and laughed and the guys ridiculed and mimicked the creature. The calimari was tasted, followed by a piece of bread dipped in olive oil and grated Romano cheese. There may not have been an overwhelming conversion to the taste of calamari that day but it certainly was a day in which even food proved to be humorous.

The meal was consumed with much laughter and story telling. Arthur led his group back to the piazza San Giovanni in front of the Duomo. There they were to meet Ambrogio who would take them to the bus.

When they crossed the Via dei Cerretani they couldn't find Ambrogio and the bus was indistinguishable from the many others pulled up next to the Duomo. Huge crowds of young people carrying various banners, announcing where they were from, were gathering on the Piazza San Giovanni. They stood directly before the stairs on which Michelangelo would lounge with friends to talk idly of art, life, and love. The students began talking with other students around them. They learned that the young people were from all parts of Europe and had come for a Youth Rally celebrating, *Lo Spirito ci invia,* the Spirit comes to each of us. Today was the culminating event beginning with a prayer service in the Duomo.

Before Arthur had time to discuss the event with anyone, his students were coming to him arm in arm with students from England, Ireland, France, Germany, Poland, and Italy. John brought along a couple of lovely lasses named Maureen and Kara. Rich had two guys in tow from Italy. Franco and Luigi were students at the University of Florence. Jessica brought Michelle and Antoine from the French group to be introduced. Soon Arthur was surrounded by a host of well wishers, all inviting him and his group to accompany them to the rally. Arthur and Maura were impressed that their students were so eager to be part of the celebration. Ambrogio was forgotten and the American group, as they were now called, became part of the rally. No sooner than the decision was made to accept the invitations than the gigantic doors of the Duomo opened.

Four acolytes robed in white stood on either side of the double doors through which the Archbishop of Florence passed, followed by guest clergy. Each had a turn welcoming the assembled youths in a variety of languages. The assembly was told the service would be conducted in Latin, English, and Italian. Another white-robed server brought forth a large book bound in golden metal. The Archbishop called upon the assembly to bow their heads and pray. In an instant hundreds of chattering students became quiet as field mice. The Archbishop then chanted in Latin.

> *Gloria in Excelsis Deo. Et in terra pax…*
> Glory to God in the highest and on earth peace…
> We gather to praise thee, to bless thee, to adore thee, to glorify thee, and to thank thee O Lord God, heavenly King.
> And today we pray as we do in every prayer through our Lord, Jesus Christ who lives and reigns with you and the Holy Spirit One God forever and ever.

A resounding sung AMEN swept across the piazza and Arthur was delighted to hear his students had joined the others. A blast of trumpets was heard from within the Duomo, followed by the sound of the organ. Resounding through the Duomo and spilling onto the piazza a melodic and familiar hymn from Arthur's own youth, *Veni Creator Spiritu*, flowed.

Maureen and Kara arranged for the little American contingency to process directly behind Ireland. In turn, Franco and Luigi made sure that Italy's rather large representation followed them. Once arranged, they processed into the Duomo.

Upon entering, acolytes distributed a small lighted votive candle to each member of each national group. Each candle had a label with the title of the ralley, *Lo Spirito ci invia,* flanked by the symbol of the pope on one side and a fleur-de-lis, symbol of Florence, on the other.

"Ah the Medici has not been forgotten to history," thought Arthur as he received his candle and saw the lily symbol.

It was the same symbol as on the bronze ball of the coat of arms of the Medici Palazzo which had been burned by the lightning strike on the eve of Lorenzo de Medici's death. His students recognized the symbol from their visit to *The World of Michelangelo and the Medici* exhibit. It was the same symbol given to the Medici by the King of France to be used on the Medici coat of arms and for Florence.

Once everyone had gathered in the pews, the votive candles were held high and swayed as the assembly sang a hymn. It looked like a sea of light with wave after wave washing up on the shore. Never had his students participated in a service of such magnitude, yet so personally uplifting and moving. He saw their faces glow in the candle light like Botticelli angels, but they also glowed with the joy so often missing from the spiritual life of young people.

That same look could be seen on the adults accompanying the youth and even on the faces of Agnes, and Maura Kennedy.

The Archbishop of Canterbury, the President of the World Council of Churches and the Cardinal-Archbishop of Firenze, on behalf of the Holy Father, told the youths they held a light — not only the light they elevated to heaven, but the light within their hearts. They called upon them not to fear sharing that light of faith, truth, and hope with others.

Later, when the candles were re-lighted near the end of the service, they were reminded of their roll in the future of civilization and the cause for world peace and understanding. After the final blessing, the recessional began. Arthur soon realized the recessional was really the beginning of a procession from the Duomo to the Piazzalle Michelangelo across the Arno River, a distance of a mile and a half.

His students were so caught up with the message and fervor of the assembly that he decided to remain in the procession. With a large banner proclaiming the coming of the spirit preceding the procession, and a replica of the cross often held by the late Pope John Paul II, they wound their way through the streets of Florence. Starting on the west side of the Duomo they connected to the Via dell' Orioulo, a small street which led them to a nondescript piazza named Salvemini from which they could just see San Ambrogio Church, where the tomb of Francesco Granacci was located.

The organizers, not wanting the young people to travel on major thoroughfares, had the procession winding down narrow lanes and streets which added a sense of adventure and wonder as they made their way through centuries of history rising on all sides of them. Briefly processing on Via Pietrapiana they turned right onto Via M. Buonarroti. The procession made its way past *Casa Bounarroti* which Arthur's students had heard so much about in the classes he held prior to departing for Europe. Arthur could hear them talking about various parts of Michelangelo's life as they approached his home. The procession took Via delle Pinzochere to Santa Croce Church where the tomb of Michelangelo resides with some of the most famous persons of Italian history, science, and the arts. Notable scholars such as Galileo, inventors such as Marconi, writers such as Dante are entombed or memorialized within the Church of the Holy Cross.

As the enormous procession continued, an occasional hymn was sung. One such song was *Come to the River*, an American gospel hymn. Appropriately it was sung as they approached and crossed the Arno. Rather than taking the Viale Michelangelo, which was the direct route to their destination, they took the river route, *Lungarno Benvenuto Cellini,* and connected to a winding pathway through a park called *Vialle Giuseppe Poggi*. This route kept the procession's participants with their back to the city across the river. When they made their way up to the Piazzale Michelangelo, with its bronze copy of his *David* looming in its center, they would turn and then see a spectacular view of the Renaissance city of Florence spread beneath them.

The sun cast a golden glow across the city turning its stucco buildings with tile roofs into shining *palazzos*. The dome of the Duomo rose over the city and the tower of the Palazzo Vecchio, where the original sculpture of *David* originally stood, poked its way over the Uffizi Gallery which bordered the river.

Judging from the gasps from the youths and the adults, they were impressed by the sight. After some moments of soaking in the view, the final talk, prayer, and blessing were offered and the assembly dismissed. Arthur learned during the final talk that the youth rally was inspired by *Il Divino*, Michelangelo Buonarroti. No one in the history of art had shown the vibrancy, energy, beauty, and faithfulness of youths better than the one who first brought appreciation for the contributions of youth to the canvas or statue.

Arthur could not have hoped for such a presentation had he planned it himself. His students were surrounded by history and faith. What was even better, those next to them and who were just like them were taking solace in the surroundings.

The day ended. Students said their farewells and exchanged little business cards with their names, addresses, and e-mails on them. Arthur's group, not being an official part of the rally, had none to distribute. Seeing their dilemma Arthur, Agnes, and Maura tore pages from their note pads and passed them out to their students. They hastily wrote down the information and exchanged them with their new friends who had so graciously and warmly accepted them into their youth rally. The final hugs were given with promises to write. As the crowds departed down Viale Michelangelo and Viale Galileo Galilei, his students stood waving until they could no longer see their new friends.

Arthur looked out over a fence in front of the piazzale to enjoy its view once more. Turning, he called to his students and organized them for a photo op. He composed the picture just so with the adults flanking the students. He asked a departing acolyte if he would take the picture. As the photo session ended, and Arthur's thoughts turned to walking back the mile and a half to the bus, a familiar face appeared.

"Ambrogio," Agnes called out. "How did you find us?"

It didn't matter. Before he could answer that he followed the other buses. The students were all talking to him at once. Each had a story to share of the day.

The adults welcomed being driven to the Hotel Alessandro.

Ambrogio followed the Viale Michelangelo across Ponte San Niccolo and followed along the river until the famous Ponte Vecchio. He took a right turn and then a left onto Santi Apostoli, a very narrow street only a block from the river. In a minute they were parked in front of a narrow building Ambrogio identified as the former Palazzo Rosselli. The Hotel Alessandro occupied the second floor and up he told the group. He proceeded to conduct a mini history lesson on its origins.

"The Palazzo Rosselli was built in 1507 by an acquaintance of Michelangelo and for the family which bears its name. Cosimo Rosselli was a well-known artist of the Renaissance and a member of that family. That architect who called Michelangelo a friend was Baccio D'Agnolo. Today, the hotel is run by the Gennarini family, though the Rosselli del Turco family still owns the palazzo. Just go on in and I will take care of our luggage," Ambrogio concluded.

Arthur led the group off the bus gathering them around the front of the Hotel Alessandro. To the left, as they faced the plastered walls accented with brick arches over the windows and doorway, was a sculpted plaster relief of the *Madonna With Child*. Above the Madonna was a plaster relief of Jesus which reminded Arthur of the famous painting by Solomon called the *Head of Christ*.

The double doors were trimmed in a highly polished wooden frame. The reception area was on the second floor. Arthur thought it best to go to the check-in desk with Maura and Agnes and then call up the students. When they walked through the doors they found a very modern-looking environment of bright white walls on which were hung framed prints of Renaissance Florence. A single stairway curving up to the reception area was to their left. They followed it up to the reception desk where a young man sat looking out the window behind him. Agnes and Maura were talking about the rally and service. They both thought the experience was a terrific way to introduce the students to Florence. Arthur was not involved as he was looking around at the precisely placed décor. When he approached the desk, Arthur noticed that the young man could not see the students below. Rather it was the building across the way which offered any kind of view. Then he saw the fresh flowers filling the window sill and a ceiling fan gently rotating above the clerk. To the right was a large gold-trimmed mirror which was added to give an appearance of width to the narrow area.

Antonio jumped up as soon as he heard footsteps coming across the tile floor. "*Buon Giorno, avere il permesso.*"

"*Buon Giorno, io sono Americano Arturo Colonna,*" replied Arthur.

"*Ah, si Professore Colonna* we are expecting you. *Dove e studenti?*"

"My students are below. I thought it best to register first," Arthur answered.

Antonio understood his meaning and went about assigning the rooms. The entire hotel had twenty-five rooms, one suite and an apartment. By the time the registration was completed everyone had a room. The suite, which he thought would best serve Maura, had already been assigned to other guests so another room was given to her. The apartment, which he desired for himself and his sons, was available. Maura was given the single room with a bath. Agnes la Straga took a room which had a loft. She was across the hall from the apartment. When all was settled, Maura went to fetch the students. It wasn't a minute before the chattering group made its way up the staircase. Antonio was pointing out the lounge on the opposite side of the reception hall when the students began to clog the staircase. Arthur called them by name and distributed the keys.

In the midst of this process three men walked out of the lounge.

"Signore Colonna, how nice to see you again," a charming Anselmo Roselli said.

Chapter 14: The Savonarola Confraternity

The proverbial expression *a feather could have knocked me over* understated Arthur's reaction upon seeing Roselli and his two henchmen Pietro and Andreas. An awkward silence followed the initial meeting. Agnes concealed herself behind John and Rich. His students, not knowing what to do, stood like immobile bulging-eyed zombies.

"Why Signore Roselli, I…well I thought we were to meet in Milan?"

Roselli explained that he was notified of the plane's rerouting when he checked on Arthur's flight arrival time.

"So not wanting to disappoint you and of course your students, we drove here to my family's ancestral home."

Arthur looked around the reception hall and into his sons' eyes, which were just as bugged out as the rest of his students.

"This hotel is your family home?" he asked Roselli.

"No, no Signore Colonna or may I address you as Arturo? Is that not what my loyal assistant, Signora la Straga, calls you?" Then stretching his neck a bit, he caught sight of the black dress and pulled-back hair.

"Oh there you are Agnes, do come out and join the reunion."

Not intending to offer Roselli the slightest indication of fear or nervousness, Agnes stepped between John and Rich while rummaging through her purse. She pulled out a brush and smoothed back the few loose strands she had pulled out before squeezing through the boys. She greeted Roselli with the sweetness of pure cane sugar.

"It was Signora Colonna who insisted I accompany her husband," Agnes explained. "The signora knew that he always needs someone to keep him on time and on task."

Arthur nodded as if the story was true; the boys almost blew it by scowling at her. Luckily, John and Rich caught Arthur's "get with it" look and confirmed the invitation.

"How right you are Signora. You should have seen our mom all upset that she couldn't be with Dad because of our sister's wedding and all and then having to take our relatives around Britain."

Arthur thought they were laying it on a bit thick but, Roselli, casting of a look of understanding to Pietro and Andreas, indicated that he swallowed the story. This inspired Agnes to add a little more sugar to her words. She joked about the hotel being Roselli's ancestral home.

Roselli called to Antonio, the desk clerk. "You…young man, is this not the Palazzo Roselli?

Antonio confirmed that the building was indeed the Palazzo Rosselli. Too bad he didn't spell it, and the group did not pick up on the slight difference in pronunciation. The real family who owned the Palazzo belonged to the Rosselli del Turco branch which was the only legitimate branch. It was Nicolo Rosselli del Turco who had graciously come to the group's rescue when CIE Tours called for help.

How Anselmo came to have a similar family name spelled with only one "s" is a long story. The double-s Rossellis are descended from the painter Cosimo Rosselli. His claim to fame was his painting of the *Adoration of the Magi*. It was near the time of his death, in 1507, that the palazzo in which they stood was built. Over two hundred years later, in 1722, the last Rosselli heir, a woman named Pellegrina de Stefano Rosselli married Chiarrissimo del Turco and she blended the names into Rosselli del Turco. Antonio could have explained this had he been he asked for further details, which he was not. He was sent back to his desk by Anselmo Roselli, of the one-s branch.

As a result of this very selective information, a new-found respect for the man with the palazzo was beginning to sprout among the students. Roselli could see the admiration growing in the eyes of Arthur's students, except John and Rich who look confused, if not disbelieving. Roselli ignored them and chose Ryan O'Donnell out of the student group. His strawberry blonde hair and big blue eyes couldn't be missed as he stood just behind the chocolate brown hair and eyes of the Colonna boys. Anselmo walked right up to John and Rich and pulled Ryan out from between them.

"Now here is a young man who seems to understand the importance of family history," Anselmo Roselli pompously announced.

He placed his arm around Ryan's shoulders and squeezed.

"Tell me young man…what is your name by the way?"

Ryan was only too willing to share it, since he was now the center of attention.

"*Va bene, mi amico* Ryan O'Donnell, would you like to hear more about my family?" Roselli kindly asked. Ryan said he would, and then paused to look at Arthur.

Arthur could not be rude and deny Ryan and the rest of his students a chance to learn a little history. He told Roselli that perhaps they could gather in the restaurant of the hotel and he could conduct the presentation he could not do in Milan.

It was settled. Roselli and his thugs continued down the stairs passing and greeting each student personally. Arthur announced that they were all to gather in two hours in the restaurant on the lower level of the hotel.

Maura, leading the students upward to their rooms, left Arthur alone with John, Rich, and Agnes. He sent the boys downstairs on the pretext of finding the restaurant, but actually to find out if Roselli was still in the building.

Arthur asked Agnes to come to the apartment when she had settled herself. "There's something amiss here and I need to find out what it is."

"I'll be there shortly Arturo," she said and walked upstairs as John and Rich returned. They reported that the jerks had left the building. The term jerk caused a stir from Antonio who cast an eye their way.

Arthur noticed the look just given to his sons. He gave them a little push to the stairs and they went to the apartment. The staircase changed from brightly polished wood to a terrazzo cover, the type seen in many schools built before the 1950's. Arthur compared the stairs to those in one of his schools in Waukegan which was built in 1928. When they got to the top floor they saw Agnes opening the door to her room. Rich and John noted her convenient location, just across the very narrow hall from their apartment. Hanging on the corridor walls were prints of various scenes of Renaissance Florence. One was of the very palazzo in which they stood. Another was a scene depicting the burning of the Frate Savonarola.

The boys took gruesome delight in checking out the Savonarola print and reading the inscription under it.

"Look Dad, it's a picture of the Frate who burned the paintings and books," Rich called out.

"And now it's him who's the victim of the torch," added John.

Arthur was not to be distracted. There was much on his mind as he entered the high-ceiling apartment with large glazed doors opening onto a small balcony with a small pot of red geraniums. Arthur missed those details as his eyes scanned the high wooden-beamed ceiling. Those beams were the only remaining original interior structure of the palazzo-turned-hotel. Why they were of such interest to him, Arthur could not answer. Maybe it was their age, for they were there in 1507 when the palazzo was built.

While Arthur studied the ceiling beams, the boys brought the suitcases to the two bedrooms. Rich and John would sleep in the larger bedroom and Arthur in the other. After depositing the bags, John opened the balcony doors and stepped out onto it. Directly below him was the Via Santi Apostoli. He leaned over to look up and down the street filled with people after the afternoon rest.

A soft sound of flushing came from the apartment. He turned and Rich came out to join him.

"Dad is freshening up, as he calls it."

"Oh… hey look down the street." John, intent on his own thoughts, totally missed Rich's witty remark about their father's bathroom visit.

"You can just see the top of the Uffizi gallery. I can't wait to get in there," John excitedly said.

"Well you shouldn't have to wait long. One of the presentations is going to take place there," Rich informed his brother.

"Really Rich? Are you sure? When? Did Dad mention it or are you just saying it?"

"Hold on Johnny. I had no idea that it really was that important to you."

"Well it is. The only other place which is more important is the Academy of Art where the real *David* stands."

"The real *David*…as in there are fake ones?"

John turned to look at his brother with disbelief. He always knew Richie was more comfortable with numbers and making great visionary plans, but his ignorance regarding the *David* in Michelangelo's own city was astounding. John conducted a little lesson on the balcony. The lesson was the story of how, after the original work of the master stone cutter stood outside for centuries, it was decided to protect it by bringing it indoors into the *Galleria del Accademia belle Arti*. A copy was carved to stand in the original location in front of the Palazzo Vecchio.

"Is that so? Well I'll be…hey look who's coming down the street towards the hotel!" the half listening Rich shouted.

John obviously lost the moment to teach and looked over the balcony railing once more. "Get Dad. I think it's Roselli and the Giuliano Brothers."

"Johnny, get a grip. They're just walking, not plotting to kill us. Let's wait and see what they do," insisted Rich.

The boys leaned over to get a better view. The three men walked casually, seemingly without focus, to their hotel. They were engaged in an animated conversation, their arms flying about and their fists punching the air around them.

"Oh my God Johnny, I think you're right. They are planning to kill us. Look how Andreas is punching the air. Pietro had to duck or get clobbered," a frightened Rich concluded.

Now it was John's turn to tell Rich to calm down.

"That's just the way Italians talk. You know they're emotional."

"Well we're half Italian and we don't do that," replied Rich.

"We're American, idiot, through and through. Anyway when was the last time you saw Dad or Grandma talk with their hands?" countered John.

The exchange continued about how Italian their family was. In the meantime, the three Italian men came to a stop below the balcony, just to the side of the hotel entrance. Their voices carried up to the boys.

John heard the voices first. He cupped a hand over Rich's mouth.

"Rich, do you hear something?" They were silent as they turned their heads and held their hands up to their ears.

The three were speaking English.

Roselli was speaking. "Andreas, I want you to spread the word to the confraternity that we cannot meet in my palazzo."

"Anselmo, this is not really your palazzo. It belongs to the Rosselli del Turco family."

"Perhaps now it does, but one day it will be mine. You can be sure of that, my sarcastic friend. Now go and do what I told you to do," demanded Anselmo Roselli.

Just as Andreas was departing Roselli pulled him back.

"You had best tell them that we'll meet at the Piazza del Savonarola at eight o'clock tonight."

Andreas headed off towards the Piazza della Signoria. Anselmo turned his attention to Pietro. It was he who would help Roselli collect an important document he had to share with the confraternity.

"We must get that Colonna gang out of the hotel tonight," Roselli declared to Pietro who rubbed his right fist into his left hand.

Seeing what Pietro was doing he said firmly, "No Pietro, not yet. Anyway I was supposed to conduct a class with his students which now I'll have to reschedule."

They entered the hotel.

"That's it. They are going to kill us!" a panic-stricken Rich shouted then covered his own mouth.

"They're in the hotel now. Let's go and get Dad," John said grabbing Rich to follow.

Arthur, approaching the balcony doorway, was almost toppled over by his sons storming into the apartment.

"Whoa...and just where are you going in such a hurry?" Arthur asked.

"Oh we didn't see you standing there. Sorry about that," John said as he helped keep his father from falling over.

"Dad, it's you...good...they're going to kill us for sure," Rich interrupted.

When the son with the most control in the family appeared so disoriented and panicky, it was time for Arthur to pay close attention.

"Rich, did you say someone's going to kill us?"

"Dad, it was Roselli and his henchmen. We heard them talking below the balcony," clarified John unsatisfactorily.

Arthur was getting alarmed.

"You heard them say that they're going to kill us?"

Just then there was a knock at the apartment door. Rich jumped so high that when he landed it was topsy turvey over the couch. But that didn't stop him. He ran back to the balcony window. On a shelf next to it was an alabaster souvenir statue. This one, was of the *David*. He grabbed the statue by its legs with both hands and held it high.

"Go easy with the artifacts Richie. I don't think our murderers would announce their arrival with a knock. Now John, you go answer the door. Rich you stay right where you are at the ready, just in case I'm wrong."

John made his way to the door. Rich, with statue in hand, stood ready to pounce. Arthur took a seat on the sofa as if expecting Antonio to come up with room service. John pulled open the door so hard that it swung out of his hands and crashed into the wall.

"*Buon Giorno, Giovanni*. Did I catch you at a bad time?" asked Agnes pleasantly.

John's cheeks turned scarlet.

"No Signora la Straga. Not at all. We were, well we were just talking about Roselli."

Agnes smiled but from the corner of her eye she could see Richie with statue at the ready.

"And Ricardo, do you intend to hit Signore Roselli over the head perhaps? After all he just called to cancel the presentation tonight not to threaten you."

Rich returned a sheepish grin as Arthur asked about the cancellation.

Agnes swished her way into the sitting room as Richie, also with red cheeks, replaced the *David* statue on the shelf. Arthur stood and greeted the assistant curator, inviting her to be seated at a round table with four chairs in the center of the room. She told him of Roselli's call and Arthur explained he was just hearing about Roselli's plan to murder the whole lot of them.

"*Madonna mia*," Agnes exclaimed while crossing herself. "Arturo, you joke of course?"

"Well I think so Agnes, but right now I'm not sure. Perhaps the boys could enlighten us a bit more about what they overheard."

Rich and John grabbed the empty chairs and plopped themselves down. Rich became a bit long winded about how he found John on the balcony and how his brother had covered his mouth and so forth. John finally got a word in and explained that Roselli had sent Andreas on a mission of some kind.

"Right," confirmed Rich. "He was to find a confraternity...whatever that is."

Agnes' eyes lit up but she said nothing. Arthur saw the illumination in her eyes but he remained silent.

John explained that Rich was correct. Roselli did tell Andreas to arrange for a meeting of the confraternity at the Piazza Savonarola.

"And it's to be held at eight o'clock tonight," added Rich.

Arthur and Agnes exchanged a look and both gave a comforting smile to the boys. Arthur rose and retrieved his shoulder bag. From it he withdrew a laminated detailed map of Florence. He spread it across the table.

"Agnes do you know of such a piazza?"

"*Davero*. Indeed I do. It should be on the outer edge of the city on the opposite side from where we entered the city from the airport by the fortress."

"Okay, here it is. It really is way out there, past the Gherardesca Gardens."

Everyone was bending over the table staring at the monument image over the green space with the words "Piazza Savonarola" printed on it. Arthur asked two questions: What is this confraternity? Why choose a place so far from the hotel for their meeting?

"Oh we can answer the second question easily," said John.

Then Rich said, "Sure, Roselli said that they couldn't meet in his palazzo."

Arthur and Agnes laughed about the 'his palazzo' part. Arthur shook his head.

"And when were you going to inform us of this bit of information?"

The boys did not understand why the tone was a bit harsh. They explained that they were waiting for the appropriate time to tell what they heard. Arthur thought that now would be that time. Rich and John told them about the second part of the conversation below the balcony. They told how Roselli said that they needed to get the Colonna gang out of the hotel.

"So that's why he canceled the class. But why would Roselli want us out of the hotel? He already changed the meeting place for this confraternity group."

"*Si* Arturo, but that's at 8 p.m. What if he wanted us out before that time?" reflected Agnes.

Each of the four offered their opinions until they exhausted the possibilities and decided they would save Roselli some time and the hotel some kind of disturbance.

"We shall take the Colonna gang away from the hotel. We shall take an evening stroll around the Piazza Signoria, have dinner and then..." Arthur paused in thought.

"And then what, Dad?" asked the boys.

"And then we shall arrange to have Ambrogio pick us up and take us to this Piazza Savonarola to see what our friends are up to."

Agnes expressed concern about having the students at the piazza. Arthur felt confident the confraternity meeting would not create a scene in front of so many witnesses. The plan was set, but the answer to the first question was yet to be given. It was Agnes la Straga's turn. From her black leather purse she pulled out a leather-bound book. She explained it was the journal of Marsilio Ficino, the teacher of Michelangelo. It was thought to be long lost in the 1960's when the Arno flooded its banks and many works of art and precious manuscripts were lost or damaged in the Uffizi and surrounding museums. She pointed out that a friend of hers, who works on restoring old manuscripts in the *Museo di Miserologia e Litologia,* had given it to her. It was one of many documents and books waiting to be restored after the flood.

Arthur gave Agnes a questioning glance which she reluctantly answered "*Va bene* then, a member of the Order of the Magi like me."

The boys were still on the museum part of the story as John's eyes lit up.

"Hey, I know where that is. It's right next door to the University where I attended last year." He did not let the mention of the Order of the Magi get past him. "And what's this about an order? Is that like a confraternity?" John asked.

Agnes shot a glance at Arthur.

"Well in a way, an order could be like a confraternity in that they are both groups of people who pledge to follow certain rules," he told his sons.

"Oh, like a fraternity then."

"*Si, davero Giovanni*, but in answer to your statement about the museum; it's true that it is next to San Marco, now also a museum. But at one time the church was the place from which the Frate Savonarola took control of the city of Florence. And that brings us to the first question about the confraternity."

Agnes opened the journal and began to answer the first question.

"The year is 1498. The Frate and his followers has had Florence in his grip for over three years. Another burning of the vanities was planned. The aging Botticelli came to the home of Marsilio with a letter... a home which is empty of the poet Angelo Poliziano who died just as the Frate came into power. On the desk where Marsilio made his journal entries two candles burned in pewter holders. He writes about how he at first thought that Frate Savonarola was a savior for the city which had fallen into excess. But now he writes about the cruelty of the Frate and of the destruction of all free thought and expression in art and writings," She began as once again Renaissance Italy was brought forward as if they could actually see the scholar Ficino writing in his journal.

"The time has come to bring balance and sanity to our beloved city. Many have had to flee the city. The power of the Frate strangles creativity and freedom as no Medici has ever done and so severely was it done. Piero, the unfortunate one, looks like a saint in comparison to the Frate," Marsilio writes as the knock on his door distracts him from the journal entry.

Standing in the doorway was the aging Sandro Botticelli. In his hand he holds what has become a familiar correspondence from their friend in Rome.

"Sandro, my friend you needn't have come out at night. The youth bands are scouring the city right now for vanities for the fire."

"It's no matter. Whatever they want they may have Marsilio. It is a blessing that our friend can work in Rome away from all of this insanity, though needed, to be sure."

Marsilio was horrified to hear the great artist speak of his work in such a manner. He chided him and then offered him some wine and a comfortable chair. They opened the letter from Michelangelo. It spoke of the reception his *Bacchus* statue had received. First, how Michelangelo was crushed when the cardinal refused the work he commissioned, then how that rejection brought fame to his work. The letter relayed that a great number of commissions were now offered to him. However, it was the one offered by the French ambassador to the Holy See which was of particular interest.

"He wants a life size Holy Virgin holding the body of our dead savior across her lap," Michelangelo wrote. He told them of his yearning to bring forth from the stone what was imprisoned there in such a way that God would be glorified.

Botticelli lowered the letter. "So our friend sees the value of work for God."

"Sandro, my friend, to work with stone, to paint, to carve in wood that which elevates the minds and spirits of people to God is without question a noble and glorious undertaking. But my friend it does not mean that this is the only way to glorify God or to inspire humanity."

Before Marsilio could continue shouts were heard in the streets outside the house.

"The pope has excommunicated Savonarola," was being shouted throughout the city. Rebellion had broken out against the Frate's cruel rule.

Marsilio was overjoyed. "Our friend, Sandro, he can come back to us now. I shall send for Granacci at once to plan his homecoming. Botticelli, however, only saw more violence and oppression ahead.

"You have not seen the rest of the letter Marsilio. Our friend wants me to communicate this news to Lorenzo di Pierfrancesco, though he doesn't use their family name any longer. Still, he's one of the Medici branches who will fill the vacuum when the holy Frate falls."

"Savonarola is not holy and the Medici who does remain is not the same as Piero. So let us be glad and rejoice that our city will once again be free."

"And within the year the Frate Savonarola was arrested, tried, and convicted," concluded Agnes. "He was to be burned at the stake. But Pope Alexander VI, the very one who brought him down, took mercy on him and let him be hanged before his body was burned."

John asked if the sketch in the hallway showed a dead Savonarola being burned. He was told yes though many did not realize it at the time. Agnes said that unlike what he did when he actually burned people alive at the stake, he was treated more humanely; if one can call torture, hanging and burning a dead person civilized.

"Okay, the Frate is dead. What has this got to do with the confraternity and the legend of the Magi?"

"According to Marsilio Ficino, everything," Agnes answered.

She summarized what Marsilio wrote later. Although the Frate was gone, many of his followers did not give up his cause. They formed a cult called the Confraternity of Savonarola. They would meet in secret to create spells to curse those who brought down their leader. They sought to find the secret of the Magi gift which they thought brought power to the Medici. They wanted to destroy it and the powerful family forever.

"Holy cow! Then you think Roselli is part of that confraternity?" asked Rich.

"Ricardo, not only do I think that, but I believe he is the leader of the confraternity."

Arthur, John, and Rich sat in stunned silence. "Why would the Magi ring be so important to the confraternity?" the boys finally asked.

The answer might be discovered by following a simple plan explained Arthur. They would get the students out of the hotel, just as Roselli wanted. They would go to the Piazza Signoria for dinner. They would go to the Piazza Savonarola to see what Roselli and his confraternity was up to. Agnes would tell Antonio that the group would go out to eat and not use the restaurant. The boys would spread the word among the students and Arthur would speak with Maura.

Within the hour, Arthur was leading his band of students towards the Ponte Vecchio where he promised a shopping excursion at the many gold shops on the bridge. It turned out they would go to dinner at a charming restaurant which Ambrogio picked out. It was on the edge of the Piazza Signoria. Since they would be eating outdoors the view beyond their table would be of the great pieces of sculptures surrounding the piazza, in front of the Palazzo Vecchio and in the Loggia.

As the last of the group exited, the desk clerk picked up the house phone.

"Signore Roselli, the Signore Colonna and his group have gone out for dinner and shopping."

"*Mille grazie, Antonio,* you will be rewarded handsomely," came Roselli's reply. He placed the phone down with a smile. "The Colonna gang has departed. You needn't cut the power to the hotel."

Piero looked disappointed.

"Get your tools. We need to get into Colonna's apartment and then to the meeting" Roselli ordered.

The two made their way downstairs to the reception desk. On the desk lay the key to Arthur's apartment. Roselli placed an envelope next to it and slipped the key into his hand. Antonio purposely had his back towards them, looking out the window. Only when he heard footsteps on the stairs did he turn and notice the envelope with his name on it. As Roselli and Pietro's footsteps faded, the clerk placed the envelope into his pants pocket and resumed his daydreaming.

With Arthur and his students gone, Roselli and Pietro were almost alone in the hotel. Most of the service staff were setting up the restaurant for the evening meal. Anselmo had free reign once he reached the upper level. He entered the apartment using the key, took a quick look around the sitting room area and headed for the balcony. Once at the doorway he turned and paced back towards the entrance door counting his steps as he did so. When he counted ten he looked about again.

"Pietro there is nothing here but furniture."

Pietro was totally confused and posed a question as to why that was a problem. Anselmo replied it was a problem because the document which they sought could not possibly be in the room since all the furnishings were modern. He pulled the chair away from the table and sat down to think. Meanwhile Pietro scanned the room once more from his position at the balcony door. All he noticed were the wooden beams supporting the ceiling.

"Anselmo, you are right. I too have seen nothing but those beams on the ceiling. We had better…" suddenly he cut off his own words. "The beams! Anselmo, the answer to our dilemma is the beams."

Roselli bolted up from the chair. He ran to Pietro, threw his arms around his huge body and told him he was a genius, which pleased the thug very much. The compliment pleased him; the hug was awkward. Pietro never expected his boss to be so demonstrative. Anselmo was beyond caring how his underling felt. He was looking at the beam directly overhead trying to solve the next obstacle. How to reach the beam? He circled the table directly under the mid-section of the beam. After a moment of thought, he picked up a chair and set it on top of the table.

"Pietro, you're quite tall. Climb up on the chair," he directed. "See if you can reach the beam."

Pietro, though large, was quite nimble. He had no problem getting up on the table and then the chair. Anselmo was elated.

"*Magnifico*, Pietro wonderful," he softly yelled. "Now, take the hammer and tap the beam until you hear a hollow sound."

Covering a six foot span of his outstretched arms Pietro tapped the beam. Almost directly above his head was an echoing sound rather than the usual thud of solid wood. The beam, which had been varnished, painted, stripped of paint and refinished a number of times, had held up well over the centuries. No one had ever listened for sounds from its hollowed interior and the small panel covering the hollow section was so well concealed that any visible crack seemed due to age.

Roselli handed up a flat-head screwdriver which Pietro used to chip away the sealant keeping the panel in place. As he did so, pieces of the dried substance fell onto Roselli's head; he didn't care. Each fragment meant he was a step closer to his goal; to his enlightenment. It was done. Pietro could place the screwdriver into the gap and pry open the cover. He looked excited as the light filtered into the crevice as it had not done for 500 years. It illuminated a rolled up piece of leather which was tied with thin laces.

"Anselmo, there's something in this wood."

It was difficult for Roselli to control himself. He wanted to climb up there himself and be the first to hold whatever lay there. He knew that his sense of balance would never make that a real possibility. He had to direct the recovery.

Back in the reception area, Antonio was still dreaming. He was looking up and out the window when he heard running footsteps up the staircase. He turned toward the stairs as John bounded up the stairs to the counter.

"Antonio, my father forgot his camera and cannot possibly tour without it. So I was the lucky one appointed to retrieve it."

The desk clerk could hardly breathe, let alone speak. John inquired as to whether or not he was feeling well, for the clerk had turned red then pale with fright. For the longest moment, the clerk muttered about cameras and the beauty of the city which needed to be preserved and told John he felt fine.

"Just a little reaction to some of these flowers, pollen or something, I guess," he said.

John understood his plight as his two little nephews had similar allergies.

"Then if it's okay, may I have our key? Time is wasting and Dad needs that camera."

"The key, of course, the key…" Antonio stuttered. "I have it right here."

The clerk walked to the key cupboard and fumbled around in it. Mercifully the phone rang and he answered it. He supplied the room rate to the caller and then, while still fumbling for the key, dialed the apartment number. Roselli was startled and Pietro almost tumbled from the chair without having the prize in hand. The phone kept ringing.

"*Mama mia*, does not that clerk know that Colonna is not here. Why does he put through a call?" Roselli asked no one in particular.

It continued to ring. Roselli looked at the caller ID screen and saw that it was the desk calling. "*Idioso*, it's he that calls the room."

Roselli picked up the phone ready to tell the clerk just what he thought of the disturbance.

Before a word on his part could be uttered a whispering voice spoke, "The Colonna son is back and coming up to the apartment."

There was a click and no further sound. Roselli turned white.

"Pietro get what you see out and hand it down to me. The Colonna boy is coming up."

Pietro grabbed the leather bound packet and dropped it down to Roselli who caught it despite his panic.

"Now get down. We need to hide."

Running footsteps were audible through the door as they replaced the chair back on the floor.

"Quick! To the balcony!" and he pulled on Pietro to follow him.

He climbed out onto the balcony railing and onto the brick ledge, which surrounded the façade of the palazzo. Flattening his body against the building, he directed Pietro to do the same even though for Pietro, being such a large man, it presented a whole new set of issues. The thug managed to hang on and made it to the bedroom window affording him better footing and balance.

The door swung open and Johnny ran right into his father's room. He grabbed the camera off the dresser and made a beeline for the door. His shoes crunched the pieces of the dried wood cement. He paused, thought to himself that the room must not have been cleaned, and continued on. As he closed the door he noticed that the chairs were askew.

"Funny I thought Rich had arranged everything just so before we left," John mumbled.

In an instant he was gone. Roselli and Pietro managed to climb back onto the balcony and into the room to glue the panel back in place. Pietro had rather enjoyed the thrill of walking on the ledge. Roselli, however, was sweating profusely; but he ignored his personal plight for they had accomplished what they had set out to do. Never a thought was given to the residue they left behind, nor to the chairs being out of place. They left, depositing the key on the unattended front desk next to the key John had just left.

John caught up with the group as they made their way along the Ponte Vecchio, the Old Bridge. Arthur gathered his students at a place empty of shops to look out over the Arno River. He explained that this old bridge, on which the likes of Michelangelo and the Medici walked, was the only survivor of several bridges which crossed the Arno in Florence. During the retreat of the Nazis in World War II, as the Allies approached the city to liberate it, the others were blown up.

"Only this one survived and served as a symbol of strength and endurance for the city in the final days of the war."

As he concluded, John ran up with the camera just in time to record the group sitting on the Ponte Vecchio with the river and city behind them.

During the photo session, Roselli and Pietro made their way towards the San Marco church complex now serving as a museum. Rather than cut through the Piazza Signoria, they made their way to Santa Trinita and its piazza, the very one where Michelangelo and Granacci had first seen the ladies chorus of the *Carnivale*. Turning up the Via de Tournabuoni, they headed towards the Palazzo Corsi behind which was the building they were seeking. Out of breath from running like two excited school kids, they knocked on the door of the brownish stucco building. The faded red painted door opened slightly and an elderly man peeked out of the opening.

"Long live Savonarola," Roselli firmly stated.

The door was opened wider by the gray-haired gentleman. He was dressed in clothes more fitting a monk in a cloister. The man beckoned them to follow him. They were led up a staircase into to a small library off the hallway. On the outside wall was a heavily draped window. On the wall opposite the door was a series of bookshelves filled with ancient bound books. To their left, was a fireplace over which hung a painting of the Frate Savonarola. On each end of the mantle there was a candlestick holding a burning candle. In the center of the room was a rectangular wooden table surrounded by six oversized cushioned chairs. The two at each end had chair arms. Roselli guessed the furnishings to be seventeenth century or older.

At last their guide spoke in Italian as the two stood next to the table.

"Then you must be the one whom I was told would come with something for the confraternity. Do take a chair and make yourself comfortable."

"Si Signore...what may I call you?" asked Roselli.

"I am Girolamo Orsini and you must be Anselmo Roselli, of whom we have heard so much of as late."

"Indeed I am Signore. My colleague, Pietro Giuliano and I have here what may well be the answer to our centuries of searching."

"*Va bene*, then let us see this treasure," the smiling Orsini responded.

Sitting at an outdoor café in the Piazza Signoria, Arthur and his students were marveling at the wonderful meal they were enjoying on a beautifully clear warm evening. The piazza was aglow in lights. Some were shining on the fountain with Neptune as its centerpiece; others shone on the Palazzo Vecchio; others were shining on such masterpieces as the replica of Michelangelo's *David*, Donatello's *Judith*, and Cellini's *Perseus and Medusa*. The group had visited the Loggia, and walked around the fountain, splashing their hands in it. Now they sat with dishes of gelato, which Arthur felt was one of the greatest gifts given to ice cream lovers. While they were enjoying twilight time as the sun began to set and the lights in the piazza became more pronounced, Arthur decided it was time to share the plans for the evening. He needed to make it sound like an adventure rather than a possible danger.

He first told of the rise of the Frate Savonarola which kept Michelangelo away from the city. He then talked about the burning of the vanities which happened in this piazza. Next he told about the Frate's downfall, and execution in the Piazza and the scattering of his ashes in the Arno River to prevent his remains from becoming relics. Finally, he told them about the legacy the Frate left and the followers which still adhered to it. The students, rather than being frightened, enjoyed the story as they would a horror flick.

Arthur explained they were going on an adventure through the streets of the city so they may get a feel for its spirit. The students put down their tiny dessert spoons. Their eyes were focused on Arthur.

"We are going to walk to the Piazza Savonarola where Ambrogio will meet us and take us back to the hotel. This way, we can enjoy the city at night."

Ryan immediately called out, "You mean they dedicated a plaza to a guy who destroyed Florentine art?"

Arthur explained the dedication was less to what he did than to what many thought he stood for and it was fitting that they visit the site.

"Can you believe that?" Ryan turned to Danny and Jessica sitting on either side of him. "This guy must have been one awesome guy."

His classmates raised their eyebrows as he backtracked.

"I mean even though he was like a Hitler-type person."

Arthur, listening in on the comments, replied to them.

"Yes indeed, the Frate was a powerful force during the Renaissance, so even after he was executed for his heresy and cruelty there were those who clung to his teachings. Many believe that Michelangelo himself could never quite get Savonarola's teaching out of his thoughts."

"Mr. C. are you saying that his order continued to preach his message?" asked Kristin.

He explained that no public preaching was tolerated.

"However, a group was formed from out of the Frate's religious community in San Marco, the same community to which Michelangelo's brother Lionardo belonged. I have reason to believe a branch of it still exists. We may, perhaps, see some of them in the piazza this very night."

Every guy in the group was now on his feet including John and Rich.

"Let's get to that piazza," they called out. "Come on Mr. C., we want to see these Nazis of the Renaissance."

The girls, though just as excited about the prospect, were more controlled. They wanted to know how far they had to walk, and how many of that Savonarola group might be there. They also wanted to know what they should do if they actually met any of them.

Arthur thought these were all valid inquiries, and, after settling down the boys, he suggested they discuss the girls' questions while they walked to their destination. In a flash, the entire group was up and ready for the jaunt across the city. Even Agnes and Maura were excited. John was selected to lead the group since he had first-hand knowledge of the city. He led them toward the Duomo and up the Via Ricasoli, which changed names several times along the route. They walked along almost nonexistent sidewalks towards the University of Florence which adjoined San Marco. Within the church-turned-museum were preserved Savonarola's room with his furnishings.

From San Marco museum they cut through the *Giardino dei Sempuci* to get to Via Gino Capponi. That route took them to Piazza Savonarola through a residential neighborhood. Once there they followed Arthur's directions as to how they were to react to any confraternity members who might show up.

John had no indication that he led their little group within two blocks of Roselli who was rolling up the manuscript back into its leather wrapping. Roselli and Pietro had no clue they walked through San Marco just ahead of the Colonna gang to enter the piazza just a few minutes before Arthur and his group.

When Roselli entered the piazza, he saw Andreas surrounded by about a dozen people. They stood to one side of a pillar dedicated in the eighteenth century to the Frate's memory. It was all the proof that Arthur would need to verify that there were followers of the Frate's teachings two hundred years after the memorial was dedicated.

Roselli walked up to Andreas and handed his briefcase to him. He opened it and took out the rolled leather pouch. The group, whom Andreas had invited formed a semi-circle in front of Roselli, flanked by the Giuliano brothers. Behind them was the memorial. They looked like any typical tourists. Some were dressed casually like university students. Others were stylishly clothed with tailored suits and dresses and famous Italian shoes. Two were dressed like Girolamo Orsini, with a loose fitted black tunic over black pants.

Roselli gently removed the packet from the briefcase. At that moment John, Arthur, and his band walked into the piazza. John, seeing Roselli lifting something up into the air, motioned to the group. They were to stay put and to listen. The group took seats wherever they stood and watched with wonder as the confraternity began its proceedings. When Roselli lifted the document up into the air the members knelt on the ground for a moment. The night was still; not a breeze to be felt. The stars illuminated the heavens and the moon, almost full, reflected the sun's light onto the piazza like a spotlight on a set.

Roselli spoke and the Colonna group watched and listened intently. No other soul was about. The night belonged to the confraternity; or so they thought. One of Arthur's students, without his approval, made his way closer to where Roselli stood.

"Behold the words of the Frate," proclaimed Roselli.

There was a gasp that spread among the members.

"The Frate again calls upon his followers. We are to find and destroy, once and for all, that so-called gift which brought power to the abusers of government and art. They, who instead of perfecting the beauty of ideas, valued perfection of form, the human form, instead."

Roselli paused and looked into the eyes of those gathered. He saw in them a yearning for action. Out of the corner of his eye he spotted a red-haired lad, easily distinguishable in the bright moonlight.

"You," he called out. "Do you wish to perfect the beauty of ideas?"

Ryan was petrified. He could not move. His tongue swelled in his dry mouth; he could not speak.

Roselli stepped down from the monument. Pairs of eyes belonging to the members of the confraternity followed his every step. He walked directly to Ryan, took hold of his arm and forced him up to the top step.

"Look at this fine young man. He is well groomed, his hair is combed. He dresses with taste and were he to speak I would say his words would be eloquent," Roseilli said as he presented Ryan to the confraternity.

The members applauded lightly so as not to attract attention, even though as far as they knew no one was within shouting distance. Beads of sweat sprouted across Ryan's brow.

"Look, my fellow members. His innocence is revealed in his composure."

The members now laughed softly.

"Dad, that's Ryan up there," Rich whispered.

"Don't do a thing, we can't endanger Ryan." They sat and watched.

John, in the mean time, made his way towards Ryan, hidden by a row of hedges.

Maura became distraught because a student was caught in the midst of those people.

"Arthur, can you go and make Ryan come back?"

"Should I do that now he would be in far greater danger. Now listen to me. It was he who went to them. They did not come and take him. Therefore no harm will come to him if he plays along."

Roselli was talking about the manuscript's message and seemed to be ignoring Ryan. Roselli assigned several in the group to meet with him at the Biblioteca Merucelliana to study some writings preserved there from the Frate and people of his day. They would compare notes from the library with the information on the manuscript with Girolamo Orsini at his home. Abruptly, the meeting was over and the members disbursed. Roselli turned to leave as well and noticed the lad was still next to him.

"Well young man, you're still here."

Ryan was able to nod yes.

Roselli interpreted this as his desire to want to know more. He invited the lad to the Orsini home. Having one of Colonna's students in the confraternity would give him first-hand knowledge of what Arthur was up to.

Never had Ryan been accepted for who he was. Never had he been complimented because he was sort of a preppie. Never had he been called bright. Ryan accepted the invitation, and, after being given the time and location for the meeting, slowly made his way back to his classmates. "Anselmo, I think you have an admirer," laughed Andreas.

"It seems that student of Colonna will help us to capture the gift."

"Then you knew all the time?" asked Pietro.

"Gentlemen, one doesn't forget such red hair in a land such as ours," answered Roselli as he accompanied the brothers into the darkness beyond the piazza.

Arthur and Rich ran to Ryan who was now sitting on a bench with John hovering over him.

"Ryan, are you okay?" a frantic Arthur asked.

Ryan seemed to be coming out of a trance. He said that he was fine and that all Roselli talked about was some kind of paper Savonarola had written.

"You know, he liked me; thought I was smart and well dressed."

Rich and John couldn't help but laugh much to Arthur's regret.

"It will be fine Ryan. Come on back and we'll have a gelato and talk about what happened here," Arthur suggested.

He gave instructions to Rich and John to escort Ryan back to the group. Arthur followed along at a slower pace while posing a question to himself.

"How powerful could this gift, which Agnes and Roselli seek, really be?"

Chapter 15: The Giant Lives

The students swarmed around Ryan, who sat in the rear of the bus. Each unloaded a barrage of questions about what the confraternity really talked about and what sinister plans they had concocted. In all his answers, not once did he mention the invitation to the Orsini house. In a short while the bus pulled onto the Via Santi Apostoli and stopped in front of the Palazzo Rosselli. Instead of being reprimanded for not obeying the rule of staying together, Ryan was being treated like a hero; a spy of sorts, who went under cover into the den of the villainous confraternity.

All the excitement of the clandestine meeting, watching it and Ryan being in the middle of it all, served to get the students quite wound up.

"Now would not be a good time to send them to their rooms," Arthur told Maura.

"Not unless we want to be up all night trying to keep them quiet," Maura agreed.

They pondered what to do next as the youths bounded off the bus talking excitedly about their adventure. It didn't matter it was past 10:00 p.m.

"Hey, let's ask to walk back to the piazza," suggested Mike.

"Great idea," agreed Danny.

Arthur was not about to have them roaming about the city with the nightclub crowd. He needed an alternative, and quickly. He asked his sons to speak with whoever was on duty in the restaurant and arrange for a late night snack. He asked Maura to mingle with the students and suggest a get-together of some kind. He asked Agnes to find Roselli and invite him to conduct his presentation at the stroke of midnight. Arthur hoped that would add just the right air of mystery.

Agnes was not thrilled to enlist the very person who threatened her search for the ring of the Magi. However, Arthur pointed out Lorenzo de Medici's practice of keeping one's enemies close, and she understood. Arthur added that his students were in spy mode and what better way to keep them controlled than to have present the very person who made them feel like covert agents.

"Arturo, you should have been what you call a covert agent."

"Agnes it's called being a teacher. Do what is necessary to catch your students' attention," Arthur reflected.

The night clerk, Lana, could not have been more cooperative. She ensured all was made ready for gelato and Cokes in the restaurant. They walked downstairs and entered a large rectangular room with patches of exposed brick in the stucco walls. Windows on one end allowed one to see the feet and legs of passers-by.

The tables were covered in white and maroon linen. Regina and the kitchen crew served the gelato and Cokes. Salvatore chipped ice from a large block for those who asked for *il gaucio*. Eva and Diana scooped the gelato into glass goblets which they served from a long table. By the time Rich and John returned with Arthur's computer and projector, the students were happily reliving what they called the Piazza de Savonarola caper.

John flipped the switch on the projector and the head of Michelangelo's *David* appeared on the wall behind Arthur. He explained that this night was different in many ways. The students laughed and said things like "you can say that again."

Arthur plowed on with his thought.

"Different in that you stood on a hill with a copy of the *David*. You ate on a piazza in front of a copy of the marble *David,* and you learned of a mysterious group of people who have, for centuries, been bent on the destruction of what the *David* stood for. Tomorrow you shall see the master stone cutter's masterpiece… in person."

There was some short lived snickering as Arthur became more and more passionate about the sculptor's feelings and beliefs as he produced "the Giant" as he called his *David*. The teacher was in full gear now with Agnes at his side to add details, those garnered from her long relationship with the Order of the Magi and their research.

Arthur continued. "When you are introduced to the *David* tomorrow, I want you to understand what Michelangelo felt when he brought life to a piece of marble; a piece of marble which had been poorly cut from the mountain in the quarries of Carrara. In fact, it was almost ruined by previous attempts to sculpt it. I want you to look at David's face and the curls upon his head."

He paused, pressed the button, and projected the full statue as seen from the back side.

"I want you to see the sling ready to slay Goliath and the tenseness of his stance as he readies himself for battle with the Philistine giant."

Some giggles ensued as Kristin commented on his cute rump.

"And Kristin as that interests you so much, you may give us your thoughts on how the artist might have carved such a cute… as the Italians would say, *coulo*."

The roars of laughter and Kristin's red face pushed further back in their minds the threat they had witnessed earlier. Even Ryan laughed and was not nearly as somber as he had been since their return from the piazza.

Arthur pushed the button again and now David was shown from a front view. It brought about instant silence from the boys and Arthur knew why. Joke they might about their family jewels, or junk, but to discuss it seriously as a work of art was beyond their abilities even after hearing of Michelangelo's dissection efforts at Santa Trinita. Arthur was pleased with the silence for it was Agnes la Straga's turn to bring them back in history. She was to bring them to the point where Roselli, if he showed up, would begin his story. She began quietly, waiting for the students to focus on her as the projected image changed from the *David* to the *Pieta*.

"Frate Girolamo Savonarola was gone. Michelangelo was carving the beautiful, serene, and moving *Pieta* of St. Peter's when he received a letter from Marsilio Ficino through Botticelli. Its contents revealed the Frate's death and the void of leadership in Florence.

Because of his obligations, it would be almost three more years before he returned to Florence. Finally, in 1501 his friend, Piero Soderini,was made Gonfalonier of the Republic, the head of the government, for life. It was springtime when the famous Florentine sculptor returned to his beloved Florence…" And in a short time her words brought the students back in time.

Granacci was pacing in front of Casa Buonarroti for almost an hour. A runner had arrived to tell Lodovico Buonarroti that his son was close upon the city limits. Lodovico had, in a rare moment of graciousness, allowed Michelangelo's long-time friend to be present for the anticipated arrival. Granacci's heart pounded with joy, but he did not want his friend's father to see such excitement in him. At last the cart pulled by a single horse turned onto what is now called Via dell' Agnolo. Michelangelo sat quietly next to the driver until he spotted Granacci down the block. He jumped up, upsetting the horse so much so that the driver had difficulties bringing the cart to a halt and calming the animal. Michelangelo didn't wait, but jumped from the cart running towards his friend and his father's house. Tears streamed down their faces as they took each others arms and held them tightly.

"You look well Buonarroti. Roman life has not hurt you in the least."

"You should one day come to Rome my friend, and see its wonders," the beaming Michelangelo suggested.

"I, the maker of carnivale artifacts in Rome? I don't think so."

"*Idioso*, you have skill better than what I saw in the pope's palace."

The tears flowed and the talk of art went on a moment more. Then Granacci pulled his friend close to him. "Welcome home my friend," he exclaimed as he swung his arm over the younger artist's shoulders.

"*Mille grazie Francesco*, my dearest friend."

"Come now, wipe your face of your womanly tears. Your father waits impatiently for his famous son."

"Whose tears are wetter, is all I will say friend. Lead on."

At the doorway, Francesco stepped back allowing Lodovico to see his son without interruption. The son, who so longed for a father's love embraced his stoic father.

He could have sworn that he felt Lodovico tremble a bit. Could that be possible? Could he really be excited that he has returned?

"You look well my son. Not like me; I am in poor health and each day the running of this house becomes more of a burden."

"But I send you money Father. Has it not helped?"

"Oh Michelangelo if you only knew of the burdens I have endured. Your brother Buonarroto works the farm like an animal. By the way, he will be here tonight. And Lionardo with those followers of Savonarola in San Marco finally begins to see the light too late. He will be here tonight as well."

"Then this night is one to be filled with joy for the Buonarroti family will be united once again, however briefly."

"How say you Michelangelo? You plan not to stay in Firenze?"

"I must work if I might send money Father. I need work."

Francesco stepped into the light from the shadows with the news which would change his friend's plans.

"Michelangelo, there is a block of marble. It has been sitting in the courtyard of the Board of Works for the Duomo for a hundred years."

Michelangelo interrupted his friend acknowledging that he was well aware of the poorly cut Carrara marble and how the Tuscan sculptor Agostino di Antonio di Guccio had attempted to work on it only to further damage it.

Francesco continued with such excitement in his voice that even Lodovico, the sour one, became more and more interested in the words being spoken. He said that the Board was talking to Andrea del Monte San Savino about how it could be made into a statue for the Duomo.

"But the fool wanted to add more stone to it and create a prophet of sorts. So they chose to think awhile on the proposed plan. Then they heard of your return and I am here to invite you to meet with them tomorrow at the *Operai del Duomo*."

"Michelangelo's eyes were ablaze. His father's eyes sparkled with gold coins envisioned. In the presence of his father he took hold of Francesco and gave him what you Americans would call a bear hug." Agnes paused as she recognized the desire of the group to ask questions.

"Was it really damaged or was that legend?" asked Breanne.

"Did Michelangelo choose what kind of statue it would be?" asked Mike.

"Did Granacci help him get the job?" questioned Jessica.

"How come Michelangelo seemed to be a huggy type of guy when his father seemed so aloof and cold?" the now emboldened Ryan put forth.

Agnes answered each question truthfully, especially that offered by Ryan. He had hit upon a crucial aspect of Michelangelo's developing ideas on the expression of love and friendship. Then she continued with her talk.

"The next day Michelangelo went to meet with the *Operai del Duomo*. He presented his plan to create a David without adding more stone to the damaged block. By August 16, 1501 the contract was signed and

Michelangelo began his search."

A hand jutted into the air. Maribeth was waving it frantically. Agnes stopped and asked her to present her question. "What do you mean when you say he began his search?"

Agnes replied that Michelangelo began his search for models. These he would sketch and then prepare wax models of them before he even touched the marble.

Another hand went up. Danny asked how many models the artist used for the statue.

"That remains unknown as far as the preliminary search goes. For the final form there was only one model."

And then Agnes la Straga continued her story despite more questioning eyes. One of those pairs belonged to Arthur. Agnes looked into those eyes but continued her tale and soon the images of sixteenth century Florence formed.

Michelangelo appeared at the Board of Works for the Cathedral of Santa Maria del Fiore in the morning before a single soul was about. He wanted to inspect the marble piece before he spoke. As he was running his hand along the jagged edge where Guccio had made his attempt, Granacci showed up.

"I thought you'd be here bright and early. Well what do you think?"

"What I think Francesco is that whoever blocked this piece was incompetent; not to mention poor Guccio who tried to work with it."

"Then it's a hopeless cause?" a disappointed Granacci asked.

"I didn't say that my friend. It has life within it. I can feel a David wanting to be released, yearning to be brought forth," Michelangelo replied correcting his friend.

"Buonarroti don't get all poetic with me; I'm a humble person who paints. Just answer the question. Can you create something out of it?"

"You belittle yourself and you don't listen. Did I not say that a David yearns to be born from the stone?"

Francesco Granacci smiled. It was a smile of satisfaction. A smile that verified his faith in his friend; one which indicated that he knew Michelangelo would not pass up a chance to prove the experts wrong. For a century they had proclaimed the stone useless. Now one came along to announce that it had life within it. He joined Michelangelo as he circled the stone over and over again rubbing his hand across its surface.

Finally, Michelangelo went inside. Once again he told his story of the stone having life. The Board listened intently. They questioned him on whether he would need to add stone to the block to perfect it. Michelangelo answered with a definite "NO." He would create a David from the block as it is. The *Operai del Duomo* looked at each other. They were thinking of a prophet for the marble.

Michelangelo stood rigidly and placed both hands on the table behind which the members of the board sat. He gazed into their eyes, each one individually.

"I tell you it's a David that yearns to be released from that stone."

Granacci, standing just outside the room, audibly gulped. His friend was about to throw a tidy sum of a commission to the wind because he wanted to carve a David.

Michelangelo remained standing, waiting. The members were speechless and kept looking at each other, but no counter argument came forth from any of them.

"*Va bene*, Michelangelo Bounarotti son of Lodovico, a David it shall be. A contract shall be drawn up for 400 ducats. Mind you, this project is to be completed in eighteen months."

Michelangelo took on a softer attitude. He even smiled as he told them that he had better get to work.

"Just build a shed around the block and I shall work where it now sits."

He almost ran out of the room, passing Granacci with such speed that it seemed he had lost the commission rather than having been offered it.

Running to catch up he called out to him. "Michelangelo, what's the hurry?"

Michelangelo turned, but kept his movement walking backwards as he spoke. "I have not a minute to lose. They gave me only eighteen months to create the David. I need to find models for the piece."

For a month, he and Granacci combed Florence to find young men who would fit what Michelangelo envisioned for his David. It was often the practice to use different models for particular aspects of a statue or a painting. The sculptor sketched the particular aspect needed, then created a wax model of it and then put it together to make it whole. They would then remove surface stone on whatever side the wax model or live model offered. That was the common practice.

Michelangelo was not common in anything, let alone how he

approached his work. He worked with such intensity, using both hands with such force when he chiseled, that he accomplished in a few minutes what many could not do in hours.

After a series of searches throughout the city and several sketches of an arm here, a leg there, a face of someone else, the twenty-six-year-old stone cutter was not pleased. Rather than sit in Lodovico's house to discuss his displeasure, which would only upset his father, he met Granacci with his sketches in hand. In a corner of a favorite inn which they frequented near the Piazza Signoria, they sat discussing the merits or lack of merit of the chalk drawings. It was when they were so absorbed in their discussion that he entered the inn, put on an apron and began to clean vacated tables.

He was an extremely tall young man perhaps eighteen years old. His thick, wavey, black hair hung in curls about his clean-shaven face. His oval, chocolate brown eyes surveyed the room to make sure each customer had been served. Seeing Granacci and Michelangelo in the corner, their heads buried in large sheets of paper and only two cups on the table, the lad walked up to them.

"*Scusi signore*," his polite voice filtered into Granacci's consciouness first. He glanced up. The lad continued.

"May I bring you something?"

Even underneath a tunic and apron, the rippling muscles were clearly visible. The eyes of the artist appraised the lad. He poked Michelangelo.

"I think you should take a look at what stands in front of us," Granacci suggested.

"Granacci, can't you see how this arm twists but no muscle comes out…" was all that Michelangelo said as he spread a sheet of paper across the table.

"*Si, si* I know my friend but I also see an arm that bulges with muscle tissue."

"What are you talking about? Have you been drinking before you met me? The drawing shows nothing of which you speak."

"*Idioso*, I tell you to look up and see what your drawing does not show."

Protesting the disturbance, Michelangelo looked up from his drawings. The lad smiled and offered to serve him if he should desire some food. The words were not heard. Michelangelo stood and walked around the table. He took the candle from the table and held it up to the lad's flawless face glowing in the candlelight.

"Such a face so full of feeling, so full of conviction," murmured the stone cutter.

The lad was feeling quite uncomfortable and shifting from one leg to another. "Signore, perhaps I should come back later?"

Granacci sat back and watched the genius at work, soaking in every detail of the form before him.

This, he thought, *was what Savonarola could not understand. This is artistic genius creating new life from stone in the human form first given life by the creator. This is why Michelangelo is called Il Divino.*

The lad had had enough of the artist's goggling. He turned to leave.

"*Scusi*, I have other tables to attend to."

Michelangelo stopped his pacing. He placed his hand upon the lad's shoulder.

"Your front is as good as your back," the stone cutter commented positively.

"What? Are you crazy?" the astounded lad squealed.

"No, lad, but I am a sculptor and I see within you the fire and intensity of my David."

The lad shivered and trembled. "Not the Florentine just returned from Rome?"

"The very one lad. The very one…then you have heard of me?"

The lad's voice cracked as he spoke.

"Who has not heard of the creator of the *Bacchus* and the *Pieta* of St. Peter's," the lad said as he crossed himself. "*Il Divino* they call you."

The lad knelt before Michelangelo and kissed his hands.

Now the artist trembled. Throughout his life, Michelangelo sought perfection in his work. He never felt that his work was good enough. He would leave unfinished works he determined to be imperfect or lacking inspiration. He hardly thought of himself as the Divine One who brought life out of stone and paint.

Granacci took control of the situation which now involved two trembling people.

"I know, let's all sit down and have a talk. How about that?"

The lad and the stone cutter looked at Granacci. Michelangelo grinned and the lad nodded yes. It was the lad who spoke first.

"They say your *Bacchus* appears so full of drink that he appears to sway and about to fall and yet is solid and balanced."

"Is that what they say, indeed? Did you hear that Francesco? They say my *Bacchus* is a drunkard."

"Well Michelangelo he is the god of wine and so forth."

"Well indeed he is. What else do they say young man?" asked Michelangelo.

"They say in the *Pieta*," he paused again to cross himself. "Well they say it is a miracle that from a formless block of stone you should be able to bring such perfection."

"You honor me too much. Give credit to the subject as well. Our Lord who died for us is being held by his loving mother. How can such a subject be anything but perfection?"

"*Il Divino*, you don't understand…I mean perhaps I was unclear. They say you brought to life in stone what nature is scarcely able to do in the flesh."

The stone cutter once again trembled at the words being spoken. He insisted that he only did what was asked of him. He decided to get to the point of his studying the youth so intently. He asked the lad if he ever heard of the Board of Works at the Duomo. He was pleased to learn that, though poor, the lad actually attended school. He had been tutored by Marsilio Ficino himself. A bond formed between them as Michelangelo explained how Ficino once tutored him in the Palazzo Medici. The revelation backfired causing the lad to become more awe struck.

Michelangelo turned to Granacci.

"Help me out here Francesco before the lad swoons."

"Yes, divine one. Whatever you request." Francesco quipped. "You boy…listen up. The divine one here has a proposition to make to you."

The lad stood abruptly. "Just because I work in an inn does not mean that I accept propositions."

"Sit down you fool. It's not that kind of proposition. It's…well it's a job offer."

"I'm sorry." Then turning to Michelangelo he expressed his contrition. "I should have known better Master Buonarroti."

He pulled out the bench on the other side of the table and sat his six-foot, four-inch frame down. Michelangelo explained to him the job offer. He talked of the marble at the Duomo and the David which yearns to be freed from it. He even spoke of the money the lad would earn for posing as a model. He held no punches. He told the lad of the long hours which would be involved. He also said that the offer would be taken back should what he would see under the lad's clothes did not match that which was exposed.

"Now lad…by the way what is your name?"

"I am called Davide Mettzini," the lad replied meekly.

Michelangelo looked at Granacci. "His name is even David. Can you believe that?"

"Well, Davide, what do you think of the job offer?"

"I think that I'm happy I will pose in summertime."

The three laughed and ordered a drink to toast the beginning of a new life in an imperfect stone.

As the images of that meeting faded in Arthur's mind, he began to understand better the issue of how many models were used for the *David*. Arthur thought, *So that's what Agnes meant when she said for the David there was only one model. The two drawings for the David, which had appeared in the exhibit in Chicago were of the rejected models,"* Agnes, as if reading his thoughts, glanced his way and after taking a sip of water she continued her story.

"It was a bright September day. The heat of late summer had not yet built up. Michelangelo was in the shed near the Duomo preparing his drawing materials. The shed should not be confused with tool sheds one may find in a backyard of your American homes," she began. "It was more like a cabin in the middle of a garden, surrounded by brick walls affording privacy for the work to be done. And soon the class was back in Renaissance Florence.

There was a knock on the door of the shed. Michelangelo called out. "Come on in."

Davide Mettzini opened the door and entered a world he could only have dreamed about. And yet it was just a wooden structure with a workbench, the marble in the middle and a platform of sorts next to the stone.

"*Buon giorno* Davide, do come in. I'll show you what needs to be done." When they got to the platform Michelangelo explained that it was there that he would stand as instructed while he created the drawings. "Eventually you'll be replaced."

The lad turned pale. *Replaced already before they had even begun?,* he thought.

Realizing that he had misspoken the artist tried to make amends.

"Listen lad…er Davide, I mean that I shall create a wax model as never before seen. I don't think you would be able to pose for the hours I would need you as I carved the stone."

It worked; the lad understood. The stone cutter set up his easel with pad, chalk, and ink. Davide removed his clothes and neatly folded them, placing them on the workbench. Michelangelo peered out from behind the easel.

"Good grief. He's another Francesco in neatness."

"Master Buonarroti what do I do now?" Davide asked though not timidly, as he looked forward to being immortalized in marble.

The artist stood up looking over the easel. It was as he expected. Davide's form was developed in a fashion that he had envisioned for his passionate, young, and robust stone David. His chest showed just the hint of ribs. His hips were narrow as a boy's, not yet fully a man's, as were his genitals. His arms and legs were strong and firm, muscles bulging beneath the skin.

"Good lad, jump in that tub of water in the corner."

Davide looked puzzled but walked over to the trough-like tub. He turned and watched for further direction.

"Jump in and let the water cover you. Then come over here to this platform. Don't worry it shouldn't be too cold, since it's been hot these last several days."

Before the stone cutter had finished speaking Davide jumped into the tub and out again. Dripping from head to toe, he stepped onto the platform and into immortality. As the water dripped from his body, Michelangelo saw crevices and muscles flexing. These he caught in his sketches. After a couple of hours standing in one pose and then another, Davide was told to take a break and get something to eat. He was to return in the afternoon. Day after day this same routine was followed, although most were without the water plunge.

On September 13, 1501 Davide showed up, as usual, early in the morning. He entered through the gated area and found Francesco Granacci in the shed with Michelangelo.

The two artists were standing on either side of a full-sized wax model of the lad. He began to take off his clothes, when the master turned to him.

"Davide, there is no need for that. You are completed. Come here and look at yourself."

The youth took the few steps to stand between the stone cutter and the painter. He walked around the wax figure.

"Do I really look like that?"

Michelangelo was taken aback. He asked if the lad was not pleased with the depiction.

Davide was emphatic in saying it wasn't a displeasure but a wondering if one would see him as a warrior about to do battle.

Francesco nudged Michelangelo. "The boy is astute my friend."

Michelangelo explained his desire to show Davide just before the battle with Goliath, hence there is no head at the lad's feet.

"You, Davide, will never be recognized as the one who gave the inner presence to the stone, but you will for all time be looked at as that warrior ready to fight for freedom for your beloved city, our city...*Firenze.*"

Tears streaked the lad's cheeks for two reasons. His time with Michelangelo was over, and he would return to his mundane duties in the inn to earn what he could. He knew the time would come to end the modeling, but he didn't realize that he would come to admire and love Michelangelo so much that parting would be so upsetting.

"Then the boy king of Israel means more to you than a bible story?" he asked the master stone cutter.

"Davide, it means much more. Why do you weep? You said it pleased you. If this wax model is acceptable, wait until the stone becomes the Giant."

The youth told the master artist he would miss him when his time in the shed was over. This touched Michelangelo's and Francesco's hearts, for they saw in the youth admiration and devotion to his friend. The stone cutter found it difficult to express the purpose of this morning gathering. As he tried to make clear his reasoning, he caused these friends to choke back tears once more. He gave up on words and picked up his hammer and chisel.

"Watch now... for the birth of the giant is about to begin."

He chipped off a piece of the marble where the chest of the giant-David would be located when completed. The marble piece fell to the floor and bounced to a stop at the lad's feet.

"Ah, see Davide, it knows its soul belongs to you." Michelangelo picked up the marble piece. He quickly filed down the sharp edges of the trapezoid-shaped chip and then placed it into Davide's hand. "It will bring you luck my boy, so keep it with my blessing."

It was an emotional moment, so profound that no more work could be planned for the day. They decided to celebrate the upcoming birth of the Giant. As they drank on the Piazza Signoria, a crowd gathered around the master stone cutter. The attention was not at all pleasing to Michelangelo, but Francesco and Davide took delight to be in his shadow. Soon all but a few left the artist to his thoughts and wished him well. There were four who did not leave. They sat a discreet distance away.

As the sun began to set, Michelangelo decided he must return to the shed and secure it. From that moment on, the marble would be closed to anyone's view until it was near completion. The three took a leisurely walk back to the shed, pausing at Donatello's bronze doors at the Baptistery of the Duomo. It was as if Michelangelo had to pay some homage to the master artist of earlier days. Following them were the four men from the piazza, of noble-looking character but with villainous hearts.

When Michelangelo arrived at the gate the three entered the shed and said their good-byes. The master would stay alone with the wax model to plan his next move. Francesco and Davide left and went back towards the piazza. The four who lurked around the corner of the brick wall waited for Michelangelo to leave, but seeing that he was not going to do so, they made their way to a small house near San Marco.

They reported to others gathered there that the heathen statue was about to be carved. Those assembled were members of the Confraternity of Savonarola. The members pledged to attack the statue when it was completed and damage it enough to make it a worthless piece of stone. The focus then shifted to snuffing the life from the model for the outrageous statue. Something must be done about him as he struts around the city boasting of his being a warrior for Florence. Shouts of agreement rang through the house and spilled onto the streets so that when Francesco, on his return to escort Michelangelo back to Casa Buonarroti, passed by he could hear the cries and shouts though not understand their intent. It was clear they were shouting about the new David, so he ran for the shed to warn his friend that there were those who would seek to discredit his work.

"Francesco, the Frate may be gone but his shadow of doom looms over the city to this day. Don't worry yourself. The Board will ensure that the giant is kept safe," said Michelangelo to calm his friend.

"That relieved Granacci and they bantered about awestruck Davide and how he adored *Il Divino*. Into the night the two friends walked, laughing about Michelangelo's new status as a role model," concluded Agnes.

Almost everyone had a hand up as she finished and all had the same question in mind. Kristin got it out first. "Signora la Straga, what happened to Davide Mettzini?"

Agnes answered that no one knows. His name was lost to history except for a brief mention in Marsilio Ficino's journal. "What history knows is this," said Agnes. "On February 28 in 1502 Michelangelo called the *Operai del Duomo* to the shed. Granacci and Davide stood off behind the statue. A large cloth veiled the gigantic sculpture. The board members formed a complete circle around the statue. Michelangelo and Davide pulled the cloth off and the members were astounded. What had begun in September with a chip chiseled from the chest now had the form and appearance it would have in its final glorious stage. So impressed were the board members, they gave Michelangelo his full commission and summoned a contract for more when the statue was completely done.

"Piero Soderini, a friend of Michelangelo's, was present with the board. He had been chosen Gonfalonier of Justice for life. When he saw the magnificent piece, he worked hard to secure other commissions for his friend even before the statue was completed. One of those commissions was to carve twelve statues of saints for the Duomo in Siena. One might say, knowing how vast such an undertaking was when he was working on the David, that it would be foolhardy to accept. But not Michelangelo. The first statue was already started; a St. Francis in marble. The statue was begun by Piero Torrigiani, the very one who gave Michelangelo his broken nose. And now the Stone Cutter Genius was to make right the ill attempt of Piero. It would be the only piece of the twelve completed. It would give Michelangelo the satisfaction of restoring in the destroyed marble, that which Piero had destroyed in the flesh.

"But I go off our topic; let's try to answer Kristin's question. On that February 28th as I said, Davide was present. When it came time to actually move the statue to its permanent location, he was not present. But wait... let us ask Signore Roselli about that part of the story. See, he comes to us now."

Chapter 16: An Unprecedented Assembly

The clock in the restaurant was striking midnight as Roselli walked in. Pietro and Andreas were close behind. The brothers took seats near the entrance.

"*Signora la Straga e Signore Colonna*, you see I got your message and here I am."

The students were itching to ask questions about the confraternity; however, Arthur had different plans. He wanted the students to first hear of the *David*'s debut. He wanted his students to hear about what was probably the most illustrious meeting of artists in the history of the world. He wanted Roselli to present this, for then there might be a chance to determine what that document he had at his meeting contained.

Arthur welcomed Roselli cordially and formally introduced him to the students, though they already knew him. He expressed his regrets for the late hour but assured Roselli of the attention of the students, who were excited to hear his presentation.

Roselli approached the podium and Agnes moved to sit next to Arthur. Arthur's sons thought she could have sat next to Maura Kennedy but she chose their father and this annoyed them.

"*Bella studenti*, as I look into your faces I see the hand of Botticelli and perhaps, gentlemen, the masculine vigor displayed on the ceiling of the Sistine Chapel or in the Giant itself," he began.

The boys felt pumped that they would be compared to such figures of strength and the girls giggled to be compared to the Botticelli *Venus*. Luckily for Arthur the over-the-top comparisons did not impress these street-wise kids for very long.

"*La Signora* has taken you to the first showing of the Giant. It was

February 28th, 1502. But it would be another year before the finishing touches were finally completed. Michelangelo left two spots on the giant unfinished just to demonstrate the progress of the work from raw marble to the highly polished result of almost two years of chiseling, chipping, and polishing. Now you may ask yourself, only two years to make such a marvel? And I would answer that Michelangelo, or *Il Divino* as his contemporaries called him, was highly gifted and quite strong. Though left-handed he chiseled and chipped with both hands and could more speedily bring forth the figure from the marble."

Roselli was on a roll. He presented the lead up to that day of January 25, 1504 flawlessly. He even introduced the students to the *Doni Tondo*, a circular painting of the Madonna with child and nudes in the background. This, one would think, was done to demonstrate the power and creativity of Michelangelo and his ability to multi-task. But what Roselli did was to project a close-up of the painting. Then he pointed out one of the youths in the background.

"Look closely at his features. Are there not similarities to the *David* in facial characteristics and body structure?"

The power to convince people to see something which is not really there is a gift and Roselli had the students hooked; particularly one red-haired one with whom he had an appointment later in the day. He knew they were now questioning Agnes la Straga's insistence that the model for the *David* had disappeared after the second unveiling on June 23, 1503. If that was true, then how did the same model appear in a 1504 painting?

He had planted the doubt successfully; he went on with his show. He painted a spectacular picture for Arthur's students. He continued with the second unveiling on the eve of the Feast of St. John the Baptist, Patron Saint of Florence on June 23rd. He correctly presented how grand an affair the event was. The Giant, as Michelangelo called his statue, was to become a symbol of Florentine freedom. With Savonarola gone, the Borgias in Rome eyeing Tuscany, and the Medici family becoming active, the menacing Giant was to be a constant reminder that the City of Florence was ready for combat; ready to defend its freedom. Throngs of people filled the area around the shed. One side of the shed had been removed so that the statue may be better seen. Michelangelo stood within the remaining walls of the shed. Next to him was Granacci and behind him was the Board of Works. Even the stone cutter's father and brothers were present. There too was Davide Mettzini, standing between

Michelangelo's brothers. All were ready for the unveiling. All waited for the moment eagerly. Roselli brought the students back in time with his descriptive words.

"Francesco, you know I do not hold up well in these types of ceremonies." Michelangelo, who was never truly satisfied with his work unless he thought it to be perfect, was a nervous wreck. "What if they don't like it?"

"Michelangelo," Granacci whispered. "Get a hold of yourself. The whole city will be coming to see your masterpiece and you will be famous; even more famous than that wizard Da Vinci."

The prayer and speeches concluded. Piero Soderini and the Heralds of the Signoria of Florentine government pulled down the cloth revealing the warrior youth poised for battle, looking into the distance at his enemy. The *David* stood unclothed with nothing but a sling held over his shoulder ready for battle. The master stone cutter intended every area of the young warrior to send a message. Each tensed up muscle, the look on his face, the wide-open eyes, the flared nostrils, the stance, the positioning of the legs with body weight shifting ready for action, the sling at the ready, and the closed fist — they all spoke volumes. The Giant-David was truly casting his terrible glare to Goliath and the Philistines in the distance. However the *terribilita,* or a work which brings about awe, grandeur, and excitement, was introduced by Michelangelo to deliver a different message: "Beware: Firenze is ready to fight."

The unveiling was a success. The crowd went wild with admiration; the *terribilata* worked.

"There still remain finishing touches here and there," Michelangelo told admirers who came up to congratulate him. He would take several more months to add those final touches. On that June day he was forced to talk about his work and views on creating art.

Piero Soderini asked the master stone cutter to define the art of sculpting. Piero was a friend so Michelangelo could relax and talk as one would to a friend, revealing his inner most feelings. He told him that sculpting was the art that works by force of taking away.

What he meant could be better understood by what he said later to a fellow Florentine artist who commented on his work as an expression of Michelangelo's thought:

Michelangelo had said, "Now there, my friend, is where you are wrong. A statue, instead of being a human thought invested with external reality by stone, is more truly to be regarded as something which the sculptor seeks to find inside his marble. It's a kind of marvelous discovery."

Having given his all for his Giant on that June day, he slipped away through the crowd to hear what ordinary people were saying about his work.

It may be that Michelangelo felt the need to perfect the statue, but the officials of the Duomo were so impressed that they called for a *practica,* or advisory meeting, to discuss the permanent placement for the Giant.

That meeting took place on January 25th, 1504 when two dozen of the most famous Renaissance artists met to give advice to the Government of Florence.

The cold, clear, crisp day arrived. Some of the most important painters, sculptors, architects, engineers, and Florentine leaders were arriving at the *Operai del Duomo* for the discussion.

Granacci entered Casa Buonarroti excited as a school boy. Lodovico was just leaving the house to watch the gathering.

"My son refuses to come to the meeting for his *David*. Perhaps you could talk some sense into him," the flustered father said as he flung his hands into the air and continued on his way.

Granacci ran up to Michelangelo's room and threw open the door. This time, a fully clothed Michelangelo lay across his bed dressed as if he were a laborer on the farm. The familiar boots, still frayed, were on his feet.

"Buonarotti, are you crazy? Get yourself washed and present yourself to the assembly."

"No. My work is not completed, so I will not go. Here's what I intend to do. I shall go to the shed and refine the Giant a bit more," he insisted as he pulled off his tunic and began to wash.

"You are mad. The greatest artists of the age are here and you will not address them."

"I have informed Piero of my desire that it should be displayed in a safe place so that it cannot be damaged. You see, I took your warning from those shouts you heard last year," Michelangelo countered as he dried himself and slipped the rumpled tunic back over his head.

"At least that is something you did correctly. You must listen my friend." Granacci paused and sat on the edge of the bed. He took one of

Michelangelo's hands into his own.

"This hand, your mind, your vision, have created a marvelous work. The Giant lives as sure as I take breath, Michelangelo. It lives and speaks to all who see it. It is a symbol for our beloved city. To those who would conquer us it says, 'stay away'."

"My, you are eloquent this morning. It must be the crisp air."

Granacci bolted up. He went to the dresser, took the basin and threw its contents out the window. He poured more water into the basin.

"Michelangelo Buonarroti, I have come at your own father's bidding to pour my heart out to you and you ridicule me," he said with bruised feelings. "It would be good if you would also wash your hair."

The stone cutter was the one who now jumped up from the bed. He ran to Francesco and pulled him around to face him.

"*Idioso*, don't you see what this gathering intends to do? They will strut like peacocks to show their power. They will present their grand ideas with eternal wisdom. In the end, no one will agree; for that is how all Florentine discussions end."

"*Si*, I see your point. But still, it's your work my friend. Besides, the wizard himself has come. Da Vinci is here. Soderini already has you two in competition for that fresco for the Palazzo's salon. Should you not speak with him?"

"There will be time for that but not in conjunction with the Giant. Let him give his opinion. When no decision is reached they will come back to me and I shall have the final say. Now does that please you?" And with that he once again removed his tunic as Francesco pushed his head into the basin and washed his hair.

"Michelangelo I should know better than to try and out-think you. However, you still needed to wash. Now, I shall walk with you to the shed."

As the young artists made their way to the shed where the *David* waited, the notable assembly was called into solemn session. The Chief Herald of the Signory, Governing Council, Francesco Filarete, rose to speak first. He presented the government's view.

"There are only two places where the statue may be set up. The first is where the Donatello *Judith* now stands next to the entrance door of the Palazzo Signoria. The second place would be in the courtyard of the Palazzo where the Donatello *David* now stands. As far as I'm concerned it should be there since the right leg of Donatello's *David* is imperfect."

Leonardo Da Vinci sketched, as the others spoke, waiting for his turn.

The wood carver, Francesco Monciatto, proposed it be placed where it was originally intended, at the Duomo.

Sandro Botticelli and Cosimo Rosselli rose to their feet simultaneously. "I second the motion," they cried out so forcefully that Da Vinci dropped his pen and paid attention to their words. It was clear why Botticelli would want it at the Duomo for he viewed it as a religious piece. If the statue were on holy ground, it would be safe from those who still followed Savonarola and who would attack it because of its nudity.

The council was hardly solemn after that outburst. One artist after another made impassioned pleas for its placement at their preferred location.

Giuliano San Gallo, the famous architect, spoke.

"I agree that the Duomo would be ideal for reverential reasons. However such a location would be too open and the elements would cause harm to the statue. It would be best to place it under the Loggia dei Lanza, so that it might be protected."

A furor rose as to the religious significance and the secular symbolism. Soon the air was filled with expressions of theory.

When the Second Herald of the Signoria spoke, he got the discussion back to location and not theological or political theories.

Angelo Manfidi caused a greater row by stating, "Placement of the *David* under the middle arch would cause disruption to ceremonial occasions."

So he voted for the arch under which the *Judith* now stood.

It was clear where the government wanted it placed; both Heralds had the location of the *Judith* in mind. But the debate was not over. The painter, Fillippino Lippi, suggested the piazza in front of the Palazzo would be best. The jeweler, Silvestro, agreed with Lippi.

Giovanni Piffero, the father of Benvenuto Cellini, wanted the courtyard; he thought the loggia would make it easier for vandals to damage the statue.

And so it went until Da Vinci, the wizard of the early Renaissance, could take no more.

He once again placed his sketching pen down. Those who looked over to him noticed that he had made a drawing of the *David*.

"It would not be a problem to place the statue in the loggia if it was done properly. Proper placement would not interfere with ceremonies."

A quiet spread across the room. With great hesitation the painter Piero di Cosimo rose.

"It would seem we are at an impasse. Where is the master sculptor? Should he not be here to give us his opinion? Should it not be he who chooses the location?"

Leonardo Da Vinci smiled with consent and soon the entire council was of the same mind. In an instant Granacci was sent from the assembly to fetch the master stone cutter.

When he entered the shed, he found his friend atop a scaffold. He was working on the hair of the Giant.

"Michelangelo, they are calling for you. You were right; they are of the opinion that you should choose."

The stone cutter placed his hammer and chisel into his belt.

"I think I'll leave this little area of marble unfinished. Then everyone will know it's my work and how the stone originally looked."

"Wonderful, whatever you think. No one will see the top of the head anyway. Did you not hear me? They want to see you."

"I heard you and I'm coming down to go with you, have no fear. But let them stew for a bit longer. I need one question answered."

"*Si*, whatever you ask. But please ask it and let's get on our way," pleaded Granacci.

"Was the debate between theological and political thought?" asked Michelangelo.

"*Si*, it was. How did you know?"

"What did I say this morning in my father's house?"

The illumination in Granacci's face indicated that he remembered.

"You said they would eventually call upon you. And now they have, so let's go!"

"Okay but one more question. Should I wash the marble dust off first?" a smirking Michelangelo asked.

Along the way, Michelangelo prodded Francesco for more information. They entered the *Operai del Duomo*. Representatives of the Wool Guild were present since it was they who came up with the money to finance the project. The Assembly stood as Michelangelo made his way through the finely dressed artists and governmental leaders in the ragged tunic and leggings of a workman; his tools still hanging from his leather belt.

As he passed his elder, Da Vinci, he paused. "I have chosen the Battle of Cascina for my fresco for the Palazzo."

"Good choice Michelangelo. You are good with fusing throbbing life with colossal grandeur. As for me I have chosen the Battle of Anghiari."

"*Va bene*, Master Da Vinci, we shall decorate the Palazzo with the victories of our past."

Off the stone cutter went to take his seat next to the Chief Herald of the Signory. As if Michelangelo now needed an introduction to such an august body he was nevertheless presented to the assembly. He rose, taking a small woolen cap from his head as he did so. The marble dust fell from it like a little snowfall. In the back of his mind he thought, *Maybe I should have washed better.*

In the end he sided with the government. It was a significant political statement to do so. The Giant-David was to be moved to the Palazzo and set where the Donatello *Judith* now stood. The date of May 14th, 1504 was set for moving the giant.

That winter and spring moved too quickly for Michelangelo as he tried to perfect the Giant each day while creating the cartoon of the Battle of Cascina. Da Vinci was hard at work on his Battle sequence but then he was already an accomplished and renowned painter. Michelangelo's glory came from carving marble. The *Doni Tondo* was the only Michelangelo painting known at this point. And so the cartoon, a chalk and ink sketching of the battle scene, would be prepared first.

On May 13th the shed was torn down and the arch over the courtyard gate removed so the Giant could be moved out of the Opera and into the street. The statue was suspended on a device which would allow it to flow back and forth as the moving scaffold on wheels was pulled by forty men.

"At midnight on May 14th they rolled the Giant into the streets of Florence. It would take four days to move it to the Piazza de Signoria and up to the Palazzo. On the 18th of May in 1504, at noon, it was mounted on the pedestal where the *Judith* had once stood. The entire city cheered." Roselli concluded his presentation and opened the floor to questions.

Danny Garcia rose. He politely but firmly stated that Mr. C. had told them that there had been an attack on the statue during that moving process. "Why didn't you mention it?"

Roselli made it clear that what Arthur had said was rumor and never proven in history.

"On the contrary Signore Roselli," began Agnes la Straga. "In the

1898 biography, by John Addington Symonds, there is a passage which speaks of the attack."

Roselli was not at all happy with her contradiction but had to address it.

"You are correct. However, it is but a sentence and the action came to nothing so it is unimportant to the story we present tonight."

He thanked Danny for the question and pursued others.

Agnes smiled at Arthur, who nodded, and sat herself down.

Maribeth spoke next. "Signore Roselli, you mentioned the youth who posed for the statue. Whatever happened to him?"

Roselli actually liked the question. He played up the youth's presence in the *Doni Tondo* painting, therefore obliterating Agnes' theory of the lad's mysterious disappearance. He explained that as with many who served in such capacities they are lost to history. He offered a theory that after he posed for the Madonna painting he went off to pose for other artists and went on to live his life in the shadows, as most of us do, as far as history is concerned.

The clock struck one and Roselli caught Arthur's eye.

"I think your teacher is ready to send you off to bed. I understand that you have a big day tomorrow as you will visit Casa Buonarroti and the Academia where the actual *David* is enshrined. Be sure you look closely at the two wax figures of the *David* created by Michelangelo."

He did it again. Roselli had placed doubt in the young minds. There really was more than one model for the Giant-David.

Arthur rose to thank Roselli and asked his students to get some rest, for tomorrow would be a big day. Roselli was gracious and left immediately. As he passed Ryan on the stairway leading up to the reception area he whispered to him

"And later today I shall meet you, right?

Ryan stopped in mid-step. He looked around. The students crowded the staircase trying to get past him. Roselli poked him to move along and not draw attention. Ryan got the hint and moved. Jenny and Jessica passed him up noting that he was a bit pokey. Danny, who was Ryan's roommate, was chatting with Mike and told him that he'd see him in the room. All of this hardly registered. He turned to face Roselli who remained next to him clogging the narrow staircase.

"Sure I'll be there," Ryan assured Roselli.

Roselli, smiled with delight. He slipped him a paper which had the directions to the Orsini house on it.

"It's not far from the *Academia del Arti* so you shouldn't have a problem. Just look for Pietro standing outside."

He made his way through the students and towards his suite. John and Rich took note of the conversation between Roselli and Ryan, and, as soon as the curator left, they flanked Ryan. Their presence caused Ryan to break out in a sweat. The boys noted this, too, since Ryan was usually the picture of cool perfection.

"Hey Ryan, what did Roselli have to say?" asked Rich.

"Nothing much. He asked what I thought of his presentation; stuff like that."

"Really, he valued your evaluation that much? You're quite the expert on history lessons then. I'll try to remember that for tomorrow. I think we'll get a lot of it," commented John.

"Whatever John. See you tomorrow," Ryan ran to catch up with Danny who was at the door of their room.

John commented that they should keep an eye on Ryan tomorrow. Rich agreed that, after seeing his reaction on the Piazza Savonarola with Roselli and then seeing his chummy talk tonight, they could take no chances.

"On the other hand," John said after some thought. "Perhaps he really is star struck that such a big shot takes an interest in him. Let's not get Dad all bent out of shape for now."

Rich agreed. They entered the room to find Agnes and their father seated at the table having a cappuccino. On the table were photos of the Ramsey brooch. Arthur asked if the boys were okay. He thought they looked strange. The boys were hard-pressed to find a suitable answer, so they just stumbled their way through saying how tired they were.

"Right, so get yourselves to bed. We're just winding up here anyway. Got to keep a step ahead of Roselli, right Agnes?"

"*Si, Arturo*, he's one smart cookie, as you Americans would say."

"Dad, do we really say that anymore?" the dry-witted and sarcastic Rich asked.

"Richie, the signora only meant that Roselli is smart."

"I know what she meant," Rich replied coolly as John pulled him towards their bedroom.

"Just hold on. Something is bugging you guys. I can tell. Let's have it."

"Dad it's late and the morning will be here before you know it. Let's just drop it," John almost pleadingly said.

By this time Agnes was feeling quite uncomfortable. She could tell the boys were not pleased to find her in their father's room. She also felt it wasn't her place to add fuel to this growing confrontation. Arthur was not about to let the issue drop. One thing he and Donna had always agreed upon was that all issues would be settled before they said goodnight. That practice was just as valid with his sons as with his wife as far as he was concerned.

"I want you two to come and sit right here by us," commanded Arthur.

"Good God, you are such a *gabadost*," John muttered as he made his way back to the table dragging Rich behind him.

Agnes tried to suppress her laugh in hearing John speaking the Italian word meaning very stubborn. The boys noticed her vain attempt and that aggravated them more.

"Listen boys, the last thing I need, or any of us need, is division in the ranks. Too much is at stake. We need to know what was written on that manuscript Roselli flashed around earlier tonight. There's also this new information from Alun. Let's have it. What's bugging you? And while I'm at it, we don't use the Lord's name in vain in this family, so stop it."

John and Rich began to fidget in their chairs. Their father stared daggers as them. He had used that method since they were little and it always made them collapse in their defiance. This time was no different.

They sputtered out that they thought their mom was a good wife, that she loved their father, and that no one should come around and try to break them up.

"Heavenly hosts, is that what this is all about." Now it was Arthur's turn to sputter almost incoherently. Agnes stepped in.

"*Giovanni e Ricardo*, there is no doubt that your mother is most fortunate to have sons such as you who come to her defense even when it is unnecessary. Believe me, in this case, it is not needed."

Arthur finally found words and looked into his sons' eyes with affection and trust. He explained that Agnes was in the room only to plan tomorrow's events. The cappuccino was just that, a warm drink to keep them awake as they planned. His sons looked at him askance.

"You know what I mean. We're tired and we had to think clearly. Now boys I think you have something to say to Signora la Straga."

John and Rich apologized for being presumptuous. Agnes told them such gallantry on behalf of their mother needed no apology. She went on to say that she could only hope that one day someone would love her enough to come to her defense.

Having resolved the issue, they retired to face the new day with a fresh outlook. The red-faced boys went off to their room. On the way, Rich turned and shared what they had seen pass between Ryan and Roselli. John regretted his brother's decision. Both Arthur and Agnes renewed their worries over the danger which may lie ahead. Arthur's mind was spinning with how to deal with the situation. He determined it best that Ryan not be left alone at any time. If that meant bringing in some of the other kids to keep a watchful eye on Ryan, then so be it. The boys assured them that they would be like glue on paper when it came to Ryan.

Chapter 17: The Spirit of David

In most homes and many hotels in Italy there are no screens on the windows. When the morning breezes rolled into the boys' room they brought along a few friendly and pesky flies. The buzzing around their heads finally forced them to wake up and swat them away. Rich looked at the clock. It was 9:00 a.m.

"Holy cow! Johnny get up! It's already nine o'clock."

The two ran around their room gathering their clothes. They were in and out of the shower, shaved, brushed, and dressed in record time.

John was panicking. "Where's Dad? Make sure he is up."

Rich ran across the sitting room. The open balcony doors reminded him that they hadn't told their father about the crunchy stuff on the floor and the chairs at the table being out of place. In a blink, he knocked on his father's door, opened it a crack and saw an empty bed.

"John, he's already gone."

This was a relief. They didn't want to think about the students running around the hotel without their father present.

"Great, let's get something to eat."

"EAT?" screamed Rich. "We're supposed to be glue on paper with Ryan and God only knows where he is and we're still up here."

Taking two steps at a time they reached the lower level with a bounding jump which thundered their arrival across the wooden floor. The entire group, busy chatting about the day's activities, looked up to see the two staggering into the restaurant after the last jump. Agnes waved to them. She and Arthur were seated with Maura. The boys waved back but decided to sit with Danny, Ryan, Patricia, and Kristin. Patricia said yes immediately when they asked if they could join the table. She still had feelings for John, though she would never give him the satisfaction of saying so.

Arthur walked up with Maura at his side. Each carried a plate of food. Agnes was behind them with glasses of orange juice. Arthur leaned in between the boys.

"I thought it best that you slept in after the excitement of last night."

"You guys are getting preferred service this morning," said Maura. "Had a rough night I hear."

"Yeah you might say that," Rich commented with bowed head.

No sooner had the adults left than the others wanted to know what had happened last night. The boys told them that they had had an argument with their father but it was okay now.

"Hmmmn…" began Kristin. "I bet it involved that la Straga woman."

"Cool it Kristin, the signora is okay. Trust me," answered Rich.

"Well I just thought…"

"We can relate," chimed in John. "But really she's all right with us and with our dad too, if you know what I mean."

The girls both looked at each other and nodded that they knew exactly what John meant. Danny hadn't a clue as to what they were talking about. And as for Ryan, all he kept doing was looking at his watch.

"Hey Ryan what time is it?" asked Rich.

"Oh…I don't know let me look. It's 9:45."

The boys and the others just looked at each other and then at Ryan who was a million miles away again.

As the ten o'clock bells rang in the campanile of Santo Trinito down the Via Apostoli, Arthur announced that it was time to visit the bathrooms and then meet in front of the hotel. By 10:15 everyone was gathered and they were off to the *Galleria del Academia*.

They had arranged for Ambrogio to meet them there later with the bus to take them to Casa Buonarroti. Arthur thought a good walk in the warm morning sun would be just what the doctor ordered for everyone. Once again, John led the way. He took the route which allowed the group to pass San Lorenzo and the Medici Palazzo, both of which had played such an important role in Michelangelo's life. Arthur assured them they would get to enter the church and palace once they visited the *David*. The group turned onto Via de Gori. On their way to Via Ricasoli, Ryan suddenly grabbed his stomach and announced that he had to get back to San Lorenzo to find a bathroom. Arthur played along in the most gullible manner possible. He told Ryan the group would wait for him at the corner of the Medici Palazzo.

"John, go along with Ryan."

"Really Mr. C., that won't be necessary. I'll be right back," Ryan insisted. "It's only one block."

Ryan ran off, still holding onto his stomach, towards the church. Soon he was out of sight and the group chatted about Michelangelo living in the Medici Palazzo from age thirteen to seventeen. Arthur pointed to the spot where the bronze balls of the Medici coat of arms would have been. He reminded them they were the ones they had seen in the exhibit back in Chicago. As Arthur continued his improvised review lesson, telling of the lightning strike on the Medici coat of arms on the eve of Lorenzo's death, he gave a sign to John and Rich. They slipped away and ran towards the church of San Lorenzo.

Ryan had entered the church and was running down the center aisle of highly polished marble. The pillars on each side brought one's view directly to the sanctuary, but that did not interest Ryan. He was looking for another way out so that he could double back to the Orsini house. Ryan tripped over the grave of Cosimo Medici, grandfather to Lorenzo de Medici, to whom the Magi ring was first given. It was he who would form the Confraternity of the Tre Magi. The members of that confraternity would take charge of Lorenzo's funeral. They made up the core membership of the Order of the Magi as the confraternity would come to be known after the fall of the Medici.

Ryan was picking himself up when John and Rich quietly entered and hid behind one of the giant pillars lining the nave. They watched as Ryan spotted a side door and ran to it. The boys were right behind, never losing sight of him as he made his way out. Ryan found himself in a line of tourists entering the *Capello Medici*. He managed to cut through the line and headed down towards the Palazzo Corsi behind which was the Orsini house. It was no short run from San Lorenzo to the Orsini House, but Ryan made it. He spotted Pietro standing outside and stopped in front of him, panting fiercely. Pietro, never the sensitive type, grabbed him by the shoulders and guided him into the house. John and Rich watched from a secluded doorway in the Palazzo Vechietti across the street. Their objective was to find a way to get into that house and see what happened to Ryan.

Pietro led Ryan up the wooden staircase to the second floor. They entered the library where Roselli had met with Girolamo Orsini before the confraternity had gathered at Piazza Savonarola. Ryan was a little nervous, but also excited. It was always Arthur's sons and Danny who got all the glory. He was just the pretty preppy boy; okay for girls to fawn over but untouchable as far as the guys were concerned. He was just too pretty. Ryan scanned the room. He recognized the Frate Savonarola from the slides Arthur had shown. In fact, the painting was a duplicate of the photo in the presentation. Roselli was seated at the large table and rose when Pietro entered with the lad.

"Ryan, how nice to see you again. Let me introduce you to our little group," Roselli stated, as he began the introductions. "At the further end is our host, Signore Orsini, the scholar who conducts our research and finds the information we need."

Ryan looked at Roselli with questioning eyes as if to ask *what kind of research does a confraternity need?* But he remained silent and instead asked "how do you do?" to the elder gentleman.

"This is Signore Giorgio Gaddi. Let us say that he ensures we remain safe in our work. Here is the lovely Signorina Anastasia Gillespie. She coordinates our efforts to the data we collect to make sure we are following the right path to our goal. And you already know Pietro and Andreas Giuliano, our enforcers.

"Lastly is our esteemed Signore Raphael Ruffolo who is an expert on art history and legendary art objects. *Signorina e Signore* this is Ryan O'Donnell from the United States."

"*Mi piacere Ryan,*" they answered in unison.

Roselli invited the student to take a seat next to him. He explained they were studying a very old document and he could be very useful in helping them find an important art object. Ryan was dazed by the attention, but managed to say that he had no idea were art objects might be found.

"*Non importa,* Ryan. You know more than you think. If you would cooperate with us, you would become part of a team that will find a treasure beyond belief," Orsini confided to him.

The lad's entire persona took on a glow which emphasized his bright pink polo shirt, gleaming white pants and white tennis shoes.

"Okay, tell me what I have to do," the now thrilled lad said.

"All in good time my boy. First we must induct you into the confraternity," Anastasia counseled with a smile.

As Ryan was being introduced, John and Rich made their way to the Palazzo Corsi which adjoined the Orsini house at the rear. The four story palazzo had long ago been turned into apartments. It was ideally located in the city centre near the most famous buildings of Florence including the Duomo and San Lorenzo Church. The boys decided to try and get into the fourth story apartment hoping that a rear window or balcony would allow them to drop to the third floor of the Orsini house. There was a small office on the ground floor where they found a pretty young signorina with raven hair and blue eyes typing on the computer.

"*Scusi signorina. Parla inglese?*" asked John as he leaned onto the corner of the counter smiling so sweetly that the bored girl's disposition had to soften.

"*Si*, I do. May I help you?"

John spun out a tale very slowly so she could easily comprehend his English. His brothers and father were coming to Italy soon and wished to rent a self catering apartment in City Centre accessible to all the museums and business areas. He explained that he and his brother were here with students this week and were to inquire about likely spots for him.

"By the way, my name is *Giovanni e lei?*"

"Angelina Rosatti."

"Well then Angelina Rosatti would you have a sister or cousin for my brother here. He's so shy. Not good with girls."

Rich could have whacked him in the head, were it not that he knew it was just a line. Rich was sensitive about his shyness around girls once they got beyond the friendship stage. While his brother smoldered, John continued his tale and soon he had a key to the fourth floor apartment to inspect.

"*Mille grazie*, we won't be but a few minutes. When do you get off work?"

"In an hour," Angelina replied.

"How convenient. See you then."

The boys ran up the stairs to the fourth floor. Unlocking the door they quickly scanned the neat and clean apartment. At the other end of the long living room was a large double door opening onto a small balcony. Richie was still griping about being portrayed as the idiot brother when John, already on the balcony, told him to find a bed sheet. Still grumbling, Rich ran to the adjoining bedroom and found an extra set of sheets in a closet. He brought the top one to John.

"Johnny, just because you helped to make a movie doesn't mean that we can do this kind of stunt," he cautioned.

"It's not a stunt, Richie. All we have to do is lower ourselves just a few feet onto the roof below and find a way into the building. It's a piece of cake," John assured his brother.

By the time he calmed his brother, John had the end of the sheet tied around the balcony railing.

"I'll go first. Make sure the knot holds and then come over yourself. I will help you get down."

Rich did as he was told and watched John lower himself quite carefully down the sheet, letting go and falling the last couple of feet.

"Okay Richie, come on down. I'll catch you."

"I can do it without help," he said while he climbed over the railing.

He too let go at the end of the sheet and fell into Johnny. As they both lay on the roof, each rolled to the edge to peer over and look for a likely entrance.

"Guess what John?"

"What?"

"We should have taken an extra sheet to get down to the windows under us if there are any."

"Nice time to think of it, Rich. Hey get a look at the Dome of the Duomo, kind of neat isn't it?" the artisitic John distractedly commented.

Rich remained unimpressed and nervously peered over the edge of the roof.

"There's a long balcony over here, but I don't know if we can jump onto it."

John crawled over to where Rich hung partially over.

"Yep, it's a balcony all right. Any suggestions?"

Rich offered a plan and they decided to try it. John would hold onto Rich and lower him over the side. The distance to the balcony was not too great so he could just let go and fall onto the balcony. To get John down, they decided they would use both of their belts to create a rope tied to the decorative molding atop the palazzo. As John was climbing down the belts, one belt became loose and dropped Johnny down to the balcony with a thud and a buckle to his head.

"Are you all right?" a concerned Rich asked.

John said yes; Rich put the belt back on. Luckily, John didn't need a belt to hold his pants up. The boys peered through the French doors into a formal sitting room. They tried the door handle; it was unlocked. Still on the floor they crawled beneath the fluttering curtains. Realizing that there was no need to crawl, they stood up and stepped onto a rug-covered marble floor. Gilt-framed portraits of people from centuries ago lined the walls. A giant mirror hung over the fireplace. The furnishings were plush, what their mom would call baroque.

Quite alone in the room, they moved quickly toward the door, opening it a crack. They saw a hallway and a staircase to the right, about three feet from them. John stuck his head through the opening between the door and the door frame. Seeing no one, he motioned that they should move to the staircase and listen for voices. They did not have to wait long. Ryan's voice was easily distinguishable. He was answering a series of questions about Arthur and the students. He was telling the interrogator that he knew nothing about Signora la Straga. Rich whispered that this would have been a good time to have Dad's golden leprechaun coin. The king would come in handy right now. John nodded agreement as they tiptoed down the stairs towards the sound of the voices. A door came into view. Once at the last couple of stairs, it became parallel to them. It was slightly ajar. They could see Ryan and several other people sitting around a table. Each of them asked questions.

Just as Rich and John were deciding what to do next, Roselli appeared in the doorway.

"Now Ryan, it's time to be inducted into the confraternity. Please, if you don't mind, climb onto the table and lay down on your back," Roselli kindly directed.

Ryan felt feelings he had never before experienced. Tingling in his stomach, like being on a roller coaster, was the only one he recognized. He climbed onto the table.

"Good lad, now we are going to remove your lovely shirt, but don't worry. You'll get it back," Raphael said as he helped the lad remove his shirt.

He felt another emotion never before experienced. This time it was not a tingling of anxiety but one which tickled pleasantly when the human hand touched his skin. Still, he allowed his shirt to be removed. As Ryan reacted to these sensations, a person took hold of each of his ankles and wrists, all the while Roselli calmly spoke about Ryan's contribution to a history-making event. Ryan stopped fidgeting. The boys saw his legs stop moving and the people holding his ankles exerted very little pressure.

Soothing and restful music was playing. The boys could not identify it, but knew it was neither classical nor new age. A woman holding a wooden box came into sight. Roselli opened the box and removed a silver blade. The woman took out a silver vial.

"Rich, he's got a knife. We have to do something."

"Johnny, follow my lead. We'll make a diversion and then we'll walk in as if we should be there. When all hell breaks loose make a run for it."

Rich ran down to the main level, opened the front door, and slammed it shut.

He ran back to John on the stairs. In a moment all the activity stopped. Roselli lifted the knife slowly. Several drops of blood fell back onto Ryan's chest where the curator had made a small cut into his flesh. He paused, gave a nod and waited.

Pietro and Andreas swung open the door and ran into the hall and headed down to the main floor entrance as John and Rich crouched on the stairs. Seeing nothing, they ran out into the street. John made a beeline for the library door, as Rich ran down the stairs to lock the door before joining his brother. Ryan was sitting up now, shaking his head. The boys rushed Roselli and Anastasia, knocking the knife, the box, and the vial from their hands. The confraternity watched, stunned, as the ivory-handled knife and silver vial fell to the floor. They were momentarily shocked and immobile.

"Ryan! Get out of here right now!" yelled John.

Ryan jumped up on the table, ran to the empty end and jumped off behind Rich. Rich grabbed a chair, held it in front of Roselli and demanded he let Ryan go. After a brief tussle with Girogio, John grabbed the knife and held Girogio and Raphael at bay with it.

Ryan, despite pain from the bleeding cut, saw a candelabrum on a side table. He grabbed it and threw it out the window. It crashed onto the street below. Candle pieces and shattered glass scattered everywhere. A crowd of tourists formed in front of the building, blocking Pietro and Andreas from the main door. Looking for another way in, they ran to find another entrance.

Roselli and Anastasia moved backwards towards the fireplace and the painting of Savonarola. With crowds forming below, they would do nothing to bring more attention to the situation. Orsini had moved to the fireplace and armed himself with a brass poker. Roselli explained that Ryan had come of his own free will to help make history. It fell on deaf ears. John insisted that Giorgio and Raphael join the others at the fireplace, brandishing the knife in their faces. Ryan reached from behind

Rich and over the table to grab his shirt from the document-strewn table. He felt the crunch of what he thought to be paper as he took his shirt and held it against his wound. He and Rich now took cover behind John. They all three backed up towards the library door.

"Now Roselli, I don't know what you're up to with your confraternity, but you can't have Ryan. We're leaving, so just stay where you are," commanded John.

The three nearly flew out the door and down the stairs. Unlocking the door they ran into the street, plowing through the tourists.

The confraternity members fell over themselves as they tried to run down the stairs. Their progress was stopped by the swarming tourists drawn by the broken window and the candelabrum on the sidewalk. They made a hasty retreat back to the library.

The three boys ran like the wind through San Lorenzo church to the Medici Chapel where members of the Medici family, including *Il Magnifico*, were buried. They ran into the *Cappella Medici* where a guard insisted Ryan put on his shirt while they were in this holy place.

"*Va bene*, no problem, signore," an obedient Ryan answered.

He took his shirt and shook it out before pulling it over his head. The parchment twisted within the shirt fell to the marble floor before the simply decorated tomb of Lorenzo de Medici.

"Hey Ryan what's this?" asked John, as he picked up the yellowed parchment with Italian writing on it.

"Holy crap…" he covered his mouth and apologized to the guard. Taking the boys to the side of the chapel, Ryan explained it was some kind of writing of Savonarola himself or one of his followers… he wasn't sure.

"Rich, Dad needs to see this. Ryan, are you sure that you're okay?"

Ryan pulled up his shirt and pressed a tissue taken from his pocket onto the cut.

"I'm fine John. I can't thank you enough," he grabbed hold of John so tightly that it was difficult to breath. "You guys saved my life. I didn't even think you liked me."

"Good grief Ryan, your pink shirt may be a bit much but we think you're an okay guy. Don't we John?"

John coughed out agreement as Ryan released his hold. But then it was Rich's turn to be hugged. The guard, thinking that the boys were about to become too physical, soon put a stop to it.

"There will be none of that nonsense in here boys. Get going," he said in Italian, but the three of them caught his intent.

John looked around the chapel thoughtfully and reverently.

"Well it looks as if the Medici and the Frate are at odds again guys."

Folding the document gently, he slipped it under his tee shirt with the head of *David* print and motioned that they should all leave.

Arthur and the group were anxiously walking around the Accademia entrance when the three arrived at the entrance area.

Maura Kennedy noticed Ryan appeared a bit pale. "You look peaked, are you ill Ryan."

He assured her that he was fine and that something had just disagreed with him but that he got rid of them.

"Them?" she asked.

"I mean it," he clarified.

Maura never noticed the red blotch forming on Ryan's shirt but Arthur saw it.

He asked the boys if everything was under control.

"I think we're safe now, Dad. But boy, do John and I have a story to tell you!" Rich whispered.

"I can't wait to hear all about it, Rich. Perhaps we should go into the Academia now. We'll discuss it at dinner if everything else is okay. Oh, and give this bandage to Ryan. I think he needs one."

"No problem but can I have your shoulder bag for awhile? I picked up something and it would be better kept in the bag."

Arthur gave Rich the bag after he removed the velvet pouch which held the golden coin of the leprechaun king. He placed the pouch in his pants pocket. John slipped the document out of his shirt and into the bag.

Arthur and his sons got through security and entered the Accademia. His students gathered behind him with Agnes and Maura bringing up the rear. He was about to present one of the highlights of the tour, a highlight for which the students had been preparing to encounter for weeks. Arthur reflected on the time when he and Donna had first visited the Galleria. It was during a post graduate course he had taken at Loyola University's Rome campus. They had been awestruck.

Now, once again, here he was at the Giant's doorstep. This time, given all they had been through, there was a feeling of wonder and an attachment to the work, as if they knew the giant personally.

The group entered the long gallery. On each side were unfinished marbles begun by the master stone cutter. *St. Matteo*, the only part of a twelve-part project begun for the Florentine Duomo, was easily identified. Towards the front was a roughed out version of the *Pieta,* but this one had Nicodemus handing down the body of Christ to Mary. Directly before them, standing on a pedestal under a semi circle dome held up by replicas of ancient Roman pillars, was the *David.*

Arthur couldn't help himself: "Behold our friend the Giant; the *David* of Michelangelo."

Realizing how melodramatic he had been, Arthur quickly told his students they were free to roam the Galleria and take a close look at all the pieces. His students, however, were awestruck. Perhaps it was due to the preparation presentations, or a feeling of closeness they had created. Whatever it was, they stood where Arthur had stopped them. Whenever a group of seventeen-to-twenty-one-year-olds pause in awe, for any length of time, one can legitimately feel a sense of accomplishment. That accomplishment was exactly what Arthur and Agnes felt. To give him his due, Roselli could have felt that way also for his part in the presentations.

"Okay, we had best take a closer look at the works. The day has taken longer than expected so there isn't much time."

"Right Mr. C.," said Mike as he began to stroll alone down the gallery towards the *David.* In an instant, the entire group re-animated and swarmed the *David.* Each tried to sneak a touch but most could only reach the base or feet. Soon, some of the girls realized that by posing in such a way in a photograph it would seem they were patting the *David*'s rump. It became the thing to do. They talked Danny and Arthur's boys into doing it for a laugh. Ryan felt too embarrassed to play along and the other guys simply refused to even pretend to do such a thing. Ryan stood in front of the statue looking at it and holding his chest now and then as a twinge came and went.

Arthur and Agnes joined them at the statue, on either side of Ryan.

"So what do you think, Ryan?" Agnes asked gently.

The lad came out of his mesmerized state. "Oh, hi. What do I think? Well I think that Davide Mettzini was one hunk of a guy as Jenny would say."

Jenny, overhearing her name, came over.

"So Ryan do you agree with me, about the *David* I mean?"

Ryan and Arthur laughed. The rest of the students gathered around them.

"So what's so interesting?" the guys asked with one voice.

"Not what you think, *idiosi,*" answered Kristin.

Mike finally reached the group after his slow walk up to the statue. He had examined every unfinished Michelangelo work and the *David* from a distance, soaking in every detail. The football player took a position behind Ryan.

"Hey what's going on?" he asked.

Ryan told him that nothing in particular was happening. They were just admiring the statue and commenting on the model they had learned about, he told Mike.

Mike looked up at the statue. "Mr. C., look at his face. Doesn't it look exactly as… well as Signora la Straga described it?"

Arthur agreed. He said once again how *David* was looking towards the Philistines. He was not the victorious warrior yet. He was getting ready to make his move and that look, his stance, served as a warning. Arthur reminded them that was the scriptural interpretation. What they had heard last night was the political statement of how this statue was meant to deliver to the Borgias of Rome and other European leaders who had their eyes on Florence the message of "stay away, we will fight for our freedom."

Mike was still on the biblical story. "Mr. C. didn't David become the King of Israel?"

Arthur confirmed that he had.

"Well then, if he's Jewish, how come he's not…you know like the rest of us guys?"

Arthur, at first, hadn't a clue as to what he was getting at but all the guys and girls knew. Johnny was doubled over with laughter trying to control himself. Rich made his way around to stand next to Mike.

"Mike it's called circumcision," he whispered to him.

"Thanks Rich. Mr. C., how come the *David* isn't circumcised?"

Arthur, now realizing the humor in Mike's question, smiled. Could it be the guys were asking a real question based on Jewish faith tradition in a serious manner? Arthur dwelled on his reflective question for a moment while they all waited on him for an answer. Usually, when one sees a picture of the statue it's from the waist up or from the back. No one in their group, except Agnes and he, had ever seen the entire statue close up.

"So this is what a teachable moment means." He thought to himself.

He walked through his students so he might face them with the statue behind him. Time for a mini-lesson. There were few other tourists in the area; it was almost closing time. Those still around, however, took an interest in what was going on and came to hear him. Arthur began with the scriptural tradition. He explained that Jewish boys were circumcised to identify them as the chosen of God. Today, and for centuries, this was done when they were infants. In the days of King David, however, there is still debate suggesting the ceremony came at a later time. Supporters of the late circumcision theory use the *David* as an example. Some thought Michelangelo was wrong not having his statue circumcised. So not to make the Stone Cutter Genius appear uninformed, his contemporaries sought possible reasons for Michelangelo choosing to show a young man in the role of David without being circumcised. Arthur pointed out the stone cutter could have gone to the Temple Israelite not far from here to seek a model.

"But he didn't and we don't know why. Perhaps it was because they would not allow their sons to pose in the nude. It's more likely Michelangelo created the *David* in a Hellenistic, that is Greek, or maybe a Roman manner. If that was true, he would definitely show the *David* without clothes and uncircumcised. Anyway, those are the theories. Speaking of theories, we shall see in Rome Michelangelo's painting on the Sistine Chapel ceiling. That work was deliberately done to merge Greco-Roman art with Christian interpretation, and then some."

Arthur's attempt to change the focus to artistic interpretation failed.

"Oh, so the guy we learned about…you know, that Davide Mettzini person, was an Italian Christian and they didn't circumcise, so the statue isn't done that way," Mike figured out.

Mike was a straight-A student when it came to math and science. His understanding of the events leading up to this statue being sculpted as it was did not develop because he was slow on the uptake. Rather, it was because such discussion would never have been conducted in an American classroom. He had one more question.

"So we're Christian Mr. C…" before he could finish the guys became fidgety and started to moan aloud.

They knew what he was going to ask. By asking, the issue became personal and made the guys feel uncomfortable.

Mike plowed through to make his point, as he would on the football field, despite the moaning and groaning of his buddies.

"So, if what you say is true, then why are we circumcised?" he asked while ignoring the mumbling of his classmates.

The tourists, who were from Britain, were enjoying this exchange immensely.

Arthur had switched from religious tradition to artistic interpretation, and now he switched again, this time to biology mixed with history to answer truthfully while remaining sympathetic to the guys' sensibilities on the subject.

"In America during World War II," he taught, "the practice of circumcision became a medical issue. It was felt that removing the foreskin from the penis would enable the soldiers to keep themselves cleaner and healthier. A massive program was initiated in which men who were not circumcised would form a line. The doctor worked his way down the line. He cut off the foreskin from each man in assembly-line fashion until all were circumcised."

The groans became louder. Arthur had not achieved delicacy. The guys, adding a bending motion, sought to protect themselves. Arthur, like Mike had done, continued on as if nothing was said.

"Babies of course were being circumcised for the same reason in most big city hospitals. By the time all of you came along, it was a common medical practice."

The guys, however uncomfortable at first, had lived through the explanation and the girls were respectful to their classmates' discomfort. Thankfully, it was time to go and check out the art work in another wing of the gallery. Arthur pointed to the time and directed them to go. The guys quickly took the lead, almost running into the adjoining wing.

Arthur was left alone standing before the *David*. "How much you have seen over these five centuries," he thought. "If only you could speak."

He reached his hand up, stretched a bit and tapped the toes of the Giant.

"Hey that tickles."

Arthur thought he was hearing things. Looking around, he saw no one was near the *David*. His group had gone to an adjoining gallery.

"You down there. Would you mind touching me again?"

Arthur was sure he heard a voice coming from the statue. He walked around to the back and checked behind the pillars.

"It would be just like Johnny to pull a stunt like this," Arthur mumbled aloud.

"Mr. C., come on, tap my leg or something."

Arthur spoke aloud but very quietly.

"I don't know what kind of game you're playing but I'll go along with it. Where do you want me to tap you?"

"*Mille grazie* Mr. C., just hold onto my leg if you can reach it."

Arthur said nothing more as he maneuvered near the pedestal to reach for the leg. He was well aware how ridiculous this would look if his students came back for him. He placed his hand on top of the statue's foot. He felt warmth instead of cold marble.

"*Mille grazie* again, Mr. C., I think it's working now."

The voice ended as a person jumped off the pedestal. Arthur turned to chase after the shadowy figure and bumped into a rather tall young man with coal colored hair and large chocolate brown eyes. His ribs were just visible under his smooth skin.

"Listen kid, when the guards come in here and see you like…well like you are, I'm afraid they'll cart you away to jail. I think your little joke is over now. Where are your clothes?"

The youth seemed to be processing Arthur's long sentences, then he spoke. "I have no clothes."

"Don't be ridiculous lad. How did you get in here like that?"

"Well I've been this way for over five hundred years."

Arthur became dizzy. He sat on the floor leaning against the pedestal of the *David*.

"Five hundred years, you say?" The question came out so softly the tall youth bent down to better hear. Arthur looked into the lad's face.

"You can't be…you're not…it's impossible."

The lad sat next to Arthur. Both were concealed behind the statue. Should anyone come into the main gallery, they would not immediately be seen. The lad asked Arthur if he minded that he addressed him as Mr. C. Arthur told him that was fine. He realized, with a start, that he was carrying on a casual conversation with the youth.

"Listen, young man, are you sure you're feeling well? I mean no one can live for five hundred years."

"I don't know about that but I can only say that since 1503 I have been trapped… a part of the giant made by the master."

"Oh no," Arthur grabbed his head with both hands. "I knew all this intrigue and legends and Roselli stuff would get to me."

"Do you know of legends? I know one which the master told me about."

Arthur looked into the lad's eyes and saw that he was being truthful. "But how…how could you have been part of the statue? And why, after all these years, did you decide to come out?

"I can't answer the last part of your questions but I can the first one. Why don't you ask me who I am?" the inquisitive youth inquired.

"Because if you are who I think you are then you're Davide Mettzini. You were the model for Michelangelo's Giant-David," Arthur said as if there could be no other explanation.

"Ah…then you do know me. I have not heard anyone say my name for hundreds of years."

Arthur assured him that he knew him very well. Arthur said he would like to discuss everything with him, but first it would be nice to know how he got out of the marble.

Davide could only say that he suddenly felt warmth instead of the coolness of stone. After the feeling of warmth, he could hear himself speak when before he could only hear himself think. When Arthur held his foot for that long time, Davide found he could move and that's when he fell out of the statue.

"And so here I am, Mr. C."

"Yes and you speak English well. That certainly is a bonus."

"Oh, I speak many languages. You pick up a lot listening to people for five hundred years."

Arthur felt that would be true. "After all," he commented, "what else did you have to do?"

Davide's face grew sad. It was clear the lad could do nothing while in the statue and felt he had missed out on life. He stood up and walked in front of the statue, looking up into its face.

"Do I really look like that? So fierce, so defiant, and so strong?"

"Davide, the master stone cutter was Michelangelo. I'm sure he had you assume expressions of strength and conviction so that his Giant might say something more than the obvious conflict he was about to have with Goliath. As for the strong part, you are a fine specimen of masculinity. We must get you dressed. I'm afraid you cannot walk around like this in today's world."

For the first time Davide looked down at himself and folded his hands in front.

"I see what you mean. I only looked this way when I posed for the master and when my soul was taken from me."

A whole new revelation was available for Arthur to delve into, but first things first.

"We need to present you as a new member of our tour group. You can keep your first name, but just plain David. I'll shorten your last name to Metz, if you don't mind. All my students know of you and I'd have to explain too much."

"*Si* that would be fine Mr. C. I shall be David Metz, *va bene*. I like it."

"Good, our next issue is how to dress you. You're pretty tall but some of my students are tall as well so we can get some of their clothes to share with you."

"These students, they carry these clothes with them, yes?"

Arthur answered with an emphatic, "No." Arthur placed his hand on Davide's shoulder. "Don't get sad. We'll figure something out."

Davide explained that he wasn't sad, just warm. When Arthur touched him again he felt the sensation of warmth which awakened his soul in the first place. It was not just human flesh touching flesh, it was more than that; it rushed throughout his being.

Arthur removed his hand for fear of injuring the lad. Davide made it clear he felt no pain; just warmth and comfort. The clothing issue was on the back burner for the moment. Davide wanted to know how he had fallen out of the statue, and why now?

Arthur hadn't a clue. He placed his hands in his pockets. He nervously turned the golden coin from the leprechaun king over and over within its pouch. He smiled.

"Well Davide, I think I can answer how your soul was awakened."

He pulled out the pouch and took out the coin laying it upon the velvet pouch. Davide looked in wonder at its fine delicate crown and shamrock imprints. Arthur hastily explained the coin was a gift. He told Davide that inside the coin was a shamrock used in Ireland by St. Patrick to preach the good news.

"*Sì*, I know of this saint. Many of that land have been here to look at the Giant."

"As you say, *va bene*. Patrick preached the truth and the shamrock became a symbol of that truth. Somehow the plant he held became fused with the power of his words. I believe it was the power of truth which flowed from me holding this coin into you. As they say, the truth shall set you free. Here you are; free of the marble."

Davide became emotional. He embraced Arthur, repeating over and over again his thanks for freeing him.

The Galleria was absolutely silent, only Davide's weeping was heard until Johnny came running in to find his father.

"Dad, there you are. We've been looking everywhere for you. Everyone's on the bus and …" he stopped talking when he saw Davide. He ran up to his father and looked at the naked youth.

"Dad, the dude is nude!"

Chapter 18: The New Student

John was unable to say anything more. He eyed the naked guy standing next to his father with a burning stare. For the first time Davide felt unclothed and walked behind Arthur.

John regained his voice, "Dad, like I said, the dude is nude. What is a naked guy doing here with you?"

"Well Johnny, it's like this…" and Arthur introduced Davide Mettzini, the model for Michelangelo's Giant-David.

As soon as Arthur mentioned the name, Johnny knew what was coming. Nevertheless, he could barely speak at first. Here was the son of Arthur, who had fought a joust and talked with Leprechauns, he thought. Why couldn't there be a spirit…ghost…soul named Davide Mettzini? Johnny accepted the reality before him and apologized to Davide for making him feel uncomfortable.

"Listen Davide, there's a gift shop in the lobby. I'll run there and get you something to wear, but I don't think they have pants…er Dad what are we going to do about that?"

Both John and Davide waited for an answer that didn't come. While John ran to the gift shop with his father's charge card, Arthur paced. Davide followed Arthur pacing a few steps behind him. A moment later, Richie ran in all aflutter; Ambrogio was being told to move the bus by the *guardia,* the police. Like Johnny, Richie squealed to a halt. He looked around to make sure no one else was around.

"Dad," he called out. "There's a guy behind you."

Arthur looked up, but before he could speak Rich blurted out the obvious once more to a mortified Davide. "Dad, the guy is naked."

"Richie, I know. Get over here and lower your voice."

Rich ran over. "What do you mean that you know? And where's Johnny?"

Pushing up into Davide's face, he asked what he had done with his brother.

Davide was crying now and Rich felt like a jerk. "Take it easy guy. I mean, I was just worried that's all…you know about my brother and …well and everything. Dad, help me out here."

"I was about to. That is before you jumped in with two feet in your mouth."

Rich handed Davide his hanky, something his mother insisted that he always carry. Davide thanked him and wiped his eyes. He looked at the wet spots on the cotton cloth. "This is the first time since that awful night in June that someone has been able to comfort me."

Rich looked at him with questioning eyes leveled right into his eyes to avoid anymore tears. Arthur was explaining who Davide was when John returned with a bag.

"We have two minutes before they clear out the joint, so let's get going. Davide, this is all I could find in size large." He pulled out a shirt with the print of the *David* on it.

Davide smiled, "*Mille Grazie.*" He pulled it over his thick black curly hair. "It looks good, no?" Davide asked.

John told him that it looked just like his and it was good. "Now about the bottom part."

Davide pulled up on his shirt and looked down. Arthur and Rich looked at each other.

"Giovanni, you have pantaloons for me?"

"I'm afraid not. What I do have is a pair of Ralph Lauren plaid shorts, courtesy of Ryan who you can thank later." Arthur and Rich exchanged a look again.

"Oh, Ryan carries around a change in his backpack, just in case he gets dirty. Oh…and here's a pair of flip flops."

"Well, God bless Ryan's need to be neat," Arthur happily added.

As Arthur called for the blessing, Rich demonstrated how to slip on flip flops and also how a zipper works. Finally, Davide was ready to join the group.

"I look like, you know, what they call a tourist, eh Ricardo?"

"Most definitely. Let's hustle before our driver gets arrested."

As they walked out, John and Rich pointed out that Davide was calling them by their Italian names. How then, they asked, can we pass him off as a David Metz? A quick name change was needed. He was given the name David Metziano. Davide liked it, but was disappointed he was no longer an American tourist.

"Don't worry about that," said John, "Our last name is Colonna and we're as American as apple pie,"

Now, for the first time in five hundred years, Davide walked onto a street in Florence, wondering how a person could be an apple pie. The motorized vehicles did not scare him as he had heard of such things from tourists talking while viewing the statue. They fascinated him; all he had ever seen were earlier versions when the statue stood in the Piazza Signoria. When they moved the statue in 1873 into the *Galleria del Accademia,* that was his last look of the outside world.

Back at the Orsini house, Roselli and the others were back around the table. Pietro and Andreas had discovered how John and Rich got into the building. They had just come into the library to show the group the route the boys had taken. Roselli, Anastasia, and Giorgio accompanied the brothers to the third floor. The others waited in the library planning the story they would tell to the police, should they show up. It was inevitable they would show up since Ryan tossed the candelabrum out the window.

Pietro walked out onto the balcony. "If you come out here and look up you will see a leather strap hanging from the roof."

Roselli and the others took turns viewing the strap. Anastasia asked how they got to the roof of Orsini's house. Andreas took them to the corner of the hallway. Attached to the wall was an emergency ladder. Andreas climbed up and unlocked the emergency exit door to the roof. He pulled himself up onto the roof.

"If you look up through the opening, you can see a white sheet flapping in the wind."

"Yes," called out Roselli. "We can see it."

"They climbed out the window of the Palazzo Corsi and onto this roof using a bed sheet." explained Andreas.

"The youngsters are clever Anselmo. Now what do we do?" asked Anastasia.

"You mean before or after we kick their bloody asses?" he angrily asked as he threw a punch into his own hand. This resulted in litany of obscenities from the pain filling the air.

Back in the library, Girolamo Orsini and the others were crawling around the floor searching frantically.

"Roselli placed it on the table; I am sure of it," Orsini insisted.

"It must be here somewhere, Orsini," said Raphael. "Keep looking."

"Perhaps that punk knocked it off the table when he jumped off it," Orsini replied. "Look behind the bookcase."

They were taking books off the shelf when Roselli walked in. When they told him what had happened, he ran to the window. The candelabrum was lying on the sidewalk; a small crowd stood around looking first at it then up at Roselli. He sent Andreas to fetch the candelabrum.

"Take this napkin. Do not, do you hear, do not rub the candlestick."

Andreas took the cloth and ran down the stairs. Roselli watched him collect the candelabrum and pick up the pieces of broken candles. When Andreas had made sure all the pieces were collected he returned to the library where everyone had reseated themselves. Roselli held a cell phone in his hand. He told the confraternity he would call the police and report a group of young vandals had broken into the house and attempted to steal artifacts. He would trump those American students and their teacher by calling the police before they did.

"Let me do all the talking," Roselli said as he flipped his cell phone shut. Everyone sat and watched the candelabrum as if it could talk.

When Davide boarded the bus, he made quite a stir among the girls with his curly hair, broad shoulders and big eyes. "He's sorta hot," said Kristin," if it weren't for those shorts."

Davide overheard Kristin and he said in passing that he was not hot. In fact the day was quite comfortable for him. Then he turned to be introduced to Ryan so that he might thank them for the use of his shorts.

Now the girls were really buzzing. "Why would he be wearing Ryan's clothes and a Johnny-type tee shirt?"

Arthur hoped the blarney he was about to spin would answer everyone's questions. Arthur introduced Davide Metziano as a student who was backpacking around Europe. Arthur explained he had seen Davide lying on the ground in a small courtyard just when the group had left to go to the next gallery. Arthur told the group that a gang of thugs had stolen Davide's money and roughed him up, ruining his clothes in the process. That was why he borrowed Ryan's shorts and Johnny's shirt until his family could be contacted. By the time the bus pulled up in front of the Casa Buonarroti, Davide, the new student in their group, was being welcomed like an old friend. John and Rich would be his pals and not leave his side in case he said something which needed explanation.

"Just stick to talking about the weather and the museum where the statue is located," the boys advised him.

As the group got off the bus, Arthur took Ryan aside and told him they would need to talk about what happened. Ryan nodded.

"Please stick close to my sons. We've had enough surprises for one day."

"Right, Mr. C," and he went to join the boys and Davide.

Casa Buonarroti, like most middle class homes of the Renaissance era, was nothing to look at on the outside. There's not even much inside to make it noteworthy other than the fact Michelangelo lived there. The group went through the house like one would do when visiting George Washington's home at Mt. Vernon.

They went from room to room looking at this piece of furniture or sketches which the master had drawn. They saw *The Battle of the Centaurs*, a bas-relief sculpture the master carved at age fourteen. They meandered through the house. In one display case were two wax figures. They were the ones Roselli had mentioned in his presentation the night before. They created quite a sensation and Agnes was soon trying to answer the question: Did they prove multiple models were used for the *David*?

Ryan, the boys, and Davide entered that room. As soon as Davide looked into the display case, tears welled up in his eyes. Richie searched for his hanky, but realized Davide still had it.

"Signora la Straga, if I may, perhaps I can help," Davide said as he choked back his tears.

Agnes was happy to let someone else handle the question, though she was uncertain why a lad could answer them.

Davide begged everyone's pardon for his emotions. "You see," he went on to say. "I have a very special feeling for these pieces because I have not seen them…" he caught himself.

"I mean, I have heard so much about them and the theories about them, all my life. Like Giovanni here, I too am an artist."

John beamed his pleasure at being called an artist by one who actually knew a master of all artists.

The guide downstairs closed the museum as Davide started his story.

"I am told that you have all heard about a person who posed for the master stone cutter. His name was Davide, as is mine. A good name for someone to have…yes?" He continued without waiting for a reply. In a flash Davide had the students mesmerized and envisioning sixteenth century Florence.

Davide walked into the shed as he did every morning. He neatly folded his clothes and prepared to jump into the trough of water. He looked over to Michelangelo who was consumed with making small wax models based on his previous sketches.

"Master Buonarroti, I'm ready," Davide called out.

"So you are. Jump in the tub, but today I wish that you come out of the water slowly. I wish to teach you something special."

Davide plunged himself under the water and then little by little rose from the water until he stood upright in the tub. Michelangelo asked him to turn in a circle slowly. Davide slowly turned himself as Michelangelo sketched each move and turn and angle. Over and over again Davide turned and more sketches were created. Just as Davide was tiring and his skin wrinkling, Michelangelo told the lad to dry himself and come to his workbench.

"Good morning Michelangelo," called Granacci as he entered the shed. Noticing Davide at the tub drying himself, Granacci offered him a greeting as well.

"Ah Francesco, I was just about to teach Davide how I sculpt. It would not hurt you to listen as well."

"Well, *Il Divino,* I would be delighted."

On the workbench, Michelangelo laid out a series of sketches and two small wax models. Francesco and Davide flanked the stone cutter, who pointed out the wax figures.

He was not happy with the position or pose of the wax figures. When he saw Davide rise from the water, he knew how his *David* must be given life. He would prepare a life-size wax figure from which to carve the statue. More than that, he would let the life within the stone come forth, as if rising from a bath one section at a time, each side being exposed in stages.

"Just as a person lifting himself from the bath waters," he said taking the small wax figure and immersing it in a pan of water on the bench. "Of course you must visualize this entire process taking place vertically."

"And that's how Michelangelo decided to carve the statue which would make him the most famous sculptor of the age," concluded the newly-named Davide Metziano.

Agnes stood with her mouth open. The students looked into the display case once more and turned to look at Davide. They wanted to know how he could know such a detailed story, but they said nothing. They knew it was true by the emotion in his voice and the truth shining in his eyes.

"*Scusi*, I got carried away."

"Nonsense Davide, you presented the story beautifully, didn't he Signore Colonna?"

"Indeed he did Signora la Straga," Arthur responded, not quite honestly since he came in late for the story. The copy machine had given him some problems.

The curator of the Casa Buonarroti museum came up the stairs.

"I'm afraid that it is closing time. I must ask that you depart," she requested politely.

Arthur was most accommodating, scurrying his students to the waiting bus. Ambrogio wanted to take a direct route back to the hotel but Arthur asked him to divert to the Duomo. Davide had asked to pass by the Duomo and Arthur could not say no; no matter how eager he was to get back to the hotel so he and Agnes could study the document Ryan had taken from the Orsini house.

During the short ride Davide sat next to Johnny. Rich and Ryan were across the aisle. On the way, Davide asked about flying machines. He had seen hot air balloons crossing over the Piazza Signoria and had heard tourists talk of carriages bigger than the one in which they rode.

"They called them jets," he went on to say. "Did you know the wizard Da Vinci planned to make a flying machine?"

Before either of the boys could answer, Davide spotted the green marble Duomo and its dome. He jumped from his seat; Rich was right behind him, not knowing what the sixteenth-century youth would do. He need not have worried. All he did was go to the front of the bus to get a better look.

"Ricardo look! It's Santa Maria del Fiore. There on those steps, I would sit with friends after my time with the master. They would ask me how the statue was going and I would say nothing other than, 'the master works without fatigue.'"

Ambrogio cast the lad a questioning glance. Rich decided it best to take Davide back to his seat before the glance became a question. "Listen, Davide, I'm sure my dad will bring us back here so that you can get a better look; maybe even tomorrow."

"Si, va bene tomorrow then," and he walked slowly back to his seat casting a look back towards the Duomo.

Arthur, witnessing the entire incident, called up to Ambrogio to pull over next to the cathedral. "Listen everyone, you've been cooped up in a museum all day," he said, as he glanced at Davide.

John leaned over to Davide and whispered, "And someone amongst us for almost two hundred years."

His remark brought a smile back to Davide's face.

Arthur continued. "And so I think since we have a bit of time before the hotel has dinner ready for us we might just walk around the Piazza San Giovanni and maybe even circle the Duomo."

Davide jumped up and gave Arthur such a hug that they tumbled into the seat and onto Agnes. "Oh Signora, *scusi*! I beg your pardon."

"*Non importa Davide*," and she brushed his hair from his face tenderly.

Davide having trapped Arthur under his large body and over that of Agnes became flustered. Arthur was struggling and yet imagining what his sons were thinking when John pull Davide to his feet as the students knelt on their seats to better see the unfolding drama. With an arm wrapped around the reddened cheeked Davide he led him off to Rich and the others.

Agnes on her part pushed gently on Arthur who quickly rolled off her and sat beside her. She smiled as she expressed her thought of what the future would hold for this lad.

Arthur attempted to explain that he could be one who is really spirit but still had a soul with form and substance.

"But whether he was a soul in spirit form or a spirit with soul, or however we may choose to explain his presence, the reality is that he is here in the twenty-first century with us."

Rich was watching what had become a rather tender scene as well. Ryan tugged on his sleeve as a child might. "Rich, would you mind if I walked with you around the Duomo? I just can't answer questions right now, if you know what I mean," added Ryan.

Rich understood how Ryan was feeling and suggested he join him, his brother, and Davide. He was pretty sure Davide would not be asking

Ryan about what had happened at the Orsini house.

The doors of the bus opened and the students spilled out onto the walkway next to the cathedral. Breaking up into their little groups, they went their separate ways; some into the Piazza and others towards the back of the Duomo. This time, Ryan was with guys and not the girls. Davide was leading their little band and the four found themselves on the steps of the Duomo where they had walked during the Youth Rally.

"Here is my spot," Davide called out as he ran up the stairs off to the right and plopped down next to the entrance door. "This is where I used to sit for hours and talk about the master's work."

Rich and John collapsed on the stairs with looks of "Now you've done it" on their faces.

Ryan stood directly in front of Davide, who was now caressing the stone stair and the marble base of the wall. "Then you're from Florence, Davide?"

"*Si, Firenze* is my home."

"But I thought you came here backpacking."

Davide's eyes grew wide with terror as he finally realized what he had said. The stunned silence stretched on and on until quick-thinking John rescued them all with one of his fantastic tales.

"You're *potso* Davide. I think when you got robbed they hit your head too hard. You're remembering those days when you were a kid, you know before you moved to…to Verona."

"*Ah si, Verona*! That's my home now but I shall always love *Firenze* as I was born here."

Ryan didn't quite swallow the story. He wanted to ask about who that master person was, but he chose to let it go; much to the relief of Davide and the boys. John and Rich pulled Davide up and led him toward the Baptistery in the Piazza.

Davide ran up to the bronze doors whose panels were designed by Donatello. He rubbed his hands across them. "You know, Michelangelo was a great admirer of Donatello."

"So we've been told by our dad," remarked Rich casually so as not to encourage another slip of the tongue.

"Speaking of Dad, I see him at the door of the bus. We had better get back," suggested John.

The walk had reinvigorated the group. The chattering bunch left the bus and walked into the hotel sharing their thoughts of the *David* and pulling up digital pictures on their cameras to share with one another. Maura led them directly to the lower level toward the restaurant. As they walked into the dining room, Roselli was there with several men. Two wore business suits and two wore fatigues and carried machine guns.

Maura let out a yelp of sorts as she saw the guns. A man in a black suit spoke to calm their fears.

"*Buona Serra, dove e Signore Colonna?*"

"I am right here," Arthur called out from the back as he quickly made his way up to the black-suited man. "What is the meaning of this? My students are frightened half to death."

In reality they were perhaps surprised by the machine guns. It was not shocking since they had seen armed police around so many of the buildings which housed precious artifacts.

"*Mi dispiacere signore Colonna.* I did not mean to upset the *studenti*. My name is Nunzio Baronni. I am the detective assigned to investigate the complaint made by Signore Orsini."

Arthur became red in the face. "Orsini, how dare he. Why he... he... well, he should know better."

The students were becoming frightened; they thought Arthur was so angry he couldn't speak. His difficulty was not because of his anger but because he didn't know what he could reveal of the truth of the incident.

"Please let us all sit down and have what you Americans call a chat, no?"

"*Si*, that would be fine with me," answered Arthur. "Maura, see that our students get seated please."

Arthur and Agnes sat where they were told – at a table with the detective, the other suited man who took notes, and Roselli. The armed guards positioned themselves on either side of the doorway.

"Should not the boy be here as well?" Nunzio asked but commanded at the same time.

"The boy?" asked Arthur.

"*Si*, come now Signore Colonna. The O'Donnell boy is involved in this complaint. I would need to speak with him."

"Very well," said Arthur. He called to his sons to bring Ryan to the table.

As the boys made their way a man in a gray suit accompanied by a woman in a blue skirted suit attempted to enter the restaurant. The guardia crossed the doorway with their machine guns.

"How dare you. I am Captain Cosimo Bartelli. Remove yourself at once."

The guards came to attention. The two passed and walked directly to Arthur and the detective. Once again he introduced himself and his aide Lt. Maria Cellini.

The detective stood for his superior officer and introduced himself, Arthur, Agnes, and Roselli.

"So then you are Signore Colonna, the professore who called me."

"*Si*, Captain I am he. It was nice of you to meet me at the hotel so I didn't have to come to the station."

Roselli could not help himself. "You called the *polizzia*?"

"Of course, Anselmo. I had to report the finding of an important document, didn't I?"

"But I called to report a stolen treasure."

The captain interrupted their exchange. "Perhaps we can be of help to each other and avoid any embarrassing situations. Please have a seat. And you lads can join us."

John, Rich, Ryan, and Davide who hovered near the table pulled up chairs.

"Where shall we begin?" asked the captain.

Arthur jumped in before Roselli could utter a sound. He explained that just a few hours ago he found a lad who had been beaten and robbed in the courtyard outside the *Galleria del Accademia*. He introduced Davide to the captain and then continued his story.

"It seems that when his attackers took everything from him, even his clothes, they dropped the very thing they had obviously stolen earlier. Davide had fallen on it, concealing it from their view. They ran off towards the University." he told them. "They are probably using Davide's clothes instead of their own."

Davide smiled as if the story was told exactly as it happened. John jumped in to back up the story.

"Right. David told me he was wearing a rather expensive polo shirt in…yellow, and khaki pants. It was an American brand name wasn't it Davide?"

"*Si, Americano.*"

"What kind of shoes did you have on Davide? I can't remember." John had gone a bit too far. Davide hadn't a clue as to what brand names were.

"I know," Rich claimed. "You know how I like shoes for every occasion, so when he told me about his K Swiss I laughed, because that's what my father wears."

Roselli could not believe what he was hearing. *What is Colonna up to?* he asked himself. He decided to play along.

"Those thugs who attacked this poor lad must have been the same ones who climbed over the Palazzo Corsi's roof and onto the Orsini house frightening poor old Girolamo half to death," Roselli concluded, seeming to be in complete agreement with the tale just told.

Arthur could not have been more pleased. What he didn't need now was a lot of questions.

The captain seemed to accept the story which both his and the dectective's assistants had taken down. "Now I will only need contact information for you, Signore Roselli, and you, Signore Colonna, in the event we do find these thugs."

Roselli was not about to let Colonna have his document. "Wait a minute what about the so called paper this lad fell upon. What happened to it?"

"Please forgive the oversight, Signore Roselli. Richie if you could hand me the shoulder bag please. I think I can resolve the Signore's concern."

He placed the bag on the table and opened it dramatically. Gently removing the faded parchment, he handed it over to Roselli. The look in Roselli's eyes was all anyone needed. The document was authentic. The entire restaurant was so quiet one would have thought Roselli was laying to rest a loved one. He gently opened the document to make sure it was the one he sought and then again folded it. He slid it into his brief case.

Roselli closed his brief case. "You did have it then."

Arthur feigned surprise and once again explained how it came into his possession and how he felt the police should be called.

The captain was delighted that the Florentine police could be of assistance. He complimented Detective Baroni and his staff for doing their job well.

"After all they didn't know about Signore Colonna's call," he explained.

With apologies to Davide for his unfortunate encounter and verifying that Roselli, on behalf of Signore Orsini, was satisfied, the police departed.

The hotel staff immediately served dinner. They had been intently watching the events unfold from the kitchen. Now that all was well they breathed a sigh of relief. As the food came forward, the student chatter began and covered a very softly spoken conversation between Arthur and Roselli, standing with his brief case in hand.

Roselli was covering up the events with an exaggerated apology for a misunderstanding on the part of the confraternity. Ryan was restrained by John and Rich holding his arms, or he would have gotten into Roselli's face and called him a liar. The boys whispered to him to remain calm and wait. Their father would surely have something in mind and he would explain his plan later.

"Again, Signore Colonna, I repeat how sad we are that Ryan was so frightened. His actions and words told us he desired to become a follower of the Frate Savonarola."

The boys could feel Ryan tense up, but he held himself back.

Arthur glanced at the boys who nodded that everything was under control. Agnes, to make sure, went to Ryan to stroke his head and comfort him after his ordeal. She was quite convincing.

"Signora la Straga you have a knack for comforting people. But I have bothered you enough with all of this." He patted his brief case and turned to Agnes again. "I'll meet you in Rome where we must evaluate the exhibit and plan the return of the artifacts."

"*Si, Signore Roselli*, in Rome then, in about two days?" she inquired.

"*Va bene*, I will be staying at the Hotel Michelangelo." Off he went up the stairs and into the night with Andreas and Pietro. They had been waiting outside.

"Colonna is up to something, but I don't know what. You will watch his every move," Roselli said to them.

With the restaurant and the group almost back to normal, Arthur asked Davide, Ryan, and his sons to follow him upstairs to the lounge. He and Agnes led the way.

Agnes and Arthur, having removed a vase of flowers from a decorative table, were pulling it into the center of the room when the youths came in.

"May I help?" asked Ryan first. The others followed his lead and brought some chairs to place around the table.

Arthur's shoulder bag laid in the middle of the table as the small group took places surrounding it; no one but Arthur knew why. Before Arthur could address why he wanted them to meet, Ryan just had to say his piece.

"Mr. C., you know Roselli was lying right? I mean…yes okay I was kind of excited about being a part of a mysterious club."

Ryan was quite nervous now and touched his blood stained shirt. He wasn't referring to the incident, but more about revealing his inner most feelings.

"Nevertheless," he continued when Davide, of all people, placed his arm over Ryan's shoulder as a sign of encouragement. Ryan calmed down. He looked at Davide, but said nothing. If he had spoken, he would have said that was the first time a guy friend had offered him a gesture of friendship.

"Like I was saying…it's true I wanted to be somebody, anybody who might be respected or well liked…you know, popular. Anyway, I did keep the rendezvous a secret."

He turned to the boys to tell them how sorry he was his actions had placed them in so much danger. Each gave him a pat on the back and told him that it was really quite exciting; to which their father raised his eyebrows and widened his eyes as only he and his daughter Jana could do effectively. They just grinned back and urged Ryan to go on.

"Like I said, I did want to go meet Roselli and his bunch, but not for the reason you think."

Arthur and his sons looked quizzically at Ryan.

"You guys never mock how I dress or how fussy I am about my appearance."

"Oh, right. Well we have a sister like that…oh gosh, I didn't mean you were girlie or anything like that," John commented.

Davide, hearing John's comment, leaned over to Agnes and in Italian asked what this girlie word meant. She smiled and told him that it wasn't important, just some American way of talking. Agnes didn't want Davide worrying about wearing clothes borrowed from Ryan.

Arthur expressed his pleasure that Ryan felt comfortable enough to share his story with everyone. Ryan made it clear that he wasn't finished. "Oh, then do go on Ryan."

The lad continued his reasoning of the why he went to the Orsini house. He told them about the document, which Roselli had held up in the piazza, and which the police had just returned to him.

"I wanted to find out what it said. Then I was going to come back and tell you and Signora la Straga," he paused and looked into the face of each person around the table. "I was going to be the hero and tell you all about its contents. Not only did I not get to do that, but I almost got carved up in the process and Roselli has the paper back."

He leaned back in his chair, dejected and disappointed. Davide, who was in the chair next to Ryan, now let him sink into him as he tried to hide the fact that he was crying.

Agnes, with outstretched arms went to him and tenderly spoke "*Mi amico*, what you did, though foolhardy, was heroic. You have nothing to be ashamed about. Lift your head high and be proud of who you are, just as Michelangelo himself was told to do many times."

"*Si*, the master would get down on himself often. Granacci would encourage him and make him smile." Davide added.

Arthur coughed. Ryan raised his water-filled eyes and looked directly into Davide's. He sat erect in his chair. "How do you know that?"

"Ryan, it's a well known historical fact." Arthur deflected the question. "But to get back to your lament if I may." Arthur took his shoulder bag and removed some white papers. He asked if anyone remembered that he was late to hear Davide's story at Casa Buonarroti. He was late because he had asked to use their copy machine.

"So you see, Roselli might have the original but we have its copy."

"*Bravissimo*!" shouted Davide though not quite sure why.

Ryan's face lit up with relief; as did the boys who had risked a lot rescuing Ryan and who had felt a little down because they didn't get the document either. Arthur spread three sheets of paper across the table.

"So that's why you let Roselli have the original," exclaimed Rich.

"Clever lad," Arthur commented. "Now all we have to do is translate it from the Italian."

Agnes and Davide looked closer at the pages written in what Agnes recognized as the early stages of the developing Italian language. As Davide read the first page, his face turned ashen. As he read on his cheeks became red. Agnes could not translate the early Italian as quickly as Davide could read it. Arthur, Ryan, and the boys were getting concerned by the quick changes in Davide's coloring and expression.

John couldn't stand it any longer. "Davide what does it say?"

Davide looked up, "*Scusi*, it's just that whoever wrote this lived during my time."

Now Ryan turned ashen. "Rich what does he mean, his time?"

Rich tried to cover by saying, "Davide didn't always get his English words right," but Ryan didn't buy it. It was clear to Ryan, in the short time they had all known Davide, that his English was not the problem. Davide was picking up that he may have said something he shouldn't have said. He turned to Agnes for help and she looked at Arthur. Rich glanced at John for help, and no one answered Ryan's question. All of the guilty silence confirmed Ryan's hunch that something more than an ancient document had been discovered.

Rich broke the silence. "Okay everyone, we need to get a grip. Dad, what do you think? Should we just hear what this writing says and explain it to Ryan?"

Ryan thought Rich's suggestion was great. "I knew there was something more to this paper."

"You have no idea Ryan, just how much more there is than what's written on this paper," John commented.

They fell silent again. Ryan looked at everyone twice before Arthur finally decided to share the truth. Arthur explained that everything Ryan was about to hear must be kept absolutely secret. When Ryan agreed, Arthur continued. He told Ryan that the story about Davide's assault and robbery was a cover story so Roselli and his confraternity would not know the truth.

Ryan rolled his eyes; he had already figured out that the story he had been told was a lie. "I didn't think people took other people's clothes in an ordinary robbery. At least not since the story of the Good Samaritan was told."

Relief spread around the table. Perhaps Ryan could hear the news and not go off the deep end. They had second thoughts when Ryan asked his follow-up question.

"So then, Davide, where do you really come from?"

Davide's eyes darted around the table. Arthur interceded at this point.

"Ryan, perhaps if you knew Davide's real name, everything might make sense to you. Let me introduce you to Davide Mettzini of Firenze."

Ryan, though not completely understanding, did have a look of "Oh, now I see." He thought Davide was a descendent of the model for the *David*. Davide, himself, explained that he was the actual model who worked with the master stone cutter. Ryan's acceptance of what he was being told began to falter. They presented the theory of how the cult of Savonarola developed, and they talked about historical events, such as the tub of water in the shed, which few could possibly know. None of this eased Ryan's anxiety. Finally, Davide picked up the papers from the table.

"I think part of what's written on this sheet may help everyone understand better."

Davide Mettzini addressed the events on the evening of June 23, 1503 during an unofficial public viewing of the nearly-complete *David*. Piero Soderini, the Gonfalonier of Justice, addressed those assembled. *Il Divino,* Michelangelo, stood on the other side of the Giant, opposite Piero. It was evident the statue meant more than a simple depiction of Biblical events. The Giant would stand as a symbol of Florentine freedom. Even uncompleted, everyone present could appreciate the message of the Giant-David; the expression on his face and the qualities of his posture suggested he was ready for attack. The viewing was a huge success. By the time the crowds departed, word had already spread throughout the city about the Giant who spoke to the world of the glory of Firenze yet never uttered a sound.

"The crowds had dispersed and only Michelangelo, Granacci, and I remained," revealed Davide to Ryan's amazement.

"You're kidding, right?" asked Ryan. "You just want to make me feel better with a fairy tale."

"Ryan, you must open your mind as you have never done before," Davide said with his hand on Ryan's shoulder. With a steady stare into the confused lad's eyes, he continued. "I was there and witnessed the viewing ceremonies. The viewing was held to promote the greatness of the master's genius, and to create a stir of anticipation and longing for this symbol of Florence. It worked."

Ryan gasped, but Davide went on telling everyone about the events which happened after the ceremony ended. The garden area was empty. Nothing remained but the footprints of the crowds who had gathered. In the streets surrounding the Duomo however, several men lurked, cloaked not only by darkness but by dark hooded robes. As the crowds dispersed, these black-robed symbols of darkness and ignorance made their way towards the shed where the Giant-David, illuminated by torches until it glowed, loomed in majesty.

The shadows created by the flickering light seemed to dance on the shed's walls and over the three who remained in the shed.

Il Divino, Granacci, and Davide followed the shadows' rythym and danced around the shed. Granacci imitated the moving shadows as if the Giant had come to life.

"Michelangelo look. The Giant lives," said the euphoric Granacci.

The master stopped in mid-twirl as the shadow of the Giant-David seemed to move and tower over Granacci.

"Ah, Francesco, it does indeed. But, there is much to be done, my friend, so that its living message may be offered to all who view it. And so, we should be on our way."

"Davide, would you mind closing the workhouse?" asked Granacci. "I would like to walk *Il Divino* home and speak of a commission which has been offered to me." This time the term *Il Divino* was used sincerely.

Davide was pleased to do whatever was asked of him. His days of modeling had ended and his new position as a helper to Michelangelo's brother, Buonarroto on the family farm, did not begin for another week. Alone with the Giant now, the lad resumed his dance imitating the shadows on the wall. New shadows, which crept into the garden and into the shed, went unnoticed. Davide jumped up to each torch to extinguish it with a flourish and a laugh, as if he were extinguishing evil in his beloved city.

The creeping shadows followed along the wall where shadows were deep and dark. Davide was at the last torch; the one by the door. Only candles burning on the workbench were left to offer a soft glow to guide him after he extinguished the last torch. He jumped one last, gigantic leap to reach the torch. He covered it quickly and descended, not to the earthen floor, but into the outstretched hands of the creeping shadows which took on all-too-human strength and form.

A woolen blanket was thrown over the captured youth. It muffled his cries for help. Although he fought valiantly, there were too many arms twisting him tightly into the blanket, making it difficult for him to breathe. Davide could feel a large hand searching for the front of his head. Once found, the hand forced part of the blanket into the lad's gaping mouth. As his mouth was held, other hands lifted his body and yet others took his ankles. He kicked his feet, but all he accomplished was to toss his sandals into the darkness.

He heard a commotion outside his confined space. He heard clay pots smashing and metal tinkling as they hit the ground. He was thrown onto what he believed was the workbench with such force that he groaned with pain. The hands removed the blanket from his ankles, and then from his knees, and then from his waist. He tried to kick his freed legs but they were still held by strong hands. The many hands continued to remove the blanket and it was getting easier to breathe. They had just uncovered his head when the door crashed open and someone entered.

His couldn't see, but he could hear a voice different from those around him.

"The order forbids you to do this!" yelled the voice.

The one holding Davide's head answered. "The frate's memory is insulted by this thing of a boy who dares to make mockery of our leader's teachings."

Davide's eyes focused in the candlelight. The shimmering light swept across the face of the one who entered, who was now standing at his feet.

Davide bit the hand which held his mouth. "You are the master's brother…"

The large hand stuffed a cloth full of marble dust into the lad's mouth. "Shut up you vile son of Satan." And he ended his command with a slap to the lad's face.

"I order you to stop!" cried out Lionardo Buonarroti.

"And I, Filippo Pazzi, tell you that the voice of the frate calls to us to cast the soul of this thing from its body."

Lionardo pleaded to deaf ears. He insisted that the Frate Savonarola would never have condoned such action. He was countered by examples of those who were burned at the stake at the frate's insistence.

"I shall report this to the order instantly. Until then, I order you to do nothing to this youth."

And with that, he left. The one who had held his waist followed to the door. He looked out into the darkness, shut the door gently and barred it from within.

Davide's heart was beating so fast he thought it would jump out of his chest. The one who had held his waist returned and placed his hand on his chest.

"The heart beats too fast. The creature may die before we can extract his soul."

Filippo removed the cloth from Davide's mouth. The lad sputtered and coughed until saliva streamed out of his mouth and down his chin

"Give him some special wine."

The one who felt his heart walked into the darkness and returned with a cup; one often used by the master stone cutter as he worked on the Giant. Filippo lifted Davide's head, forced his mouth open, and poured the drugged wine into his mouth. The youth choked and coughed, but even so, some of the liquid was swallowed. He made one last heroic effort to release himself from the grasp of those who held him on the workbench. The effort took his captors by surprise, but in the end it only resulted in his tunic being torn from his body. The marble chip which Michelangelo gave him fell to the floor unnoticed. His torn tunic was then used to tie him down on the workbench. Davide was dazed, but lucid enough to understand what was happening.

His four captors chanted something Davide did not understand. The one who had held his ankles kept staring into his eyes as they chanted about a soul needing to be freed from its sinful vessel. Another came up to the table holding a wooden box with a gold plate on its lid. Filippo opened it and withdrew a shiny, short-bladed knife with an ivory handle.

He held it up so the blade reflected the candlelight. The others stopped chanting and the silence was as frightening as the blade. Davide expected Filippo, at any moment, to thrust the blade into Davide's heart and kill him.

The confraternity leader did no such thing. He slowly lowered it towards Davide's chest until the sharp tip just touched his flesh. The cold metal on his skin caused his drugged body to twinge.

Filippo carved a symbol into Davide's flesh. Deeper and deeper he cut into the chest until blood first trickled and then flowed from the wound. Davide could feel his soul slowly leaving his body. Some of the blood was collected in a small vial. The eerie chanting began again as the blood was collected in the tiny silver vial. Davide could now see his body tied and stained with blood lying on the workbench.

Filippo turned and looked up into the face of the Giant-David under whose gaze this deed was being performed. Then he turned and spoke to Davide.

"Since you have desired to be the *David*, so you shall forever be a part of it; never again able to walk this earth, but to see it through the stone which shall be home to your soul."

He let the blood in the silver vial drip onto the foot of the unfinished Giant. As the blood spread across the carved foot, Davide felt his soul pulled into the marble. He saw his limp head turn to the right. His wide-open eyes looked at the Giant. His hands opened and his body went limp in its cloth ropes.

The imprisoned Davide screamed, but nothing came out except to his own ears, which were no longer made of flesh. He could see. He could hear. He could feel the cold stone of his prison, but he felt no pain from his wound. He had become one with the Giant-David. The statue had been given his own soul.

The singing had long since stopped. The black robes were wrapping the mortal remains in the blanket. Filippo replaced the vessel and knife in the wooden box and handed it to one of the others. He gave orders to take the body to Santo Spirito and place it in the morgue.

"The monks will see it as an unclaimed body and bury it in a grave for those without family." He told the others.

They lifted up the tall and limp body of Davide and carried it into the moonlit night. It would be placed in the morgue where Michelangelo had first learned of anatomical structure, human tissue, organs, and muscle.

The soul of Davide, imprisoned in the Giant, was left alone. Only the moonlight, filtering in through the shutters over the small window, kept him company. He screamed, but could not be heard. Lionardo Buonarroti returned with members of the order at San Marco. Seeing that the shed was empty, he felt relieved.

"So we did scare them away. I can only hope that the youth was released."

"No, I'm here! Look at the statue! I'm here! I'm right here in the statue!" Davide continually yelled but no one heard him. The brothers from San Marco left.

The morning light spoke of a glorious day. It was the Feast Day of St. John the Baptist when all Florence would be celebrating their saint's Feast Day. The events of the previous night were reported to Michelangelo. He and Granacci ran to the shed. It was obvious someone had broken in. On the floor below the workbench Michelangelo saw a marble chip. He knew instantly it was the one he had given to Daivde.

The master's heart pounded as he checked over the Giant. Davide's soul, trapped within the marble, again tried to communicate his presence to no avail.

"Francesco, come here!" cried out Michelangelo. "Look on the foot of the Giant."

"Michelangelo, I think it's blood, but we should call Marsilio Ficino to verify."

The stone cutter knew it to be blood and needed no verification. His heart sank as he realized that Davide was probably the victim. He had been alone, locking up, when they had left. He showed the marble chip to Francesco. Then he sent his friend away to inform Piero Soderini of the break-in and to ask him to create a plan to secure the area so such an incident could not recur. He desired to be alone in his grief.

Alone now with the Giant, the master stone cutter took chisel in hand and worked on that foot where the blood had been poured. His tears fell upon the stained marble as he chipped, ever so lightly, until only the brightness of the Carrara white marble was visible.

Davide felt each stroke of the chisel, each rubbing of the marble. If he could have cried he would have; his heart was broken as he saw his master, the one he adored, mourning for him.

When the stain was removed and the area brought to a high polish, Michelangelo sat at his workbench with quill and paper. He placed the marble chip before him and wrote a sonnet of sorrow, probably one of his first. It would be common in his later years to write love poems and sonnets of sorrow for those he loved; such as when his father died many years from this day of June 24, 1503. When the sonnet was finished he read it to the Giant-David. Within, Davide's soul sank into depression when, after having read it aloud, his master placed an edge of the paper into the candle flame. It burst into flames and Michelangelo let the burning paper fall to the ground where he stomped on it with his boot.

For weeks Michelangelo had everyone he knew searching for Davide. Michelangelo buried himself in his work. When he worked on the Giant, it brought joy to Davide's spirit to have his master near him. But much of the time Michelangelo was also engaged in creating a portion of a cartoon, a drawing in detail, of his battle scene for the Palazzo Vecchio. This he would show to the Signoria of Florence who was to commission the project with him and Leonardo da Vinci.

Months passed and the *David* was finished to a highly polished state except for two spots.

The day had arrived to move the David to its permanent location. It was midnight on May 14, 1504 when the door frame of the *Opera dei Duomo* was torn down to make room for the rig holding the suspended statue. Michelangelo had chosen the time, for he was certain that another attack on the Giant was forthcoming.

Just prior to being lifted onto the rigging ropes, when the statue was alone, those same black-robed confraternity members slithered their way into the confines of the courtyard and pelted the statue with rocks. The spirit-like soul of Davide was shaken but the statue itself remained undamaged. Piero had ordered a guard from the Duomo and they arrived just as the attack began. They chased off the so-called vandals.

"And so I was moved to the Piazza del Signoria. For centuries I have watched the world about me change, losing all hope that I would ever be released from the stone. And then this day Mr. C. came and touched the exact spot on my foot where they had poured my blood and I was freed," concluded Davide Mettzini, tears flowing from his eyes for the second time in 500 years.

Ryan was speechless. The others, though they knew the truth, were moved by the story of how his soul became one with the stone.

The lounge was as silent as a tomb; Davide sensed Arthur's desire to speak of his sorrow for the lad, but could not bring himself to do so. Davide spoke again.

"Today is my new birthday, so we should be happy. I am free again."

Well that was all Johnny had to hear. His heart was in his throat and he was choking back tears but it was not in his nature to show such emotion. Even though all about him shed their tears freely, he could only force himself to levity. Thus he jumped towards Davide, flung his arm around him and pulled him up from his chair.

"I vote for gelato and cake to celebrate your birthday," John proclaimed as he thumped Davide on his back. "I think we should go back to the kitchen and scrounge up something."

Everyone welcomed the invitation to celebrate; it would give Davide an opportunity to distance himself from the horrible memories. It was Agnes who interrupted, for a moment, to call their attention to the other writing on the sheets.

"Davide, you told us about the second part of the manuscript; but I see something different written on the other page. Do you agree?"

"*Si, Signora la Straga*, but it's nothing, just something about a ring which belonged to the Medici. The master had spoken of it but just telling a tale that's all."

Arthur and his sons froze in their steps. Tugging on Ryan, the boys and their father turned and resumed their seats.

Chapter 19: The Destiny of the Ring

It wasn't gelato or cake but the idea that the whereabouts of the ring might be mentioned in the document that focused Arthur and Agnes' attention. It was the other section of the document which would bring to Ryan, in particular, knowledge of another part of the story woven with the Medici legend. Arthur wasn't quite sure that Ryan could handle more.

But then he thought, *What could be more profound or awesome than a soul being encased in stone?*

Arthur decided Ryan would be brought into their full confidence. After all it was his question back in Chicago which first brought the issue of a special Medici ring as a historical item into question.

Once again Arthur spread the three pages across the table, this time directly facing Davide. "Now Davide, if you would, please read the passage."

The lad read it, as Agnes helped with unfamiliar words.

"Today we received word that the villain Piero de Medici was killed. The news being spread was that he drowned in the Gagliano River while engaged in battle. Thus are we saved from his return to our city. The body was to be taken to the Abbey of Montecassino for burial. I made my way from Naples so that I could accompany the entourage feigning grief beyond measure. The Magi ring was still on his finger. I never let its view leave my sight as we transported the body with his hands crossed over his chest clutching his sword. On the day of the funeral rites I was chosen to help cover the body before entombment. What would you have me do with the ring? I am in Naples and from there I shall go to Ischia and then to Capri. I tell those near to Piero that I travel to mourn in private. How goes it with the so called *Il Divino?* still working on the blasphemous statue?" David came to a pause. "Well that's all, except for his signature. His name was Domenico Pazzio."

"Not quite all Davide," interrupted Agnes. "There is a scribbled note on the margin next to where the question posed is written."

"Can you read it Agnes?" asked Arthur.

"I think so, Arturo. Do you have your magnifying glass with you?"

Arthur took the glass from his shoulder bag and handed it to Agnes. She placed it over the notes. "It says, 'Domenico apprehended en route from Ischia, taken to Rome. Ring stolen by Confraternity of Tre Magi.'"

"Dad, not another confraternity?"

Agnes explained to Rich and the others again that the Tre Magi, or what many call the Three Kings, confraternity was the group which had buried Lorenzo, *Il Magnifico*.

"No doubt members fought alongside Piero to restore the Medici and were then assigned the funeral rites as they were upon his father's death nine years earlier. The Order of the Magi would evolve from that group."

Ryan's head was spinning. The boys were somewhat relieved that they didn't have to face another confraternity and that the order was the one to which Agnes belonged to and therefore on their side. Davide, of course actually knew of the Tre Magi group as they existed in his time. What he didn't know was the importance of the Medici ring to the Tre Magi Confraternity.

Arthur, however, was already planning to recover the ring. He had remembered something which might affect Davide's existence in the twenty-first century; something recorded in Marsilio Ficino's journal. Something which may change the lives of Agnes la Straga and her Order of the Magi and Anselmo Roselli and his Confraternity of Savonarola. There was only one problem. If he was thinking this way then why wouldn't Roselli, who had the original documents, also have similar insights?

First things first, thought Arthur. He had to address the confusion and nervousness amongst the young people. He didn't want to place what he was thinking on their overburdened shoulders; least of all on Davide, whose very life might be altered by what he thought was possible. Arthur agreed they needed to have some of that gelato to celebrate Davide's new birth and then, perhaps, lay out step-by-step what they learned from the document and how to proceed from there. All his plans needed to be accomplished while touring Italy with a group of students who must be kept ignorant of what was really in Arthur's mind.

In the kitchen, John generously dished out the raspberry gelato while Rich poured Cokes for everyone. They all eagerly waited for Davide's reaction to this unique ice cream treat. No one knew if Davide could even eat, being something other than a human being. *What an introduction to food after 500 years*, thought Arthur.

Rich handed Davide a small, plastic gelato spoon. The sixteenth century lad understood and scooped out a heap on the spoon. All eyes were riveted on him as he lifted the dripping gelato towards his mouth. They helped him in spirit and when the spoon neared his mouth, they, too, opened their mouths. Davide's lips touched the frozen yet soft treat and engulfed the spoon. He pulled it from between his closed lips, empty of the gelato that Arthur called the "new nectar of the gods." He let the cold sweetness melt on his tongue and then swallowed. His eyes widened; a grin spread across his face.

"There was nothing like this in my time," said Davide who began devouring scoop after scoop until the dish was empty and he looked for more.

"Easy dude," cautioned John. "That famous build of yours will go to pot if you take too much. But what the heck; you haven't eaten in 500 years, so go for it."

John brought him another helping. As if experiencing gelato for the first time, Arthur, Agnes, Ryan and the boys ate ravenously as well, 'to show support for the lad,' they said. They all washed it down with Cokes, Diet-Cokes for Arthur and Agnes.

The carbonation tickled Davide's fancy and caused him to release a loud belch, which John thought was superbly done.

"That was wonderful. When do we get more?"

"I think you have had enough for your first day, Davide. Tomorrow is another day," advised Arthur. "Before we retire let's just review what we know from this document and from the Ficino journal."

Arthur took out a pad from his bag and wrote as he spoke, making a list. By the time he had finished thinking aloud and sharing his thoughts the list included:

1. Piero died with the Magi ring still in his possession.
2. The ring was stolen at his funeral.
3. The writer Domenico took the ring with him to Naples.

4. Domenico intended to go to Ischia and then to Capri.
5. Somehow the Tre Magi Confraternity intercepted him at sea and took him to Rome.
6. The ring was in the possession of the Tre Magi group.

"Okay, so now where is the ring?" Arthur asked.

Agnes thought it would have been brought to Rome, since that's where they took Domenico.

Ryan thought it was wherever the Tre Magi Confraternity was headquartered at that point in history.

Rich thought that it may have ended up in Capri anyway since the ship was going there.

Davide and John were still trying to outdo each other in consuming Coke and belching. Suddenly, Davide's eyes began to water. The group thought he was getting emotional again, but it turned out he needed to pass water, as Agnes referred to it.

"Boys, what goes in must come out. John, take him to the bathroom and show him how to use it. There was no such place as an indoor restroom in Renaissance times."

In a flash, all four were on their way to the men's room. One could hear Davide expressing hope that he could keep it in until they got outside.

Arthur was alone with Agnes. He expressed to her his concern that Davide's time on earth may not be permanent.

"After all he's really a being of some kind. Though he has to have his soul for that is what gives uniqueness and divine spark to humans."

"*Sì*," responded Agnes. "He's a spirit-like being, but not ghostly as was Timothy of Syria when he appeared to Lorenzo de Medici. Davide's form has substance."

"*Veramante*…truly there is a difference between Timothy and Davide, though both would be… or both have a soul, though separated from its human body."

The miraculous nature of what they were discussing, how to refer to what they were seeing in Davide -- a spirit being with his soul intact or his actual soul with form and substance -- was now beyond Arthur's thought process. What he did know was that the Magi ring was a divine gift and it possessed the power to free a soul or divine essence of humanity, in need.

"Agnes, the lad may want to be released so that he may enter his heavenly reward. He may have no choice in that matter. If Roselli's gang finds that ring, you can be assured they would use it to imprison Davide or someone else, like Ryan, or even my sons. We must find it first so Davide may have a chance to stay with us or not."

Agnes agreed that finding the ring was essential so Davide didn't have to remain on earth, free or not, forever. She aptly pointed out that the soul does not die. She also pointed out she was an art historian, a curator of museums, and a scholar of legends; she wanted the ring to assume its rightful place in history. To that end, she suggested they pay a visit to a friend of hers in the Vatican Library.

"And while we are there, perhaps he could shed light on Alun's story of the Ramsey brooch and Michelangelo's connection to it," she added.

Arthur readily agreed to such a meeting. They would be going to Rome anyway. As for tomorrow, there was a slight change of plans. After breakfast, they would set out for the Ramsey Villa before going to Arthur's ancestral village. There they would meet up with his family and give the kids a day off from history and art and intrigue so that they could enjoy the villa and its amenities. He pointed out that since Roselli was sure to follow their every move, doing something touristy would frustrate him.

Just as they finalized the activities for the day, the four guys returned and John announced to all that Davide knew how to pass water.

"And we didn't have to go outside, either," he added with a giggle.

They decided it was time to rest. Agnes bade Arturo and the guys a restful night. Arthur thought it best for Ryan and Davide to stay in the apartment with the boys and him.

"Ryan, you and Davide will stay in John and Rich's room with them. Danny will probably wonder where you are, but we'll explain that tomorrow. For now, my sons will supply you with what you may need."

"No problem, Mr. C.," Davide responded with a Johnny flair for words.

The apartment was cool. Someone had opened the balcony doors and the night air gently flowed into the sitting room. Arthur went directly to his room as did the youths.

The boys' comfort in their sexual identity was put to the test. There were two large beds in the bedroom. The entire environment impressed Davide, who had not seen how people actually lived their every day lives for centuries.

"Ryan, you and Davide will bunk over there," John matter of factly ordered. "Rich and I will sleep here by the window."

Davide pulled off his souvenir shirt with the imprint of the *David* on it. He unzipped the shorts with a sense of accomplishment and stepped out of them. He folded them neatly and placed them on the dresser. Lying across the bed, he remarked that he had never felt such softness. The other guys were in and out of the bathroom and dressed in sleeping shorts. Rich, having a variety of them, lent a pair to Ryan. When they noticed Davide sprawled across the bed they collectively gasped.

"Hey dude. We don't sleep that way where we come from," noted John. "Rich, get him a pair of shorts, pronto."

In a minute Davide had his sleep shorts on and was redeposited on the bed. In another minute, slumber had brought them into a dream world. For Davide, it would be his first restful sleep in five centuries.

Arthur quietly listened for nonsense. He walked across the sitting room and onto the balcony. Taking a deep breath of air and looking up into a starry sky, he became convinced that the ring of the Magi must be found for Davide's sake. He turned and re-entered the room. As he walked, there was something crunching under his slippers. He looked up at the beam above him. "So that's where you were hidden, eh?" Then he looked at the chairs, still not returned to their proper places. "And I'd be right." Off to bed he strolled, very pleased with himself.

"Hey Davide, are you getting up this morning?" Rich yelled from the bathroom. "Johnny, make sure he's okay, will you?"

John meandered to the other bed and looked at the sleeping Davide. "He's breathing, so I guess he's okay."

"*Idioso,*" as Agnes would have said, "wake him up!"

"Hey dude, it's time to get up." John shook the bed. When that didn't work, he bounced on the side of the bed that Ryan had long-vacated when he had returned to his regular room to get a new outfit for a new day.

"*Bellisimo, ah Giovanni*…is not this day wonderful?"

"Yeah it's just peachy but Dad…er Mr. C., has a lot for us to do today. Get ready."

Rich walked into the room and suggested Davide take his shower now while Rich looked for some clothes which might fit. Looking at Davide's six-foot, four-inch frame, Rich thought he might have more luck finding shorts that fit. Davide had gone to the window and was hanging over the edge looking down the Via Santi Apostoli. He noticed the dome of the Duomo and heard the bells of Santo Trinito declaring that it was 9:00 a.m.

Rich grabbed him by the arm, fearing he was about to lean out too far and plummet to the street. Davide turned and smiled.

"Do not fear for me Ricardo. I am just born again. What am I to do now?"

"You are to wash yourself and then dress yourself. I have laid out some clothes for you."

Davide looked at the bed and saw a pair of khaki shorts, a tee-shirt and what he thought was another pair of sleep shorts. He picked those up first.

"And these, I am to sleep in these tonight, *si*?

Rich laughed and explained that those are worn under the pants or in this case the shorts. "Hey, I bet that's why they're called underpants."

Rich saw that he was proud of himself for figuring that out. The normally dry-witted youngest son had made a crude joke without the instigation of John and that was a first for him. Noticing Davide's confusion he became himself once more.

"Davide, go and wash, then put these on. After you've done that come and put the rest of these clothes on. As for shoes, I think that we'll have to borrow a pair from Ryan. He has big feet like you."

John was ready and decided to go fetch Ryan and his shoes. "I'll be right back if Dad asks."

Not fifteen minutes later the four of them were sitting around the table waiting for Arthur. Arthur came into the apartment from the hallway, not from his room.

"*Buon Giorno figlii*, Ryan and Davide. Today I have a little surprise for you. We're going to visit the villa of Alun's family. There you can play bocce ball, swim in the pool, walk in the vineyards up on the hill, or even ride horses. Afterwards we'll head out for the ancestral village of the Nannini family on Cookie Grandma's side.

"Sounds good to me. When do we go?" asked Ryan.

Ambrogio will pick everyone up at ten o'clock, right after breakfast. "Get a move on," said Arthur

Three of them made a beeline for the door, almost knocking Arthur out of the way. Davide didn't move. Arthur walked up to him to ask if he felt all right.

"Mr. C., I wish to go and see *Il Divino,* Michelangelo."

"What…" was all that could come out of Arthur's mouth.

Davide explained. He told Arthur how he watched the Piazza Signoria. Day after day, year after year, he watched from his marble tomb of the Giant. He told of the time the arm of the statue was broken, due to a riot in the Piazza. He had a glimmer of hope that the master would come and repair it himself, but he was in Rome then working for the pope. An apprentice was sent to repair the Giant. More years passed until one day great shouts, accompanied by loud cries of anguish, swept across the city and into the Piazza. *Il Divino* was dead. News had come from Rome that the Son of Florence, the world's greatest artist, had died. From the Palazzo's main entrance, next to which the *David* stood, he heard the solemn announcement made.

"On the day, Friday the 18th of February, 1564 at twenty three and a half hours, Michelangelo di Lodovico di Lionardo Buonarroti Simoni left this present life, having died in Rome. He was eighty-eight years, eleven months, and fourteen days old. His body was deposited in the Church of the Apostoli were it shall rest until March 2nd, at which time he shall be brought home to his beloved city by Simone de' Berna. Thereafter he shall be brought to San Piero Maggiore to rest until his burial at Santa Croce."

Arthur understood what Davide wanted. He wanted to go to Santa Croce Basilica to visit the grave of Michelangelo.

"It's okay my boy, to miss one whom you loved. We shall visit Santa Croce before we move on to Ponte Buggianese."

Davide smiled, leapt from his chair and ran after the boys.

Agnes was already seated with Maura when Arthur entered. His sons were mixing in with the students; Ryan was telling everyone about the trip in the country; Davide talked about the visit to Michelangelo's grave.

Jessica, already enamored with Davide, remarked to Kristin and Maribeth that he was a bit morbid.

"Good grief; getting all excited about seeing the tomb of a dead artist."

Maribeth always looked on the bright side and suggested that perhaps Michelangelo inspired him. Very soon the talk changed to what they would bring on the outing to the villa and which boy would look best in a swimsuit.

Arthur sat himself between Maura and Agnes and went over the change in plans.

"I think this visit might take longer than anticipated so have the kids bring a change of clothes. I think we'll need to stay overnight."

"Arthur," began Maura. "That's an added expense. It's not part of the tour."

Arthur told her there wouldn't be an added cost since he was sure his family would bunk up together and free up some rooms for the kids. That settled, the next issue would be keeping an eye out for Roselli and company. But he couldn't refer to his thought because of Maura being present.

"Oh, that will be fine then. By the way, Danny came to me this morning and asked why Ryan was switched to another room," Maura commented. "He was afraid that he had done something to offend Ryan."

"Far from it, Maura," Arthur replied. "I just felt that Ryan having been…er sick and Davide being new might need to be watched over."

"I'll be sure to explain that to Danny," she said. "It will make him feel better."

Then she announced the students should pack an overnight bag for the trip to the Tuscan countryside. The students were to go to their rooms, pack, and place their bags on the bus. They would be walking to Santa Croce, before they boarded the bus, so that Arthur could show them other sites along the way.

As all these details were being announced, in walked Anselmo Roselli and the Giuliano brothers. The brothers went directly to the buffet table; Roselli went to Arthur's table.

"*Buon Giorno*, Signore Colonna, Signora la Straga," he nearly sang the greeting. "And what are your plans for this fine morning?"

Arthur and Agnes remained tight lipped but it was too late. He had already overheard Maura's announcement.

"Perhaps our paths will cross. Andreas and Pietro have a yearning to see Tuscany."

"But they're Italian," Maura commented.

"*Si*, quite true; but as with you Americans, sometimes one doesn't appreciate where one comes from. In their case, they are from the Rhegium area and they have never visited past Rome." With that, Roselli bade farewell.

Arthur made an excuse to leave so that he could throw a few things in a bag for the trip. Agnes was on his heels as he began to climb the stairs.

"Arturo, what are we going to do?"

Arthur turned to Agnes, who was in an obvious state of distress. He assured her that Lorenzo de Medici's advice to keep enemies close at hand would be the approach for the day. He pointed out that he certainly would have read the manuscript by now.

"He probably thinks that somehow we knew what it said else why would we have given it up to him so easily. Anyway Agnes, we always knew that Roselli would be following us. And now, he just about confirmed that for us."

They reached the top floor and Agnes was at her door. "So Arturo, Roselli following us to learn what we know will also allow us to figure out what they know."

Arthur opening the apartment door turned and affirmed her thought.

"And by the way, our jaunt to the country will add to their confusion for there is nothing remotely connected to the legend of the Magi ring where we are going."

The bells of Santa Trinita were announcing that it was 10:00 a.m. The students had their bags on the bus. John would lead the group, but this time, Arthur had a specific route he wanted taken. First they would cut through the Uffizi Gallery. Then they would circle the Piazza Signoria and walk behind the Palazzo Vecchio to Santa Croce. John motioned to follow him as he began the trek along Via Apostoli which led right into the Uffizi Courtyard. As soon as they entered the courtyard, Arthur, who was bringing up the rear with Agnes, rang Johnny on the cell phone.

"Quick, get everyone into the first gallery entrance and make it fast."

John enlisted Rich, Ryan, and Davide's help in keeping everyone together so that they could enter the building speedily. It wasn't long before an entrance presented itself along the narrow passageway separating the wings of the Gallery.

"Welcome to the Uffizi *studenti*," Marcella, the guard inside the door, said. She had greeted them in English.

John was surprised. "How did you know we were Americans?"

Marcella answered she was quite sure all but one was American. That really shocked John, but when she pointed to Davide dressed in American clothes, he was very impressed.

"Oh I see. We're that obvious then?"

"*Si*, but not to worry. We love Americans."

Rich was urging John to get through security and stop flirting, when he noticed Davide had wandered off. He panicked, thinking the Renaissance guy was walking within the clutches of Roselli with no one to protect him. Rich ran out the door and turned left. There, standing before a statue in a niche, was Davide.

"Davide, what the heck are you doing out here alone? You scared us half to death!"

Davide, totally immersed with viewing the statue, hardly heard Rich. "You know, this statue isn't very accurate."

"What?" exclaimed Rich as he nervously looked up and down the Uffizi Piazzele.

"The master almost always wore his boots. I saw him in sandals like those portrayed here maybe once or twice. And that's when the boots were being repaired. Of course this is when he was quite a bit older than when I knew him back in 1501."

"Well, I'm sure they meant well. See how nicely the cape drapes over his shoulders?" Rich said now trying to motivate him to go back with him. "Really Davide if you want to get to Sante Croce, we must get a move on."

"*Si, Santa Croce*; then let's go, *andiamo*."

The whole group had passed through security and entered by the time they returned. Arthur stood in the doorway and peeked outside one more time. He was waving them on to come quickly. He had seen the Giuliano brothers running down the courtyard looking into each doorway for signs of his group. The youths ran through the doorway to join up with the others.

"I think we've given them the slip, Agnes." Arthur then looked around. A sign over the arch announced the next room to be the Botticelli Gallery. "I think the kids should see this. After all, they have heard all about Botticelli and his being a loyal follower of Savonarola to the point of destroying his own works as symbols of vanity."

When they passed into the gallery he noticed his students gathered in a semi circle facing one of Botticelli's paintings. It was the *Birth of Venus*. The students recognized it immediately. What impressed Arthur even more, as they moved on, was their recognizing the painting with the famous Botticelli cherubs.

Ryan's cheeks were pinched by Jessica as she compared him to the little angels. Soon every boy was having their cheeks tweaked likewise.

As the laughter subsided, Arthur heard heavy footsteps. He gave a sign to the boys to get a move on and they herded the group onward. Arthur abruptly stopped in his tracks. He was passing the *Adoration of the Magi* by Botticelli when he realized the faces on the figures were Medici family members just like those in the *Capella de Magi* in the Medici Palazzo. The people represented were dressed in Renaissance attire and not as first century Middle Eastern people. On the left hand of one of the Medici was a ring.

"Agnes, Botticelli has placed the ring on the Medici's finger. He must have known about the legend as well."

"That would not surprise me since he was of the older generation and would have heard about the story since his youth. But why is that important?"

"I don't know. The building in the background looks like a Roman ruin. Obviously it's not the stable of Bethlehem. But then again, it was painted in 1475 which was the year of Michelangelo's birth. What do you suppose that could mean?"

"Arturo, I think you're reading too much into the painting. We should get to Santa Croce."

By the time they caught up with the group, John was leading them outside behind the Palazzo Vecchio.

At that moment, Andreas and Pietro had found their way into the Botticelli Gallery.

John decided to circumvent the Palazzo and had everyone going down the *Borgo dei Greci* which led them directly into the Piazza Santa Croce. The Giuliano brothers, he had hoped, would take the route through the Piazza Signoria, which, because of the tourists, would delay their progress. He took particular delight in causing the thugs a bit of annoyance.

Four blocks later, the group strolled onto the piazza across from the Basilica. The façade, with its three portals and towering peak in the center, was not there in Michelangelo's day. Why a six pointed star was chosen to dominate the center peak was unknown. In Arthur's mind it symbolized what could be called the stars of Florence who are buried within. As they entered purposefully through the center door the eyes of the group were drawn to the opposite end of the exceptionally wide nave to the simple Franciscan cross suspended over the altar for Eucharistic celebration. When one approaches the *Cappella Maggiore* it is filled with gloriously colorful paintings depicting the art and saints stretching back to the twelfth and thirteenth centuries.

Behind the pillars, supporting high arches and stone walls leading to the beamed ceiling and dating back to the thirteenth century, are entombed the great personages of Florence in eternal slumber. Arthur led the group first up to the sanctuary and then turned them around.

"You may now make your way back along the side aisles. Take time to visit the illustrious people whom you have read about in history."

The students were off. John and Rich, accompanied by Ryan, followed Davide who made haste to reach the entrance. Arthur knew where he was going and advised the boys to make sure that he had support around him if needed.

As at the Uffizi Piazelle, Davide stood with fixed gaze. This time, his face was glum. Tears welled in his eyes as he stood before the enormous tomb of Michelangelo. A colorful marble curtain, with blue at the peak on which was affixed a golden crown, flowed down to the sides of the monument. Its cloth-like appearance turning from blue to red trimmed in gold. Cherubs held open the marble curtain revealing a painting of Christ being lowered from the cross. Moving downward to the mid level was a marble bust of Michelangelo executed in the Roman style. Below the bust the simple gray marble sarcophagus resting on a large marble base. At each end and in front sat three women clothed in flowing robes. They represented Michelangelo's three areas of expertise: Painting, sculpture, and architecture.

The boys were reading the inscription under the sarcophagus on the marble base.

It told of Michelangelo's accomplishments. The rendition was created by Giorgio Vasari who adored Michelangelo and had written a book about Renaissance artists within the master's lifetime. By the time Rich and John were whispering to each other about the translation of the inscription which they held, Ryan had joined them. He was still rubbing his cheek. "How's he doing?"

"I can't tell. We're staying a little distance away so as not to disturb him," answered Rich.

Davide turned and asked that they come and stand next to him. He reflected on an April day in 1564.

"I had been entombed in the Giant for almost sixty years. Florence was changing in front of me. The master had achieved such fame that the city was abuzz constantly about his great works. I heard about the ceiling in the Sistine Chapel in Rome, of the dome for the new St. Peter's and his *terribilata* painting of the Last Judgment. Oh, how I yearned to be able to see his works, but then that announcement was made that the master had died."

A single tear trickled down his cheek which he wiped away with Rich's hanky. "I can see it…the funeral, as if it were yesterday. The Florentine Fine Arts Academicians had elected Michelangelo Prime Academic, or what could be called the Head Father and master of everyone. The body of the master arrived on April 10, 1564 and was brought to the Church of San Pier Maggiore. I knew the church well for it was but a short distance from the Casa Buonarroti where I had visited a number of times. Word spread through the city like a raging fire. For two days the church was filled with those paying their last respects to the one who had, more than even the Medici, brought greatness to *Firenze*."

Davide continued to paint the picture of what happened and soon the boys were back in Renaissance Florence.

It was April 12 and the church's funeral rites were just ending. The coffin of the master stone cutter and painter was being draped in somber cloths of purple and black. As was customary the confraternity to which one belonged was responsible for carrying the deceased person to the final resting place. In Michelangelo's case, the Academy had that privilege. The young members were assigned to carry the bier. Each vied for the honor. The route passed the Casa Buonarroti and then went straight down to the Basilica of Santa Croce for burial.

The crowds had become so huge, however, that a longer route was quickly designated which went through the Piazza della Signoria and then past the Ufizzi and to the river Arno where it followed its banks until it reached Santa Croce. Older members of the Academy were given torches, and in solemn procession, the bier was carried through the streets of Florence. *Il Divino*, Michelangelo, had come home to rest. As the coffin was processed, the people genuflected and crossed themselves as if the pope or a saint was passing by.

Walking slowly down Via Ghebellini, they turned left at what is now the *Bargello*. Several blocks more they walked, changing bearers of the bier as was necessary and thus spreading the honor of holding the Master Stone Cutter, Academic Father, Artist, and Architect; indeed the light of their world. The incense rose giving a sense of holiness to the scene. The cross led the procession and reflected the setting sun and torch light. All of this ceremonious procession could be seen approaching the Piazza

Signoria. Davide, trapped within the Giant, had a better view than most people, as the statue stood high above the crowd. As the procession passed the Palazzo Vecchio it paused in front of the Giant-David. The spirit of the youth within screamed in agony, born of sorrow, and his inability to reach out and touch the coffin being held before the statue.

The procession moved and the bier was shadowed by the Uffizi towering on each side of the entourage. The torches' glow was all that could be seen. The crowds were in a grieving frenzy as the master's bier was brought to Santa Croce. The piazza in front of the basilica was filled with throngs of people of every status, sharing the same emotion and reverence for the master stone cutter. Slowly the academicians walked as the hands of the crowd reached up to touch the pall covering the bier. Some even tried to kiss the cloth, rocking those who carried the coffin.

The procession finally entered the church and processed down its long, wide aisle to the sacristy. The bearers gently placed the coffin on a table to remove the lid. The older academicians wept along with the young ones who removed the lid. Everyone took a step back, expecting a smell of death from one who died three weeks ago. Surprisingly, only the aroma of sweetness emanated from the coffin. The bearers crossed themselves for surely the master deserved the name given by all to him, *Il Divino.*

They peered into the coffin and saw a peaceful Michelangelo dressed in a black damask gown wearing his boots and silver spurs. His French-styled cap was of silk and was circled by a black velvet ribbon. Those in the sacristy knelt in reverence and then brought the open coffin into the main church for the mourners to view. The members of the Academy, in Italian fashion, touched the master's body. Each left, awed by the sensation of having touched not a rigid corpse, but a soft and lifelike body. The feel of his cheek, the smoothness of his forehead, were as if he had just passed into eternal life. Each touched the master with the respect and adoration which Davide had yearned to impart, but could not. The budding artists walked away thinking that perhaps a part of the master's talent might be infused into their being.

At the end of the day, the coffin was resealed and placed in a temporary tomb with the simple inscription of *Il Divino Michelangelo* carved in the marble.

"Oh I heard so many stories as the crowds who witnessed the burial came through the piazza and shared their experiences," Davide said as he finished recounting what he had heard those many centuries ago. "Rich, I think I may need another one of these." And he wiped his eyes once again.

Rich assured him that he could have as many as he wanted. He placed his arm around Davide and suggested that they get out of the church and into the sunlight. Ryan and John agreed, so the four walked out the main doors into the sunny day.

"Let's go sit by the Dante statue and wait for the others," suggested John.

No sooner had they plopped themselves down than they saw Pietro and Andreas running across the piazza. Davide and Ryan became frightened. John told everyone to just sit and talk and ignore the thugs.

"They wouldn't dare do anything in broad daylight. Anyway, it's all part of Dad's plan to get them off course. He'll have them following us all over Italy and they will never know when we get to the place where we actually want to be."

The Giuliano brothers ran into the far right door which led directly to the tomb of Michelangelo. Arthur and the group were just moving away from the tomb.

Arthur saw the brothers and continued to walk slowly toward the door. He was a bit nervous at not being able to see all four of his boys. Without the slightest concern, however, he led his group right past the brothers and even offered them a *"Buon Giorno"*.

It seemed the brothers were counting the group as they passed by. They had noticed the missing ones. They did nothing until Arthur left the church. Then they exited from the other side door facing the piazza, the one near to the Dante memorial.

Now they stood just outside the portal. To their left, they saw Arthur walking with the group. They looked right and there were the four youths.

Ambrogio was standing just beyond the Dante statue on Via San Giuseppe. The bus's motor was running. As they ran for the bus, the group began calling dibs for this or that seat. As this distraction passed the Giuliano Brothers, the four boys made their way behind the memorial and ran to join up with the others. By the time Maura and Agnes boarded the bus everyone, was in a seat and the thugs were barely down the stairs in the Piazza.

John could not resist hanging out the bus window and waving good-bye to Andreas and Pietro. Luckily he could not hear what they said, but he recognized the gesture of the arm and hand. He dropped himself into the seat next to Ryan. "I think those guys are talking to us with their hands." Ryan peered out and laughed.

In a short time the bus crossed the Arno River and was below the Piazzale Michelangelo as they made their way into the Tuscan countryside.

Arthur expressed another concern of his with Agnes. He told her they should be planning on what to do with, or for, Davide. He was free, but no one knew for how long; and he was really not truly human. He had decided to speak to his wife about adopting the lad, so to speak.

Agnes was also concerned, but she felt Davide should not be taken out of his native land and brought into an even more formidable and different culture.

He accepted her observation, with thought. They continued to review options for the lad. Meanwhile, the subject of their discussion was at the back of the bus telling Ryan and the boys how he, inside the *David,* was moved from the front of the Palazzo Vecchio into the Galleria dell' Accademia in 1873 after almost four centuries of standing outside in the elements.

Arthur and Agnes were delighted to see Davide share his tales with at least some of the group. They felt that by relating his stories to the guys he was able to relieve himself of some of his burden. The other three offered the responses he needed to keep him going.

Fifteen minutes later, the bus stopped next to a very narrow road. There was a small wooden sign with an arrow pointing up the narrow paved road. Over the arrow, they could read: Villa Montebellini. Everyone was looking out the windows. On one side of the bus they could see the dome of the Duomo, off in the distance. On the other side they could see the green rolling hills with several similarly designed villas.

Arthur went to the front of the bus to speak with Ambrogio. The driver felt that he could not get the bus up the road.

"Perhaps that's why there's this parking area at the road's entrance," he explained to Arthur.

"You're probably right. Let me call my wife to find out how they got into the grounds."

In a minute he was talking with Donna, who was all aflutter about how lovely the villa was and how gracious the Ramsey family was for letting the family use it.

"Listen, I hate to cut you off, but I have a busload of students and heaven knows who following us," said Arthur.

"Good grief Arthur, what have you gotten yourself into now? Are the boys okay?"

"Yes everyone is fine. We even have a new kid with us, his name is Davide Mettzini. Anyway, how did you get to the villa? The bus won't fit."

Donna explained they had a couple of mini-vans that just fit. She would send Chris and Ron down with the vans to pick up the luggage and whoever wanted to ride.

"I bet your students might want to walk the mile up here. It's truly a lovely walk and the views along the way are outstanding."

Arthur felt her suggestion was just what the doctor ordered to get a little exercise in after a morning of touring Santa Croce. He addressed his group and explained they would walk the rest of the way. Arthur added that those who didn't wish to walk could ride in the vans which his elder sons were driving down. Having all the details arranged, Arthur felt a tap on his shoulder.

"Mr. C., am I allowed to speak with your other family members?"

Arthur turned to answer Davide's question. He told him of course he could, but perhaps he should leave out the part about his just being released from the marble. Davide understood and rejoined the boys and Ryan. Ambrogio came up next and suggested that he return to Florence, since it was not too far, so that the bus could be parked more safely. He would pick up the group later the next day. That was an excellent suggestion, for whoever might be following might think that the day's outing had ended and the bus was returning to the hotel. The bags were transferred into the vans, which had just pulled up. The boys were already introducing Davide to Ron and Chris, when Arthur approached. Maura boarded the van for the ride back; Agnes opted to walk with the students.

"Listen carefully; Davide is a very special lad. He's much older than you think, but naïve about the world around him," Arthur explained to his son and son-in-law.

Arthur was having trouble explaining the situation without letting the cat out of the bag. His son and son-in-law looked at him strangely but answered, no problem, they would keep an eye on him.

"Just follow the road. It will lead you directly to the villa," instructed Ron. "It's about a mile."

"By the way, the kids have their noses out of joint because they couldn't come with us," added Chris.

"Thanks, I'll be ready," said Arthur, grateful for the heads-up.

As the vans pulled away, Arthur and Agnes gathered the troops and began the trek up to the villa. They took the rear, but were relaxed since there was no sign of any confraternity members around the villa. If the Giuliano brothers or Roselli followed, they would have to check out all the hill top villas in the area.

At John's instigation the youths began to run, then walk, then run again. Agnes and Arthur were soon left in the dust.

They finally had an opportunity to talk about Davide's future and what they should do next to keep the Magi ring from getting into the wrong hands. They decided they would continue their tour and go on to Rome. In any case, Agnes had that friend at the Vatican Library who might be useful.

Chapter 20: All Roads Lead to Rome

The walk was spectacular. The cypress trees lined the road nicely and framed the views of Florence in the distance and vineyards across the hills. When the group stood before the villa itself the urban kids' jaws dropped. The three story villa with its golden hued plaster walls and hunter green shutters framed the family who anxiously waited.

As the student group crossed into the garden leading to the villa proper, the four grandchildren could not stand it any longer. Connor, little Arthur V, and Riley made a dash for the boys and Olivia to her papa. The rest of the students cheered as the little boys took flying leaps into their uncles' arms. Soon the little boys and their uncles were tumbling across the lawn as Olivia and Arthur walked up into the circle of his students who were enjoying seeing the boys rolling around the grass. Davide was enthralled with the scene and was soon drowning out the other's cheering with his own.

"*Benissimo, d'accordo!*" Davide shouted.

John whispered something in Riley's ear and Rich did likewise into little Arthur's ear. In a flash both boys jumped up and attacked Davide and Ryan, pulling them down by jumping on their backs.

"Boys. They never grow up, do they, Papa?" a haughty Olivia asked.

"Oh, sometimes they have to. But perhaps they need your help," Arthur suggested.

That was all she had to hear. Instantly, she jumped onto the pile sprawled on the lawn.

Now the other students were shouting they wanted a turn but Donna and the mothers of the children showed up and the rough housing and wrestling came to an end. Reluctantly, all four boys got up to greet Signora C., as Davide called her as he kissed her hand.

But there was more to that kiss, than the holding of a hand. She was the wife of the one who freed him. But even more, her caring hazel eyes, curly red hair and broad smile took him back to his own childhood. Donna had become for him the mother of whom he had only a faint memory. She instantly took a liking to him. He felt the blood rushing into his cheeks with a sense of warmth when Donna pulled down on his shoulders and kissed him on the cheek. His eyes sparkled with delight. The blushing indicated that he had not known such a welcome in a family setting. Even with his beloved Michelangelo there was but an occasional hug. Now he stood within a circle formed by the entire family and with them felt the emotion of the moment as each in turn came to welcome him to the family with a hug. Davide, for the first time in centuries, felt wanted and once again took out Rich's hankerchief to wipe his eyes.

The students couldn't quite figure out why this meeting was so emotional. The girls could not help but cry and the guys kept shifting from one leg to the other trying to keep their emotions in check. They never looked Davide in the eye; they would have seen tears and that would have been the end of control for them.

Donna felt this first meeting was becoming too much for Davide. She began the introductions to the family. Afterwards, Donna directed the kids to the veranda where she had set up a lunch of fruit, sandwiches, cookies, and lemonade. In an instant, they sat down for the picnic and soon everything in sight was consumed.

By unanimous vote, they decided to go swimming. The youths were ready to dash off but froze when they realized they didn't know where to go. They looked to Mrs. C. for guidance. Donna informed Arthur that the students' rooms where on the second floor.

"Jana and Tricia used the list of names you faxed to assign rooms," she told Arthur and his students.

In an instant they were off to change into their swim suits. All save Ryan, Davide, and their sons, who didn't quite know what to do.

Donna continued to explain room assignments. "Our room and the boys room are on the third floor," she began.

"Ah, you do mean the four boys right?" asked Arthur as he glanced over to Ryan, Davide, John and Rich.

"Four? I was thinking about…oh, certainly, the four boys," she stammered out correcting herself. "You will see John and Rich's names on the door, but it's for all of you."

And with that the four ran off.

Donna knew something was up as they walked off the veranda and into a sitting room. The sitting room was decorated with sheer curtains draping the floor-to-ceiling windows, and a marble hearth over which a gilded mirror hung. There was a small table that held a pitcher of ice water, flanked by two chairs. Donna poured out a glass of water for her husband.

"I think I need to hear something. Am I right?" questioned Donna.

Arthur smiled and began his story of how Davide came to be part of the group.

Ambrogio was parking the bus near Palazzo Rosselli. He took the short walk to the hotel and informed Antonio he would be staying one more night. He would pick up the group's bags; they would not be returning.

"*Si, signore*, that will be fine," replied the lad behind the desk. "We are sorry to lose all of you so soon."

Ambrogio told him that the decision was made by Signore Colonna. "The group will be off on the next leg of their journey when they leave the villa tomorrow."

Antonio's eyes lit up as he questioned where the group would be staying. The driver answered vaguely that it was one of those villas beyond Piazzale Michelangelo. With a wave, he was off up the stairs to his room.

"We have an early start tomorrow so, *Buona serra.*"

"*Buona serra, signore* and have a pleasant tour tomorrow." As soon as Ambrogio was out of sight he picked up the phone. "Signore Roselli I think I have some news which you may want to hear."

Roselli thanked Antonio and promised a special packet for him. Within a couple of minutes he was on Via Santi Apostoli waiting to be picked up. Several small black cars pulled up behind the Giuliano brothers. Out of them stepped the confraternity members. Roselli informed them they must scour the hills outside Florence. The Colonna group was in a villa on one of them. "We must find out where their next stop is."

With that, the scouting mission began.

Donna was the one gulping down water now, as Arthur finished his story of how the Confraternity of Savonarola had trapped Davide's spirit in the marble of the *David* statue.

"Arthur, the poor lad. What on earth can we do to help?"

"First, we must treat him like any other youth. Then, we must never let him know that his time on earth may be limited. Let him enjoy being with his new friends as long as he can."

Donna thought it best not to upset the family right now; she felt she should tell them the truth when Arthur left. They were scheduled to meet up with the family again in Pompeii; by then, heaven knows what would be taking place, and he would need all the help he could get.

"Now go and make sure that our four boys are comfortable. They'll have to bunk together; after all, this entire place only has eleven bedrooms," and she laughed at her own sarcasm.

Arthur reappeared on the veranda having found the boys' room empty. The veranda seemed deserted since it now contained only the four boys, Ron, and Chris. Everyone else was changing, judging by the laughter and nonsense coming out of the windows.

"Hi dad," began Rich.

Davide stood up as Arthur walked towards them. John pulled him back into his seat.

Nevertheless, Davide insisted Mr. C. take his chair; he would get another. Arthur reassured him the empty chair across from them would be fine; however, he took the one offered to him by Davide. He barely had a chance to sit when John blurted out that Ron and Chris knew the truth.

Arthur thought for a moment. "Well then I guess the four of you should go to your room and get ready to swim. Not you two however," he said, pointing to Ron and Chris. "I need to explain your mother's plan to you first." The four boys ran off and Ron and Chris sat down.

The four black compacts were racing up and down the hills for about two hours when Roselli and the Giuliano brothers finally came across the small parking area at the bottom of a narrow road. The sign read Villa Montebellini. Roselli suggested they walk from the bottom so as not to attract attention should the Colonna group be there.

"Remember, we need to find out where they are going next."

Half way up the hill, they knew the splashing, laughter and chatter they heard came from a group of young people. They looked for a way to avoid the pool.

Pietro and Andreas split up, making a large circle around to the back of the villa where the veranda and terrace were. Roselli made his way towards the other side of the stone staircase and lay motionless between the cypress trees listening to the students frolic.

The four boys came bouncing down the stairs, towels in hand. "Hey, Jessica what do you think of Davide?" yelled John.

Jessica flushed with rosy cheeks. She thought the orange Hawaiian swim suit looked wonderful. Everyone in the pool began to mock the look of the new Adonis. They pretended to swoon, especially the guys. John took control of this matter; he cannon-balled himself directly into the group. Davide froze at the pool's edge.

Everyone shouted for Davide to jump in.

He turned to Rich and Ryan in a panic. "What do they expect me to do? Fall as John did? And right on top of girls. I cannot do such a thing."

Ryan tried desperately, as the shouting continued, to convince him to do exactly what John had done. "It's okay. Really, Davide. The girls won't mind at all."

As this scene played out, Arthur appeared on the second-floor terrace where the Roses had invited Maura, and Agnes to join them while the kids had some fun.

"So here's where you've gotten yourself to. Trying to get away from the clamor no doubt?" Arthur joked with the women.

As they talked about the next leg of the tour, Pietro Giuliano made his way to the veranda directly below the terrace. Donna and her daughters entered the second-floor terrace just as they were about to discuss their itinerary.

"Jana, Tricia, and I think that we'll leave the pool supervision to Ron and Chris…I was going to add Arthur, however, I see that he's already here."

With their arrival, the subject changed to the view of the Duomo in the distance and a recap of both tours so far.

Down at the pool, Ron and Chris came running down the stone stairs with their children. Davide was still motionless at the pool's edge. "Hey Davide watch out," someone yelled as the three little boys grabbed hold of him and took him into the pool with an enormous splash, delighting everyone.

Once in the water, the little ones had no chance of being entertained by Davide, for he was surrounded by the big girls. The little boys made do with their uncles, Ryan and the other guys. Unfortunately for Ron and Chris, they had been told to act like adults and supervise.

Davide, never having been in the company of women his own age, didn't quite know what to do. He was a quick learner and began to demonstrate something he learned when he was modeling.

"Modeling…as in posing for an artist?" an excited Kristin asked.

"You mean someone photographed you? Like for a magazine ad?" questioned Breanne.

Davide was now getting unsettled again. Photos he understood, but the innuendo of posing was what shook him up. The follow up questions were even more disquieting.

From Patricia came, "So Davide, how did you pose?"

Then Jessica cut to the chase. "Is it true that models had to…well you know, pose in the nude?"

Davide explained as best he could and once or twice almost let loose with Michelangelo's name, but he caught himself in time. The eavesdropping ears behind the stairs were sharp, and heard every cut off syllable.

"It wasn't like what you're thinking at all, ladies. I just came to work, took off my tunic…er clothes and jumped in the water, well just like what we're doing here. Would you like me to show you how?"

The girls were giggling so much, that the guys had come over to check out the situation.

"Now watch and I'll show you how the master sculpted…"

"The master…is this guy for real?" asked Mike.

John and Rich told the guys that Davide posed for a very famous professional artist; he couldn't divulge his name, and therefore called him by such a title.

A double circle was made around Davide as he floated in the center. He immersed himself and slowly let himself come out of the water, turning as he did so.

"See it's that simple. The master brought the life out of the marble as if it were coming out of bath water. Even Vasari said so."

"Who's Vasari?" asked Dena.

"Oh some dude who wrote a book on art; didn't my dad tell you about him?" John said.

The games resumed. The guys taught Davide how to chicken fight by carrying someone on one's shoulders.

"Hey John, this dude is kind of…well he doesn't get out much does he?"

"Danny, he's like an orphan and has had to work most of his life."

Up on the second-floor terrace, Arthur had his map spread out on the table. He explained that Ambrogio would pick them up tomorrow after loading the bags from the hotel onto the bus. He proposed showing the kids the tower of Pisa and then having lunch in Siena on the way to Rome.

"Dad," began Jana. "Where are you staying in Rome?"

Arthur was hesitant to reply; he was almost embarrassed.

Tricia asked if he had forgotten.

"No I haven't forgotten. It's just that…well when I tell you…the hotel's name is the Colonna Palace."

"You're kidding" was the general exclamation shouted by everyone. Even Donna hadn't heard and was taken aback.

"Dad this is great. Do we have relatives running the place?"

"No Tricia, it's named after a very famous Italian family. In fact Michelangelo is said to have been in love with someone named Vittoria Colonna."

Even the Roses got into the conversation, and Agnes squirmed in her seat knowing what inevitably would come up. Jana brought it up. Marilyn made it clear that, years ago in her Art History classes at the University of Wisconsin, her professor had taught his students that Michelangelo liked men.

Arthur started explaining Renaissance thought about love and then realized that Agnes knew much more than he about the historical era. Agnes made it clear that though sonnets and poetry written by the master stone cutter were often filled with expressions of love for a particular young man, historians such as Condivi, who was Michelangelo's biographer when he was still alive, never attributed the words used to actual action taken. Renaissance men thought of love, as did Plato, in a manner rather different than we do today.

"Love was just expressed passionately in Renaissance Italy. But truthfully, even if he did love Tomaso Cavelieri, who was with him when he died and was like the son he never had, or Francesco Granacci, whom he certainly loved as his dearest friend, would that have made his artistic genius any less moving, or inspirational, or magnificient? Michelangelo did write sonnets depicting love as spiritual, platonic, or physical. He also loved Vittoria Colonna. If you read the poems they exchanged with each other you would see that clearly. After all is said and done, the historians feel that Michelangelo led a chaste life for most of his almost eighty-nine years."

"Wait a minute Agnes, if you please. Speaking of Vittoria Colonna, I think I have something here which may help this discussion," said Donna.

She left for a minute and returned holding a velvet box. When she opened it inside lay the Ramsey brooch which Kathy had worn. All eyes became glued to it, as none had really seen it so close up.

"Kathy didn't want to take it with her so she asked that I watch over the brooch," Donna explained.

"Signore, it is indeed just like the amulet which I wore to your daughter's wedding," Agnes noted. "But there's something different other than this is a brooch."

Agnes turned over the brooch and looked intently at the back side. She noticed that the gold backing could actually be opened. With Donna's permission she gave it a tug and it revealed a hollowed area behind the marble piece at the center of the brooch.

"So it's true what Alun said," Agnes began. "This is where Mary Stewart, the soon-to-be Queen of Scots, hid the safe conduct given to her by her mother-in-law, Catherine de Medici, Queen mother of France and mother of Mary's young husband, King Francis II, who had died."

She handed the brooch to Donna who passed it around. When it was handed to Jana she gave out a yelp of sorts.

"Jana, did the pin stick you?"

"No Mom, it's just that there is something written, or rather carved, into the back of the marble," Jana explained.

"What?" exclaimed Arthur and Agnes.

"Look Dad, here at the top; almost covered by the gold holding it in place."

Arthur took the brooch and held it up with the sunlight at his back illuminating the carved letters. He told the awe stricken women what he saw.

"There's a 'V' followed by the Latin words *amo te* and then an 'M'," Arthur reported.

"Arturo," exclaimed Agnes as Donna looked rather keenly interested regarding her form of address to her husband. "This is a monumental historical find."

"Well, it certainly proves that the shy Michelangelo may have intended to have more than a platonic relationship with Vittoria Colonna," Arthur replied. "After all, *amo te* is Latin for 'I love you'."

"Or perhaps such a relationship already exisited and this was to prove his affection for her," Agnes observed.

"Well wouldn't my art history teacher love to be here to see this discovery?" added Marilyn.

"Quite so, but how did this piece of jewelry become the property of Catherine de Medici? And how does it relate to the Order of the Magi, if it does?" questioned Arthur.

"Perhaps my friend in Rome will be able to tell us," concluded Agnes.

Pietro had heard enough. He got the information he sought and was off to find Roselli.

Andreas had already found Roselli when Pietro arrived. They were both listening to Davide's explanation of how some master artist sculpted his subject. When Pietro showed up behind the tree line, next to the stone staircase, they were looking towards the pool with intense interest. He was told to be quiet for the lad was explaining something else. This of course meant nothing to Pietro but it was quite illuminating for Roselli.

The demonstration Davide was enacting ended abruptly when Mike and Danny grabbed hold of the floating Davide. They lifted him skyward and tossed him right into the space between Jessica and Jenny. The girls were delighted and playfully dunked him as he came up. Instantly, a water war broke out with the boys choosing sides and tossing each other about. Davide, having no experience with such behavior, did know what taking sides meant.

"Enough of this nonsense. I have heard all that I need. Let's get out of here."

Quickly Roselli and the brothers traveled undetected along the tree line. Pietro finally reported that the Colonna clan was going to Rome, making stops in Pisa and Siena. Everything seemed to be working in their favor. When the plum of the report was shared, Roselli was ecstatic.

"The Colonna Palace is it. That's right by the Parliament building; I know it well," Roselli began. "More importantly that brooch may symbolize something even more important."

Feeling safe now, they entered the road and ran to the car so they could call the confraternity members and share the exciting news. Roselli called for a meeting at the Orsini house for 7 p.m.

Arthur and the women were just ending their discussion of Renaissance love when Ron and Chris came running up to the terrace.

"Dad, I think someone was spying on us."

Arthur jumped from his seat. "Where's Davide?"

The women, except for Donna and Agnes didn't quite get why he asked only for Davide.

Donna ignored everyone as soon as she heard and ran off the terrace with Jana and Tricia to make sure all the children were safe.

Arthur made his apologies and excused himself without explanation. He left with Ron and Chris. "Okay, I need to know everything."

"There's not much to tell really," Chris began. "We heard what we thought was a rustling of branches by the stairs behind us."

Ron added that they had thought the noise was created by a small animal, so they ignored it. With the chicken fight and then the water fight, not much could be heard anyway. When the kids were getting out of the pool, he and Chris had walked up the stairs to better take a head count. "That's when we saw three guys running down the roadway."

"Before we could do anything, they were out of sight and we could hear a car engine starting," concluded Chris.

Arthur assured them they did the right thing staying with the students. Since they knew about Davide, he hardly needed to add how important it was to keep him safe. He wanted to see where his sons had thought the intruders might have been lurking. They took him to the tree line above the stairs. Sure enough, they found footprints, three distinct sets.

"No doubt these belong to Roselli and company."

Looking over the ledge, as Roselli probably had been doing, Arthur could see chaos breaking out as Donna wrapped the grandchildren in towels. She sent them into the villa with their mothers. As for the rest of the group, she instructed them that water time was over; they needed to dry off and get ready for dinner. By the way she shouted the directions John and Rich knew something was up. Davide was horrified with all the confusion and shouted orders. Ryan explained to Davide that dinner was important to Mrs. C. and somehow that made sense to him. The explanation at least calmed him, and he followed the direction to go to his room quickly. Ryan told John and Rich that they would be in the apartment.

"Davide doesn't want to disappoint your mother, so we have to get him dried off and dressed for dinner…and right now."

Inside the villa, Agnes and Maura were herding the students to their rooms. Why the quickness of the action they didn't clearly understand either, but given Donna and Arthur's concern with their sons' alert, they thought it was prudent to get them inside and dressed. Especially since they were now trapped at the villa with the bus back in Florence.

As Agnes flew by Arthur with a couple of the girls, he stopped her briefly.

"Just go along with anything I say."

She nodded affirmatively and continued up the stairs. He sent word via Ron and Chris to everyone that once dressed everyone was to gather in the dining room.

The room was large enough for everyone to fit comfortably. Several small tables covered in purple and gold table cloths were spread about the room. Doors opened onto the veranda and sofas were positioned along the walls. In the corner was a white marble pillar about three feet high holding a single votive candle. The pillar was obviously taken from an ancient ruin; Agnes had studied it intently when they first arrived. With their hair still wet, but clothed and dry and full of expectation, the students meandered into the room. From the murmuring among them they had conjured up a variety of scenarios, some of which Arthur thought were quite good. He wished he had thought of them. The little boys were allowed to play with their DS games on the veranda by the door. They were not to leave the doorway. Jana and Tricia sat at the open door to keep an eye on them. Olivia sat next to Donna.

Arthur stood on the bottom step of the staircase watching everyone enter the dining room. Ryan came down with Davide at his side. Davide was wearing another of Ryan's famous label shorts, polo shirt, and sandals. Arthur could not have asked for better planning, even if Ryan had been told what his thoughts were. Behind them were Rich and John. They were the last ones to enter the dining room. He stopped the four boys on the stairs.

"Listen very carefully. I am going to present a story which you, Davide, will soon realize is not true. It is being told to protect you, Ryan and everyone in our group. Do you understand?"

"*Si*, Mr. C., *capisco*…I think."

"Well, Rich and John will help you when I'm done. There will be some excitement after I have explained the story, so be ready to be famous."

"Ah, you mean like the Giant? Everyone shall admire me?"

"Good lad Davide. That's exactly right. You shall be famous like Michelangelo's *David*. Now go into the room and sit together at that table by the fireplace."

The scene had been set as in a Sherlock Holmes movie. Sitting in the fourteenth-century villa were the cast of characters. Some knew the truth of the mystery; others knew Davide's true identity; none knew of Arthur's intentions in telling his blarney tale. Arthur entered with a matter-of-fact stride and headed for the fireplace. He placed his hand on the mantle and fidgeted with a small alabaster statue of the *David*. All eyes were now on him as he brought the statue and placed it deliberately in front of Davide. The lad looked at Arthur in confusion, but all Mr. C. did was return a smile. If it were not that the confraternity lurked somewhere out there in the hills of Tuscany, he would have enjoyed putting on this performance.

He looked into Donna's eyes and got a message of support, and he began. He apologized for the lies his students had been told. There was a collective murmur of disbelief. Mr. C. never lied to his students; of that, they were sure. He then said he was sorry the tour had to now take on some precautions which may restrict some of their freedom; he hoped once they heard the reason for those precautions everyone would support the decisions. Now everyone was confused, even Agnes and Donna who knew the truth about Davide.

The only sound was the DS games making their bings and dings as the little boys played, only half listening to parts of their Papa's story.

Arthur walked back to the table where the four boys were sitting and picked up the *David* statue again. All eyes followed him as he crossed the room, elevating the statue so that everyone could see it. "Can everyone see this statue of the *David*?"

There were nods of yes, while others spoke aloud.

"Good, because I need to tell you a story which may astound, and most certainly, will impress most of you."

Arthur started to spin his tale. He told the group that among them was someone who was just as famous as the model who posed for Michelangelo. In fact, he said, the two were so similar in character and charm that it would be difficult to separate one from the other. It was a bit over the top, but the tale was holding their attention. He strolled through the room with statue in hand. He told them of events in Europe which had now affected their little tour group. Since their arrival they had been out of touch with local news, so perhaps they hadn't heard. Arthur had heard of a news bulletin which he would share with them. Someone as recognizable as this statue of David was almost killed. He was captured and trapped for some time, when by a stroke of luck someone came and released him by mistake.

"He made himself known to me," Arthur told everyone. "I pledged that I would conceal him from his enemies and help him find his way home."

Arthur returned to the table and placed the statue in front of Davide. "By now you have probably guessed that the person who we are protecting is Davide."

Agnes could be heard above all the other sighs and shouts. "Marvelous, just marvelous…Donna he is a gem among men."

"Yes, I have always thought so myself," a cool Donna replied.

"Well, no wonder Davide was talking about modeling and Michelangelo and all that stuff. He looks like the statue, doesn't he?" Kristin asked her friends.

Arthur let everyone talk for awhile, sharing their impressions. Many of the students went to Davide and patted him on the back, particularly

Danny and Mike, who had been a little jealous of him. After a few moments, when they all calmed down a bit, Arthur resumed. He revealed the rest of the story. He told of the need to keep Davide safe from those who sought to kidnap him. He told of the need for secrecy, even from authorities, for Davide wanted to enjoy life for a while as an ordinary guy. Ultimately, when the tour ended Davide, would have to leave. That was the only actual lie Arthur spoke. He had every intention of keeping Davide in the family in some manner.

Off and on throughout this story, Davide cried. He had never felt such loyalty and compassion in his short life. Ryan, then John, and then Rich did their best to perk him up and made jokes of fighting off the jerks.

Everyone made it clear they would do what was necessary to protect Davide; of course, that only made him cry more. Davide's reaction made the girls' hearts break. At one point Ryan took him out onto the veranda. That's when John and Rich asked everyone not to make such a fuss.

"Let's just treat him like one of us," requested Rich.

Donna arose and announced dinner should be ready shortly; what better way to make him feel at home than to eat with his new family. The boys went to get Davide, who was being shown how to play a DS game. And after a quick game against John, the four boys entered the dining room again to enjoy a meal of homemade gnocchi and sauce made from recipes from Arthur's mother and grandmother.

The apartment, in which Donna, Arthur, and the four boys were staying, filled with the morning sunlight. The polished floors reflected the sun's rays onto the smooth ivory walls. The sheer curtains fluttered with the breeze through the window which framed a spectacular view of Florence. The dome of the Duomo and the tower of the Palazzo Vecchio were easily identifiable. Arthur and Donna sat at the small breakfast table, enjoying the view.

They were reviewing the day's plans. The first excursion, including both the family and the students, was a visit to the family village and the house where Arthur's great-grandparents had lived prior to immigrating to America. As the villa awakened, and family noises drifted in, Arthur got in a few final thoughts.

"We are to meet in Pompeii, and maybe then go on to Sorrento and of course Capri. I promised the kids a swim in the Mediterranean. The family can see Rome after I get my students on the plane and heading back to the States. We could have a good-bye time without the fuss of students and curators and confraternity members."

"I see," began Donna half heartedly. "And what if you can't find this ring? Then what happens to us, your students, and poor Davide?"

Arthur soaked in the sadness from his wife's face directly into his heart. He mustered up a happy face before he responded. "Well there's always the gold coins, if all else fails."

Donna smiled. "And I thought there was to be no magic in our lives for a while anyway."

Arthur kissed her gently and went towards the door. The rumbles of running steps were becoming stronger and soon the little boys would be at the door. He turned with one last word on the subject.

"And besides, we have Michelangelo's Davide on our side so, what's to worry about, eh?" He opened the door just as the little ones came running through.

"Hi Papa! Hi Grammy!" and they headed for the boys' room.

In an instant havoc broke out as they jumped on the four sleeping lads.

"Uncle Johnny wake up! We're going to the family house today," yelled Connor.

"Uncle Richie, come on get up!" called Riley as he jumped up and down on the bed.

Arthur V headed for Davide and Ryan and soon they were being tormented to rise and shine.

Donna decided it was time to retreat from the chaos and head into the kitchen where the Roses were making breakfast. She missed Davide coming out of the room, his hand being held tightly by little Arthur V, and crying again.

He looked at Arthur, "I never had a little brother before, Mr. C."

"Well lad, I think you have one now."

His new brother pulled him to the window where his Papa stood. "Davide, you're from here. Can you name all those buildings out there?"

Davide swung open the doors and walked onto the terrace. Little Arthur jumped into his lap and looked up to him in a way which had always been reserved for Rich and John. Arthur had to turn away for a moment. Emotions swelled inside him.

"All this kid ever wanted was a little attention and some love, just like his master" Arthur thought to himself.

As Davide named the palazzos and churches, the others staggered out of the room into the sunlight, covering their eyes until they got adjusted to the brightness.

"Sunny Italy. I think that's what the flyer said about the tour," commented Ryan. "And apparently they knew what they were talking about."

A moment later, the uncles, Ryan, and the little boys joined the two on the terrace; Arthur looked away once again. Then, as he had done for his wife, he put on a happy face to cover up his true feelings of concern.

"Listen up guys. Today is a busy day, so don't mess around too long. And you, my precious ones, are to go to your mothers right now for your breakfast or we'll never get on the road."

"Food!" the little boys yelled as they abandoned uncles, old and new, and ran off down the stairs.

The four boys sat shocked and Arthur laughed. "I wish *you* would listen so obediently when I gave a direction."

The still red-eyed Davide now looked pained. "'Mr. C., I always listen to you."

"Yes Davide, you do," Arthur replied patting him on the shoulder, realizing that he had hurt the lad's feelings. "I just meant it as a joke for my sons."

"*Va bene*, then I shall lead the way to get dressed, no?"

"*Sì*, and as for you others, take the example to heart," and with a grin from ear to ear he paraded out of the apartment and down the stairs.

"Good, Dad is gone," began Rich as he closed the apartment door.

"Dudes," began John. "I think we're in big trouble and Dad won't let on. We need to stick together at all times, especially in Rome. I heard on the news last night that big crowds have come to the city. It seems that all those youth groups which we met in Florence are now going to Rome to pray with the Pope at a special gathering."

Ryan and Davide returned to their chairs on the terrace. The morning breezes buffeted the four with a gentle reminder that it was early in the day, before the warmth of the sun really heated up the day. They huddled as if on a football field.

"Now, I mean it Ryan. Forget the girls. Well at least tell them you can't go off with them," ordered John, who of all people would find such a direction almost impossible to follow were it not for the circumstances surrounding them. "And that goes for you too Davide."

"*Si, Giovanni* as you say…no problem. I sound like an *Americano*, no?"

Rich added his two cents worth. He reminded them of the visitors yesterday who, in all probability, were Roselli and his thugs.

"And wouldn't they love to get their hands on you, Ryan, and Davide too."

Ambrogio entered the villa kitchen and walked through to the dining room. It was humming with chatter about the day's activities. Arthur chided him for not calling so that he could be picked up, instead of walking up the hill. He replied that the walk was good for his heart. He and Arthur walked out onto the veranda to talk about the route and to ask if Ambrogio had seen any cars following him up to Montebellini. The driver assured him he saw no one save Antonio the desk clerk as he left the hotel.

The breakfast eaten and the kitchen tidied up, it was time to board the bus and vans. Ron and Chris were to follow the bus. The grandkids begged to ride on the bus, so that's where they would be. Donna decided to ride the bus and get to know Agnes better. The Roses and the family would follow in the vans. Just before the walk to the bus, Nancy lined everyone up in front of the villa, set her camera timer, and preserved the moment.

No one would have guessed that in the adjacent villa, across the vineyard fields, was a blue Alpha Romeo which would be part of the entourage. The motor was running and Andreas was in the driver's seat waiting for Roselli who had just walked out of the doorway with Pietro. They had told the residents they were lost. The time it took for directions to be given to Ponte Buggianese was just long enough for the bus to be loaded. As Roselli opened the car door, he could see the top of the bus slowly pulling out into the street.

"At no time are they to see us," he directed while entering.

Forty-five minutes later the bus, followed by the family vans, pulled onto a single lane street lined with centuries-old buildings, one of which had a sign reading *Doretti Farmacia,* or drug store. The sign created quite a stir; Doretti was Arthur's mother's maiden name. As interesting as that was, they were looking for Arthur's grandmother's family, the Nannini family. After a quick stop at the Town Palazzo, or City Hall, they found their way to a house nestled on the outskirts of the village.

Arthur's great-uncle, John Nannini, had called the cousins in Italy to announce that his nephew and family were coming to the village. Barbara and Roberto were ready for them when they appeared at the door. The house was like any other farm house in Italy. It had a neat stucco façade with accent arches that created a gateway into the family garden. The garden was surrounded with flowers of every type, but primarily red geraniums. Inside there were four bedrooms, a large kitchen, a living room and a sunroom. The sunroom overlooked the garden. The house was charmingly decorated with ceramic plates on the kitchen wall depicting various aspects of Tuscan life. One plate showed a field of sunflowers. These were cultivated on huge acres of land and their oil and seeds were harvested. Olive trees and sprigs of olive branches were also depicted in scenes. On the mantelpiece over the hearth were candle sticks and a statue of the Virgin Mary in a group to the left; a statue of the *David* sat on the right.

Barbara's daughter, Rosella, was a teacher and could speak English. She and her husband, Sergio Balduco, served as interpreters and guided the large group to ruins behind a series of townhouses. Each townhouse was currently occupied by Nannini family members. In the middle of another huge garden of vegetable plants and flower beds, was a golden plaster façade of a building on which a small porch extended off the second floor. An iron staircase descended from the elevated porch to the paved driveway lined with flower pots filled with red geraniums and rose plants. The space in front of the façade served as a carport.

"This," began Rosella, "is the ancestral home of the Nannini family going back over 300 years. Here lived Arturo's great-grandparents, Maria Cleofe and Armando Piacientino before they left for America. Here also lived Cleofe when she returned with her two-year-old son. That son is the uncle of your mother, Arturo; the one called *Tio Giovanni Nannini*."

She went on to share a story of Arthur's grandmother and her brother, John.

"Your grandmother arrived at Liberty Island in New York City with her parents when she was eight years old. There they waited to go on to Ellis Island to be processed as immigrants. Even at that tender age the young Ida Nannini knelt on the ground and kissed the soil. She vowed that she would never return to her homeland. Years later, John was born, and your great grandmother Cleofe began to miss her mother and family in Italy. She took the two-year-old John back to Italy. Grandma Ida stayed with her father in America and never returned to Italy. When the Facists under Mussolini took over the government of Italy the family could not get back to America. Then the war broke out across Europe. It was during World War II that your great-uncle had to be smuggled out of Italy for he was a natural-born American. Had the Nazis, who were then in control of most of Italy, found him, he would have been sent to the death camps. Through the tears of his mother's broken heart he found his way back to the Untied States. There he was reunited with his sister, Ida. Her daughter, Wanda, the mother of the one you call Mr. C. would eventually be married to Arthur Colonna, Jr. Great-uncle John was drafted and served in the Pacific theater in the Army. He fought with heroism in the Battle of Guadalcanal."

The entire gathering stood in silent wonder as the tales of heroism and immigration were shared. More than ever, Arthur's students and his own children had a deeper appreciation of why he was so interested in legend and history. His own ancestor's story was a source of inspiration.

As the bus pulled up to board the group, Arthur, Donna, and their family walked to the rear of the golden-hued façade. There they found the home to be a ruin. Its brick walls starkly revealed and beams broken and fallen throughout the structure.

"These are our roots kids, so take a picture, collect a piece of its brick, and never forget where we came from," said Arthur, quietly.

After the good-byes and hugs all around, the bus with the students was on its way to Rome. Arthur's family stood on the pavement in front of the ruin waving and shouting "See you in Pompeii."

Arthur was a little misty eyed when he asked Ambrogio if the road they traveled would take them to the Eternal City.

"Arturo, don't you know? All roads lead to Rome."

Chapter 21: Candlelight in the Eternal City

Ambrogio was correct; all roads do seem to lead to Rome. In Arthur's case the road also took them through Pisa, with its famous leaning tower, and Siena, with its famous Medieval Piazza del Campo and the Duomo, for which Michelangelo carved the St. Francis statue. As they drove along the A1 autostrada, the student's chatter was focused not on famous sites but on the little deli John found close by the Piazza del Campo. What made this shop so intriguing was its name: Nannini and Co. So far, the Colonna boys had found a hotel named after their family and now a significantly large chain of shops. Of course, no one knew any of the people involved with operating either the hotel or the store, but it was great fun talking about them and their possible connections to the family.

And so the students talked and talked of the boys who made movies and who now were connected to hotels and shops across Italy. It was a pleasant diversion for Davide. He preferred not being in the spotlight. Davide was enjoying seeing his native Italy, which he had not seen during his short life in Florence.

The bus was now in the province of Latium, where Rome is located. Crossing into Latium was quite emotional for Davide, as he had never left the outskirts of Florence. Now he was to see those famous places for which his master had created some of the most artistically renowned works in the world. He couldn't help but to barrage the boys and Ryan with questions about the New St. Peter's, the Sistine Chapel, the Vatican, San Pietro in Vincoli (home to the Tomb of Pope Julius II adorned with Michelangelo's Moses statue), and the Capitoline Hill complex which was designed by the master stone cutter. All of these places he had heard about from tourists conversing about his master's works as they visited the famous *David*.

John, having studied art in college, was the only one who could even try to answer Davide's questions. John delighted in sharing a story that even Davide may not have heard concerning his master.

The story dealt with the sculpting of the *Moses*. It was to be one of many statues for the tomb of Pope Julius II who had interrupted construction of his own tomb several times while he had Michelangelo create other masterpieces, such as the Sistine Chapel ceiling. And so he set up an introduction to his planned dramatic story. He presented some background on how the *Moses* came to be made. John explained it was to be the centerpiece for the tomb of Pope Julius II. The pope's final resting place was to be in the church near the Colosseum called St. Peter in Chains. Normally, the pope would be buried in the crypt under St. Peter's in the Vatican, but since it was under construction that was not possible.

"Like he did with you, Davide, your master searched Rome for just the right look for his *Moses*. In this case, however, it is fairly certain that many men contributed to the final look of the patriarch of the children of Israel. He sits, with a look of disdain, grasping the Ten Commandments under his right arm. His eyes flare out, opened widely, giving a look of reproach to his children, Israel, who had wandered from the commandments. In 1515, just as he completed the statue, your master struck the knee of his Moses and exclaimed, 'Now speak.'"

Now Davide's eyes flared open in shock. "You mean there is a soul trapped within this Moses statue as well?"

John had to set poor Davide straight. He explained that what Michelangelo was doing was a dramatic act to prove that his work brought life to the marble. He didn't need someone's spirit or soul to give his work lifelike form and expression. In the end, John's great attempt at drama fell flat because the lad took it literally. John finally told him that he could judge for himself; they would be visiting the church, while in Rome, and Davide could see the *Moses* for himself.

Before John was further questioned, Ambrogio pulled off the autostrada for a refreshment stop at the beautiful town of Orvieto, with its spectacular cathedral. After the brief stop, they were on their way once more. John shuddered to think what questions would be thrown at him by his new friend. Happily, Davide came up with a story of his own.

Like John, the sixteenth-century lad tried to set a dramatic picture.

John was quite proud he had created a storytelling clone of himself. Ryan and Rich, however, were truly interested in Davide's story; it was from the perspective of an eye witness.

It was May of 1504. The statue had survived the attack from the Confraternity of Savonarola. After four perilous days being hauled along the stone streets of Florence, each bump causing the Giant to sway to and fro from the huge wooden beams holding the statue above the carriage base, the rig finally arrived at the Piazza Signoria in early morning. The forty men who had pulled it to the piazza dropped to the pavement in exhaustion, but their rest was brief. Their goal was to place the Giant on its pedestal by noon. By 11:30 a.m. the Giant was suspended over the platform which would be its home for almost four hundred years. With expert accuracy they lowered the Giant. At exactly noon, it touched the top of the pedestal. The forty men joyously cheered as the sound of stone landing upon stone echoed across the piazza. Leaving the rigging still around the statue, they went off to drink a toast to their successful transfer of the symbol of Florentine freedom and their faith.

Michelangelo stood nearby with his friend, Piero Soderini. When all was quiet he and Piero walked around the statue to ensure that it stood where it should. Piero stopped in front of the statue. For the longest time, he looked up at the face of the Giant-David. Finally, he spoke.

"Michelangelo, *mi amico*, please come here. I want to show you something."

The Stone Cutter Genius walked to a place to Piero's right. He looked up, as his friend had. "Piero, what do you see up there?" Michelangelo queried.

"I see a nose too large for the head and overall presence of the statue."

The master said nothing but he climbed up the rigging and scaffolding surrounding the statue. When he reached the level of the statue's head, Michelangelo took out his hammer and chisel from his belt. He also held something in his closed fist.

Michelangelo went to work on the nose. With hammer and chisel he seemed to pound and file. As he did so, clouds of marble dust fell off the nose and sprinkled down to where Piero stood.

Taking a cloth from his belt he wiped off the Giant's nose. "So then, Piero, how does it look from down there?"

"Oh you have definitely improved its appearance my friend. It is indeed a masterpiece to behold."

Ryan, Rich, and John sat in amazement as Davide delivered his final image. The lad realized that the three had taken the story the wrong way.

"Don't you see *mi amici?* The master played a joke on his friend. He never touched the nose at all. He carried the marble dust up with him enclosed in his fist."

Suddenly John began to laugh. "You really got us going Davide. You'll do okay in our world." The others agreed.

Davide's introduction to the world of funny stories was short–lived; a commotion was spreading through the bus. They were driving along the Via Flaminia; the city of Rome surrounded them. To the right flowed the Tiber; to the left spread the Villa Borghese, with its gardens. The dome of St. Peter's was seen beyond the river.

"Look Davide, see that dome over there? That is what you call the new St. Peter's and it was designed by Michelangelo."

"*Ah si*, it's magnificent, Ricardo. Are we to go there?"

"Si Davide, we most certainly will be going to St. Peter's. Trust me, my dad will have us in every part of this city."

Ambrogio was now announcing that they would be traveling down the Via del Corso, which was the Via Flaminia with a different name. Ambrogio pointed out that the Corso would take them through the Piazza Colonna, off which the group would be staying at the Colonna Palace Hotel on Piazza Montecitorio. Across from the hotel would be the Italian Parliament building. He added a special note.

"Today I shall take you right through the heart of the ancient city onto the Via dei Fori Imperiale and past the most famous ruins from ancient Roma."

Soon, each of the places which Ambrogio had referred to came into sight. They drove through the gates called the *Santa Maria del Popolo*. The gates were flanked by two identical churches: Santa Maria dei Miracoli and Santa Maria in Montesanto. In the center of the piazza was an Egyptian obelisk. They entered the Corso, which was one of the main arteries of the city for business and shopping. The streets were packed with people and remained so all the way down to the Palatine Hill.

Directly in front of them, before the bus turned towards the Forum Romano, appeared a huge gleaming white marble monument. Ambrogio narrated its history; it had been built to honor the first king of a united

Italy. His name was Vittorio Emanuele II. He could be seen astride his bronze horse. Behind the statue was a colonnade of dazzling white Brescian marble pillars holding up the canopy. On each flank sculptures of Winged Victories on chariots topped a miniature reproduction of a Roman Temple's entrance.

"This monument contains the Altar to the Fatherland and the Tomb of the Unknown Soldier," Ambrogio pointed out. "You can see two fountains at the very bottom of the monument." What he didn't point out, and which Agnes la Straga did, was that the monument was built on the site where Michelangelo's house, known as the *Macel de' Corvi* (Slaughter House of the Crows) stood. A replica of the house could be seen a short distance away.

During the driver's commentary, the crowd of shoppers and tourists grew denser as young people streamed onto the Corso. Groups of youths, who held national flags and banners, swarmed all around the Palatine. These groups had come to Rome to celebrate International Youth Day. They represented youth groups from around the world, and Arthur's group was soon to become a part of the experience. The students were yelling out names of the countries whose flags they could identify. When they saw the flag of the United States, they went wild. Hanging out the windows of the bus they shouted greetings. They spotted the Italian flag and saw Luigi, whom they had met at the Duomo of Florence prayer service.

"Mr. C., look; it's Luigi and the kids we met in Florence," called out Danny and Mike.

"Luigi, we're here in the bus," shouted Jessica. "Look over to the street."

The Italian youths made their way to the curb. The Americans joined them, when they saw Breanne waving a tiny flag of the United States out the bus window.

Arthur asked Ambrogio to stop the bus. He conferred with Maura and decided he would take the group off the bus. They would walk around the Forum, and then to the Colonna Palace Hotel.

Arthur's students streamed off the bus and into the open arms of the Italian and American youths who gathered around them. In a minute they learned that a candlelight procession was planned at sunset. From the Church of Santa Maria in Aracoeli on top of the Capitoline Hill, the groups would descend from the main portal down the hundreds of stairs to the Piazza de Campidoglio. From there, they would process through the Forum and around the Palatine Hill.

Arthur watched the excited youths reunite, and, upon hearing of the challenging stairs and walk to follow, turned to Maura and Agnes.

"Are we up to this after such a long day?" he asked, knowing his answer was yes.

Agnes was up for it, but he could see in Maura's eyes that she was not sure.

"Maura, why don't you go to the hotel with Amrogio and make sure the preparations for our stay are done right."

"Arthur, you are intuitive. I'd be happy to check on our reservations. Thanks for the reprieve," Maura replied with a smile.

It was settled. Arthur's group would be part of the now joined Italian and American groups and take part in the procession. Davide was overwhelmed with the sights and sounds of the Eternal City but when he climbed the stairs up onto the Campidoglio, designed by the Master, himself, his emotions took over. The boys and Ryan made sure he was always involved with the group, trying to ease his reflections on the life work of his beloved Michelangelo.

They had been dropped off next to the Roman Forum, so Arthur suggested they walk through it on their way to the church high above where they stood. They walked down the Sacra Via passing the ruins of temples and Rome's ancient government buildings, including the famous home of the Vestal Virgins. They came upon a small ruin, still covered with a roof; it had no walls, just support pillars. On a large rock underneath the stone roof lay a bunch of flowers. Agnes explained this was where Julius Caesar, after being assassinated in the Senate chamber, was cremated. The group was standing where Marc Antony had delivered his eulogy. She pointed to the intact building behind where they stood.

"Here is the curia, the main section of that ancient Roman Senate chamber; the seat of Roman law."

As Agnes spoke, Arthur rummaged through his brief case bag and pulled out a folder. "I've found it."

Agnes looked at him, puzzled as to what caused such excitement.

"Danny, please come over here," Arthur requested.

He and Danny talked quietly in a corner of the ruin. The other youths had run to the Senate building hoping to enter it. But they could only peer through an iron gate. The sunlight revealed a mosaic floor made of black and white marble chips. The marble floor covered the rectangular room which was very plainly ornamented. Scattered around the floor were fragments of sculptures and pieces of broken marble. Two huge, solid, iron doors could be seen folded open on either side of the gated area.

The conversation ended, and Arthur called back his group. The leaders of the American and Italian groups returned too. Arthur explained to Frank Miller, the leader of the American group, and Libby de Cenzo, the leader of the Italian group, that he had planned a dramatic reading for his students when they visited the Forum. With their permission, he wished to conduct it now. The leaders were pleased to cooperate. The students took seats on various pieces of stone and marble blocks which encircled a large platform rock. Danny was standing on top of that large rock. Being a Drama major, Danny was invited to perform the Marc Antony's speech over the dead Julius Caesar. Danny delivered Shakespeare's immortal words in the actual spot where, over two thousand years ago, the people of Rome had gathered to bid farewell to Caesar.

When Danny finished his recitation, the youths applauded and cheered his performance. Many of those visiting the Forum were attracted to the large crowd which surrounded Danny. They joined the audience to hear the words Shakespeare wrote for his character, Marc Antony. Like the young people applauding, they were impressed by Danny's reading. The would-be actor achieved a bit of fame and a taste of what he hoped to achieve.

It was time to make their way to Santa Maria in Aracoeli. They approached the church from the bottom of the immense stairway. Its façade concealed the opulence of the art inside. All they saw when climbing the stairs was a very ordinary brick exterior. When they entered, they saw the gold of Christopher Columbus gilding its ceiling and amazing art work going back a thousand years.

Sitting in the plush arm chair in the tastefully decorated lounge of the Colonna Palace Hotel, Maura sipped her cappuccino. Being away from that climb and long walk was appreciated as she thumbed through a guide book on Rome. She hardly noticed the three men who entered the marble accented lobby from the piazza. The men walked up to the reception desk and inquired about vacancies. When they were told that there were none, the well-dressed man became slightly indignant.

"Madam, I am Anselmo Roselli, the curator of the world-renowned exhibit called *The World of Michelangelo and the Medici*," certainly there must be a suite of some kind available."

The young woman became quite flustered. She had no idea what a curator was, nor who Roselli was, but his presence and language obviously was quite persuasive and commanding. The two thugs who flanked him added a bit of anxiety to the encounter. Ava called for her manager. He approached, concerned that his clerk was being intimidated. When he saw the formidable trio, he became apprehensive.

Roselli gave the manager no time to speak. "Now then, I presume you are here to arrange for accommodations."

"Signore, I shall do my best, but, as Ava told you, we are booked full."

"Now listen..." Roselli looked at his name badge. "Listen Signore Frazzini, I have a most important meeting at the Vatican Library."

The manager paused and reviewed the registry. He perused the computer monitor looking at dates and bookings. After a few "hums" and "ehs" he spoke.

"I see that we do have a vacancy in one of our suites, but that won't be until tonight. Then, of course, we must have time to prepare the room for new guests."

"Indeed, I would expect nothing less from your fine establishment," Roselli now charmingly commented. "We shall be pleased to receive the key later tonight."

"Si, you may leave your luggage here and I shall have the suite ready for you by 9:00 p.m., *va bene?*"

"Most assuredly, Signore Frazzini," Roselli replied. "We shall return at nine, ciao. Oh and by the way our colleague Signore Colonna is here correct?"

"Well I can't say. However, he is due to be here."

Roselli did not push the manager. He turned to leave as Maura rose from her chair. She had heard pieces of the conversation, but when she heard the name Colonna mentioned, she thought it prudent to listen more closely. She made her way to the lobby. The Giuliano brothers and Roselli were turning away from the desk to leave. She ducked behind the red damask drapes, peering out ever so slightly. When the trio left, she approached the manager who was busily working on the computer entering Roselli's registration.

"*Scusi*, Signore Frazzini, I am Maura Kennedy, Arthur Colonna's assistant. Were those gentlemen looking for us?"

The manager confirmed that they were, but quickly added that he gave out no information.

"You are a sweet, dear boy to protect our privacy. May I have a piece of paper?" she asked in an unusually flattering manner.

After receiving the paper she jotted a note to Arthur about the newest guest at their hotel.

"If you would be most kind and place this in Signore Colonna's box." She walked to the elevator.

The prayer service had just ended up on the Capitoline. The bishop had spoken about the legacy of Christianity and how their procession would lead them to many of the sacred places where the church would be established. St. Peter's would be the last of those visits, tomorrow, he told the huge assembly.

The acolytes and cross bearer, began recessing from the church with the student pilgrims following and the Bishop and several priests following them. The two acolytes lit candles held by youth pilgrims standing next to the aisle, as they passed by. The youth, in turn, lit those next to them until the whole church was filled with flickering candlelight. The fading sun cast a reddish glow in the church as the groups organized themselves to follow the cross outside. The procession of student pilgrims, teachers, choir members, and clergy began to sing the hymn *Salve Regina*. Each national group slowly made their way under the lavish vaulted ceiling. Down the stairs, hundreds upon hundreds of candle-bearing youths processed until they reached the Campidoglio. Past the bronze equestrian statue of Marcus Aurelius they walked, their candle glow bouncing off the statue and illuminating the intricate pattern design of Michelangelo's plan on the veranda-like expanse, Typical of most processions and parades, a delay occurred just as they reached the statue.

Arthur's group, with the American and Italian youth, was now on the veranda surrounded by three palazzos. Two of these were designed by Michelangelo and the other's façade was created by the master artist.

The students were admiring the patterns on the stone paving as the sun's fading rays emphasized them quite dramatically. Danny grabbed hold of John.

"John, take a close look at this pattern. Where did you see it before?"

John scrutinized the design spreading across the Campidoglio plaza. "I remember seeing this pattern about a year or two ago, Danny. And it wasn't here."

"And you're right," Danny, who sought to enter show business, replied. "It's the pattern used on the stage of the Kodak Theater where the Oscar presentation took place."

"Danny, that's quite good. I remember it now because, of course, my dad never misses the Academy Awards Show."

"One day, I hope to be up there accepting that golden statuette. And trust me, if I get up there, your dad will be remembered."

John began to thank Danny for his pledge of a tribute when Agnes and Arthur walked by. "Dad, look at this keen design by Michelangelo."

It only took a glance before Arthur realized what he was looking at.

"Agnes take out your photo of the brooch, if you would."

Agnes did as she was asked and watched Arthur hold it and glance down at the Campidoglio Piazza paving. John and Danny were now joined by Rich, Ryan, and Davide. They formed a circle around Arthur as he studied the design. Arthur looked up, and, catching Danny's inquisitive eye smiled, announced that it was indeed a masterful work and quite wise of the Academy to use the master's design to honor motion picture artists. Danny was delighted that Arthur had seen what he saw and went off to share the news of his discovery with Kristin and Jessica.

As soon as he left the little circle, Arthur announced that the brooch was the same design as the piazza. It was a trapazoid with a twelve pointed star.

"And this is important why?" asked Rich.

"It means that this design symbolized something and that may very well be the Order of the Magi, if I am correct," Arthur answered with excitement.

"Perhaps when we meet my friend at the Vatican Library we shall learn more," added Agnes.

Just as Arthur was about to offer more of his thought, the procession started up again. His idea would have to wait for that meeting in the Vatican.

The throng of youths reverently moved through the gigantic stone statues of Castor and Pollux standing next to their horses. They broke into song. The familiar *Come Holy Ghost* hymn rang out behind the Victor Emanuele Monument. The youth groups made their way into the Forum and they turned right to follow a route circling the Palatine Hill. The columns of the Sacra Via, and the Colosseum in the distance, were illuminated in gold and white lights. The flickering candles approached the Arch of Constantine. As they passed under it, each group paused to honor the Roman Emperor who legalized Christianity in the Empire.

The long snake-like procession turned right to circle the Colosseum and a marble slab recognizing it as holy ground where early Christian martyrs were fed to the lions, or fought animals and gladiators to the death. It was in the Colosseum that great gladiatorial combats, circus shows, and even naval battles took place. The floor of the Colosseum could be flooded to create a lake on which small ships imitated great Roman sea battles. On this night it was the blood of the martyrs, who consecrated the ground on which it stands, who would be remembered in prayer and song.

It was the American group's turn to lead the singing and they broke into *When the Saints Come Marching In*.

The group then turned onto Via dei Annibaldi which led to San Pietro in Vincoli. Davide was getting excited. After John's story of the *Moses*, he was most eager to see it. The groups processed down the nave to the gold and crystal box which held the chains St. Peter wore in prison both in Jerusalem and in Rome before he was crucified. The story has it that he asked to be crucified upside down as he was not worthy to die as his savior had. After the groups paused in meditation at the gold box, they exited by a side door.

The route allowed them to pass Michelangelo's *Moses*, the central figure in Pope Julius II's tomb. Carved in 1515, it was not placed until 1545, when a much smaller tomb was finally readied long after the Pope's death. Davide found himself drawn to his master's work. He knelt before the tomb, looking into those eyes filled with fury. He saw the muscles flexing beneath the prophet's robes and in his bare arms. Several of the youths asked John and Rich if he had a special devotion for the pope who made Michelangelo paint the Sistine Chapel ceiling. Rich, in no uncertain terms, made it clear that Davide's devotion was to the Stone Cutter Genius who created the *Moses* and ordered it to speak.

Ryan joined Davide kneeling next to him. "We have to go now," he told him.

Davide's eyes, welling up with emotion, looked into a pair of caring blue eyes belonging to one who felt the sorrow the lad was experiencing. "*Va bene*," then Davide crossed himself and rejoined the others.

The procession made its way through the streets of Rome. People hung out their windows to view the spectacle and to pray with the youth who paused at every shrine along their way. Down the final, narrow alley-like street, housing little shops with souvenirs and hand crafted artifacts, they processed. Once they entered the Piazza della Rotunda, they had almost arrived at their final destination for the night. Before them, in majestic beauty, stood a massive floodlighted portico and huge dome on top of the round building. That dome was once the largest in the world and crowned an ancient church. Even before it had become a sacred place, it was a temple to the gods of Roman mythology. This mighty symbol of the blending of antiquity with Christianity is called the Pantheon. It is one of the few buildings of ancient Rome still completely intact from the days of the emperors. Its presence exemplified the absorbing of pagan culture into the belief system of Christianity. It housed the tombs of the Italian kings since Italy's unification, as well as the tomb of another famous Florentine Renaissance artist, Raphael.

Once all the groups had entered, the bishop intoned a hymn of glory. Once the *Gloria* was concluded, the final blessing was bestowed and the youth groups were free to explore the church and piazza before returning to their lodgings.

Arthur's students bade farewell to their American and Italian friends. They made plans to meet in the colonnade of St. Peter's, on the right side, "tomorrow when all the groups would gather to pray with the pope." Their chosen meeting place was the very beginning of the famous Bernini columns. The colonnade was named because Bernini had designed them. He was the artist who came after Michelangelo and ushered in the Baroque period.

Arthur and Agnes guided the students around the circular building, drawing their attention to the hole in the center of the concrete dome. It was placed there to allow light; when it rained the water fell into crevices in the floor which channeled it out of the temple. They stopped twice as they walked from shrine to shrine.

Agnes explained that remains of martyrs taken from the catacombs are buried within the walls of the Pantheon. That act saved the building from being destroyed.

They stopped to pay their respects to King Victor Emanuele II and to sign the book at his tomb, provided by the House of Savoy. Arthur explained how the Savoy family provided Italy with its kings after unification. Until, that is, they got a bum rap when Mussolini came into power, Arthur informed his students. The dictator allied Italy with Nazi Germany in the years leading up to World War II. Crown Prince Umberto hated Hitler and refused to give up his room when the German dictator visited Rome. Mussolini ignored the prince's refusal and forced the prince to give up his room. Prince Umberto later became King Umberto and set up a government against Mussolini. In 1943, the dictator was captured by Italian partisans and hanged. Eventually, thanks to propaganda from political groups coming into power in Italy at the time, not the least of which was the Communist Party, a popular vote forced the Kingdom of Italy to become the Republic of Italy in 1946. The House of Savoy is exiled to this day. Arthur concluded a rather passionate but brief overview of the Royal family's demise.

No one, except for Donna, knew Arthur held such strong feelings in favor of the House of Savoy. Nor did they know about his efforts to help King Constantine of Greece retain his throne. Arthur was still in communication with the King of Greece, writing essays while in college based on books lent to him by the King. These articles promoted the king's cause. The king still lives in exile in England. Arthur always felt that if only he could write persuasively, like Thomas Jefferson, he would have gotten his articles published in Greece, where people who did not have a voice in removing the king might now have one in the matter.

His little outburst over, Arthur led them on. When they reached the statue of *Madonna del Sasso,* they saw a light shining out from underneath the aedicule. It shone on an ancient sarcophagus containing the remains of Raphael. Agnes translated the Latin inscription for the group.

"Here lies Raphael: our great Mother Nature feared to be conquered by him in his lifetime, and to perish herself on his death."

She told the group they would be seeing his work in the Vatican tomorrow as part of the Vatican Museum and Sistine Chapel tour.

"Our appointment to visit St. Peter's is at 8 a.m., so we should probably be getting back to the hotel."

Arthur concurred and gathered his troops together, once again finding Davide mesmerized, this time at the tomb of Raphael.

"They say he greatly admired my master. Over the years I have heard many people talk of how he imitated the master's work."

"Tomorrow you can judge that gossip for yourself, Davide, but for now we must say good-bye."

Back through the piazza the group traveled when suddenly Mike began to shout. "Look, Mr. C. look, it's a McDonalds right in the middle of ancient Rome."

Excitement spread like a wild fire. Arthur had no choice but to take them into the McDonald's. Now the favorite photo setup was the student flanked by the Parthenon and McDonald's. Everyone had to have one of those photographs. Inside, cameras flashed until the manager informed Arthur that photos were not allowed. Arthur apologized and explained they were unaware of the rule, but that this was a most special time for his students. The manager asked his name and when he told her, Arturo Colonna, the entire work force could not do enough to provide them with the service and food they required. "*Italiano, sì?*" she had asked.

"Well Italian-American to be sure," Arthur replied. He hadn't realized they were standing only a few blocks from the Piazza Colonna and their hotel.

As the students ate and watched the sacred cats of Rome climb across the ruins bordering the Pantheon, Arthur and Agnes spoke about their meeting the next day in the Vatican Library.

Arthur wanted to have the busy day planned in every detail; especially the part when they would meet Agnes' friend in the Vatican Library. Agnes would have Marsilio Ficino's journal. Arthur would have the copy of the Savonarola manuscript and the other documents Agnes had given him in Chicago. The challenge was to put together all the information to determine where the ring could be today. All of this had to be done before Roselli arrived at a similar conclusion. Arthur's advantage was that he felt confident he knew the symbol for the Order of the Magi and Roselli did not.

Across the Tiber and facing the thick walls of the Vatican, another group was planning its next day's events. Roselli and the confraternity members sat around a table in a meeting room of the Hotel Michelangelo; literally a stone's throw from the border of Vatican City; an independent and sovereign nation in its own right. Over and over again they read the manuscript taken from the beam in the Palazzo Rosselli in Florence. Like Arthur and Agnes, they had not arrived at a conclusion with which they felt comfortable.

Roselli told the members that he and the Giuliano brothers would be staying at the Colonna Palace Hotel; whenever Arthur left, someone would follow. The other members would stay at the Michelangelo Hotel until Roselli contacted them to enact the second part of their plan. The first part of the plan was their meeting with the Director of the Vatican Library.

"The Monsignor Ottavianni is a professor of Medieval and Renaissance literature and a well known archeologist," Roselli explained. "If anyone had ever heard of the whereabouts of the ring, spoken about in the document, then it would be he."

Girolamo Orsini was fuming with hostility. Being in Rome and having to confront yet another Colonna, even though it was only one from America, was making him angry. The ancient feud between two powerful Roman families, the Orsinis and the Colonnas, seemed to be resurrecting itself. Roselli recognized this anger and would use it to reach his own ends. Orsini was well respected by the director because of his ancestral roots and his work to connect legend with Renaissance art.

Roselli laid out the plan. The papal event was scheduled at three o'clock in the afternoon. Members of the confraternity would attend it for the second part of the plan. To deflect any connection to him, Roselli arranged for a meeting with the monsignor in the morning. The meeting was to be held at the Piazza Colonna.

Orsini could not control himself; he protested and refused to attend a meeting in any place bearing that name. "Why not meet at the Medici Palazzo next to the Borhgese Gardens? Even that would be better than something named Colonna."

Anastasia tried unsuccessfully to calm the older gentleman. Raphael pointed out the irony of defeating a Colonna in his own ancestral land. That too, fell on deaf ears. No one could deflect Orsini's objections. Roselli finally caved in and told the group he would call the monsignor and change the location to the Medici Palazzo. Luckily he had connections with most of the curators of the Palazzos; the change would not be difficult to make.

Orsini's color came back to his face and he seemed to become more relaxed, now that he got his way. He began to understand Roselli's thinking.

"So then, what will happen once the second part of the plan is implemented?" Orsini asked.

The chatter on the piazza in front of the Pantheon continued. Some of the students were taking photos at the Obelisk of Isis. It stands in the middle of a fountain designed by Giocomo della Porta in 1575. Arthur and Agnes sat a little distance from the rest of the group. As they discussed the activities for the day, he was preparing an outline of the day's itinerary.

In order to get to St. Peter's for their 8:00 a.m. tour appointment they must leave the hotel no later than 7:00 a.m. He wanted to walk the students past some of the important sites of Rome on the way to the Basilica. The tour, including a trip into the crypts to view the tomb of St. Peter, would take about an hour. Afterwards, they would go directly to the Vatican Museum for a tour that ended in the Sistine Chapel. Everything was to be concluded by noon so they could have lunch and return to the Piazza San Pietro by 2:00 p.m. when the gates would be dropped and the students would enter the piazza to wait for the pope's arrival. The Holy Father was to conduct the closing prayer service with the youth of the world.

Agnes expressed concern that the day was so tightly planned that the slightest alteration could throw the whole plan out of whack. "For instance, how are we to meet with my friend, Monsignor Ottavianni?"

Arthur explained that he thought the meeting would be less conspicuous if held during the tour perhaps in one of the rooms of *The Raphael Stanze.*

"This way the director could be seen consulting with a tour group and offering insight, rather than holding some kind of clandestine meeting."

"Bravo, Arturo. You thought it out well."

With that settled, he called the students together for the walk back to the hotel.

Davide suggested they relight their candles and have their own procession back to the hotel. With candles held high, Arthur's group wound their way down narrow streets to their hotel. All along the way, they were greeted with cheers and welcoming words. For a moment, Davide felt he was participating in the funeral procession of the master stone cutter; that was a happy thought for him.

Upon entering the hotel, as everyone headed for the elevators, the clerk handed Arthur a note.

Chapter 22: The Pope Riots

Arthur hardly slept that night after he read Maura's note. He sat in the roof top dining area while it was still dark, going over the plans for the day. He checked his bag to make sure the copies of the documents were still there; as he had done several times already. Only when the workers came to set up the breakfast buffet did he stop and look out over the Eternal City, still wrapped in a cloak of darkness before dawn. The dome of St. Peter's glowed in floodlights, a brilliant symbol for all of Christendom.

Back in the suite the four boys were groggily meandering in and out of the bathroom as they made ready for a very packed day.

"Now everybody, listen up. My dad is meeting with this guy."

"Johnny, how do you know dad is meeting with someone and we don't?"

"Get real Richie. I looked at his notes."

Davide expressed confusion and Ryan said not to worry because he was just as confused.

"Okay, John you have our attention. So what did you find out?"

John revealed what he had learned; including the meeting with Monsignor Ottavianni.

"Davide, if my dad is doing what I think he's doing, then I am pretty sure you are involved. So the bottom line is this. None of us lets the others out of sight today. In fact we are like flies on glue paper; inseparable."

Rich was dazed to see his Peter Pan of a brother, who wouldn't admit growing up, actually acting like a mature, rational, thinking adult.

"So what's this meeting about, Johnny?"

"If I'm right, and I'm always right, the Signora la Straga and Dad need this historian guy's guidance on what's on those documents he's been carrying around."

Ryan thought that what John presented was logical. "But guidance on what?"

"Why the legend of the Medici ring, of course."

"Oh, I see now." And indeed Ryan and even Davide began to see. The latter one, in truth, knew more about the legend than he had shared.

Davide walked to the door.

"I think Mr. C. is on the roof waiting for breakfast. Perhaps we should go and keep him company."

He walked out of the room, forgetting entirely about what had just been promised about sticking together. The others ran after him. John grabbed his shoulder and turned him around.

"Dude, you already forgot our pledge to stay together."

Davide expressed his sorrow. He had many things on his mind, what with everything that's been happening and now the secret meeting and talk of legends. The elevator door opened and the four of them entered in silence. Three of them looked at the melancholy lad, trying desperately to figure out what brought on this mood.

As they left the elevator and walked across the hall and through the doors leading to the roof top dining area, the sun was bathing its new light across the Eternal City with the brightness of hope and wonder. Arthur was seated at a small table by the hot tub. It afforded a better view when seated and eating. Seeing the four boys, he rose and called them over. Cheerily he instructed them to go and get something to eat while he gathered a couple of more chairs. The boys only looked at his shoulder bag, in which those papers were kept.

Arthur hadn't been a teacher for so many years to not sense that something was up. "So why's the bag so interesting to you this morning?"

None of them wanted to lie, so they stood frozen and said nothing. This added to Arthur's concern. "You really need to tell me boys."

"No dad, you really need to tell us something," corrected Rich.

Arthur looked at the bag as the sun rose slightly higher into the blue sky causing a burst of light to reflect from the hot tub's water. Arthur pointed to the phenomenon which had just taken place. He asked them if they had seen that burst of light reflecting off the water. Of course they had. He compared that burst of light to an idea popping forth in one's mind. He called it illumination.

The boys were seated now, in a state of bewilderment. They did not comprehend his flowery language, comparing sunlight and water to forming ideas.

"Okay, let me tell you straight," Arthur began to say.

"That would be helpful, Dad," interrupted Rich.

When Arthur finished explaining how the library director might have insight into the location of the real Medici ring, and how that ring may possess certain properties—powers which in turn may affect life, the four boys were nodding understanding. The three boys then looked at Davide, for now they understood why he had become depressed.

Then Arthur dropped the other shoe. He told them about the note from Maura, which alerted him to the presence of Roselli and company right in their hotel. The boys looked at Davide.

"Hey dude, don't you worry about a thing, including Roselli. We'll be there for you and no matter what powers this ring may have, my dad and the guys won't let it do anything to you which you don't want to happen."

John grabbed Davide and gave him a huge bear hug. "Let's eat." And off the two walked like Siamese twins, inseparable. Ryan and Rich followed along, leaving Arthur to wonder what had just happened.

While the four boys were getting breakfast, the roof top terrace was filling up with his other students. Agnes came out last with coffee in hand.

"*Buon giorno Arturo*, how goes the morning with you?"

"Well Agnes, I just don't know. I think the four of them have just become the Musketeers."

Agnes looked at Arthur with a grin which indicated she hadn't a clue what he was talking about. He told her about his morning, which began before daybreak.

"*Ah, si*, the Musketeers to be sure, Arturo...all for one and one for all."

Just before leaving the roof top terrace, Arthur gave the orders for the day; the number one item was that their group was never, under any circumstances, to be separated. The newly-formed four musketeers smiled at each other; they had already established that rule. He told them of the crowds which they may expect and the need to stay close to one another. He told them of the surprise walking route. They were to visit the Trevi Fountain, before the crowds came out, throw their coin into its pool and make their wish to return.

The famous fountain, with the god Oceanus being pulled by two Tritons in his chariot, was soon found, not more than three blocks from the hotel. Suddenly, as they turned a corner, there it was. Almost no one was around as they ran up to the edge of the basin to toss in their coin while a friend immortalized it on digital memory card. From the Trevi Fountain, Arthur led his group along a small city street, looking for the Via Vittorio Emanuele which would lead them to the Vatican. Now, standing on the corner of Via Vittorio and another nameless street, they looked up at the Villa Colonna. The group was excited about another family connection. Arthur kept emphasizing it was not a relative, given that the family emigrated so long ago. If they had waited a little longer, perhaps they would have noticed the blue Alpha Romeo pulling onto the grounds. Better yet, they may have noticed its occupants.

Within the car, Roselli was blasting Andreas for having taken him and Orsini to the Colonna Villa, when their appointment with the director of the Vatican Library was at the Medici Palazzo several blocks in the other direction. Andreas tried to explain but all his excuses fell on deaf ears. Roselli and Orsini, sitting in the back seat, were reviewing the Savonarola manuscript and asking the same questions Arthur and Agnes had asked.

"Does the note in the margin mean that the ring is somewhere in Rome, or back in the area around Naples?" Orsini was confident that if anyone would know it would be Ottavianni.

Arthur and his merry band walked along the Via Vittorio Emanuele enjoying the waking city. Groups of youth with their flags held high appeared along the way as they made their way towards Vatican City. Arthur turned right onto the Corso del Rinascimento so they might walk through the Piazza Navona. Within that piazza, the generation after Michelangelo, who worked during the Baroque period, created a number of wonderful fountains, palazzos and the Church of St. Agnes in Agony. Here he told his sons, and the other two Musketeers, of the day their mother and he first arrived in Rome for his post-graduate studies.

"It was mid-July and scalding hot. Your mother, as she did in Washington D.C. in those days before five children, sat on that fountain called the Fountain of the Rivers. She refused to move until we got something to eat. As you can see, there are a number of outdoor cafés. At this one, right here, we sat down. We ordered a dish of gelato because we had heard so much about it. That's when I fell in love with Italian ice cream."

"So you're here in Rome. Sitting in front of Bernini's masterpiece and the water is flowing over stone carved centuries ago and what you fell in love with was ice cream?"

"Richie, that's not what I meant..." Arthur began to say trying to redeem himself.

"Rich's right, Dad, you are not the eternal romantic. There's no doubt about it," chimed in John with a laugh in his tone.

Agnes, for the first time, lost her professional composure, giggling then laughing over the exchange of views on love. In the end, Arthur saw the humor of the story too and joined in the laughter, with a reddened face.

The story spread throughout the ranks. Jenny ran to the Fountain of the Rivers. Imitating Mrs. C., she demanded refreshment. Danny knelt before her, begging her to move on. She, feigning a fainting spell, leaned over a bit too far and plunged into the waters of the fountain's basin. Everyone was shouting and screaming and laughing as Danny pulled her out. Maura and Arthur ran to her just to make sure it was only a laughable incident.

"Don't worry, Mrs. Kennedy, I'm only a little wet. I mostly fell on that rock."

Jessica offered her a pair of shorts she had in her bag. Arthur pointed out that shorts were not allowed in St. Peter's.

"There must be a shop somewhere around here," Maura Kennedy suggested. "We'll stop at one after they open."

The slightly wet Jenny, arm in arm with Danny, skipped off down the piazza.

"Now that, Arturo, is love ready to bloom."

"Indeed Agnes, I shall remember that the next time my wife and I have a dish of gelato."

Having left the piazza, the group wound their way to the Tiber and followed it to the Bridge of Angels. Here they crossed the Tiber. It took them to Hadrian's tomb, or what is called Castel Sant'Angelo since the miracle of Pope Gregory the Great. Arthur presented the story of the miracle which resulted in a bronze statue of the Archangel Michael sheathing his sword being placed on top of the fortress.

"The pope was leading a penitential procession asking for God's forgiveness and His ending the plague which threatened to wipe out the people of Rome. As the procession crossed the bridge, the very one we're standing on, the Archangel Michael appeared above the emperor's mausoleum, now a fortress. He sheathed his bloody sword as a symbol that the plague had run its course and Rome would be saved. The pope had a statue of that vision created and crowned the castle with it."

The students, walking toward the Archangel Michael, and walking under the gaze of the angels lining the bridge, each holding an instrument of Christ's passion, felt a sense of spiritual awakening and reverence. That was exactly what Arthur had hoped as he turned left down the Via Conciliazione toward Piazza San Pietro.

Because of the International Youth Days and the appointment schedule, those coming from their appointment, or those about to enter were the only ones in the area. Slightly after the groups entered the embrace of Bernini's Colonnade, so named because it seems to act as the arms of the church reaching out to embrace the world, they arrived at barricades. They presented their reservation and stood in line to wait their turn. Arthur's group was no different. They took their position next to one of the two fountains flanking the Egyptian Obelisk which supported a cross in which is held a piece of the true cross. Agnes had taken their time in line to talk about the colonnade, the fountains, and the obelisk.

She identified the two large statues on either side of the stairs leading into the basilica. One was St. Paul and the other was St. Peter. Lining the portico was Christ Triumphant, flanked by his Apostles. On top of the colonnade a procession of statues, representing the Communion of Saints, stood looking down on the pilgrims gathering in the piazza. As she pointed out the various saints, the bells of St.Peter's rang out announcing the time was 8:00 a.m. It was their appointment time and they walked forward.

The newly dubbed Four Musketeers, however, stood in place. Davide's eyes were riveted on the sight of the dome. "You say my master designed it?"

John assured him that he had and soon he would see the colorful uniforms of the Swiss Guards that he also designed. Then he would enter the basilica and get to see the *Pieta* which first brought him fame.

"So don't you want to see all the neat stuff?"

"And don't forget, we're going to get to climb up into the dome and look out over the city," added Rich.

Davide began to move, locked arms with his comrades and they in lock step strode across the piazza and up the stairs into St. Peter's.

Arthur gathered his students under the portico. He wanted to give to them an experience they would never forget as they entered Christendom's largest church and one of its holiest sites. Two Swiss Guards, dressed in their gold- and blue-striped uniforms with fifteenth century silver helmets and chest plates, cooperated in enhancing the moment. They opened the immense bronze doors.

The students stepped into the world of the Renaissance and the Baroque periods but more than that; they stepped into a house of God, which millions believe was built upon the rock that Jesus, himself, had named (Tu es Petrus, and upon this rock I shall build my Church. Matthew 16:18).

Arthur watched the newly-formed four musketeers to see if their reaction was as his was when he first entered St. Peter's Basilica. He thought of himself walking into the largest church in the world with his wife during those post-graduate study days. He had thought just its immense size would overwhelm him. Quite the opposite had happened. He had been amazed as the natural light from the dome flowed down onto the *baldacchino* over the papal altar drew his attention to the altar itself before all else was noticed.

Now he eagerly watched his sons and students for a similar flow of focus.

"Agnes, watch the musketeers and the others," he said. "You know, from the perspective of the time you first remembered entering St. Peter's."

"Ah, I see Arturo. You wish to see if Michelangelo's plan works on young people, *si*?"

"*Si*, Agnes exactly that."

The two stepped to the side and let their band of students walk past them. The Micelangelo touch was working. Each pair of eyes was drawn to the area of the dome over the papal altar. The steams of natural light illuminated the area in a halo of radiance.

"Look Agnes, see how their eyes are drawn to the altar. They know they are on holy ground," Arthur whispered so his four boys did not hear.

"*Si*, Arturo. Now comes the second revelation of the church, no?"

"Si Agnes, most definitely. Now they will notice that they are surrounded by centuries-old shrines, sculptures, tombs, and paintings."

As the words came forth from his lips, Arthur's students began to look about the church. Some had their eyes drawn to the vaulted ceiling with its panels of gilded designs similar to those back in Chicago at Our Lady of Sorrows.

"Johnny," began Rich. "Look, the ceiling is just like the church in Chicago."

"Rich, you mean the one in Chicago is patterned after this one."

"Okay Mr. Know-it-all, you're right. St. Peter's is only, what, three hundred years older right?"

"Exactly. Hey where's Davide and Ryan?"

Richie became excited that they had lost the other two until they turned around and spotted them standing before the very first shrine to the right as they entered the church.

"I should have known. Come on Rich. Let's go to them."

As they made their way toward the shrine, John pointed out how the whole shrine had a red marble background to offset the brilliant white Carrara marble of the unadorned cross behind Michelangelo's famous *Pieta* sculpture.

Davide practically ran into the bullet-proof protective glass wall separating the statue from visitors. Ryan purposely kept a distance. Davide fell to his knees and gazed into the serene eyes and face of the Virgin Mary, followed the flow of her garments to the Lord Jesus, her son, whom she held. The face of Christ was peaceful. His suffering was now over.

As this took place, Arthur and the rest of the group were told to follow to the right and up the side aisle.

John and Rich, arriving at the shrine, paused next to Ryan. They soon found themselves kneeling without thought or planning. It happened as Davide began to pray.

"Holy Madonna, Mother of Christ," he began while remembering, too, *Il Divino,* who had brought life out of the stone.

His fervent devotion so affected the three that they joined Davide in prayer. No longer on a field trip, no longer chasing after legendary artifacts, they felt what those who through the centuries must have felt.

Agnes came upon the scene of young men unabashedly praying in a shrine usually filled with noisy tourists. She was moved to tears but had to tell them that they must move on so other groups could enter. She tapped John on the shoulder.

"Right, okay. We're coming."

The four boys stood, locked arms, and followed her to the center of the dome area.

They found Arthur there, under the dome, with the group. Maura had just touched the foot of the thirteenth century St. Peter statue, as is tradition when one visits St. Peter's. So often has that bronze foot been touched that it has a permanent golden shine. Everyone wanted to have their turn touching it, so Arthur lined them up.

Soon the youths, including the four boys, were like any other visitor, being photographed touching the foot of St. Peter. They looked closely at the tomb of St. Pope Pius X whose body is enclosed in glass. They marveled at the Shrine to the Chair of St. Peter created by Bernini.

This shrine, located behind the main altar, encases, within its gold and bronze complex, a wooden chair. The Chair of St. Peter, or the *Cathedra Petri,* is the symbol of papal authority. The *Cathedra* of a bishop, anywhere in the world, symbolizes their teaching authority.

Arthur led them into the crypt to walk among the tombs of the popes. Afterwards, they climbed into the dome and walked outside its rim to see, laid before them, the arms of the church, gleaming in the early morning light, reaching out to embrace the city of Rome and the world. Arthur pointed to the end of the colonnade on their left. That is where the group was to meet the Italian and American groups when all the groups gathered to welcome the pope and pray with him during the concluding service of International Youth Days. Already they could see flags flying as groups made their way to the Piazza San Pietro.

In the ornate salon of the Medici Palazzo, Monsignor Octavianni sat on a plush red velvet chair next to a gold and silver gilt table. About him were frescoes depicting the life of Pope Leo X, who was a Medici and the same age as Michelangelo. The monsignor was well aware of the significance of being in this particular salon; so did Roselli, who was seated with Orsini on the other side of the table. It was the brother of Pope Leo X, Piero Medici, who last had the Magi ring. On the table was the manuscript written by a follower of Savonarola. Octavianni assured Roselli that it had every appearance of being a Renaissance-era document. Roselli cut to the chase.

"Does this mean that the Medici ring really exists?"

The monsignor thought, while pondering what was written on the aged parchment.

"Naturally, there is no one who has studied Renaissance history who hasn't heard of the Medici ring legend." But then he added, "Even so, until you presented this document there had been no recent research on it, or search for it, of which I am aware."

Roselli pushed onward. He invited the monsignor to help him in his search. He presented the idea of searching for the ring in the context of placing the ring, if found, in the collection of *The World of Michelangelo and the Medici* exhibit.

"Would it not serve to add a thrilling side to often told legends? Would it not bring in huge amounts of visitors to enjoy the art of the Renaissance, which ordinarily would not be the case?"

Ottavianni could hardly refute the case being made by the curator of the exhibit which had achieved such world-class status. At the same time, he wanted to think over the proposal; to have the researchers and historians of the Vatican involved in the search. He affirmed Roselli's position that such a find would indeed enhance the exhibit's attraction to a broader audience.

"As for enlisting the Vatican's active support and financing of such a project, this would have to be discussed at higher level in the Curia."

Roselli was well aware of the workings of Vatican bureaucracy, but there was one final question.

"*Sì*, I understand the need to present the plan to your superiors. However, if I may present one more question?"

"*Sì*, most certainly Anselmo, do ask it."

"If you, in just reading this report of the theft of the ring, were to search, where would you begin?"

The monsignor paused in his usual style of reflection. He took the parchment in his hand, gently turning it to read the notation in the margin.

"Roselli, if I were you I would begin right here in Rome."

Excusing himself so that he might attend to the Youth Groups coming to the Vatican Museum, he walked with the curator of the Medici Palazzo Galleria down the great hall and to the simple doorway which opened onto the street. Ottavianni's car stood ready at the curb with his driver standing by the open door. He bade a good morning to his host and was off to the Vatican.

Roselli and Orsini sat quietly until the director of the library departed. Roselli gently folded the document and placed it into his brief case.

"And so the old fool thinks I would search all of Rome for the clue, does he? When I have, available to me, one who has already figured out where to seek the ring, and one who may just have been there when it was originally lost?"

Orsini didn't understand Roselli's final statement but he certainly understood what he meant about running around Rome searching archives in this or that library or palazzo.

"I take it that the second part of our plan should be enacted."

"Si, my dear Orsini," replied Roselli. "I shall make the call as soon as we leave the Palazzo."

The bells of St. Peter's began to chime the nine o'clock hour as Arthur and his students made their way down from the dome. Cutting through the colonnade, the group followed the immense stone Vatican wall which led to the museum's entrance. At one section of the wall, work was being done to the street. Old stones from centuries back were scattered about as workmen searched for whatever it was being repaired. Arthur picked up one of those stones and put it into his pocket. That piece of the Vatican would be added to his collection of rocks along with those from his ancestral house and the garden of Michelangelo's house.

When Arthur and his group reached the entrance to the Vatican Museum, a black sedan was pulling up along the curb. A long line had formed which stretched back quite a distance. Arthur had arranged for a tour time, so the group stood in a much shorter reservation line.

Ottavianni, stepping out of the car, spotted Agnes la Straga. "Agnes, *buon giorno.*"

Agnes turned and saw her dear friend from the Vatican Library. She pulled Arthur along as she made her way to the old priest. As she threw her arms around him and kissed his cheek, she told him that he looked well.

"Monsignor, this is Arturo Colonna, who organized this trip for his students. He is also the author of works describing ancient legends in Ireland and Britain."

Ottavianni extended his hand which Arthur shook warmly. "I have been waiting a long time to speak with you, Monsignor."

"And I with you Arturo, if I may call you by your given name."

"Indeed you may."

"*Va bene, allora*…we shall get your students into the museum. Then when you get to the Stanze de Raphael we will have time to talk without interruption."

Agnes had a few quiet words with the monsignor concerning the Ramsey brooch. Arthur called to Maura who guided the students to him. The monsignor brought them into the reception area near a huge spiral staircase, which led to the various museum galleries. Up the twisting staircase went the students. Ottavianni elected to take the elevator with Agnes.

"We'll meet you in the courtyard by the Belvedere *Apollo*," Agnes told Arthur.

Arthur waved with his Vatican guidebook. With each step, Davide became more agitated and excited.

"How soon until we get to the Sistine Chapel?" he asked the boys.

They told him the chapel was almost the last part of the tour. Davide's expression changed, but the three boys perked him up by telling him that they would first see a statue which Michelangelo inspected when it was found by Pope Julius II, buried under the dirt of ancient Rome. It worked. Davide cheered up; anything that dealt with the master stone cutter was a good thing.

When they walked out into the courtyard, they realized this grassy piazza was elevated above street level. To the right was a gigantic head of the Emperor Constantine; in the center was a globe-like sculpture. Beyond that was the Belevedere *Apollo* alcove housing one of the most famous statues from antiquity. Agnes and the monsignor stood waiting. Agnes presented the *Apollo* to Arthur and his students, giving them a short explanation as to why it was considered such an important work. She summed up the art world's view by quoting Bridgette Hintzin-Bohlen, art historian and writer, who wrote, "It represented the supreme ideal of art among the works of antiquity."

The monsignor guided them into the Galleria of Antiquities where they would see the statue of the *Laocoon*, an original and intact marble sculpture of ancient Rome. Davide was excited; this piece was connected to Michelangelo. The priest-cum-director explained how it was found during excavations being promoted by Pope Julius II, the very pope who brought Michelangelo to Rome after the triumph of the *David*.

"What a sad day that was for the city of Florence, Francesco Granacci, and me," Davide whispered to his fellow musketeers.

Ottavianni, overhearing Davide's whispered message, picked up on it.

He told the story of how Michelangelo came to Rome to work on a magnificent tomb for Pope Julius II.

"When Michelangelo got to Rome and after he had chosen marble pieces to begin the sculptures for the Pope's tomb, the Pope suddenly had other ideas. Thus only the *Moses* which, Professore Colonna tells me, you have seen already, was eventually completed as intended at a much later date. From 1508 to 1512 Michelangelo became consumed with the art of painting, which was not his preferred medium. He was, after all, a stone cutter. And now, five hundred years later, we celebrate the creation of his masterpiece in paint."

The monsignor took the group to the Sistine Chapel. He told them he would leave it to them whether or not Michelangelo was a gifted painter, which, of course, the stone cutter had denied frequently. They entered the chapel in which the papal elections take place; the most famous chapel in the world, containing the early painted works of Michelangelo and his last effort, called *The Last Judgment,* completed thirty years after the ceiling. On the chapel's walls they would also see paintings by the master's friend, Botticelli, his teacher, Ghirlandaio, and a host of other early artists.

"When the Stone Cutter Genius entered that first day to cover the blue ceiling with painted gold stars on it, "with appropriate designs," Pope Julius II had ordered, the chapel and the world of art would not only be changed, but gifted with an expression of faith and humanity unparalleled in human history;" so the monsignor expressed dramatically as they entered the chapel.

The chapel was filled with other youth groups and tourists; all their eyes were lifted upward. The restored work of Michelangelo once more portrayed glorious colors. Agnes la Straga drew the group's attention to the vibrant life of Adam being touched by the hand of God. She pointed to God who wraps his other arm around Eve, who in his divine plan was to be brought forth to be with Adam.

The scene astounded the young viewers. She explained Michelangelo's vision of placing sibyls, or prophetesses, of the pagan world and the prophets of the Old Testament between the panels depicting the Genesis stories. That decision created a sensation in his day; and yet, the artist's vision was upheld by Pope Julius II. Five hundred years later, it is still being celebrated.

She told how Michelangelo blended the Christian understanding and the pagan understanding of man and life. The sibyls represented thought from antiquity as they announced a new way to understand mankind. The Christian belief absorbed that pagan thought. They saw in the Prophets the prediction of the coming Savior who would profoundly touch humanity, as never before, as the path to salvation unfolded. In the lunettes, the stone cutter, now painter, presented the forefathers of Christ from Abraham to Joseph, awaiting his birth. All of this was connected by the *Ignudi,* or nudes, who served to reflect Renaissance thought of the beauty of human form which reflected the glory of creation itself. And that thought was in direct contradiction to the thought of the Frate Savonarola. Michelangelo struggled to understand his teachings, which tore at his very heart and soul so much that it kept him away from Florence even after the Frate's execution.

Arthur felt Agnes had presented a succinct overview of the much-discussed ceiling. He was pleased his students seemed attentive to her commentary. All except Davide were attentive. He was in another world; one in which he was bedazzled by everything he saw.

The other musketeers noticed this trance-like state; but they just let him absorb and enjoy. The crowds shifted as new groups were allowed in and others left.

The shifting crowds forced Arthur and his group to the front of the chapel to stand before the fresco of *The Last Judgment.* Here the *terribilita* design was most pronounced as the souls showed anguish and pain, joy, and heightened expectations of being lifted into heaven by angels. Once again, Davide froze before the fresco studying every detail; soaking in every movement and expression portrayed on the souls of the damned and the saved. After he had done so, he turned to his comrades and asked if he would end up like those painted by the master. The three boys were speechless. They knew he was really thinking about himself. He, being a soul with form, must one day face the judgment as those depicted before him.

Finally, John came through with an answer. "Davide, if you had been able to finish your schooling, you may have learned that all of us will one day face judgment. Our souls will be taken to heaven, we hope, as those shown here."

"*Si*, but what about me? Have I done something so bad that I shall be with the damned?"

Now Rich and Ryan stepped in and put it all on the table. They made it clear that what happened to him was not a reflection of his deeds.

Rather, they went on to say, it was the result of others' acts. Those who did this to him deserved to ride on the boat guided by Charon to the underworld.

This seemed to lighten up Davide's mood; shortly thereafter he had a tale of his own to share with his fellow musketeers. It was the story of the day Michelangelo left for Rome after the Giant-David had been placed on permanent exhibit at the Palazzo Vecchio.

The master stone cutter stood before the Giant-David. Next to him was his closest friend, Francesco Granacci. They stood a long time looking up at the statue, as if it was too difficult to say farewell.

"So *amico*, this is it. You are really going to serve the Holy Father."

"I need to work Francesco. I need to say something with my work and if the Holy Father thinks I can do this in the Eternal City, how can I say no to him?"

"But your project for the battle scene for the Palazzo, how can you give that up?"

"I don't 'give it up', as you say. I simply must say yes to the Holy Father. He must take precedence. Anyway, already there are criticisms of my drawing as being too lewd, as if bathing soldiers was some horrible act. In Rome, I shall create a tomb for the Holy Father which will astound the world. I shall have all the marble I need to bring forth the life within them."

"I understand. And you will not have to paint because you, above all things, would be a stone cutter."

Michelangelo laughed and told his friend that he knew him only too well. Francesco placed his arm over the younger artist's shoulder and they both stood there for the longest time, saying nothing at all.

"Well that's it. It's time; my father is probably wondering what has happened to me. So Giant, guard our city well. Come along Francesco, walk me home."

"And it would be many years before I saw the master again," Davide concluded.

Just as he finished his story, Arthur walked up behind them. He waited until the tale concluded before he told them it was time to leave the Sistine Chapel, built by Pope Sixtus IV, who in 1478 had helped to plot the overthrow of Lorenzo de Medici in the year Michelangelo turned three. Had he succeeded, the probability of Michelangelo growing up in a palazzo and painting for popes would have been nil.

Today, the museum was closing early because of the papal event in the Piazza San Pietro; and as the last groups were escorted from the chapel, Ottavianni came in to take them out another way. Arthur's group was being taken to the *Stanze de Raphael;* specifically, to the *Salla della Segnatura* in which the painting of the *School of Athens* held particular interest for Arthur and a surprise for Davide.

The monsignor allowed the students, who had been standing for a long time in the Chapel, to sit before the work of Raphael. He told them about the young Florentine artist who so admired the work of Michelangelo that it had a profound influence on his own work. He explained how the painting illustrated one of the four principles of human knowledge: Philosophy. Thus in a Greek temple setting, Plato and Aristotle walked outside deep in discussion. All around them, students and admirers were listening to their every word. The monsignor walked up to the painting and pointed to a man sitting on the bottom step of the temple. The man leans against a marble plinth which serves as his desk. With pen in hand and paper under the pen he appears in deep thought. His left arm extends upward and he rests his head on his closed hand. He is totally detached from all the activity around him.

"This," the Monsignor announced, "is Michelangelo Buonarotti as he looked when he was working on the ceiling of the Sistine Chapel."

"How cool is that, Davide?" John exclaimed.

"Very, as you say, cool, Giovanni; very cool." Then he got to his knees and looked to the monsignor as he reached to touch the figure of the master. The old priest nodded and Davide lightly touched the boots of the master.

"Look guys, he wears his boots like I always said he did."

The monsignor's gasp was enough to break the silence. Davide knew he had a lot of explaining to do and wedged himself between John and Rich, trying to avoid the stares. Johnny came to the rescue of his new friend.

"Well guys, you probably guessed by now that our new friend here has a man crush on a dead artist. You know, Mike, like you have for Bret Favre, and you, Danny, for that guy who plays the son of Indiana Jones." Mike and Danny squirmed with the comparison, but that only served to support John's premise. Even the monsignor seemed to be sucked into the story; though he continued to eye Davide and then look at Agnes and Arthur. The girls responded in a totally different manner. Patricia pointed out that if more boys had role models like a Michelangelo, or even that football player, we would have a more tolerant world.

"Right on, Patricia, and thanks for your insightful thought. But now it's time to eat," Arthur said with a tone of pride in his voice.

Food always got things back to normal quickly. Arthur gave directions to Maura on how to get the students to the Spanish Steps. The route he chose would lead them to Holy Trinity Church at the top of the famous staircase. They would walk down the Spanish Steps, pause to look at the apartment where Lord Byron lived, and then go to the fountain in the piazza below. The fountain was in the shape of a boat and right beyond it was a pedestrian street. They were to take that street, walk a couple of blocks, and on their left there would be a restaurant called Rex Amici.

The monsignor said that Arthur's choice for lunch was commendable as that restaurant attracted many of the Vatican City and Curia workers.

"That building served as an inn, even during Michelangelo's stay in Rome."

John and Rich didn't know if they should leave with the others, so they dawdled and waited for instructions from their father.

"The four of you should probably go. I'll fill you in on what happens here when I join up with you. Afterwards, we'll go to the colonnade to meet the students from the Italian and American groups."

Taking their father's advice, the four musketeers joined the others on their way out.

"Monsignor," began Agnes. "Why did you want to see us alone?"

Ottavianni explained that he had been invited by Roselli to the Medici Palazzo in the morning. They were looking for information about the theft of the Magi ring.

"Madonna mia, you didn't tell them anything did you?"

"No, Agnes. I did not. However, they insisted on some guidance. I suggested they start in Rome and then proceed to Naples and the islands in the bay."

As he talked, he led Arthur and Agnes down to his office in the Vatican Archives, where Michelangelo's drawing of the dome for St. Peter's had been discovered. Once there, they sat around his desk, piled high with ancient texts and documents.

"Now, Agnes, I have kept my mouth shut for your sake. Why did I have to feel obliged to keep silent with the very man with whom you have worked for so long in creating the Michelangelo and Medici exhibit?"

Agnes leaned on his desk and took a deep breath. When she completed her story about the true nature of Roselli and the Confraternity of Savonarola, the monsignor leaned back in his chair.

"I see," was his only comment.

"Exactly what does 'I see' mean, Monsignor?" asked Arthur.

"It means that the Vatican has been well aware of the activities of the Confraternity and also, Agnes, of the Order of the Magi."

Agnes smiled, trying not to be caught at something wrong. Arthur however still didn't feel that the 'I see' was totally explained.

"Okay, so you know about these groups, so what?"

The monsignor smiled as he pulled out a journal. He opened it to the page where a colored slip of paper stuck out. He addressed the "so what" part of Arthur's question. By the time he was finished, it was clear the Vatican had been keeping tabs on both organizations for centuries. The Holy See realized the Order of the Magi was secret only to prevent others from finding the Medici ring and using it for the wrong purposes. The Confraternity, however, was a different matter. The monsignor pointed to a print of an ink sketch on yellowing parchment. He had printed it out from the extensive Michelangelo archive file after receiving a call from Agnes from the villa in Tuscany.

"Does this look familiar Agnes, Arturo?" Ottavianni asked coolly.

"Monsignor, it's the brooch of which I have a picture right here," exclaimed Agnes.

"You are correct my dear. It is also the symbol of the Order of the Magi," he informed them.

"Then Michelangelo was a member of the Order of the Magi; his design on the Campidoglio and this brooch prove it."

"Perhaps, Arturo, but what it does demonstrate is that the Order had a symbol, and this is the symbol you must seek. Because you know this, you must leave Rome today, if possible, and go to Capri. I am convinced that is where you will find the ring that is spoken of on this page written by the Order member who took the ring from the thief."

Agnes hugged the monsignor, who blushed but was gracious. "You're wonderful. We'll make plans to leave immediately."

"Well not quite immediately, Agnes. We have to attend the farewell prayer with the Holy Father first.'

The monsignor thought he could help by getting them a special pass to get up close to the pope. Arthur felt, however, that he preferred to be just one of the groups in attendance; as they all dispersed afterwards, his group would simply blend in with the others and easily get out of town.

"I see your point, but be careful, especially with that Davide boy. There is something about him which I don't understand. I hope that he's not a plant by the confraternity to learn about your plans."

"You needn't be concerned about Davide, Monsignor. I assure you that, if anything, it would be the confraternity who would want to get their hands on him," Arthur confided.

"I see," the Monsignor replied.

He led them out through the Vatican Gardens onto a small street which opened onto the piazza in front of the Basilica.

"Remember, be careful my friends. I shall be in touch. Agnes your phone number is the same, I presume?"

"*Si*, it is."

"*Va bene*, then God be with you *mi amici*. Oh, Signore Colonna, perhaps you would be kind enough to read this when you have the time. I think it would interest you."

Arthur thanked the monsignor and placed the paper in his shoulder bag. With a wave, he and Anges strode out to meet the others.

The two Alpha Romeros pulled up alongside a small water fountain crowned with a papal coat of arms. It was but a short walk to the colonnade where Arthur and his group were to meet fellow pilgrims. Youth groups were pouring into the piazza hoping to get a good spot from which to watch the pope's arrival and the service which would follow. As Roselli, Raphael, and the Giuliano brothers got out of the cars, they were almost swept away in a wave of young people singing a back-and-forth hymn. Only by clinging to the cars' doors were they able to stay together. When the wave of youths passed Roselli and the others, he issued the orders for the afternoon.

The lunch at Rex Amici was grand. It seemed that all was going well. Arthur and Agnes got there just in time for gelato and that was all Arthur cared about. As they approached the colonnade, they were caught up in wave after wave of youth groups cramming into the piazza. Arthur repeated the primary order: stick together, at all costs. If anyone did get separated from the group, they were to go to the Vatican Post Office behind the left colonnade. Then they could call Arthur or Mrs. Kennedy. He was barely done speaking when a helicopter appeared overhead.

The pope was being flown in from Castel Gandolfo, his summer residence. Cheers swelled from the thousands flowing into the piazza. As the pope disembarked, those thousands pushed forward to get closer. Arthur could hardly hear those who stood next to him because of the volume of the cheers. He caught sight of the four boys and waved.

"Stay together; don't let go of each other."

Everyone in the group locked arms and moved as one as wave after wave of pushing youths crushed against them. At one point, the group's linked arms were broken by the pushing crowds, but they stayed in sight of each other, called out to each other, and reached out to re-clasp hands.

Slithering along inside the colonnade and watching the splitting of Arthur's group, were three shadowy figures. They crept along, watched and waited for the right opportunity. It was not a problem recognizing the red-haired Ryan, the tall student called Davide, and the Colonna boys, who were linked arm in arm with them.

Another wave pushed everyone together and brought into it those who got separated. They made a formidable force. However, by the time they created the wall of people, the four boys had been completely cut off from the main group. The waves of human bodies caused the four boys to keep moving forward. The three shadows in the colonnade moved out, plowing their way through the moving mass of people.

The four boys were in a panic now; they couldn't see their father, Agnes la Straga, or Mrs. Kennedy. None of their friends were within shouting distance. They were isolated in a throng of humanity. Despite his height, Davide could see no one familiar. Their next effort was to jump up and down to get a glimpse of anyone near them. As they did so, Pietro made his move and grabbed the closest boy. Soon Rich was being pulled away from the other three.

He called out to John, who was shouting, "My brother, I can't see my brother."

Andreas attempted to split the remaining three without success. The waves of humanity had simply grown too powerful to counter. The three were soon beyond reach. Though they continued to scream for Rich, they never got an answer. The waves stopped. There was no space left to fill. The service music came over the sound system and large screens, placed around the colonnade, projected the service. The hymns were sung after the Apostolic Blessing was bestowed. Pietro pulled Richie along the outer portion of the Colonnade and onto the street beyond.

It had only been fifteen minutes and now it was over. The crowds could hear the papal blessing and the music which followed. The waves of humanity reversed themselves and poured out onto the streets surrounding the Vatican.

John, Ryan, and Davide could move and they plowed their way under the colonnade. They were still yelling out Rich's name when Luigi and the Italian youths ran into them. Joining forces, they connected with the Americans and then found Arthur and his group.

John ran to his father. "Dad, they've kidnapped Richie!"

Chapter 23: Sacrifice in the Curia

Arthur couldn't believe it when a nearly-hysterical John cried out Rich had been kidnapped. He held his son close, comforting him, saying all would work out. Ryan and Davide grabbed hold of John and Arthur. He told his son, his fellow musketeers, as well as himself, that if Rich was truly taken and not just lost somewhere in the crowds, the abductors would not hurt him.

"They will want something for his return. The thing to do now is comb the piazza, go to the Vatican Post Office, and make sure Rich isn't still around here," he told them.

Arthur had not noticed that his students created a circle around him,

John, Davide, and Ryan. Almost instinctively, they had made a protective barrier. The hopeful face Arthur put on was transparent and the father's pain showed through. Davide collapsed to the ground crying in Ryan's arms; he was sure that the abduction was meant for him and Rich was taken in error.

Not more than one block away, back at the fountain, Pietro dragged Rich towards the car. Pietro had punched Rich in the stomach, causing him to lose his breath and double over in pain, in order to have an excuse to get him through the crowds quickly. He told those who offered help that the lad was overcome with excitement and he would be fine.

Roselli, Raphael, and Andreas were standing by the cars when he dropped Rich to the ground at their feet. Roselli took one look at the lad and realized that it was one of Arthur's sons. "*Idioso*, this is Colonna's son."

"I know, but what was I to do? The crowds had broken him away from the other three, so I grabbed him; it was impossible to reach the others."

Roselli told him to put the lad in the car and to sit next to him to ensure he wouldn't shout for help. He paced back and forth trying to take this new dilemma and make it work to his advantage. Andreas had decided to help his brother and went to sit on the other side of Rich in the car. Roselli told Raphael that he needed to think. Raphael thought the lad was useless and should be dumped in the Tiber.

"Don't be ridiculous. If anything this boy will show us the way to the ring. If he can't do it, his father certainly can and will with the promise of his return. We need a place to conceal him."

Girolamo Orsini and Giorgio Gaddi stepped out of the car to speak with Roselli.

The search groups Arthur created from his own students, Italian and American youths, were reporting back. There was no sign of Rich and no one at the Post Office had seen him. The last group which reported back was Ryan, Davide, and John who insisted on going with Danny and Mike to search the area outside the colonnade. Arthur was sure that those who took Rich could not have gotten far; the crowds were still pretty thick in the streets.

The three lads were out of breath as they ran through the colonnade. They were shouting, "We found him! We found him!"

Agnes and Maura screamed with joy. Agnes grabbed onto Arthur's arm, telling him that all would be well.

Arthur was trembling as he asked John where they saw Rich and why he was not with them.

"Well we didn't actually see Richie but we did see Orsini and Roselli standing next to a blue Alpha Romeo. Dad, I'm sure that they have Richie."

"But not for long boys. Not for long. Did you leave someone there to keep an eye out?"

John told his father that Mike and Danny were keeping watch. They would also stop a guardia if any passed by. Arthur complimented them on their good planning. The four made their way outside the colonnade and along the roadway by the drinking fountain. They picked up Danny and Mike who were crouched behind the fountain.

"See Mr. C., they're over there. The old guy got back into the car and so did Roselli," Mike said, pointing toward the front car.

Arthur knelt behind the fountain. "Have you seen Rich?"

The lads told them that they had not seen or heard his son. Arthur laid out the plan. Agnes and Maura were bringing up the students to form rings at certain points were the car would have to travel once the crowds thinned out. The six of them, in the meantime, would move in on the car in the hopes of catching them by surprise unless they were willing to run them over, Arthur explained, they would be trapped in the car.

Arthur and the lads made a semi-circle and moved towards the cars, staying, as much as possible, behind other youths and leaders who were passing by. John told Arthur he was sure that it was Pietro who took Rich. Arthur felt if it was true, then Andreas was around.

"And you saw Orsini, so that only leaves that Anastasia woman and Raphael guy unaccounted for, unless of course they have already enlisted other confraternity members who may be here in Rome."

That latter thought brought a pall of doom over the lads' faces. *How were they to combat such a force?*, they all thought simultaneously. They were now within rushing distance of the car. The street had cleared out; they were now visible to the driver.

"Roselli, it's Colonna and his kids," Orsini shouted. "They're right in front of Raphael's car."

"Good, if they make a move towards Raphael, then you make a U-turn and head up the street while they are distracted."

Orsini, who did not know Rome well, asked if they should head for the palazzo. Roselli told him to first circle Castel Sant' Angelo to throw Colonna off the scent.

"But what about Raphael?"

"He'll be fine. He can take care of himself. Just follow my orders. We'll call Anastasia to make sure she leaves the hotel and gets to the palazzo."

As Arthur and the lads made their move towards the wrong car, Orsini revved up his engine. Just as Arthur and the lads surrounded Raphael's car, he swung out, brushing against Ryan, throwing him into Davide, causing both of them to be thrown to the pavement. In an instant they heard Rich's yells as Orsini sped past them. Arthur was enraged. He pulled Raphael from the car and delievered a quick punch to his face. The surprised enforcer reeled back into Mike, the football player, who turned him around, socked him in the stomach and threw him back to Arthur.

"Tell me where they are taking my son. I assure you that you will never see the protection of the police."

"Polizia, like they would protect me?" Raphael gasped out while rubbing his jaw and looking into the raging eyes of a furious father. A look, which his son and students had never before seen, glared from Arthur's eyes. Raphael trembled but remained silent as Arthur approached with clenched fists.

Orsini made his way around the Castel Sant' Angelo as instructed and headed back to the Hotel Michelangelo.

Anastasia had been alerted and was at the desk checking out when Agnes and her group walked into the lobby.

"So Signorina, you are going somewhere?" Agnes asked.

Anastasia ran through the marble lobby to the other side as the clerk rang a bell for help.

Agnes caught up to her as her students blocked the exit. She trapped the escaping woman in the corner of the lounge. Swinging her purse, she approached Anastasia with one question.

"Where are they taking the Colonna boy?"

She insisted, as Raphael was doing with Arthur, that she didn't know. There were several possible locations. Agnes grabbed the woman by her shoulders and flung her into a plush revolving chair which spun her around as she hit it hard.

The students were forming a circle around Agnes who leaned into

Anastasia's face.

"List those places for me right now or you'll become my punching bag."

The feisty little assistant curator had not realized she had such drama within her, but she was pleased that it seemed to be working. Before Agnes left the dishevled and bruised Anastasia, she had a list of locations. As she and the girls swung through the exit doors, Agnes instructed the clerk and hotel detective to call the police. "I'm sure they would like to speak with her."

"*Si signora*, immediately," replied the rather agitated clerk.

Agnes phoned Arthur who, exhausted after running after the Orsini car with the boys, could barely speak. She told him of the locations Anastasia listed as possible holding sites for Rich.

"*Mille grazie* Agnes, I'll call Frank of the American group and Luigi of the Italian group. They will contact the French and Irish groups we met in Florence. We'll send a group with police to each of the locations. As for ourselves, we shall go to the most conspicuous site but the least expected location as far as the Roman police or Vatican detectives were concerned. That way we won't be encumbered by the guardia."

The Italians were sent to the Isola Tiberina on which stood St. Bartholomew's Church and its adjoining hospital. The French would go to the Palazzo Farnese. The Irish would go to the Church of Sante Clemente under which an ancient pagan worship site existed. The Americans would go to the American Academy which is comprised of a series of palazzos dating back to medieval times.

Arthur and his band would meet up with Agnes, Maura, and their students at the hotel. Then, having everyone together, they would begin their search right where Danny had delivered Marc Antony's eulogy for Caesar.

Arthur walked solemnly toward the hotel. He feared if his understanding of Roselli was off, he might not find Rich until it was too late. John walked along side of his father with Ryan and Davide right behind them.

"How am I going to tell your mother, Johnny? Her baby; we've lost her baby."

"Dad, don't tell Mom a thing right now. We'll see her in Pompeii and Rich will be back with us, so don't get yourself all upset."

John seemed to say this with complete confidence, but in his heart a sinking feeling was all he experienced. On Arthur's part, he felt relieved that his son was so confident. They talked of what they would do after they found Richie.

Luigi and the Italians swarmed over the island; they searched throughout the shrine where the apostle is said to be buried. Finding nothing in the grotto, they left for the hospital built on an ancient Roman site.

The French were no more successful at Villa Farnese. The curator was contacted by Ottavianni after a call from Agnes. He was most cooperative, allowing them to roam throughout the palazzo and its grounds.

The Irish had been informed that the French and Italians had found nothing. Finnian Clonnard, the adult leader, was not about to have their search fail as well. The Church of San Clemente dated back to the days when the Emperor Constantine legalized Christianity. In recent times they discovered it had been built over a worship site for the eastern god called Mithras. Soldiers and warriors were especially drawn to the cult. When his group walked through the Church with its golden mosaic rendering of Christ and the Apostles, it was as if they were in the Holy Land or an Eastern rite church rather than in Rome. The curator led them down the back steps four levels to the ancient site. At each level, they searched each nook and cranny but found nothing. As they stood at the altar of Mithras, Finnian called Arthur to report the bad news.

"Okay then, thanks Finnian; I appreciate all your help. Please call Luigi and Antoine for me. If everything works out, I'll call you later."

Immediately after that call, Frank Miller of the American group called. Arthur had to report that none of the groups had found Richie. Davide became emotional as he saw the disappointment in Arthur and John's eyes. Ryan stepped forward to offer a positive view.

"Mr. C., if they haven't found anything it stands to reason that Orsini and Roselli are going to where we are going."

Arthur expressed his thanks to Ryan for thinking that they had indeed figured out Roselli's and Orsini's thinking. After all, Orsini was the ancient lore and legend scholar. He was the one who led the confraternity in their quest to find the ring of the Magi.

With Raphael and Anastasia out of the picture Roselli was on the phone issuing orders. Rich listened for names and places while pretending to be dazed from the struggle to escape from Andreas and Pietro. When

Roselli finished his last call, Rich decided to confront him.

"You know, Roselli, my dad will find you, no matter what you do to me. The entire city and every student in it will search you out."

"You may be right, Ricardo, but when we have made you one of us, I think your father will have second thoughts about persecuting me."

Rich understood clearly what he meant. Roselli's plan to make him one of them brought back the vision of Ryan lying on the table in the Orsini house in Florence. He would not allow his fear to show. He decided to address Roselli's notion of persecution.

"Signore, how can you say that my father is persecuting you? You are the one who kidnapped me."

Roselli ranted about how Savonarola's followers have been hunted down throughout the centuries since his execution. 'Our way is the right way' is what he was saying. All who didn't follow them were on a wrong path.

The lad would not let it go. "So you think that controlling one's soul is the right way?"

Roselli refused to discuss the issue. All he would say is that Rich would soon be a believer. Rich paused to search out where they were in hopes of finding an opportunity to escape. Orsini turned onto the Via Sante Teodoro next to the Palatine. The lights illuminated the Palatine. The pillars and ruins in the Forum took on a mystical appearance. The car halted next to a row of medieval buildings bordering the Forum. Orsini pulled through an archway leading into a secluded parking area.

Roselli turned and looked into the back seat. Andreas and Pietro held Rich's arms.

"And now, my young friend, what Ryan could not experience you will soon feel. You shall understand why you should follow us."

"Signore Roselli, you do realize that you are *potso?* All your crazy people could do is trap the soul of Davide Mettzini in the marble of Michelangelo's Giant-David. You may end up killing me and trapping my soul in some piece of antiquity but that's all you will do."

Roselli ordered the Giuliano brothers to take Rich from the car and head out toward the Forum.

"Ricardo, you will soon see that our abilities have improved over the centuries."

Night was stretching its cloak across the city. The gate leading into the Forum had not been locked. Roselli, Orsini and the brothers, pulling Rich along, entered without question.

They walked past the stone on which Danny had performed Shakespeare. They glanced at the flowers, now drying, upon the stone where Julius Caesar's funeral pyre burned over two thousand years ago. They stood in the silvery glow of moonlight before large iron gates. The gates and great iron doors of the Curia of the ancient Roman Senate were closed. Roselli ordered Pietro and Andreas to pull back the gates, and then he pounded on the door. The banging sound echoed throughout the Forum. The doors opened slowly as if by some automatic mechanism, however, when the black robed men became visible as they opened the doors, it was clear Roselli had planned for this moment. Roselli greeted the two men who closed the doors while another lit torches in the room.

Andreas and Pietro pulled Rich down until he lay across a broken façade depicting a sacrificial rite of ancient times. Orsini put down a wooden box as he tied Rich's ankles and wrists with velvet ropes. Rich tried to yell out. Andreas slapped his face.

Arthur and the three boys left the bus walking directly across and through the lighted pillars lining the Forum's Sacra Via. Agnes and Maura guided the other students, who followed. They had insisted on helping Arthur, so they would surround the Curia which is where Arthur was convinced Roselli would bring Rich, if Anastasia had told Agnes the correct location options.

Ottavianni had connections of his own and the group passed through the Forum without incident, walking directly to the Curia building. The iron gates were open, but the iron doors were shut.

"We'll have to rush the doors and hope they aren't locked," whispered Arthur to the three boys and Danny and Mike.

A muffled yell could be heard followed by a sound of flesh hitting flesh. "Dad, it's Richie; let's get going," John softly said as his father held him back until the students were in place.

The circle made around the Curia, Arthur gave the sign and all the lads rushed the doors. The unlocked doors opened heavily but swiftly. The two who stood guard were taken unaware and knocked to the ground; Mike landed on one and Danny on the other. Several punches later, the robed men lay motionless. Ryan tackled the third who had stood next to Orsini, holding a knife on Rich's chest. A trickle of blood ran down the side of Rich's body onto his torn shirt. John took on Pietro with such force that the much larger man was thrown onto the Senate benches and knocked out instantly when his head collided with the stone surface. Davide did the same to Andreas as Agnes led the rest of the students into the Curia only to find all the members subdued or held at bay.

Arthur went for Roselli who had grabbed the knife from Orsini.

"Stop or your son shall lose his soul forever."

Roselli dropped to his knees, the point of the knife once again cut Rich's skin. Arthur froze as new blood flowed out of Rich's chest. Rich let out a slight moan. Orsini knelt behind Roselli peering out with trembling eyes.

"And now Signore Colonna, you shall listen, *si*."

Arthur held out his arms signaling his students to stop where they were.

"*Va bene*, Roselli what's your proposal?"

A hush filled the Curia. Each student held their breath as their eyes fixated on Rich's blood. The flickering torch light bounced shadows off those frozen in place, creating an eerie atmosphere. Those tackled remained on the mosaic floor. The strain of the moment could be seen in the faces of students, confraternity members, and Magi Order members alike. All eyes slowly moved from the blood on Rich's chest to the knife in Roselli's hand.

Arthur broke the silence demanding he be allowed to place a cloth on his son's wound. Roselli told him to give his handkerchief to Orsini. The older man grabbed its edge and held it on the pierced skin.

"Again, Roselli, what is this proposal?"

Roselli looked into Rich's eyes which shot him daggers of anger. But Rich held his tongue and waited. His bound arms and legs offered him no chance to hold the cloth which he resented being held by Orsini.

"The proposal is simple, Signore Colonna."

He presented the situation as he saw it. He told Arthur they both sought the same prize, perhaps for different reasons. He spoke of how they both knew where that relic may be and that the location was not Rome.

"I propose this. I shall release your son once you allow us to leave. We shall both go to where the relic may be hidden. Whoever finds it first shall be the victor."

"Absolutely not," yelled out Agnes la Straga.

Arthur turned to her. "Agnes, my son is more important than the relic."

"Indeed he is, Arturo; forgive my outburst."

He returned his attention to Roselli. "You have a deal. I give you my word we shall not pursue you, if you release my son without further harm. But should you hurt him, you shall relive the day when Savonarola died."

"Boys, you may release the confraternity members now."

The Giuliano brothers helped the black-robed members to their feet. Roselli carefully cut each bond holding Rich. Andreas pulled Rich up onto his feet. Rich staggered, grabbing his chest. Arthur made a move to help him, but stopped when Roselli shook his knife-wielding hand. Rich gave his father a brave look indicating that he was okay. He even managed a grin in the hopes of convincing his father, but Arthur didn't believe it for a minute. There was nothing he could do without endangering his son. He watched as Rich was propped up and walked through the doors. As Rich was brought past each student, not one could look at him without tears obscuring their view.

Orsini followed the curator with the others behind him. As they passed through the doors, the students moved to close ranks behind Arthur, John, Davide, and Ryan. They watched the confraternity enter the darkness of the Forum and disappear into the secluded street lined with Medieval buildings.

Once the confraternity was out of sight, Arthur ran for the door. He, the students, and the women filled the stairs, looking into the darkness.

In the stillness of the night, they heard footsteps shuffling through gravel. A shadowy figure stumbled out of the recesses of the Forum. It stopped and held onto a broken marble block. John saw the movement and pointed.

"Dad' it's Richie."

Arthur and he ran down the stairs, crossing the Sacra Via and making their way to the Arch of Septimus Severus where Rich was leaning inside its archway. Arthur grabbed him into his arms. He cried out with pain.

"Oh my God, I'm sorry Richie! Are you okay?"

"Yes, it just hurts a little. Johnny, give Dad a hand, will you?"

John took his brother's arm while Arthur took his other arm as he walked toward the gathering students. Each offered a message of support. Jessica and Kristin, holding his bloody shirt, walked up to him, tears streaming down their cheeks.

"I don't think this is much good any more," sobbed Kristin.

Rich smiled and thanked her anyway for retrieving it. Agnes approached wiping her eyes as well.

"Ricardo, I have someone here on the phone who wishes to speak with you."

"Richie, are you there?" yelled Donna into the cell phone.

Rich weakly replied that everything was fine. There was just a little excitement when the pope riots broke out.

Donna went a little hysterical when she heard the term riot, but in the end Rich assured her that it was just a big crowd and they got crushed and trampled, but nothing serious.

"You got trampled?" Donna was now crying and calling for the rest of the family. "Your brothers and father got trampled in Rome, but they're okay."

"Richie let me talk to your father."

For five minutes the gathered troops watched the changing expressions on Arthur's face as Donna expressed her concern over his not being able to protect her babies. In the end, the mother was relieved, and Arthur told her they were on their way to Pompeii and from there they would take her and the family with them to Capri.

After a quick call, Ambrogio pulled up along the Via Foro Imperiali. John, Ryan, and Davide insisted on carrying Rich to the bus. Danny and Mike had Rich in their arms before anyone else had a chance. A few minutes later, they were off to Pompeii. As the Colloseum faded behind them, the bus passed St. Giovanni in Laterano Cathedral.

A group of youths were entering the pope's church, still open for pilgrims. St. John Lateran was the Mother Church of Rome dating back to Constantine. Arthur thought it beneficial to pay a visit to the church and use their facilities to wash and dress Rich's wound. The wound had stopped bleeding, but it needed to be cleaned. Rich, in his typical manner, thought they were making too much of a fuss. Arthur made it clear that when Rich's mother found out what really happened there would be a grand inquisition to ensure he had been properly cared for. Rich agreed that they should stop at least to say a prayer of Thanksgiving that he wasn't murdered.

"Indeed," a surprised Arthur replied. "By all means, and I know just where it should take place."

The bus door opened and they filed out onto the expansive piazza of St. John the Baptist.

Through the portico, on top of which Christ once again was portrayed with his Apostles, they strode. Arthur pointed out the immense statue of Constantine on their left. Down the 184-foot-long aisle they walked very slowly. Rich's ability to move faster was limited so Davide and Ryan locked hands, and John placed his brother on the human chair. He refused to be carried again but allowed himself to lean on them as he walked to the front of the cathedral. Turning left at the papal high altar, Arthur led them into the Cappella Colonna, so named to honor Pope Martin V, who was of that family and is buried there. Arthur felt it fitting to offer their prayer of thanks in a chapel bearing their same family name.

At the tomb of Martin V, who reunited a divided church, Arthur, his sons, Davide and Ryan, and the rest of the students all joined hands. Rich spoke the words as he presided at a public prayer for the first time.

> Lord God, thanks so much for keeping me alive. Thanks too, for bringing into our lives such good friends as those who hold our hands in this bond of unity. And thanks for our leaders, my dad, who saved me, my brother who watches over me and Mrs. Kennedy and Signora la Straga who taught me the value of love in friendship.
>
> And all of this we pray in the name of our Lord Jesus Christ.

With a resounding Amen, it was all over and Agnes, though still crying, was thanking Rich for his kind words.

"No problem Signora, it's the least I could do for being such a jerk."

After their stop to cleanse Rich's wound and dress it properly, they were off toward the city buried in volcanic ash in 79 A.D. and not discovered again until the nineteenth century.

As each of the students began to doze off after a most dramatic day, Arthur pulled from his shoulder bag the paper which Monsignor Ottavianni had given him.

Arthur told Agnes that the monsignor had handed him a paper as they left the Vatican Archives. He thought about it when they visited the Colonna Chapel in St. John Lateran. He had hoped it would provide more information on the ring's location. He presented it to Agnes so she could help translate the early Italian. Agnes was pleased to translate the writing and take a step away from the inevitable confrontation that would lie ahead in Capri.

She began checking various sentences and analyzing the source of the document. It was clear to her that it was written during the time when a woman named Vittoria had visited Rome for the first time after her husband's death. It appeared to be a journal page not unlike the Ficino one which helped them discover the truth about the legend of the Magi ring and the Medici. She read and as she did her eyes bulged from her head.

She exclaimed, "*Madonna mia*" over and over again.

Arthur asked what the writing said, but she only kept reading sentence after sentence and calling for saintly help. This continued for quite awhile. The entire bus was asleep except for Arthur, Agnes, and the driver, Ambrogio. Agnes asked for pen and paper so that she might make notes to remember details. She began to contstruct the events of the late 1520's.

Michelangelo was making plans to return to Florence. He was to design fortifications to protect the city from a pending attack. Word had come that a so-called army, raised by the German Frundsberg, had entered Italy. Many of the local City-States and Duchies did nothing to stop their advance toward Rome.

Michelangelo's activity was disturbed by a knock on the door. It was Bishop Reginald Pole who was soon to be made a cardinal. The servant was in shock as the bishop announced himself.

"Please tell your master I wish to be presented."

Michelangelo stood in his workroom, working on the marble of the *Moses*.

"Your Excellency honors me," the artist began as he lowered his chisel and hammer.

The bishop offered apologies for the disturbance but he had someone in his carriage who sought to meet the famous sculptor of the *Pieta* and the *David*. Michelangelo, ever the humble person when talking of his work, nearly blushed at the bishop's words.

"May I introduce her to you Michelangelo?"

Michelangelo had not had any type of relationship with women in his boyhood days besides the daughters of Lorenzo, and that was only at dinner time or special events. After he left Florence to engage in his life's work, he was consumed with project after project and had no time to develop a social life. Therefore, he was abnormally shy around women and never used a live female model. He could hardly refuse the soon-to-be cardinal, so he invited the bishop to bring her into his house.

The woman who entered was a charming, thoughtful person who oozed emotion and passion. Having lost her husband several months ago, she was making her way to the island of Ischia near Naples.

"Michelangelo, may I present to you the widow of the marquis of Pescara, Vittoria Colonna." Having made his introduction, he turned to bid the two a farewell, saying that he would send his coach for the lady.

Michelangelo was left alone with a woman of high education and passionate presence for the first time in his life. Just entering her mid-thirties, Michelangelo was fifteen years older than she. She explored his studio, studied the sculpture pieces in progress and spoke to him of his views on the Sistine Chapel ceiling. Within the hour they had formed a bond based on their love of art, philosophy, and theology. She was a Catholic reformer and he was a loyal member of the Catholic Church. He was, after all, working for the pope. He was torn with guilt produced by his reading of Savonarola regarding expression of one's sexuality. She had just lost her husband in a battle in Milan. He had lost, in a way, his loving friend, Francesco Granacci, who had left for Florence after the Sistine ceiling was completed. Both were in mourning, needing consolation and comfort.

Night after night they met to discuss art and theology. One night she arrived in a gown of purple covered with a cloak and hood of ivory silk. Her auburn hair and ears just showed past the edges of the hood. The cut of her dress exposed the top of her bosom. Tonight they were to talk of poetry and love. In later years, they would both write about love in such profound and passionate terms that many thought the experiences expressed actually occurred. If any two people represented the Renaissance understanding of love and appreciation of beauty in all forms, these two would be prime examples.

Michelangelo, who had probably never known physical love with a woman, experienced love on that night and then, in a wave of guilt and fear of damnation, returned to his chaste existence. Immediately after that night, Vittoria Colonna continued her journey to Ischia where she went into seclusion for several years. That day, the artist designed his only piece of jewelry, as a token of his esteem. The brooch would never be delivered. The pope learned of it and begged the artist to allow him to present it to his niece, Catherine de Medici who was to be married to Henry, son of King Francis I of France. Michelangelo, as he often did throughout his career in Rome, could not say no to the pope.

Vittoria and Michelangelo would console themselves by writing poetry and sonnets to each other. They would meet many times, a decade or more later, but of that night never a word was to be spoken between them. They may hint at it in their poetry, but Michelangelo used similar terms to describe his relationships with close male friends much later in life, especially Tommaso Cavalieri. That particular father-son relationship would last until the artist's death. The secret Vittoria withheld from

Michelangelo had never come to light.

Agnes looked up into Arthur's eyes. He waited to hear what was so amazing. She handed the paper to Arthur.

"If the writing in this journal is accurate, I would have to say that you, Arturo, and your children, have within you the blood of Vittoria Colonna and Michelangelo Buonarotti."

"Impossible, it's just impossible, Agnes. We are ordinary people who share a similar name with a noted Italian family. Besides that, we're Americans."

"Well, Arturo, everyone in your country came from somewhere else, save perhaps the Native peoples, and even they came from Asia during the great migration of peoples across the land bridge between what is today Russia and Alaska."

"Shall I try to be like Anselmo Roselli, trying to claim a relationship that isn't there, and be what I am not? No, Agnes, I cannot do that to my family. My daughter has just married a real lord, is that not enough? Shall I now come along and claim noble blood of an ancient family? For what reason other than trying to be what I am not?"

"But Arturo, look at your children; especially these who sleep in front of us. One has the artistic talent never before seen in your family. The other writes, as does your daughter Jana, like one who can create poetry and prose with ease. All of them have a temperament of humility, courage, faith, and creative vision. What about the frugality that your producer friend mocks? Is that just a coincidence, or is it genetic? Do not your eldest son and youngest daughter possess that quality as well?"

"Stop, you're driving me *potso*, Agnes. I shall not reveal this to my children and certainly never to the public. It's just hearsay."

Agnes shot him a look of "No it's not."

"*Va bene*, then it's only one source claiming the ability to trace the lineage. Anyway, we have a relic to claim and a life to restore, is that not enough for any one person?" he asked.

"I once heard your son call you stubborn and now I can see why he did. I shall honor your decision and no one shall hear of the connection from me."

"*Mille grazie* Agnes." He returned the paper to the shoulder bag. "Anyway we can now trace the history of the brooch and that will bring fame enough for any historian." Arthur muttered before he dropped off to sleep.

All on the bus were now asleep save for one whose life was to be altered should Arthur find the ring first. He pondered what he had just heard as he viewed the cliffs overlooking the sea. To his left, the silhouette of Mount Vesuvius dominated the horizon.

Chapter 24: The Miracle of the Grotto

Rich had been rescued; the price was allowing Roselli and his gang to leave. It was worth it. Rich's wounds could have been much worse. He was resting comfortably as the bus pulled into the parking lot of the Majestic Palace Hotel in Sorrento around 11 p.m. The white façade with balconies, overlooking the bay from its cliffside location, would provide quite an impressive view when morning arrived. At that moment, the impressive view was Donna, standing under the entrance canopy, with Jana, Chris, Ron, and Tricia at her side.

It was as if an alarm clock rang when the bus stopped. All the students and adults were suddenly wide awake. John hung out the window waving frantically.

"Hi Mom! We're here, safe and sound."

Maura guided the students off the bus first to allow the family to have a moment of privacy. John helped Rich down the stairs with Davide and Ryan assisting. Just this sight caused Donna to sway with dizziness so Ron had to hold on to her. She remained where she stood and did not create a fuss. Once Rich was off the bus, she and the family surrounded the boys; each asked questions about the crowds at St. Peter's.

John shot Ron a look of "it wasn't the crowds who were the problem." Ron said nothing, realizing there was more to the story than the riots in the Piazza San Pietro. Ron kept using the humorous term, Pope Riots, to ease his mother's concern for her youngest child. Even though Rich was in college, he was laughingly referred to as Richie baby. It was natural, then, for Donna to fuss over him, especially seeing how slowly he was moving.

"Richie, were does it hurt?" she kept asking. He kept replying he was just a little sore and it would be better tomorrow.

"Well it's almost morning now and you need a decent night's rest. Ronnie, please help Johnny get Richie to bed." With that order, she greeted Agnes and thanked her for helping with the situation. "And now that the kids are off to bed, you might like to tell me what really happened."

Agnes looked at Arthur, who looked at Donna, who looked back at Agnes.

"Well...?" Donna insisted.

Arthur went through the whole story; not the part about the Colonna relationship, just the part about the confraternity's attempt to carve their son up to capture his soul. Agnes ran for some water as Donna turned white and Jana screamed. Arthur helped his wife to sit on a nearby bench as Jana, with Chris' help, brought herself under control. Agnes came back with bottles of water which Ron gave to his mother, sister, and wife.

"Now we have a few itinerary changes to talk about because of what happened," Arthur stated. Donna seemed to be gaining not only her color back but also her feistiness.

"And I would hope one of those changes would be to kick the crap out of Roselli and company!" fumed Donna.

Agnes was taken aback by Donna's reaction to the threat to her sons and the other students, but she thoroughly understood the mother's anger and need to protect her children.

The students currently had no idea why Rich was abducted; they knew nothing about Davide's true identity. To them, the kidnapping had been a random act by some crazy fringe group; until the event within the Curia in the Forum. The mention of a relic got them talking and the four boys soon had a room full of students wanting to know the truth about Rich's abduction.

With their dad busy explaining the events to their mother, the boys had to make a decision.

"Listen guys, can you hold on just a minute? I think we need to have a quick conference before we can answer your questions," John requested.

The girls sat on one bed and the boys on the other bed. The four boys walked onto the balcony for a brief chat. All four thought that if their friends were to be placed in harm's way then they should know what was going on. The question was: how much should they know?

The four entered the room. Davide took a chair near the window and looked out over the lights of Sorrento. In the distance, out in the bay, the Isle of Capri was only a boat ride away. Rich took the other chair while Ryan sat on the desk. John had been elected to speak.

"Here we go, are you ready?"

The groups adjusted themselves on the beds and nodded yes. Kristin made it clear they wanted none of John's blarney stories tonight.

The lad took a different approach. Instead of telling them what was going on, John began to quiz them.

"So then, how many of you have made a connection between the exhibit we saw in Chicago and what we've encountered over here in Italy?"

Most of the hands went up.

"Good. That makes my job a little easier. How many of you understand the legend of the Medici ring? The one you've been hearing about back home and now over here?"

About four hands were raised.

"Okay, now I know where to begin." John traced all that was presented in the classes back home. He reminded them of the prints in the case which showed the Medici wearing the Magi ring. He explained what the Magi ring was and why it was so important that they find it first. He left out the part which involved Davide not being truly human. Having attended Sunday school, the students understood what a relic was. He told them about the Confraternity of Savonarola. If they got the ring first, they would use it to finance their efforts to destroy the art and the fundamental beliefs of Christianity, which they deemed too tolerant and forgiving.

This part their new friends understood quite well. Jessica offered a comparison between their goal and what the Frate had tried to accomplish. "In other words," she began. "It's their way or the highway."

"Oh it's more than that," and then John looked at Rich.

"Holy crap, are you saying the confraternity wants young people like us to build up their ranks?" an unbelieving Mike asked.

John confirmed that was exactly what the confraternity wanted to do. There was genuine nervousness among the students as many grabbed their chests.

John thought everything was settled until Breanne asked Ryan a question. "Hey Ryan, what really happened to you when you supposedly went to the bathroom back in Florence?"

Ryan was caught off guard and didn't know what to do. He looked to John and Rich for help, but received a shrug. The deadening sound of silence filled everyone's ears. Until it was broken by one who seemed not to be paying attention at all.

Davide raised his tall frame and walked to the front of the television set. He ran his hand across the TV, as if it were a pet of some kind.

"I really think this invention is, what you call, super cool."

The group didn't quite know how to receive the statement so they made some guttural sounds and smiled. John, Rich, and Ryan felt what was coming and grabbed hold of each other's hands. With a tight squeeze they held on as if what Davide was about to tell them would toss them off the balcony.

"What happened to Ryan," he began, "is what happened to Rich. Ryan, show them your cut."

Ryan nervously pulled up his shirt to reveal a slight cut. It was not as bad as Rich's because Rich and John had rescued him before greater damage was done.

Ryan told his classmates exactly what happened in the Orsini house, and how Rich and John climbed over palazzo roofs in order to save him.

The room was abuzz with gasps and all kinds of questions. Like why the heck would they want to cut you up Rich, Ryan?

Davide explained. He explained that the confraternity was a splinter group of extreme followers of Frate Savonarola. For half a millennium they have been undermining the work of Michelangelo calling him *inventor delle porcherie,* an inventor of obscene things. His work glorified the beauty of creation, but they did not see it that way. So what happened? They started the fig leaf campaign, using innocent people who meant well. They started by covering the genitals of his statues, all but the *David.* The Florentines revolted against the movement to cover the *David.* The scene of the last judgment had its nude figures painted over after the master died. Michelangelo's own friend and assistant, Daniele da Volterra, was ordered to put *perizomas,* or briefs, on the nudes. Not until 1993 when the Holy Father, Pope John Paul II, had the painting restored did the briefs come off.

He was on a roll and John, Rich, and Ryan became comfortable with his approach dealing with censorship and art. Their comfort didn't last long.

"So you see… Ryan, Rich, and I are the victims of their efforts to destroy not only the legacy of the Stone Cutter Genius, but all that doesn't fit their beliefs regarding what is proper, artistic, and holy."

Davide sat down; the students reeled from his presentation. They slowly reacted to his mention of being a victim of the confraternity. They had a variety of questions, but what they all meant was: When did you get kidnapped by the Confraternity of Savonarola?

It was too late now to back up. If Davide had to stand up for the truth, he thought, he must do so whatever the consequences. His fellow musketeers, who knew what he was about to do, could not and would not stop him. Davide lifted his shirt to show his scar; it was clear it had received a severe cut.

"Even my soul holds the scar and the pain of that night."

Some of the students were now making the sign of the cross over themselves. Somewhere, deep within their being, that expression of faith seemed to be needed.

Joe, who almost never spoke about controversial things, raised his hand as if he were in the classroom. "Davide, exactly when did you receive that wound?"

Here it comes, thought the boys; they clasped their hands more tightly and almost held their breath.

"Well, Giuseppe, let me put it this way. Remember the story of the preview of the *David* statue? You know, before they moved it."

Joe indicated that he remembered.

"Well on that night the confraternity captured my soul and ended my life."

The squeals, muffled screams, and gasps of disbelief filled the room. Each person froze, then thawed and became limp, and then froze again. John, Rich, and Ryan each took a turn embracing Davide, who had used every inch of fortitude he could muster to deliver the truth. Several of the girls were crying; a couple of the guys were trying their best to hold back their emotions.

Jessica, through her tears, had to say what everyone now knew. "Then you're not really human?"

"I don't know what I am. I think I'm a spirit with soul and form, but I don't know how long it will last."

John and Rich, since they found out about Davide, had always felt that his time with them would be limited, but they didn't realize Davide knew.

John took back the meeting as the bells from the steeple of the church in the Sorrento Piazza tolled twelve times.

"Listen, it's late. We've been through a lot and tomorrow, well later today, we have to search all of Capri for the ring. Let's sleep on it and look at what needs to be done in the morning."

Everyone agreed. After hugs were exchanged all around, the four boys were left alone to look out over the balcony towards the island of Capri hidden in the darkness.

Arthur had left a 7 a.m. wake up call for each room. By 8 a.m., he expected everyone down at poolside for breakfast and at 9 a.m. he had reservations on the hydrofoil to take them to Capri. His plan was to explore the surface, especially where Tiberius' palace once stood. Afterwards Agnes, who had contacted Monsignor Ottavianni, would have special boatmen ready to take the group into the Blue Grotto where Timothy of Syria made the bargain with Lorenzo de Medici concerning the ring.

The grandkids, except Olivia, were running around the pool. Olivia was talking with the girls of Arthur's student group. The Roses, Nancy, Anita, and Marilyn, had arrived at poolside and began talking with the students, who remembered them from the Villa in Tuscany. No one had eaten anything of substance and Arthur pointed out it was going to be a long day. The guys did their best to obey his directive. The girls were no slouches when the chips were down.

Arthur, Agnes, the Roses, and Donna were in deep conversation with the married children about the previous night's events when Kathy and Alun arrived with Sean and Grace.

"Surprise!" they called out.

Donna ran up to hug all four of them. Arthur was right behind her. He hastily brought them around to meet the students and Davide, whom they saved for last. John and Rich joined them, with Ryan in tow. Donna and the Roses wanted to hear about their travels in Italy, but they knew there were more important matters to address that morning.

The four boys took the adult children aside to explain what happened last night in their room, as Donna and the Roses kept the little ones busy. By the time the boys had finished their story, everyone was on board to do what had to be done to find the ring before Roselli and his gang. John and Rich were sure Roselli was already on the island and getting a head start, but Agnes had the Order of the Magi involved and that was to their advantage. As for the grandkids, Jana and Tricia would take them to the main shopping area of Capri to keep them safe should there be any sign of danger.

The bells were signaling the half hour. Arthur called for everyone to follow him to the bus. Ambrogio was to take them to the boat dock to save time. There would be no sight seeing this morning.

As the nine o'clock bells rang out, the hydrofoil lifted above the water and sped out towards Capri; it was on time, which in Italy was quite unusual. The Bay of Naples spread out behind them and Arthur realized why the poet said, "See Naples and die." In front of them, there appeared two gigantic rock fragments breaking the surface of the sea and reaching for heaven. These are called the *Fraglioni*. Today, they announce that a boat is nearing the Port of Tragara landing. When the ring first came to Capri, Timothy of Syria was crushed between them with boat wreckage.

Everyone in the Colonna clan knew the rocks showed where the ship carrying Timothy had crashed. The sight of them caused some anxiety, but the sea was calm and they floated smoothly to the dock. On a typical summer day the island is filled with day tourists enjoying the beauty, shopping, and beaches. Today, the Colonna group would have little time for such pleasures.

Arthur had quite a sizable group with him, with students and family; it was quite a chore to get everyone off the boat and keep them in some semblance of order. There were too many distractions. The Marina Grande was a spectacular sight with its many boats getting ready for trips to various grottoes. Arthur wanted to get his group to the top of the mountain, as Timothy had done when he was a guest of the Emperor Tiberius at the royal palace called Villa Jovis. That villa was to be a primary searching area. Arthur didn't expect to find anything since Ferdinand IV, during the 1700's, stripped anything of value from the Roman ruins to adorn his palace in Naples. Since sections of marble and mosaics were torn away, the clues they sought today could have disappeared over two hundred years ago.

To prepare for that possibility, Arthur had the foresight to pick up a modern tool to help with the search. It created quite a bulge in his shoulder bag and added a hefty weight. John relieved Arthur of that weight when Arthur asked him to carry the bag while they trekked up the many stairs to Ana Capri, the island's main town. Its clock tower displayed 9:45 a.m. The lure of the shops tugged at Jana, but she took a deep breath and passed them to make the climb up to Villa Jovis.

Roselli and confraternity members from both Rome and Florence were making a similar climb on the other side of the island. Anastasia and Raphael were part of the group; Roselli had posted bail for them. Getting them out of jail had delayed them; they had only just arrived on the island in a privately chartered boat. Luckily for Arthur, Roselli hadn't had the foresight to bring modern technology, so their mission was to find any symbol, scratched on the ruins or walls of the grottoes that may be linked to the ring.

Roselli's other plan was to find Arthur and follow him until he found the ring and then confiscate it. He never thought of keeping his word. For now, they made their way to the Villa Jovis. If a clue existed, it would have to be in the royal palace of Tiberius.

Arthur made a game of the hike up the mountainside to occupy his grandchildren. A shopping spree was offered to those who reached the Villa first. Jana and Olivia were in the lead. Chris, for the moment, had Connor and Riley in tow. Little Arthur V kept pace with his Papa. They could now see the ruins of the villa. They were about to reach the southern watch tower, which overlooked Ana Capri. If Timothy of Syria had to gauge when the fishing boats came into port, it would be from that tower. It was not Timothy who hid the ring, but the Order of the Magi who had intercepted it from Domenico of the Confraternity of Savonarola, a millennium and a half after Timothy. Arthur's theory was that the Order must have known Timothy's story and would, therefore, follow his experiences on Capri. Now that they had a symbol, the twelve pointed star over a trapezoid, Arthur knew what to look for on stones or in the ruins. With this knowledge, Arthur hoped, they would be better able to decipher where the Order hid the ring. Arthur felt that location would have a connection to *Il Magnifico's* first encounter with Timothy's spirit, when they made their bargain. That was the theory.

The Colonna band made the climb in good order and now stood on the ruins of the tower. Arthur asked John for his shoulder bag.

From the north end, Roselli and his gang were just approaching the northeast wing of the villa, where in ancient times the receptions were held. They were pausing for Orsini to catch up when they heard the laughter of the little boys announcing they were the winners of the climb. Roselli ordered everyone to keep their heads down, to listen, and to watch.

Through the archways of the south tower, the children ran and the students explored. As they did so, Arthur removed the bulge from his shoulder bag. It was a portable metal detector.

"If the ring or any other metal piece is around, this device should find it," Arthur declared.

He gave the detector to Ron, who alternated with Chris, to wave it across the walls of the ruins. The others looked for surface markings, such as a twelve-pointed star, that may symbolize the Magi and be a clue.

Arthur V, Riley, and Connor were walking on top of a wall of the villa when they spotted some people crouching behind the crumbling wall of the north wing.

"Papa," they screamed. In a flash, Arthur and the four boys were on the wall with them.

"There are people behind that wall," Connor whispered.

The four boys jumped from the wall onto the grassy area and waved to the guys to join them. Roselli, seeing the formation coming towards them, had nowhere to go but down. So Roselli stood up and motioned to his followers to move forward. He looked in each corner of the ruin in which they stood, as if no one was coming their way. In two minutes, Arthur and all the guys of his group were lining up along the edge of the wall above Roselli. Behind them were all the girls and women of the group. Behind them, was Olivia with the little boys. She had a devil of a time holding back the three little boys, but she kept telling them that Papa wouldn't let them have their shopping time if they disobeyed. That made all the difference.

Roselli finally looked up and saw the formidable line up. When Rich noticed Raphael and Orsini, he just about leapt from the wall. John and Ryan held him back.

"*Buon giorno*, Arturo, such a *bella* day for a search, no?"

"You needn't play the courteous buffoon with us Roselli," Arthur replied.

"What? No greeting on this lovely day?" then he quickly changed his attitude, like a cloud blocking out the sun, to cold and foreboding.

"Now listen to me, you would-be savior of art. We have a bargain, right?" he waited for no answer. "Well the answer is correct and I have as much right to be here as you do. So, if you don't mind I shall continue my search and you...well you do what comes best to you, pray for a miracle, *va bene?*"

Arthur turned red with fury, but his honor would not let him attack Roselli, nor would it allow him to unleash his boys on them. He turned to

Jana and Tricia and told them to take the children away from these examples of low life. As they ran off, he turned to Roselli.

"The children needn't hear someone like you. Nor do I, so good day Signore."

He led his students and family off the wall to return to the port. Roselli watched them leave. When they were out of sight, he directed the Giuliano brothers to look for the portal leading to the secret stairway of the emperor into the Blue Grotto.

On the way down, Alun, Kathy, Grace, and Sean were plotting. Should magic be needed Grace would try to see if she still possessed some skill.

Jana and Tricia were already at the port with the children when the rest of the group walked onto the pier. They were talking to Monsignor Ottavianni.

Agnes ran up to him. "Monsignor, what on earth are you doing here? I only meant I needed some of the Order to man the boats for the grotto."

"My dear Agnes, for centuries the church has been accused of covering up legends for its own end. This time, we shall get it right. Whatever happens today will be duly recorded and properly handled. I am here to ensure that it is done. What shall we do? The boats are ready."

"First we shall put life jackets on the children," Jana announced and it was done immediately.

"Next, we shall board the boats for the Blue Grotto," said Arthur with less authority in his voice than his daughter had.

The entire group stepped on the small fishing vessel and was brought to the grotto. There, they climbed into a number of row boats staffed, today, by members of the Order as steersmen. The monsignor led the way off the vessel into a rowboat. Agnes went with him. Donna and the Roses were in the next boat. They were followed by small groups of students. Arthur tried to ensure that an adult was in the students' rowboats. Next there followed the family groups. The grandchildren made the descent look so easy that the teetering adults, who almost lost their balance during the climb down, were taken aback. Finally, Arthur and the four boys climbed down and gently dropped into a red rowboat staffed by Father Armando Romani.

Above the Blue Grotto, Roselli's henchmen found the portal to the imperial staircase. Roselli ran over to divide his gang. The Giuliano brothers, Raphael, Orsini, and he would go down the stairs and wait for the inevitable entrance of the Colonna clan. Anastasia would head for the port with the members from Rome. They would board prearranged boats steered by confraternity members. They were to enter the grotto's opening and block Arthur's retreat.

The Magi Order's armada of rowboats reached the grotto entrance. The turquoise waters of the Mediterranean shimmered, as they ducked their heads, while they entered the cave. Once they entered, they were caught up in a world of spectacular blue hues reflecting up from the waters and onto the walls of the cave. Father Armando rowed Arthur and the four boys to the stone ledge where Lorenzo de Medici met the spirit of Timothy of Syria. Ron, Chris, Alun, and Sean were rowed next to the rocky portside, where they could get out, if necessary. Everyone else remained in the boats for safety. John took out the metal detector and searched around the water's edge. He walked up the imperial stairs. Nothing registered. His back ups were right behind him as he made his way along the narrow ledge where legend said Timothy had crawled when making his escape from Capri. There was a hush from everyone as the four musketeers clung to the wall, inching their way along the ledge, while John balanced the detector.

Suddenly, the gentle splashing of the water was broken with a ringing sound. Anastasia and the Romans entered the mouth of the cave undetected as all eyes were focused on the drama unfolding up on the ledge.

John became excited. "Dad, it's ringing and the dial is going crazy."

Arthur, who had gone halfway up the stairs, told him to direct the device towards one spot and then another to see which gave the greater signal. John did so. Ryan pulled out a flashlight from his pocket and shined it on the spot where John pointed. Rich bent down and laid flat. There was nothing those in the boats could do to help; the narrow ledge made it impossible for anyone to join them. They all continued to support with words of encouragement, their eyes fixed on the four musketeers.

"Ryan, shine the light here," requested Rich. Ryan did so. "Listen guys, I think there are scratches on this stone."

Davide asked if he could look. He too laid flat on the ledge.

"Rich, I see it too."

"It looks like the star which…well like the one your sister wore at her wedding," noted Ryan as he peered into the crevice. "Now what do we do?"

"Dad, I think we've found something."

"Okay John. Take the ice pick I gave you and chip at the stone. See if it loosens." Arthur stopped where the ledge met the stairs and watched with bated breath. He remembered to breathe again as the chipping of the rock echoed throughout the grotto.

John replaced Rich, whose wound was paining him, on the ledge and chipped away around the stone. Little pieces of stone tumbled down to the water below. Several pieces dropped in the boat containing the little boys, who instantly collected the rocks for Papa. As Arthur suspected the stone was not part of the cave wall, but an insert into a crevice.

"Davide, help me pull out the stone." The two of them worked at it little by little until it was sufficiently loosened to remove it smoothly. It turned out to be heavier than expected and they dropped it. The splash caused Jenny and Jessica to scream, but they only received a slight soaking.

"Ryan, hand me the flashlight."

"Okay, here you go John."

Rich now knelt down and bent over John. He peered into the crevice as the light illuminated its interior.

Arthur edged slightly onto the rocky ledge. No one noticed the figures on the dark side of the staircase. Had they not been so excited, perhaps someone would have noticed Roselli slowly descending from the portal and moving up behind Arthur.

All eyes were on the hole in the cave's wall. John stuck in his hand.

"I can feel something, Dad. It's soft."

"Soft? Whatever it is, pull it out."

John grabbed the soft leathery pouch and pulled it out. He handed it to Rich so that he could stand up.

At that moment, Roselli grabbed Arthur by the throat and the Giuliano brothers grabbed Arthur's arms. Orsini ran down the stairs calling out to Anastasia and the Romans.

Sean yelled to his Grace from the edge of the rocky platform where he and Arthur's eldest sons had jumped from their boat. "Grace! For God's sake, do something!"

"Please Grace! My dad is up there!" pleaded Kathy.

"I'm trying; nothing is happening!" Grace weepingly replied.

Soon the entire cave was echoing screams to release Arthur. In the confusion, Anastasia's boat touched the stone ledge and the Romans jumped out. They attacked Ron, Chris, Alun, and Sean. As the diversion took place Anastasia started to jump from the boat.

"No you don't little lady," and Agnes jumped from her boat and pushed Anastasia out of her boat and into the crystal clear, cold waters of the grotto. Agnes landed in the empty boat. She threw the anchor line for Anastasia to hold onto, but would not let her out of the water.

Roselli screamed for silence. His yell echoed throughout the cavern, bringing a pause in the fighting on the platform.

"Now, give me that pouch and I shall release your father."

Arthur stood perfectly calm and limp in Roselli's grasp. The Giuliano brothers, having focused on the fight, had dropped their hold on Arthur's arms and moved toward the fight scene. They froze in place when Roselli shouted his order for silence. As Rich made his way toward Roselli with the pouch, Arthur elbowed Roselli in the stomach. The resulting cry of anguish caused him to loosen his hold long enough for Arthur to swing around and push Roselli onto the ledge as he jumped backwards. Rich backed up towards the other three boys.

Roselli, instead of being filled with fear, as he had been on the ledge of the Rosselli Palazzo, became demanding. He turned to Rich, "Give me that pouch!"

"Leave my son alone Roselli," called out Arthur who approached him from behind. "You're trapped."

Rich was holding out the pouch to lure him further along the ledge and Arthur was encroaching from the back.

No one observed Davide, still lying on the stony ledge. He grabbed Roselli's leg. The curator lost his balance and lunged for Rich, hitting him in the chest. Rich lost his balance; pain swept through his chest; the pouch flew out of his hand. John grabbed him to keep him from falling.

Roselli grabbed for the leather bag, not understanding he had nowhere to step. He stepped into the air above the grotto as he reached out for the pouch. Roselli screamed as he fell. Into the waters of the grotto he plummeted, crashing his head on Donna's boat and bouncing into the blue water. The steersman, unnoticed, draped Roselli's limp body across the boat. All eyes were watching the twirling leather pouch. Everyone raised their hands to try to catch the falling pouch. It didn't fall. It was suspended in the air, not moving in any direction.

Arthur moved back to the stairs to allow the four boys to leave the ledge. Orsini and the Giuliano brothers were controlled by Arthur's sons and the Romans were being tied up with anchor ropes by Danny, Mike, and Joe. As soon as the four boys returned to the stairs, the pouch began to twirl. Its contents flew out of the sack like a shot fired from cannon. A metal box flew out landing in Arthur's outstretched hands. He opened the container and a bright silver light poured out of it.

"It's the ring of the Magi," Arthur announced to the cheers of all in the boats below.

The Giuliano brothers attempted to break away, but the four adult lads made them think otherwise. The ring floated out of the container adding its silvery brightness to the blue hues throughout the grotto.

The members of the Order of the Magi began to chant their ancient prayer and knelt in their boats. The family and students crossed themselves and stood in awe.

At the mouth of the grotto a bright light appeared; the spirit of a young lad, in willowy white robes, floated above the boats.

The confraternity members tried to back away from the sight toward the cave's wall, but their captors stopped them. Their superstitious minds thought of a scene of judgment. It wasn't an angel bringing the wrath of the Lord, but a kind and youthful presence who held out his empty hands in a gesture of welcome.

Arthur held out his hand to Davide who took it as he came to stand next to him. Both knew what was about to happen. Arthur turned back toward the vision.

He softly and simply said, "And you must be Timothy of Syria."

"I am Timothy of Syria and I have been sent to fulfill the promise I made to Lorenzo de Medici as he freed me from the ring."

Arthur looked at his four boys and across to his family and students below. Ottavianni was in ecstasy, still holding the empty pouch which fell into his boat. He watched, with devotion, as the vision spoke.

"Arthur of Chicago, are you ready to release a soul to heaven?"

Arthur could not speak. He could only pull Davide closer to him.

"You would make a fine son for any family, including God's family. I cannot decide. Davide, it is up to you."

Davide turned to his pals and embraced each one. "I need to go. I knew it would come some day. You are my family now and I shall remember you for all time."

John, for the first time in his life, could not respond except with the slightest of smiles. A trickle of a tear streaked his cheek. Ryan told Davide that he felt a bond which could never be broken. Finally, Rich touched his wound beneath his shirt and then also the place on Davide where his cut was.

"Our hearts share the same mark. You will always be remembered my friend, my brother, my fellow musketeer."

Davide turned to Arthur, "I am ready, Mr. C." Then, with an embrace and a hint of a smile, he told Timothy that he was ready.

Timothy smiled. "There is someone else who is here to take you home Davide."

In the grotto's entrance appeared another white light which brought forth a strong man dressed in a black damask gown, wearing boots with silver spurs and a black silk hat with a velvet ribbon. His salt and pepper hair was long and his beard perfectly trimmed.

"Master...Michelangelo!" Davide called out. "It's the master stone cutter Mr. C.! It is he!"

Arthur smiled, nodded agreement, and let go of Davide's hand.

Michelangelo stretched out his arms. "Come forward my son; come home to your heavenly Father."

Davide leapt from the stairs as he touched the hand of the Stone Cutter Genius. His form was no longer solid. He, like Timothy and Michelangelo, was pure spirit.

"*Arrivederci*, Signora 'C', *ciao bambini, e studenti*. Farewell *mi amici, ti voglio bene Mr C.,*" Davide called out, as he, Timothy, and Michelangelo glided toward the grotto's entrance.

There was a flash of bright white light and then the grotto was glowing once again in its blue hues. The ring stopped floating in the air above the waters of the grotto. It fell, landing in the hands of the monsignor. He stepped out of his boat, close to a state of shock. Ottavianni climbed the stairs to Arthur.

"This is yours, Signore Colonna."

Arthur placed the ring back in its silver box and closed it. He scanned all those below in the grotto and looked into the eyes of the three boys next to him.

"Well...what shall we do with the ring of the Magi?"

From the Roses, the family, his students, and Agnes, their voices shouted in unison.

"It belongs to the Church!"

Monsignor Ottvianni smiled. "Then you shall present it yourself, Signore Colonna, with all your family and those gathered here today."

The Order of the Magi broke into song, but this time they were joined by family and students. They sang, *How Great Thou Art.*

Epilogue

A promise is a promise, Arthur thought. He whispered something to the monsignor who returned to his boat. "I will see you in Rome, the day after tomorrow."

Each steersman guided a boat to the edge of the stone apron. Their passengers got out and the confraternity members were escorted into them by the guardia who had just entered the grotto. Only then did Agnes allow Anastasia to pull herself into the boat. Agnes joined Donna and the Roses.

"Signora Colonna, may I join you?" Agnes shyly asked.

"Si, Agnes, and my name is Donna. This is my sister Nancy, and our dearest friends, Anita and Marilyn. We would be honored to have you join us as a Rose.

Family and students followed Arthur and the three boys up the imperial stairs out of the blue grotto into the bright Italian day. All were still in a state of ecstasy, even the little ones, as they solemnly climbed those ancient stairs. As they stepped off the last stair and came into the bright sunlight on top of the mountain, the gentle breeze, though warm, seemed to breathe life back into them.

"Arthur, you certainly know how to create a memorable tour," Maura Kennedy observed with a smile.

After everyone was gathered on the ruins of Villa Jovis, Arthur told them why he chose to leave the grotto by the imperial stairs.

"Before this trip began, I made a promise to my students. Girls, you go to the north wing; boys, you go to the south wing. After you've changed into your swimsuits, there is a lovely beach just below us waiting for a bunch of tourists like us.

The cheers were deafening. His plan had worked. His students and family were themselves again. Like young people do, they noisily ran to change. There would be plenty of time to reflect on events; now, the important thing was to enjoy each other's company on the playground of the Roman Emperors.

Three days later, after Pompeii and seeing Rome without being hunted, it was time to relive those events and reflect on the miracle in the grotto.

Ambrogio pulled up in front of the Colonna Palace Hotel. Two motorcycle guardia escorted the busload of students and family down the Corso to the Via Conciliazone and up to the Basilica of St. Peter, sparkling in the morning sunlight.

"Davide loved seeing the dome of St. Peter's," Arthur sadly observed.

"That he did, Dad," reflected Rich.

"The dude knew what loving something or someone was all about, didn't he?" John asked aloud while looking at the dome as if Davide would appear and wave to them.

"There's no doubt about that," responded Ryan.

The four of them gave a wave to St. Peter's as if that gesture would be seen by Michelangelo and Davide. Who's to say they didn't see it; just then a gust of wind carried water from the twin fountains onto the bus as if blessing it with holy water.

With windshield wipers briefly swishing across the window, the bus turned right. They passed the area where Rich had been taken and past the other side of the little fountain. Following the Vatican wall, where the hole in the street had been filled, they arrived at the entrance to the Vatican Museum. The monsignor thought Arthur and his group would enjoy walking through the courtyard and gallerias on their way to the Sistine Chapel for the presentation ceremony.

As the Swiss Guards opened the chapel doors its famous choir sang *Ode to Joy*.

Ottavianni turned to the Colonna clan. "Just follow me and take your places in the empty space up front. Family and the Roses go to the left; students and teachers go to the right.

Arthur was that proud of his family and students as they flawlessly processed, dressed in their Sunday best, to take their places. Walking down the aisle, he recognized those who had been at the grotto. The members of the Order of the Magi were attending.

The monsignor acted as the Master of Ceremony as the trumpets announced the Holy Father. The choir sang *Tu es Petrus* as the pope took his place on a gilded chair in front of Michelangelo's fresco of the *Last Judgment*. With the prophets and sibyls, ancestors of Jesus and much of Genesis looking down on the Colonna clan and the Roses, the ceremony began.

Father Armando Romani proclaimed the Gospel from Luke, chapter ten, verses twenty-three and twenty-four.

"Blest be the eyes that see what you see."

The pope spoke of how this band of students and family had brought light to an ancient legend and faith to one who was without hope. He was referring to Davide Mettzini.

It was time for the presentation. The organ played a very familiar tune, though not the usual church hymn. Arthur's children looked at each other and motioned to their mother.

The music was the same as that played during a celebration when the Leprechaun King and the wee folk honored Arthur and the Roses for saving the symbols of the good news preached by St. Patrick. How did they know?

Arthur rubbed the gold coin in his pocket as he entered the aisle behind his grandchildren. Olivia carried the open silver box on a purple velvet pillow. The triple-banded ring of the Magi looked brilliant, but normal. There was no glow. Olivia was flanked by Connor, Arthur V, and Riley, who once again wore their tuxedo kilts.

With a tap on her shoulder from her Papa, she processed to the papal chair. The children bowed and stepped to the side. Arthur came forward, took the ring from the box, and placed it into the open hands of the Holy Father. Monsignor Ottavianni looked on without offering direction. The pope told Arthur that the ring would be placed in the Medici Chapel at San Lorenzo in Florence, so all who come to learn of the Medici and Master Michelangelo shall learn of the legend.

It was the pope's turn to bestow gifts. Each student and Maura Kennedy were called before the pope who presented them with a papal medal. He did the same for each of the Roses and Arthur's family, including the four young ones. Lastly, with a blast of trumpets, Arthur, Agnes, John, Rich, and Ryan were called forth. They were made papal knights and received medallions symbolizing their new rank.

Tears flowed freely. Arthur noticed a sixth medal of knighthood lying on the gold silk pillow held by Fr. Romani. The Holy Father announced that the Order of Papal Knight was awarded post-humously to Davide Mettzini and would be enshrined at Sante Croce in Firenze.

"For no greater love has a friend than to give up his life for that friend."

Even the members of the Order of the Magi felt a trickle of water down their cheeks. Arthur wasn't alone in wiping away a tear drop or two and remembering how Davide had done the same with Rich's hanky just a short while ago.

Following the Apostolic blessing, another blast of trumpets introduced Purcell's *Trumpet Voluntary,* to the delight of the Colonna clan. The ceremony concluded.

They all waited at the curbside for the bus to take them back to Rex Amici for dinner. Ambrogio had also received a papal medal, and now he went to get the bus. Everyone was sharing their thoughts, showing each other their medals, and praising the Holy Father for recognizing Davide.

Kathy and Alun were in a serious conversation with Donna.

"Mom, Alun and I have decided to open a couple of pubs in the Untied States. Nothing fancy, but it will require us to spend more time in the States." Donna's eyes swelled again, filling with more tears. "Oh, and the whole family will be partners and help to run them."

While this news was shared, John and Rich came up to their father with a bit of news of their own. The boys had received that morning an e-mail from the producer, Arthur Lovell, congratulating them on their discovery and honor received.

"Oh and he had a couple of ideas," John started to say.

"I'm sure he did. What were they?"

"Well the first one was that Danny and Ryan should come with us to London to audition for the sequel."

Arthur turned to Ryan and Danny who were right behind them. Their smiles indicated that they would call their parents and jump at the chance.

"And what was that second wonderful idea?"

"Well, Dad, he was thinking of a sequel to the sequel," answered Rich.

Arthur wrapped his arms around his sons, "You know boys, I think we need to find another name for you. How does musketeers sound?"

References

Though this work is a work of fiction, the hotels, museums, churches, and actual historical events portrayed are real. Many of those events did take place in the life of Michelangelo and the Medici or exist in today's world. To that end, the following resources were used to authenticate certain events in history and the life of Michelangelo, the Medici, and those who were friends of the Stone Cutter Genius.

Beck, J. H. *Three Worlds of Michelangelo*. New York: W.W. Norton & Company.

Condivi, A. *The Life of Michelangelo*. Baton Rouge, LA: Lousiana State University Press.

Firenze City Centre Map. (n.d.). Berndtson and Berndtson.

Florence, All the Masterpieces, History, Art, Folklore. Florence, Italy: Becocci Publisher.

Hintzen-Bohlen, B. *Art and Architecture/Rome*. New York: Barnes and Noble Books.

Rome and the Vatican. Rome, Italy: Plurigraph.

Symonds, J. A. *The Life of Michelangelo Buonarroti*. Philadelphia: University of Pensylvania Press.

Wikipedia. (n.d.). Retrieved from www.wikipedia.org

Wirtz, R. C. *Art and Architecture of Florence*. New York: Barnes and Noble Books.

Wright, C. *Rome*. London: Multimedia Publications.

Dept. of Tourism of Italy

Chicago, IL and Piazza Umberto I, Anacapri, Capri, Italy

Lazio Regional Tourist Board

Rome, Italy

Acknowledgements

To my legendary wife, and our children (Ron and Tricia, Jana and Chris, Kathy, John, and Rich) who bring to each day the light of truth and the discovery of joy.

To my mother (Wanda Colaianni), who indeed provided the anecdotes of the family history, my mother-in-law (Ruth Dooley) who was thrilled as each chapter was finished and to Uncle John Naninni and Cousin Linda for their tales of family history.

To the "Royal Roses" Marilyn Griffiths, Anita Christensen, and Nancy Shields whose travels with us added tales to tell.

To my sister Janice and her children who provided unending encouragement.

Special thanks to the people of Italy, the United Kingdom, and the Republic of Ireland, who through their generosity of spirit and service, inspired many of the incidents portrayed in this book.

Especially:

Palazzo Rosselli del Turco

Nicolo Roselli del Turco, Florence, Italy

Hotel Alessandra

Florence, Italy

The Colonna Palace Hotel

Rome, Italy

The Hotel Michelangelo

Rome, Italy

The Majestic Palace Hotel

Sorrento, Italy

The Westport Hotel
London, England
The Blarney Woollen Mills Hotel
Blarney, Ireland

Clontarf Castle Hotel
Dublin, Ireland
And to: CIE Tours and Travel Leaders
    Mary Pat Flanagan: m.p.flanagan@cietours.com
    Patti Speigelhoff: tripcotravel@sbcglobal.net
Join Arthur Cola on one of the tours based on his books:
The Leprechaun King Tour of Ireland
The Excalibur Tour of England and Wales
The Michelangelo Tour of Italy

About the Author

arthurcola@yahoo.com
www.arthurcolalegendarytales.com

Arthur Cola was born in Chicago in the "little Italy" neighborhood of the near west side of the city. His family moved to Oak Park, IL where he attended Oak Park-River Forest High School. While attending Loyola University, Chicago, he met his future wife, Donna Shields. Together they have five now grown children and four grandchildren. He, his wife and family now live in Wisconsin.

He has been an educator for 35 years. During that time he was a Teacher of History and a School Principal. Upon receiving his Master's Degree from the University of Southern Mississippi, he also served as a Lecturer for Barry University in Florida. His post graduate work concentrated on Educational administration and theology. He studied in Rome at the Loyola University Campus while conducting research for his current work, "The Stone Cutter Genius" and conducted tours and traveled extensively in Ireland and Britain researching cultural sites and folklore for his other novels.

While performing his duties as a School Principal, he also began writing a "Movie Review" column with his daughter for a Wisconsin Newspaper. Also during those years he began adapting novels and plays for Jr. High School students to perform. One of those productions won the "Bicentennial Award" and was performed at McCormack Place in Chicago. Part of that award winning work was his original poetic reflection titled, "What is America?"

His literary works also include the children's Christmas themed book, "Papa and the Gingerbread Man, An Adventure in America's Oldest City©." In this tale the famous cookie man is sought out by "Papa" through the streets of St. Augustine, Florida. He wishes to invite him to his grandchildren's school Christmas party. As the chase takes place the children will be introduced to some of the most famous landmarks of early America such as Castillo San Marcos and St. Augustine Cathedral. (www.amazon.com)

The prequel of *The Shamrock Crown* for older folks is titled "Papa and the Leprechaun King, The Secret Legend of the Shamrock." In this tale the hero is called upon to come to the aide of the Leprechaun King with his Irish-American wife. Together they, along with some friends embark upon a quest to save the Realm of the Wee Folk. And in the process the reader is introduced to the wonders and folklore of Ireland and the secret of the Shamrock which is sure to not only delight but also uplift the reader.

His next book is an historical fantasy for the whole family. *The Shamrock Crown and the Legend of Excalibur* is being published by The American Book Co. (www.american-book.com). This tale takes a large mid-western family on a journey from Wisconsin to Ireland and Britain as they attempt to save two of the most famous relics from ancient Camelot. The reader will encounter the Legend of King Arthur and the Knights of the Round Table in a way slightly different from that of Mark Twain in his tale of *A Connecticut Yankee in King Arthur's Court*. Arthur Cola has the family encounter the legendary characters of Camelot in the twenty-first century. Together they join forces to preserve the symbol of the most important "Message" of our time and all time.

His current work is an epic legendary tale titled *The Stone Cutter Genius*. This historical fiction with elements of the supernatural takes the main characters from *The Shamrock Crown and the Legend of Excalibur* on a new quest to recover a missing artifact of the most famous family of Renaissance Italy while uncovering the mystery of the Legend of the Magi Ring. Along the way the heroes of the tale discover how the early life of the master artist, Michelangelo, was entwined with the Medici family of Florence, Italy in the fifteenth and sixteenth centuries and now themselves…the Colonna family of the twenty-first century.

The American Book Publishing Co. (www.american-book.com)

To:

May the spirit of
Michelangelo inspire you,
May my tale add a bit
of magic to your days,

"Festa Italiana"

Happy Birthday!

Arthur Cola

7/22/11